THE SWORD OF MICHAEL

MARCUS WYNNE

THE SWORD OF MICHAEL

This is a work of fiction. All the characters and events portrayed in this book are fictional, and any resemblance to real people or incidents is purely coincidental.

A Baen Books Original

Baen Publishing Enterprises
P.O. Box 1403
Riverdale, NY 10471
www.baen.com

ISBN: 978-1-4767-8106-8

Cover art by Adam Burn

First paperback printing, January 2016

Library of Congress Catalog Number: 2014027499

Distributed by Simon & Schuster
1230 Avenue of the Americas
New York, NY 10020

Pages by Joy Freeman (www.pagesbyjoy.com)
Printed in the United States of America

To my son Hunter Wynne.
You're the reason I draw breath every day.
Thanks, my son! Love, Dad

CHAPTER 1

The dead man chased me through the graveyard.

My breath rasped in my throat as I ran for my life. With each labored gasp I tasted the Arturo Fuente 858 I'd enjoyed after dinner. Good cigars never taste as good coming up as they do going down. I ducked between gravestones and marble monuments like a scared quarterback hustling through a broken field of meth-snorting linemen. The dead man right behind me meant to do more than tackle me; he meant to snuff my life out and roll what was left of me into a hole.

I'd already killed him twice. He hadn't taken the hint.

Mud splashed up from the soaked grass as I ran. My shirt darkened with sweat and mud and my ponytail beat on my collar.

Trying to stay alive is hard work, but I've found that not dying is a great motivation to work hard.

I fumbled a spare magazine into my Glock 19. The antique crystal rosary wrapped around my left hand hindered my usually flawless exchange, but I wasn't overly worried about technique at this point.

I held the power of Christ in one hand and a 9mm pistol in the other.

The sacred and the profane.

My life in a nutshell.

I dodged sharp left around an ancient concrete mausoleum, the edges melting into the gray of curdled milk. On the other side stood a full-size statue of the Blessed Mother Mary. This was a good place to make my stand. The Holy Mother was one of my patrons. She held me close as she holds all the children of men. She'd once held the man whose body now shambled after me. The decaying flesh no longer held the original soul, now passed into the Light: the shell that pursued me was inhabited with the twisted fury of a dark spirit bound by a sorcerer's will.

A zombie is hard to stop. The undead flesh is rotting and the nerve ends don't work. Only the force of will and intention from the dark spirit keeps the body moving. They shamble, they drag, they stumble.

But they never stop and they have incredible strength.

So my Zen koan for the night was "How do you kill the undead?"

The first magazine of 9mm I'd put into the zombie didn't slow it down. When it first came out of the bushes along the bike path off Nicollet Street, I thought it was a mugger, so I treated it like one. I drew my Glock 19 from my Philly Holster Appendix Rig and put a burst of Hornady Personal Defense into its chest.

The gunfire was loud. If anyone else was out on the moonlit path, the shots would have cleared them away. Five rounds of high-performance 9mm into the upper chest would have gotten a mugger's attention, according to my gunfighting mentor Dillon, whose presence I keenly missed right about now.

The lack of effect on the zombie was what he would call a clue.

Another burst of 9mm verified my initial impression.

If not an undead, or some other variety of hostile paranormal, it was a bullet-resistant mugger. So flight was called for. I don't have the ability to fly in the Middle World, but I can run. If required.

Tonight was such an occasion.

Running isn't my thing. I consider it pointless pain except when truly necessary. In my normal day, running's not necessary. It also isn't my style. One thing I've learned in my life—and my extended spirit apprenticeship—was that you must face that which you fear.

So I stopped and turned to face it.

And to catch my breath.

The undead had been a big man. Over six feet tall. A broad frame only slightly diminished by his brief stay in the grave. The remains of an expensive dark suit rippled with pulses of the energy that kept dead bones and meat moving. He would have been handsome, with sharp pronounced cheekbones and a square jaw. Now the skin was sallow and pulled taut over the bones. The eyes yellow and red with sorcerous fury. Blackened lips drew back across yellowed teeth in a feral smile.

"Shaman..." it hissed.

"Yes," I said. "That would be me."

The yellowed shirt beneath the dark suit coat leaked

fluid from the holes my 9mm had punched in the chest. Center of mass hits don't mean much when the heart and plumbing in there no longer function. That doesn't apply to me. I'm a fragile bag of meat and water. The supernatural strength that drove the undead across from me would enable it to choke the life out of me and tear my lifeless form to pieces.

But I knew what I was dealing with.

And I knew what to do.

The rosary wrapped snug around my hand, I held my pistol in a strong isosceles and carefully aimed my Glock.

"Sword of Michael..." I murmured.

I shot twice. Once in each undead knee.

If they can't stand, they can't hurt you. Shattering the leg's bony structure robbed the creature of its ability to walk. It toppled and before it struck the ground I saw surprised rage pass across the decaying face. It went down as though praying. Then it raised its head, looked at me, and began ripping into the wet manicured sod with clawed fingers.

Two more carefully aimed shots, one for each elbow, brought it to a stop.

It raised its head.

"You're delaying the inevitable, Marius," it whispered. "Sooner or later..."

I squatted down. "Who sent you?"

A cackle like branches scraping across the icy glass of a winter's window.

"So many hate you, Marius. So many grievances... is it someone here, or someone who's come back or...?" it said.

"I compel you," I said.

The dead face twisted. It gagged from a rotting throat.

The voice changed. Sickly sweet words, obscenely feminine: "You cannot compel me, shaman. I am bound to no living flesh..."

I holstered my Glock. I took out a squeeze bottle of holy water. I took a deep breath, gathered myself and called upon the Power of Light.

"Michael, Mighty Archangel, General of the Mighty Warriors of Light on Earth, I call on you for your help... cleanse this flesh of the Dark Forces in the name of Creator God and by the power of Jesus Christ, rebuke this unclean spirit and cast him out of this vessel!" I shouted. I sprayed holy water over the undead.

The corpse rippled like a pond in a strong wind. Darkness rose out of it. Black mist on a midnight moor.

"We'll be back, shaman. We'll be back..." whispered a disembodied voice.

I continued with the clearing. "Michael and Uriel, Mighty Archangels, I call on you for your help... enclose this spirit in a super bubble of Divine Light, contain it so that it may do no more harm..."

The trees bowed as a wind rose from nowhere. With the vision that is not-vision, the seeing that is not-seeing, the gift of shamanic sight, I saw the dark spirit struggling within a bubble of light, surrounded by the Warriors of Light taking it away—

—And one mighty figure surrounded in blue light paused to look back.

Michael the Archangel. General of the Legions of Light. Protector of the Sons and Daughters of the Light.

He faded away, leaving only the memory of light in the darkness.

I stood. I replaced the rosary in the velvet bag I wore around my neck. Put the holy water back in my pocket. The corpse on the ground began to draw in on itself. A bright light in the center of the chest drew it in like a whirlpool of light. Then it was gone.

Faint and far off were distant sirens.

My strength ebbed from me. I spurred myself into a slow jog to the edge of the cemetery. I slowed to a walk on the pavement, cut across the street, and headed for home. I hurried past well-tended houses slowly lighting themselves up as my neighbors woke to the dawn.

What a night.

The Dark Forces were back. With a vengeance. And they'd sent an advance party to deal with me.

Lucky me.

CHAPTER 2

My name is Marius Winter. I am a shamanic practitioner. A shaman, though by tradition I can never refer to myself that way. Shaman is a title bestowed by the community I serve. That title is earned through serving the community in the shaman's roles: ceremonialist, artist, storyteller, healer, warrior, leader and keeper of knowledge. These roles are not sharply defined like a job title in the Middle World. In the shamanic world roles are blurred, defined by Spirit, and there are many shades of gray in the spectrum between the Dark and the Light.

Sometimes, depending on what Spirit brings to your door, some or all of those roles might merge. For instance, a healer may be called upon to be a warrior to provide the service of protecting his community from the attack of Dark Forces. This is the most dangerous and challenging shamanic work of all.

Depossession.

What some call exorcism.

For a reason known only to the Great Spirit, this is the work that comes to me.

In partnership with the healing spirits, my job is to remove the lost souls of dead humans, spirits, entities, demons and extraterrestrials from those who come to me seeking help. To send those possessing spirits back to where they came from and to be a channel for the healing of those who'd been infested by those forces.

I call myself a depossessionist.

I'd once had business cards made with that as my title along with "I depo . . . if you don't pay, I repo . . ." I ended up getting rid of them because I thought it too pretentious and the humor lost on my clients.

You need a sense of humor to survive in this business.

Shamans die doing this work. Illness, madness, accidents, heart attacks, violence done to them by the possessed, taken by the Dark Forces . . . possession. These are the risks. If you're blessed, very lucky and damn good, you might just live long enough to die of old age in your bed, surrounded by those you've loved and those who've loved you.

The latter is what I aspire to.

I have an impressive scar collection from the former.

First In Front, my Native American spirit guide, likes to point out that all my scars were on the front of my body. In the Native tradition, that meant I got them by going straight on at my opponents.

I'd like to believe that, but I can recall plenty of times when discretion had proven to be the better part of valor, which is a fancy way of saying I ran like hell.

With hell on my heels.

Did I mention that First In Front is dead? Or passed

over, as we depossessionists prefer to say. Speaking to the dead is in my job description, and despite there being a long list of entries in the *DSM* that cover that particular mental affliction (and the medications prescribed for it), in the realities I work in, speaking with the dead is just as real as a book in the hands or on the screen or stacked on the bed stand beside my queen-sized bed in my otherwise austere bedroom.

I'd like to say that my mostly empty bedroom was because of my spiritual practice, and that's part of it, but the larger part had to do with my ever-present cash flow crisis, something we practitioners have to deal with since we spend most of our time dealing with nonordinary reality, in which annoyances like rent, groceries, car payments and child support don't come into play.

My bedroom: one queen-sized bed with a carved oaken headboard done in Celtic imagery of the Horned God and the Goddess. A beautiful altar on a small table of carved rosewood holding candles, Native American fetishes, a few crystals, the power-phernalia that a shamanic practitioner accumulates. On the wall, a drum and a rattle, the tools of the wandering shaman.

"Have drum, will travel," I like to say. That might be better on a business card?

The only other thing on the wall was a carved wooden cross with the World Tree on it, a gift to me from the most beautiful woman in my world, my lover Jolene.

Jolene, Jolene . . .

And me, sprawled beneath several layers, because even in the warmest nights of summer in Minneapolis I get cold. I don't have much intestinal tract left and the crisscross of scars across my belly and chest tell a grim tale to anyone familiar with edged-weapon violence; losing so much of my guts messed up my internal thermostat so much I almost always feel cold.

It can also be the presence of spirits.

My familiar spirit guides and the compassionate and helping spirits leave me feeling warmed; the presence of less friendly spirits leaves me feeling chilled. I sat up on the edge of the bed and did my thrice-daily shielding exercises, a legacy of the Atlanteans: cup my hand at the base of spine on the sacrum and call for the Universal Force for Clearing; seal the soul gate at the base of my skull with my thumb and extend the blue energy of the Archangel Ebernox over my entire body; take my hand over my sternum and channel the essence of platinum, gold, silver, the light of the rainbows, the colors of earth . . . and for those not from this planet, the compassionate Star Beings, the colors of their home world. I felt warmth return to me as the energy shields cocooned me in their protection.

Then I picked up the loaded Glock 19 and slid it into the lockbox beneath my bed.

In my world, I have to deal with a full range of threats, from dangerous spirits to equally dangerous humans.

And now I was ready to start my day. I went downstairs into my front room, turned on the MacBook to download my e-mail, checked my voicemail (nothing) and padded barefoot into the kitchen to brew a single cup of perfect coffee in my Keurig coffeemaker. I watched the coffee decant into a blue china mug with the images of the Horned Man and the Sun God painted on it. The free trade organic Sumatran was thickly scented and black with a faint sheen of oil on the surface.

Lovely.

I took my coffee out onto my porch, eased myself into an old rattan chair with a thick cushion, and watched the park wake up. I consider the greenways of the park across the street an extension of my front lawn. At this time of the morning, in late spring, the air is fresh and clean and it's one of my morning pleasures to watch the early joggers and walkers circle the park, while a group of Falun Dafa practitioners train under the shade of the big oak trees.

I took a long slow sip of the Sumatran.

Life is good.

I checked the waiting room, which is a special crystal I keep on my porch, blessed and charged with the Divine Light of Creator God. It attracts spirits. I attract them as well, which is why I have a waiting room, so that those spirits who seek me out for help can stay within, drawn by the Light they want to return to, till it's time for me to work with them and help them cross over into the Light. Those of us who guide the dead or work with the spirits are like beacons in the dark; the more we do the Work, the brighter our personal Light becomes, and we draw . . . things.

Lost spirits looking for help. Curious elementals. Confused dead humans. Spirits of nature.

Then there's Dark Workers, demons, and the occasional vampire, werewolf and possessed human as well.

I rubbed the scar tissue on my belly where one such possessed human had opened me like a bag of groceries with a big knife. That was a long time ago and I'd learned well that particular lesson about the dangers of the Work. I live and work in two worlds simultaneously, the Seen and the Unseen, and both worlds have their own dangers.

In one, you can lose your soul. Or your mind.

In the other, you can lose your life. Or your mind.

You pays your fee and you takes your chances.

Or words to that effect.

One thing for sure, being a crazy magnet makes you appreciate the fine things in life, like good coffee and a little peace and quiet early in the morning. I wanted to linger in that, but today I needed to deal with the issues of ordinary reality like house payment, groceries, renewing my work consumables (white sage, sea salt, holy water, sweet grass, olive oil and some other unguents) and the small budget I set aside for simple pleasures like movies, Arturo Fuente 858s and a bottle of Bushmills Single Malt.

I needed some income. I used to have a regular job. But when Spirit calls you, it calls you hard. I'd left that job and a steady income behind me on the Path.

"Your needs will be met," First In Front said.

My spirit guide perched comfortably in the rattan chair beside me. He's a tough-looking man, as suits a Lakota Sioux war chief and medicine man, tall with a hawk nose and flat slab cheeks, warm brown eyes that can sharpen and narrow like a bird of prey as it strikes.

"What about my wants?" I said.

He laughed. *"Put your intention out there. What you seek will come to you."*

"I seek some income."

"You're in the wrong business, white man."

"I could raise my prices."

He shrugged. *"I took horses."*

"You also took scalps."

He nodded in agreement. *"There is that. You should try it sometime. Use that big knife I sent you."*

He had sent me a knife as a gift. In the way of spirit guides he'd led me to an old antique shop in a little town called Arthur, an Amish community in central Illinois, when I'd been on a road trip. I'd gone into the shop just as an old farmer unloaded a box of junk he'd found in his grandfather's attic. In the box there'd been a big knife, a trade knife, in a beaded sheath. I took it home for a whole twenty-five bucks. It took a razor's edge after I'd oiled and honed it up. The knife hung on the wall in my healing room.

"I like that knife," I said. "I owe you one or two. Smoke?"

He smiled.

I went inside and fetched my last Arturo Fuente 858 from the humidor on the coffee table. When I came back he smiled in anticipation. I clipped the end, struck a wooden match and carefully fired the cigar. It's an extravagant indulgence to smoke my last cigar first thing in the morning, but I've always had a problem with delaying gratification and since spirits—especially spirit guides of the Native American persuasion—love tobacco, this was the perfect opportunity to thank my friend with the gift of smoke on a fine morning.

I puffed the cigar into life and blew smoke to the Four Directions.

"I thank the Powers of the East, the North, the West, and the South. I thank the Mighty Archangels Michael, Uriel, Raphael and Gabriel, you who stand

at the four corners of the Creator's throne, you who
stand at the four corners of the World. I thank the
Great Spirit Above, Below and Within . . ."

I blew the smoke towards First In Front. The blue
smoke covered him in the chair. He leaned forward
and inhaled deeply.

He smiled. *"Thank you, my friend."*

"Most welcome, brother," I said.

He disappeared, leaving an eddy in the blue smoke.
Spirit guides are apt to do that.

I finished my smoke, an enjoyable forty minutes
or so, and then went in and checked my e-mail. The
first in my priority queue was from Jolene, the love of
my life. It was a photo of a beautiful Asian woman,
naked, bound tight in white cords tied in elaborate
knots, gagged with a beautifully folded white linen
scarf. The subject line said: "Do you like this? I do . . ."

Nothing else.

That's Jolene.

I saved that one.

I deleted the spam which offered to extend my
penis or sustain my erection or order pharmaceuticals
from Canada or buy discount jewelry. My friend Lou-
ise asked me to come give a class on basic shamanic
journeying—that would be a few dollars in the cigar
and whiskey fund—and a message from a colleague in
the Chicago suburbs asking if I was free to consult on
a difficult case she had going. There was a note from a
potential client who'd seen an article about me in the
Star-Tribune. I sent her a brief reply with my phone
number and went on through the queue. I found an
interesting one from my friend Troy who ran the American Ghost Society in Decanter, Minnesota—one of the

darkest and most haunted cities in the U.S.—asking if I'd like to tag along with him on a ghost investigation. It would appear on the Discovery Channel and be a nice promotional effort for us.

Not that my practice needed that, nor did I particularly want to promote it. Like everything in the Middle World and the Other Realms, the ebb and flow of business—though I don't think of my practice as a business—was dictated by Spirit. I'm accustomed to periods of frenetic activity in between the slack time when I had no clients, no classes to teach, and nothing but time on my hands. I take those times as blessings, as well as an opportunity to cultivate patience, and trust in the Creator to see that my needs were met.

But I was low on Bushmills, out of cigars, and down to leftovers in the fridge. So maybe it was time to pray and remind the spirits that in the Middle World we mortals needed to eat, and that required cash for groceries.

The phone rang.

I laughed. See how intention works?

I looked at the caller ID. A local number but not known to me.

"Hello?" I said.

"Hi," a woman's voice said. "Is this Marius Winter?"

"That would be me."

"I'm Maryka Owen, I just e-mailed you about a consultation?"

"Hi, Maryka. That was fast!"

A pause. "I'd like to see you as soon as I can."

I looked at the last short stub of my cigar fuming down into the gray of ash.

"How 'bout right now?"

CHAPTER 3

My healing room is a spare bedroom down the hall from where I sleep. It would have been the master bedroom; I use it for my healing room because there's a bathroom in it for clients and a big walk-in closet for storage. I covered the wooden floor with a Persian wool rug with a teal blue motif, and on top of that I put a Peruvian prayer rug that was gifted to me from a Peruvian shaman friend. Two big pillows double as chairs if I sit on the floor. I keep a folding massage table in there so I can stand and work on my clients. A few low tables line the walls with crystals: lots of amethyst, several large geodes, a small statue of Mother Mary and directly to her right, a small statue of Michael the Archangel.

There are two armchairs in there, and I moved them forward as most new clients liked to sit for their initial consultation. I lit a small bundle of sage in a blackened abalone shell and wafted the smoke with a harvested hawk feather into all the corners of the room, in all four directions, then above and below and all over me from the soles of my feet to the crown of my head. I picked up my favorite rattle from the side table and stood in front of the second altar I maintained in the healing room. Two altars might seem like conspicuous consumption, but I want and need as much protection as Spirit might muster on my behalf, so keeping an altar where I slept and another one where I worked makes perfect sense.

Besides, both altars were beautiful works of art in their own right. This one was a plain table of polished oak, with an altar cloth of brilliantly colored Guatemalan fabric with all the colors of the rainbow and the colors of platinum, gold and silver woven through it. These are the ancient colors of protection, the colors of the flag flown in Atlantis over the Sons of Light when they marched out against the Sons of Belial.

The Sons of Light were the good guys. The Sons of Belial were the not-good guys.

Both sides are still very much around.

That's what keeps me in cigar and whiskey money.

I bowed my head and closed my eyes and began to chant the ancient Lakota power song given to me by First In Front, long ago... "Hey-ya, hey-ha-ho..."

I shook the rattle, a ball of dried leather, filled with corn and maize kernels, mounted on an antler handle. The steady rhythm of the rattle fired off deeply grooved synapses in my brain and put me into a light trance, the first step in crossing over into nonordinary reality, as some modern shamans like to refer to the Spirit World, or the Other Realms.

The basic tool of the shamanic practitioner is the

journey. That's when I send my spirit into the Spirit World to negotiate with the spirits, to fight, to heal and, right now, to gather information. I always like to know something about the clients that are coming to see me. I once neglected to make a preliminary journey and that lapse nearly cost me my life in this incarnation. I'd opened my front door to a drug addict possessed by a demon I'd crossed swords with in the spirit realm; that demon sent a possessed human with a knife to finish me. One of the lessons you learn early in the Work is that you must protect yourself in this World as well as in the Next.

Which is why a Glock 19 lived under my bed, my trade knife was always well-honed, and I cultivated certain other self-protection skills as well.

From behind closed eyes, I saw with my inner shamanic vision. *My spirit rose up out of my body and flew through the air to my favorite portal into the Spirit World. It's a beautiful old oak tree, with a small hollow in it, on the shores of Lake Harriet. It's a tree that stands watch, over all those who pass by, on the shores of a lake sacred to the Lakota. I flew into the hollow and then went down, down, down . . . through the roots and then further down through a tunnel of earth that grew broader as I approached a pinprick of light that grew and grew and grew into a portal. I stepped out onto a grassy hillside overlooking a broad expanse of forest and mountains and lakes beneath a brilliant blue sky.*

This was the Lower World, the world of nature and spirit animals; home to the power animals that walk with all of us, whether we see them or not, from our birth till our passing into the Light.

An enormous white tiger sat on her haunches beside the portal.

"Hola, *Tigre*," I said.

"Hola *yourself*," the white tiger said. "What have you brought me?"

I pulled an ornate ivory comb out of my pocket. "For you, my beauty."

She bared her gleaming white fangs. "Would you?"

"I would."

I ran the comb through her immaculate and perfect fur, as only the fur of a white tiger in the Lower World can be. She's a feminine spirit and she likes her beauty aids. I never argue with the Divine Feminine, especially a spirit that embodies all the power and the wisdom of a white tiger.

She purred a deep rumble in her throat.

"So," she said, after savoring the pleasure of her combing. "What is your intention?"

"A client," I said. "Coming to see me..."

A voice behind me that sounded like he'd spent a lifetime in the Bronx making book on the horses said, "Owen, Maryka, female human type, thirty-two years old, divorced, a child, what else you wanna know?"

I turned and grinned up at the big black crow perched in the lower branches of the oak tree beside the portal. "Hey, Burt. How you doing?"

"Doing? How you doing, Marius?"

Tigre stretched her back. "He's doing for me."

Burt laughed a crow's laugh. "You remind him of the wife he'll never have."

"Oh, don't go there, man," I said.

They both laughed.

"You have the makings of a good husband in you,"

Tigre said. "It's that which you resist the most that you should examine."

"I'll examine that another day if you don't mind," I said. "So Maryka?"

"Do you want to see or do you just want me to tell you?" Burt said.

"You know she's possessed?" Tigre said.

"From her family," Burt said. "There's attack, past, present and future . . . someone close to her. There's a cloud around it . . . professional. Karma and past life issues, too."

"When isn't there?" I said. "What travels with her?"

Tigre tilted her head. "It's not with her now . . . one or two steps removed. This is the first step towards something hidden."

"She's looking for help," Burt said. "She read that article in the paper."

He cawed with amusement. "Not much for being down in the weeds are you, Marius? Better watch out for that self-aggrandizement . . ."

"It's not self-aggrandizement if it helps educate those who need," I said.

"Yes," Tigre said. "And you're getting more clients . . ."

"More people who need help," I said.

"Don't smoke so many cigars," Tigre said. "You want to be more careful with that."

"Sacred herb and all that," Burt said.

"Okay, okay," I said, laughing. "I thought I was supposed to be pure, but not too pure?"

They both said at exactly the same time in two different voices: "We never worry about you being too pure, Marius. It's the other we watch for."

"Thank you, my friends," I said. *"Is there anything else I should know right now?"*

"Yes," Tigre said. *"This is more than it appears."*

"And...?" I said.

"Just remember that."

Burt cawed and tilted his head. His eyes flared briefly with the White Light of the Spirit within him. *"I'll remind you if you forget."*

They always did.

"With love and gratitude, my allies," I said.

"He's always so formal, huh?" Burt said.

Tigre laughed. *"See you on the Other Side, Marius..."*

Yes. They would. I entered the tunnel and flew back to my body, settled into it and opened my eyes in my healing room.

This would be more than it appeared.

It always was.

CHAPTER 4

Maryka Owen was tall and willowy in a granola way. Long blond hair pulled into a ponytail, a muslin blouse over faded jeans and bright green Birkenstocks. Her big toes were each painted blue with a gold star in the middle of the nail. The other perfectly formed toes were tipped with standard red. I notice those kind of things. Small details are essential in my work. It had nothing to do with how attractive she was. Really. I serve the Divine Feminine, the Goddess in all Her incarnations, and there is a Goddess in every woman.

Really.

"C'mon upstairs," I said.

She smiled and followed me upstairs to the healing room. I waved her to the armchair on the south side of the room. I sat in the chair facing east, where I wasn't aimed directly at her. My senses work well both directly and indirectly. Having her in my peripheral vision helped me see her energy more clearly. She eased into the chair, graceful and tall, about five ten or so, the same as me.

She had nice energy around her. Her auric colors were full and fluid. Very open, which can be a good thing or a bad thing. Most of the time it was a little of both. Being so open meant she was receptive, intuitive, maybe a little psychic; it also meant she was easily influenced and extremely sensitive to energy permutations around her, whether positive or negative.

I let her settle for a minute.

"So what can I help you with?" I said.

"I read that article about you in the *Star-Tribune*," she said. "It seems . . . strange . . . that you'd be so open about what you do and what you believe. I mean, this is a big city that's really a small town, you know? I've seen you around in Lyn-Lake and Uptown, even sat by you once in Gigi's."

"Gigi's? I love that place."

She tilted her head to look at me. She had cornflower blue eyes with long natural lashes. No makeup at all, not that she needed any. Distracting to say the least.

"Me, too," she said.

"Next time I'll recognize you," I said.

I felt rather than saw the shift in her energy as she studied me with a sudden intensity.

"Does it bother you that people know what you do?" she said.

"No," I said. "I believe in what I do. I serve the community. The more people who know what I do and what I can do to help them, the better."

She nodded. "I believe that. It just seems . . . strange . . . to be talking about demons and ghosts and lost souls like it's just a regular thing."

"It *is* a regular thing," I said. "It's part of the natural order of life."

"That's a good way to see it."

"That's just how it is," I said. "So what about this part of life can I help you with?"

She took a deep breath. "It's my father."

"What about him?"

"He's come back from the dead."

"Oh," I said. "How do you feel about that?"

A blank look. "How do I . . . *feel* about it?"

Asking the right questions is an essential part of learning on the shamanic path. Education is part of my job. It's not all casting out Dark Forces or being the finder of lost children.

"Yes," I said. "How do you feel about him coming back? Assuming it's him. Is he invasive? Has he come back to tell you something he didn't tell you before he passed? Is he unwanted? Do you have unfinished business with him? How do you feel when he's there? Is it cold, or warm, or nothing at all? When does he come—"

She cut me off. "I get your point."

"I'm sorry," I said. "If I sound testy, I don't mean to be."

I had to check in with myself about that. Was I being cranky? Was there something else leaking in around the edges of this conversation? I sent my senses out, *"Tigre"* and felt my white tiger's presence and the ghost of a whisper, *"Gone . . ."*

"I'm sorry," I said. "I didn't mean to rush you . . . I just felt something."

She looked around. Her eyes were wide in alarm. "Is he here?"

"No," I said. "You're safe. There's nothing here."

"Now..." Tigre whispered. *"Something brushed through here, past your protection..."*

I have heavy duty protection on my house. Beyond heavy duty. Industrial grade. Something that brushed by my protection and then left with only a trace of a faint disturbance?

"This will be more than what it seems," Burt said.

"Thanks, Burt," I thought.

"Tell me about your father," I said. "What's it like when he comes to see you?"

Her face flushed. Anger. "I see him standing there. In my house. When I'm walking on the street. In my car, in the passenger seat when I drive..."

"So you see him?" I prompted.

"Yes," she said. "But I *feel* him, too. The weight of his disapproval. His look."

The weight of his disapproval.

"So it's like a weight on you?" I said. "You can see him, you can feel him too? It feels heavy?"

"Yes. Like a big heavy black blanket thrown over my head...I get all fuzzy, can't think straight, I'm confused..."

"Do you feel his thoughts, too? Hear them? In your head?"

She looked away and studied, too carefully, the Tibetan mandala hanging on the wall.

"Yes," she said. "I hear him all the time. Sometimes faint, sometimes loud...sometimes he's not there, but then just when I think he's gone, he comes back."

"You feel this sensation at the same time? The heavy blanket feeling?"

"Yes."

"When did he pass?"

"Last year. In the fall."

It was spring now, so it had been six or seven months. Most souls cross quickly. Some linger in the part of the Spirit World called the Bardo or Purgatory, especially those with unfinished business. They also may linger if they don't realize they're dead, and they'll cling to people or places they knew when they were alive. Those lost souls become confused and if they don't pass over into the Light, they wither away to wizened vestiges as their soul essence slips away. They're then drawn to the living and attach themselves to an embodied soul in a body, and they sip that life essence to experience life second-hand. That's always to the detriment of the possessed. They feel tired, fatigued, suffer sudden mood swings, thoughts that aren't their own, hear voices, feel odd sensations, see and experience strange phenomena... all that cluster of symptoms can mean possession.

But not always.

And if it was, it's not necessarily human in origin. There's an epidemic of nonhuman energies possessing humans that every credible practitioner knew about, but the overall presentation of this case indicated that the suffering being attached to Maryka was the lost soul of a human.

"What was your relationship like? When he was alive?" I said. I sensed the answer, but I needed to see the energy around her response.

A flush of anger. "I hated him. He..."

I nodded and looked away. It was important now to honor the wounded dignity she drew around herself.

A long silence between us. I stared into space and whispered softly, "Mother Mary..."

I'm not what most people would call a Christian. I know and honor the power of the Christ, but I have a special relationship—a deep and abiding love—for the powerful spirit who descended to earth as Mother Mary, Mother of the Christ. She is the greatest of all the compassionate healing spirits, the Queen of the Angels, and one of the greatest gifts in my life was her appearance to me in a vision. Since that time I'm honored to call on her. She brings the White Light of the Creator into the darkest corners of the universe and heals all who come in contact with her. Her special calling is to heal children and we're all somebody's child, right?

All of us Children of Men.

In answer to my prayer, she came.

A sudden brilliance as great doors were flung open and a Light beyond description poured out from behind a woman's figure, arms spread wide, and that Light surrounded and illuminated Maryka. In that brilliance, like a camera flash going off, I saw in Maryka's energy field a faint shape that shrunk into a black ball and disappeared deep into her pelvis.

Second chakra. The gate for sexual energy.

That told me about Maryka and her father.

The Light entered me at the same time; it was like water washing filthy sweat away, cooling and cleaning, and the information I needed was there, just like that. In some cases, I must journey repeatedly to gather all the information for a diagnosis. Then I need to check it out energetically in person. In other cases, like now, all the information comes in a sudden flash.

As Anton Chekhov said in *The Lady with the Dog*, "And suddenly it all became clear."

That's one of my favorite lines, and it surely applied to the world I worked in.

"I felt something," Maryka said. "Like someone touched my head...I feel light-headed..."

"A little clearer?"

"Yes," she said. "Did you do that?"

"No," I said. "Someone good and clean and powerful did. We have more work to do, Maryka...are you ready? Do you have time today? Do you have anything else to do today? After the treatment you might feel a little..."

"Treatment?"

"Yes," I said. "We have work to do. If you want to."

"You make it sound like I have a choice."

"Of course you do," I said. "You always have a choice. You're in control."

I dug out my teacher face and put it on.

"You always have a choice," I said. "My job, if you decide to go ahead, is to help *you* with your healing in partnership with the healing and compassionate spirits. It's not me, it's the Spirit of Creator God moving through me that works with you. That requires your permission and your cooperation. Even if you were in a coma or dying, I couldn't work on you without your conscious and explicit permission, or the permission of your immediate family members, and then only if you were beyond the point of being able to say yes...or no."

"Only with permission?" she said.

I knew what kind of boundary work she'd had to do. The aftermath of her father's crime on her had a lifelong impact: physical, emotional, mental, spiritual. She'd been betrayed by the one she was supposed to trust above all others and that left scars that were long and deep.

"Yes," I said gently. "Only with permission."

She considered that. "What do I have to do?"

I nodded at the massage table. "You'd lie down on that table. Fully clothed. I'd have you relax. And then we'd do the work together. I won't touch you. It's not necessary, but if it becomes necessary, I'd ask your permission first. I'll ask you some questions, and ask you to tell me the first thing that pops into your head. I'd ask you to trust in the strength of the Spirit that brought you here today looking for help."

She took her time thinking that through. That's a good sign. A healthy skepticism is always good in anyone who works with Spirit. Adversaries walk among us, and the gullible and easily swayed are the first to fall to the seduction of the Dark Forces.

"I can do this . . ." she said softly.

"Of course you can," I said. "Do I have your permission?"

She nodded yes.

I set up the massage table in the center of the room where the power converged. I smoothed the clean sheet and set a knee pillow in place.

Maryka stood. Her uneven posture read uncertainty. Muscles rippled in her thigh. She was nervous. Some of that would be the entity within her that felt me coming.

Lost souls are like that. They're often afraid. Fear is what traps them here. When they are caught, and confronted, it's fear that makes them try to hide or cling to their host. They won't fight, though.

It's the nonhumans that fight.

She lay on the table. I tucked the pillow beneath her head and adjusted the knee support. I picked up my rattle and shook it as I hummed my power song to call in my helping spirits.

"We're here..."

Yes. My faithful friends, my companions, and my allies in the Work. They honor me with their presence.

Mother Mary had told me what I needed to do. The possessing spirit had to go and pass over into the Light. Maryka, the unwilling host, needed to be illuminated from within with the Divine Light of the Creator to clear out the sludge and residue of the possession. Her energetic body and spirit needed to be healed and repaired; the pieces of her soul that had been taken away as a child needed to be found and returned to her. Depossession is rarely quick. While the possessing entity may leave quickly, the clearing and healing work afterwards always takes time. It's like taking out a bag of ripe garbage. The odor lingers and it takes time to air out. If a client has been possessed for a long time, the symptoms, though diminished, may linger. Occasionally a client gets repossessed. That's most often the result of not dealing with the spiritual issue that led to an intrusion in the first place, or not receiving proper healing.

Some people don't want to be depossessed.

Not the case here.

I shook the rattle and watched the rise and fall of her breathing deepen and slow as we both went into a light trance. After doing the Work for as long as I have, my energy intermingles with my client's (with their permission) and I help them relax and enter a shared trance so we can work together.

Shamans don't heal. Shamans are channels for the spirits to come through to do the healing and to assist the client in doing their own healing. I felt my spirits close to me, as tangible as any being of flesh and blood in the room, their power in me and through me. I felt the presence of Maryka's companion spirits as well, could see them in the lumen of my mind's eye, the shamanic vision, the coterie of loving and protective spirits that accompany all of us on our journey through the physical world. They were there to support her. When we do our Work, the veil between the Spirit World and ours grows thin and those helping beings can more easily cross to help us.

I set my rattle down. With my eyes closed I held my hands in the energetic field over her body. My shamanic vision allows me to see in a different way. I felt the being lurking low in her belly. It was tightly furled as they often are in my presence. These beings are full of fear. Sometimes they don't know where they are or what they are. They know they've been caught doing something against the Universal Laws. Sometimes they don't care.

It looked like a black ball with a knurled surface twisting tightly into itself in reaction to my vision.

"Maryka?" I said.

She spoke in a subdued whisper. "Yes?"

"I'm speaking to the True Maryka here, your True Self as you came into this flesh, the True Self never touched by the Darkness ... Maryka, direct your attention to any feelings in your belly ... do you feel something? A presence?"

"Yes," she said. "Low. In my belly."

"If it had a color, what color would it be?"

A long pause. "Black. With red all through it."

"What does it feel like?"

"Hate. Anger. And . . . it's afraid now. He's afraid of you."

"It's a he?"

"Yes."

"I want you to move your True Self to one side, Maryka. I want to speak to that male energy there. I want you to listen to him and to tell me what he says. Will you do that?"

Another long pause. "Yes. I'll do it."

"Just say the first thing you hear or feel. Don't edit or elaborate."

"I understand."

The ball drew itself even tighter.

"My name is Marius Winter," I said. "Do you have a name?"

Maryka twitched. "He doesn't want to tell you."

"Thank you, Maryka. Spirit, do you know where you are?"

"Yes," she said. "He knows."

"Do you understand that you're not in your body? Your body is gone. Do you know that you've died?"

"He knows where he is."

"What do you get from Maryka by staying in her body?"

She shuddered. "He gets to own me. Control me. Forever."

"He doesn't own you, Maryka. He doesn't get to control you. Not now, not ever. He can't do that. It's time for him to go."

"He's afraid now," she said. "He doesn't want to go to Hell. He knows he was bad . . ."

"He won't go to Hell," I said. "He can choose to go into the forgiveness of the Light. He could have gone before. He can go now. It's time to go."

"How do you know?"

"I've been to Hell," I said. "He doesn't have to go there. He can choose to pass into the Light right now."

My arm throbbed. I'd been injured there on an excursion to Hell. It wasn't a trip I'd undertake lightly. I was glad it wasn't called for today.

"He can go now," I said. I silently called on the Angels of the Crossing, and with my shamanic vision, I saw the Great Gates of the Crossing swing wide, the brilliance of the Light behind it bursting free, and the Angels of the Crossing standing there, the mighty Warriors of Light who guard souls in transition from this world to the next.

"He sees them," Maryka whispered. "Above him... he sees them...and the Gates..."

"Does he see someone there in the Gates waiting for him?"

I could see, but it's important for the client to participate in the process. It's a way of reclaiming power and soul-energy stolen by the possessing being, and it's the most direct way to involve the client in their own healing.

Her voice shook with emotion. "He sees his mother...my granny...she's there and she's calling to him, telling him he's forgiven..."

"He can go to her now...it's time for him to go..."

I watched the Unfurling, when the tight capsule a frightened lost soul draws tight around itself begins to open as a flower unfurls in the light of the sun. The black ball unfurled into the gray shadow of a man, dim, the face twisted and thin lips pinched tight, rising like smoke from water towards the Gates. The Angels of the Crossing drew ·close, both to guard him and to keep him going in the right direction. Now Maryka's father sped towards the Light. I saw him illuminated with the Light of the Creator and the beginning of the Transformation, the burning away of his transgressions, and he turned just then, with sadness and regret across his face, mouthing the words "I'm sorry..." before the Light filled him and transformed him—

—and he crossed, into the arms of those waiting for him on the Other Side.

The Angels of the Crossing turned and looked at me, as they always did, and nodded. Then the Great Gates swung shut.

It was over.

For him.

Maryka shuddered and opened her eyes. I shook my rattle over her energy field and studied the aftermath written there. There was residue. She'd have a lingering sense of the presence for a while. Deep tears in the energetic body around the second chakra, the seat of sex, that would need to heal before she could enter into healthy sexual relations again. This was the arena of Mother Mary, and I felt her Divine Presence swell in the room.

She's always near when there's healing to be done.

I saw her in my shamanic vision with her choir of angelic helpers filling Maryka with Light. The deep tears in the second chakra closed together and it began to spin. As it spun, its color began to clear and deepen into the healthy colors of the chakra as it's meant to look. The final step was her reconnection with the Divine Light we are meant to stay connected to.

I stepped back from the table and bowed my head. I am always humbled by this Work. I am grateful for the opportunity to be of service, and I am richly rewarded in these moments when I stand in the presence of grace and divinity and the Holy Spirit. When the Gift first awakened in me, I remember the first channeling I had, a clear crystalline voice that spoke to me: "Not me, God, but you through me..." That was the prayer I was gifted with long before I understood what it meant.

Not me, God, but you through me.

Maryka lay there and came back slowly to full consciousness.

"Take your time," I said. "Notice the sensation of the table against your back, the weight in your body on the table...bring your consciousness back into your body and feel yourself filled with Light..."

The shadow had left her face. Her eyes were different. Her face glowed with the Light.

"Welcome back," I said.

I left the room and came back with a bottle of cold water for her. "Here you go."

She emptied it in one long draught. "Thank you."

"You'll want to drink more," I said. "I'll give you another bottle downstairs. You should get a few more. Spring or filtered water. Lots of it. Stop at the drugstore and get a big box of Epsom salts. Find one with lavender if you can. For the next seven days, every night, pour a full quart of Epsom salts into your tub and soak in it as long as you can. While you soak, visualize any sludge in you being drawn out into the water. You'll be thirsty so keep drinking lots of water."

"What was that like?" she said. "Did you see . . . I felt like—"

I held my hand up and interrupted her. "Best not to think or talk about it now. Best to just let it go."

She stood.

"You need to take some time to get grounded," I said. "Do you know how to do that?"

"I do tai chi . . ."

"That's great. It will work fine for that. Be grounded. Do you have far to drive?"

"No."

"Best thing now is to go home and rest."

"Thank you," she said. "I feel different . . ."

I nodded. "You are. It gets better as it goes along."

She went ahead of me. I reminded myself not to be distracted by the winking rivets of brass on her hip pockets, swaying gracefully as she walked down the hall and the stairs. She paused at the front door.

"What do I owe you?" she said.

I dislike this part.

"I don't charge a fee," I said. "If you want to make a donation or gift, you can leave it in the glass bowl there."

I pointed at the conspicuously empty glass fish bowl on the old oak table beside the door.

"The article said you had a sliding scale . . ."

"I was misquoted," I said. "I don't charge fees. People make a donation or gift based on what they feel my services are worth to them. I've been paid nothing at all, and I've been paid thousands."

I hoped I hadn't emphasized that last part too much.

She nodded, two quick bobs of her head. She wrote a check and dropped it in the bowl.

"Thanks," I said.

"Thank you..." she said.

She stood there. I knew what this was about. There's this moment at the end of a treatment, especially the kind I do, where the client feels the need to disconnect—or tries to stay connected. If the practitioner is an ethical one, he'll have already let go of the session and disconnected from the outcome. It's a test for a healer to let go of the rush that comes from being a channel for the Light, to let go of the ego and not allow your clients or the community to make you into something more than just a human with a special Gift.

The temptation is always there. Especially if the client is a beautiful woman and looking to cling to the man who helped facilitate her healing.

I closed my eyes and did the visualization of Severing the Cords and saw the disentanglement of our energetic connection begin.

Oh, Spirit... why do you tempt me so?

I laughed.

"What is it?" she said.

"Private joke," I said. "Take care, Maryka. If you feel you need to call or come back, just call me. We can talk. You're already feeling relief and it will get better. Like any other healing it'll take a little bit of time."

I watched her go. Then I gave into temptation and looked at her check. Two hundred fifty dollars. I could afford a box of cigars!

And more sage and sweet grass.

CHAPTER 5

I ran my tongue up Jolene's spine, from the cleft of her buttocks to the deep muscled hollow above her sacrum. I tasted the sweetness of her sweat and juices, mixed with mine, when I'd rolled her onto her belly.

"Aaaahhhhh," she moaned. It was like the opening of a holy song.

Jolene. The hottest woman in the world in one hundred words or less: tall, six feet barefoot though she favors heels, sleek and flat-bellied, with small breasts that defy gravity, perfectly chiseled like Michelangelo on his best day would sculpt her, the palest white skin, a rich length of red hair like a scarlet wing across her back, a long muscular dancer's back that swooped down into the glory of her waist and hips, eyes shocking blue and clear, high cheekbones and strange soulful lips—a thin upper lip curved like a bow, an obscenely full lower lip she sunk her teeth into when she thought about sex, which was often.

She's a Scorpio and an avatar of the Goddess in all her passion and fury. A Wiccan Priestess in her own right, a practitioner of the solo Wise Woman's path, a master of Reiki energy work and an intuitive who worked most often with the Tarot. Cool and self-possessed to the point of otherworldliness until she came to me in bed.

I lay my cheek against her buttocks and ran my hand down the long smooth white length of her taut leg.

"I give you a lifetime to stop that," she said.

"Mine," I said.

Deep husky laughter, so sexy and surprising in such a slender woman.

"Caveman," she said.

"Always."

"Do you worship the Goddess, Caveman?"

"Thoroughly. Otherwise she might cut me up and strew me in the field."

"There's a thought. Then I'd start over with some fresh flat-bellied boy."

"My belly is flat. Fairly."

She laughed. "It's fine, Marius. I like men with substance. I like having some meat to hang onto."

Lord, Lord, Lord. I am grateful.

She rolled onto her back, reached down and lay one long-fingered hand, nails clear and carefully polished, on my cheek. It was an infinitely gentle touch, in such contrast to her raw nature in bed. Contrast, contradiction...

Yes. She's a goddess.

And I'm lucky to service her.

"I feel that grin," she said. "I know what you're thinking."

"This is complicated, dating a psychic. A man can't have a single moment of private thought."

She laughed that deep throaty whiskey laugh and raked her nails across my scalp, then tugged at my hair, loose to my shoulders after she had undone my ponytail.

A long silence, that loving silence so essential between a man and a woman that so few couples seem to master. I love the soulfulness and ease between us in these times after our loving, in the lingering.

It's a fine way to spend the afternoon.

"I'm hungry," she said.

I stroked my fingers over her cleft, parted the fine red hair and tasted her. "Me, too."

She tugged a handful of my hair. "Feed *me*, Caveman. I'll feed *you* later."

"What if I insist?"

I felt her grin swell. "What if I deny you?"

"Then I'd go all caveman on you. Mine..."

Delighted throaty laughter. "It's a dangerous thing to trifle with a Priestess of the Goddess."

"I exist only to serve. She must be served properly."

"Then serve her dinner, Caveman."

I have a problem with deferred gratification, but learning graceful capitulation to the will of the Goddess is an essential milestone on the shamanic path. Or so I tell myself about my dealings with women, who were many before I met Jolene.

"What shall I feed you, Goddess? What do you desire?"

A satisfied giggle. "Let's see ... it's too nice to be inside. Let's go out."

"Picnic? Bottle of wine, a loaf of bread, and thou?"

"No. Too buggy. Take me to . . . Lucia's."

We lingered over our early dinner, the seafood linguine special, and finished a fine bottle of Chardonnay before we went out for a stroll through Uptown.

"Somewhere outside?" I said as we entered the parking lot.

"Of course, love," Jolene said. "Too early and too beautiful to be inside."

We took the long route through town, up north on Hennepin and across the bridge into the Northeast Art District. I found a parking spot around the corner from the Ginger Hop and escorted Jolene in. She staked out a banquette with a view of the street, crossed one immaculate white leg ending in impossibly strapped shoes, and set her purse on the table.

"Macallan, sweet," she said.

I went to the bar. The bartender, Ness, a beautiful and wise beyond her years woman who was also of the Church of Jolene, nodded to me.

"Hey, Marius, how you doing?" she said.

"Ness. How's it?"

"Awesome. Let me guess . . . Macallan for Jo; Bushmills Green Label, neat with a shot glass of water on the side, for you?"

"Is it wrong to be so predictable?"

She smiled her gentle smile; she was the best bartender in town when it came to creating the hint of the confessional that only the best bartenders can do.

"Good to have you back," she said. "Haven't seen either of you in too long."

I stuffed a twenty into the tip jar as an act of

contrition and carried our drinks to the table. Jolene smiled serenely at two young college boys who gawked at her. I nodded to them as I set down our drinks.

I don't get jealous. It doesn't pay to get possessive with an avatar of the Goddess. She doesn't tolerate even a hint of ownership.

She picked up her Scotch, tilted the crystal in my direction, tasted it slowly and with full attention, eyes closed in utter satisfaction. I worship her ability to be silent. Don't get me wrong, she can prattle about her favorite TV show (*Justified*—she nursed a serious crush on Timothy Olyphant) or carry on a deep spiritual dialogue about our respective past lives in Atlantis. Her ability to hold peaceful silence is a gift that most couples never enjoy. She was happy to hold her space, sip her drink, and watch the world go by.

I love that.

It frees me up to sit and admire her, and to enjoy the men (and women) admiring her. She was all dolled up: devastating low-cut little black dress, spiky-strappy expensive designer shoes, gleaming handcrafted silver earrings.

Nothing else.

At all.

Just raw Goddess in all her power.

I sipped my drink and watched her watch me over the rim of her glass, how her lips left a crimson half-moon on the crystal edge.

Lovely.

The traffic was light outside. I noticed one car slowing as it passed us, as though the driver were looking for a parking spot. A fleeting impression of the driver: bulky, hair cropped close to a squarish head, pale skin, eyes black slashes above the turned-up collars of a leather jacket...

A sudden chill.

My eyes narrowed. I leaned forward and set my drink down.

He passed.

Jolene noticed me noticing the driver. "Someone you know?"

"Not in this life."

She's a Wiccan High Priestess. She understands that. "Human?"

"I'm not sure."

"What have you been into, Marius? Are you drawing something in?"

"There's something I feel coming..."

She closed her eyes.

So did I.

With my shamanic vision I saw First In Front standing beside us, war paint on and brandishing his knife and bow. *"Brother, take care..."*

That was enough for me. I visualized the energetic shields around me hardening the layers of energy that ward off Dark Forces. Jolene whispered a warding spell beside me. The two Powers, Male and Female, entwined to create a fierce fortress around us.

"What is it, Marius?" she said.

I tuned in. Nothing.

I sat back and picked up my Bushmills. "Let them come. Right now, I'm enjoying my drink. And you."

She was still as a graven marble image. "I love your confidence. But sometimes I fear for you, my love."

"Fear's an old friend."

"It can be useful. Even more so if you transcend it." She sighed. "You're such a male..."

"It's part of my charm."

She tilted her glass to me. "Yes, sweet. Truly said."

The dark feeling had passed, so we enjoyed our drinks.

And while I enjoyed my woman and my whiskey, part of me stayed with my watchful protective spirits who prowled around me in the unseen world.

We were safe.

For now.

CHAPTER 6

Dillon Tracy is a half-Iranian, half-Irish madman cursed with Persian fire and Irish moodiness, given to drink and violence, and more than mildly obsessed with weapons. He runs a completely illegal firearms business out of his home and covers the proceeds with a part-time job as a spray-painter in an auto body shop. He's my go-to guy for weapons and accessories, and he's the best man—in this world—to watch my back when things get iffy.

He's a boon companion and my go-to guy for long meandering conversations over drinks and cigars as well.

Dillon is long-faced, with furrowed wrinkles running from his eyes down to the corners of his mouth; tall and lanky with jet black hair worn long; an olive complexion that made his racial background a mystery to the uninformed; surprisingly mild eyes for a man with his history of violence and a deep voice all out of proportion to his lanky frame.

We'd met when he came to me as a client, looking to rid himself of a dead Viet Nam Special Forces veteran, who'd attached to Dillon when he was a Special Forces operator in Iraq, drawn by the fear and anger that had been the dead man's last emotional resonance when he passed over. After that clearing, which had been a long one, Dillon and I became friends.

He's a great sounding board, and beloved by Coyote and Badger in the Spirit Realms—powerful and cunning warrior allies. He was grounded in the Middle World, and Creator knows that sometimes I needed that just as badly as an armed friend at my back, and more to the point, he was completely comfortable believing in and working with the other realities that intersect with ours.

So when I needed a gunfighter—or a good laugh—his was the door I turned to.

He tipped his second bottle of Harp's lager at me. "Shooting zombies? You don't need special bullets for that?"

"Just plain old Remington Golden Sabers," I said.

"Good round. I thought you'd need a silver bullet and a blessing."

"That's vampires and werewolves."

He twisted his mouth in eloquent distaste. "Don't like fucking with them."

"Me, neither. I try not to if I don't have to."

"Word." He chugged down his beer. "Want another?"

"I'm good," I said.

"What you got going, Marius?" Dillon said. "You going to need me?"

I laughed at the barely concealed eagerness in his voice. "What makes you think I need you, bro?"

"I know you. I'm down. What's up?"

The joy of the fight was a trait that I loved in him, and endeared him to his spirit guides, warriors all.

"If you're not busy, I'd like you to watch my back while I do some work."

"Is this the kind of back-watching I need holy water for, or will a Glock do?"

"Both."

His grin widened as though a winch pulled on his mouth. He tossed the bottle up, spinning, caught it on the descent.

"That's the kind of work I live for," he said.

"You're quite insane," I observed.

"Takes one to know one."

"To know me is to love me."

"Yeah, whatever. Tell it to Jolene, you lucky bastard. So. When do we start?"

"Tonight. After dark."

He laughed. "Isn't it always dark when we start?"

I retraced my chase from the night of the zombie. Dillon trailed behind me, his head swiveling in the practiced scan of an infantry man, leaving me free to concentrate on the subtle feelings that came to me as I followed the energetic track of my encounter. Every place has a vibration and a certain energy to it. Events and living beings leave an energetic imprint on top of that vibration. Magic—more accurately, in this instance, sorcery—leaves a distinctive imprint. It's like a foul odor, but more than anything else it's a feeling as though the air itself had become oily and roiled with Darkness that cloyed and clung.

I wanted to backtrack to the grave where the dead

man had been animated by Dark Will. That would be the jumping-off place for a journey back along the timeline to the origin of the sorcery, to see who—or what—I was dealing with. Clearly it was something that knew me and had a connection with me. That left me with many questions: This life...or another? Human or not? Souled or unsouled? Being or thought-form?

And what was the connection with the human-looking thing that had driven past Jolene and me at the Ginger Hop?

The answers were here, somewhere. In Middle World Work, the world of magic and curses and sorcery, there's no substitute for walking the ground and sensing the energy directly, watching the movie unfold in real time with shamanic vision.

We started where I'd ended it, in the graveyard. The energy was clear here. The presence of Michael and the Mighty Warriors of Light on Earth will clear even the worst place. But the lingering essence was enough for me to track...

...random images and thoughts, becoming clearer...

...past life? No, this life...but knew you before, knows the work that you've done and the Dark Work you've undone on others' behalf... Son of the Light, Warrior of the Light...who?...

My white tiger appeared and whispered, "Follow me, Marius..."

...and I followed, the journey unfolding before me, as though I were walking like an apparition through an empty movie theater up onto the screen of a sepia-tinted film, and I was following the trace of the undead, like a ragged strip of black cloth frayed and fading into a light gray, still dissipating from

*the brilliant White Light of the Warriors of Light . . .
back to the grave it rose from and my white tiger
stood before me and bloomed with shielding Light . . .
I watched a Dark Portal open, not into the Void,
but the Dark Void beyond that . . . another dimension entirely . . . something there, something reaching
through, orchestrating, a puppet master working the
way the Dark Forces worked best . . . find a portal
in the Middle World, a human with a resonance for
and with the Dark . . . utilize them . . . obsess, possess,
influence—the lean, we called it, the ability to lean
on someone energetically—something I'd undone . . .
coming back, returning for vengeance . . .*

"Wait," Tigre whispered. "It's coming forward . . ."

*The black beyond the Darkness altered, shifted
shape . . . like a face pressed up against a sheer sheet
of black rubber, rising up out of the fabric of Darkness itself, a face carved in long obsidian plates . . .*

"Shaman . . ." it whispered.

*My white tiger stood in front of me. A huge black
crow settled beside her, black and white illuminated
from within with the Divine White Light of the Creator,
protecting me from the chill that roiled from that face.*

"Don't speak," Tigre said. "Only listen . . ."

*There was an unspoken dialogue, telepathic . . . an
array of images passing before my shamanic vision:
beautiful, tall, green crystal towers toppling and shattering beneath a wall of water, a huge tidal wave; tiny
figures garbed in white and green and silver tumbling
in the water; a temple collapsing around a huge red
crystal shaped like a prism; a wave of Dark energy
riding the wave, overcoming the heroic few holding
space for the Light, holding the Darkness back . . .*

The War.
The Sons of Light against the Sons of Darkness.
The followers of the Law of One against the follow-
ers of Belial.
. . . and now I returned . . .

"Marius?" Dillon said. "Marius?"

I stood at the lip of an open grave.

"Did I just walk over that?" I said.

"Nice," Dillon said. "You okay? What you got?"

I looked up at the night sky. Clear. A thousand stars gleaming above the city lights. An endless eternity of night. Somewhere out there, beyond space as we mere mortals called it, something pressed against the fabric of our reality and slouched towards us, ready to rend its way out of its dark womb.

"Long story, bro," I said.

"Have a smoke long, or get the hell out of here and go have coffee long?"

"Coffee long."

"Then let's do like the cowboys and Indians and get the hell out of Dodge."

"Something I need to do . . ."

I pulled a half-full Advil bottle out of my pocket and rattled it. Dillon opened his mouth, then closed it. I chanted the opening words of a Lakota power song gifted to me by First In Front as I closed my eyes and called in the Light to illuminate and clear this space of the lingering essence of evil that had been perpetrated here. I continued to rattle and felt the Light bring its brilliance into me, and felt the Darkness lifting from the roots of the grass and from the disturbed earth of the grave. When it was gone, I pulled out my tobacco pouch and offered a pinch to the spirits here, and closed with a simple prayer of, "Thank you, Creator God."

I took a deep breath. "Now we can go."

Dillon looked around, scanned the graveyard.

"Dude," he said. "Can't you afford a real rattle?"

Gigi's Coffee Shop on 36th is one of my fave coffee hangs in a town full of excellent coffee hangs. It's open and airy with Ikea tables that are the right height to work at or lean on, the food is extraordinary and cheap, the coffee excellent, and the service is committed to creating an open, welcoming atmosphere. It feels like home.

Dillon and I sat at a back table, hunched over big mugs of the house French Roast. Outside, people walked their dogs, bought newspapers, enjoyed the night air; cars flowed by.

"The story?" Dillon prompted.

"How's your belief system tonight?"

He actually considered that. "That changed forever the day you worked on me. I don't waste time arguing with my own experience. You know, you told me something that day. You remember? You said, 'Dillon, you might not believe in Spirit, but Spirit believes in you.'"

He grinned and tilted his coffee mug at me. "So what I believe is kind of irrelevant."

"Your belief is never irrelevant, Dillon."

"There you go getting all shamanic on me, dude. What I'm trying to say in a fancy way is that whether I know it or believe it, if *you've* seen it, it's good enough for me. Does that work?"

Dillon's trust is not given lightly. A man with his

background didn't live as long as he had by being naive or overly trusting.

"Thank you, Dillon."

"Yeah, yeah," he said. "This humble shaman guy thing wastes time, you know? I get it. Cut to the chase and tell me the story."

Dillon is grounded and solid, the man I trust to watch my back. But after all these years, I'm still cautious about opening up the door to the other realities to those who didn't work with them everyday. A shaman's job is to cross over into those realms and bring back information, rescue souls and soul fragments, carry the dead into the Light, do battle with Dark Forces when necessary, undo sorcery, depossess and extract. I did all those things. And a big part of the job was to journey and return with information and share it.

So I needed to tell the story.

"You know about Atlantis?" I said.

"I read the comic book."

"There's an Atlantis comic book?"

"Lots of 'em. Get on with the story."

"Here's the comic book version, then," I said. "Before Atlantis fell, there was a war. A revolution. It was led by the followers of the Law of One, the Sons and Daughters of Light, against the followers of Belial. It was a war between the Power of Light and the Power of Darkness. It was a war like any war: battles, heroic stands, bitter betrayal, horrifying defeats—and magic. Atlantis's spiritual leadership communed directly with the Creator's Light. There was a giant crystal in the central Temple of Light that channeled the Light of the Creator directly to those who spoke with the Creator—the Priests and Priestesses.

The Light powered everything—airships, homes—it moved stones and parted the water at the direction of the Light Keepers. The Sons of Belial tried to turn the power of the Great Crystal against the Sons of Light, and that conflict shattered the island's foundation and changed the energetic grid of the Earth itself. The survivors of the Sons of Light escaped from the harbors; behind them, in the Temple of Light, the Priestesses of Light who had the closest connection with Mother Earth drew on all their power to hold back the tide—but their power couldn't hold it. The wave fell, and shattered the land, and scattered the escaping boats of the few far and wide."

I saw that great wave shattering the towers, the brave few who'd returned to rescue the Priestesses crushed in the wave, the boats propelled away by the power of magic and the wind, just ahead of the huge wave of destruction.

"What happened, as a result of the Fall, was that certain Powers were released and set loose in the world," I said. "Key players from the Other Realms, here in the Middle World, some of them energetic, some of them in the flesh. And the battle continues. There was never any resolution. It's the Dark against the Light. If you're a Warrior of the Light, a Light Worker, if you go that way, you're a magnet for your counterparts, the Dark Workers..."

"So that's you. I get that. But how does the zombie thing play?" Dillon said.

"Someone who knew me before, someone with a grudge, has come through. Or is coming through. They're working through proxies. They may be ready to cross into the flesh...or they might be here already."

"Can you journey on it? Find out who they are? Give us a target?"

I grinned at my friend, leaning forward in his chair, the fire and love of battle in his eyes.

"I intend to," I said.

Dillon drained the last of his coffee. "Sucks to be you, dude. Just saying."

"There's always an upside, Dillon."

Sometimes it's best not to burden your friends with unpleasant truths.

CHAPTER 7

Hawks don't flock. Neither do shaman.

In the indigenous shamanic tradition, there may be more than one shaman in a community. Each one would be known for a specialty. Often there was competition, but shamanism is measured by actual results, not advertising, despite the best attempt of the new generation shamanic practitioners, often products of expensive training programs, to run their spiritual practices like modern day businesses complete with ads like "Shamanic healing done here! Soul retrievals done! One-month shaman course, with certificate!"

Native American medicine culture, especially the outspoken Lakota with whom I felt affinity, condemned the modern practices and coined the term "plastic shaman" or "plastic medicine man."

The old rules still apply. You shall know a shaman by his work, not by his words. It's up to the community to evaluate his work and measure the results;

shamanic practice is as pragmatic and practical as a plumber's—and should be evaluated the same way.

There is a very loose-flung network of practitioners, both in Spirit and through the modern mediums of phone, e-mail, Facebook and Twitter, that attempts to organize and consolidate contact information and referrals. Most of us have our own private network, a shamanic list of friends and practitioners we call on when we need work done on ourselves, backup, or questions answered.

I called one of my favorites.

Sabrina Murphy is a badass biker chick. She's drop-dead gorgeous: killer violet eyes, a body bursting out of ragged jeans and wife-beater tops like a teenage boy's midnight fantasy, pale skin covered with tattoos and more than a few scars from barroom brawls. She's Cherokee and one of the most powerful shamanic healers, with a particular gift for divination journeys into the Other Realms. I called her my shamanic CIA. Nothing was hidden from her for long. She'd come to the attention of the government's military psychics, like most of us do. What they called remote viewing, we called Middle World journeying. When they came round offering her big bucks, she told them to fuck off and went back to her work. They tried to teach her a lesson with their technologically enhanced remote influencing; she kicked their asses in the Other Realms and, rumor had it, left several of them injured when their machines backfired on them.

My kind of woman, all the way around.

Her voice, still sleepy at this time of day, was colored with a whiskey and cigarette rasp. "What did you get, dude?"

"It's mixed, sister."

"Cabal?"

"Could be. There's that whole Atlantean connection."

"Piss off some sorcerers lately?"

"Daily."

She laughed a deep and throaty and hot-as-hell laugh. If it wasn't for Jolene—who loved this Wild Woman—I might take my life in my hands and dally with her.

Truth is, I probably wouldn't survive it.

"You got that right, Marius," she said. "You got that whole 'fuck you and the world' thing going on. I thought you were kinder and gentler now that you've reached the age of wisdom."

"I'm not getting any wiser, darling."

"Born dumb, huh? That's all right, baby. I love you anyway."

"Thank the Creator for that."

"I thank him every day," she said.

A long thoughtful draw on her cigarette, audible through the phone.

"So," she said, "I'll look at this today. Get back to you. I'll tell you my first hit right now...old curse, Marius. Past life, not ancestral, but someone...or something...from before. I get Cabal, too. You got to watch out for the psychotronics and those convenient accidents they're fond of."

"No lie, GI."

"Yeah. Watch yourself. I'll get back to you later... cell phone?"

"Yeah."

"You should get you a prepay burner, baby. Cabal likes to..."

"I know."

"'Kay, baby. Watch yourself."

She hung up.

I powered down my cell phone and took the battery out. Cabal. That really complicates things. The Cabal is where top-secret technology, hard-core sorcery, and the amoral direction of nonhuman entities and willing humans intersect. It's cloaked in government secrecy, funded with black budget dollars and put to the service of the hidden bureaucrats who ruled from behind the puppets they slipped into place every election.

Not a pretty picture.

The Dark Forces manifest here in Middle World in all sorts of ways—the thoughtless cruelty of one human towards another, the efficient predation of a serial killer, the ruthless exploitation of Mother Earth—to hold humans in thrall through the machinery of governance, all to quash the greatest gift of the Creator: Free Will.

Freedom.

Made me want to go watch a Mel Gibson movie.

I had no clients today. That happens. My practice isn't one that lent itself to a lot of return customers. Depossession is like surgery. You go in and get the work done, help them through their recovery, and move onto the next. That's why I keep a list of practitioners to refer clients to; I'm problem-oriented and once I've done the work I'm supposed to do, I'm glad to hand the client onto those better able to further facilitate their recovery.

Right now I was working for myself, which meant I was working pro bono.

For the public good.

Lovely.

I checked my bank balances, which were bottomed out. I had to make a withdrawal from my backup stash in a lockbox I kept in the closet of my bedroom. There was a few hundred in there which left me good for right now. I took a handful of twenties and tucked them into my empty wallet, then set off for a longish walk down to Lake Harriet and then back over to Gigi's for some coffee and head-clearing. It's a nice long walk, though circuitous: from my place off Nicollet down the greenway along Minnehaha Creek, around Harriet, then over to Bryant.

And I like to walk.

I was only just down the greenway when I heard my guides whisper, *"Good time to be aware, Marius,"* and then I saw First In Front just off to my right and felt a nudge against my lower leg. My white tiger was with me.

I touched my elbow to my side and hissed when it pressed against meat instead of the comforting plastic of my Glock 19. I'd left it at home, under the bed, an oversight I was guilty of more than once when preoccupied with Other Realms' work, and an oversight Dillon had chastised me about more than once.

I took a quick look around.

Nothing...

Maybe.

One of the things a hunter knows is how to think like the hunted. When your practice involves the hunting of dark things, you learn that sometimes, maybe all the time, you get looked at. *The more you see, the more you are seen.* The Dark Forces work through humans as well as directly. I bore scars from some of the encounters with them I'd had. Protection and caution is all part of my game.

I pay attention to "maybe."

Like the man slouched down in an idling car studiously not looking at me. Waiting for somebody?

Maybe.

Maybe for me.

I don't like giving the initiative away, though sometimes the counterpunch is best. I crossed the street and headed straight for the car. The driver pulled away, not meeting my eyes. Newish Ford sedan, dealer's temporary plates.

Hmmm.

I felt the gentle nudge of my invisible—to anyone else's eyes—white tiger.

First In Front appeared in full war-fighter regalia: leather overshirt and breeches, a simple headband with coup feathers, a tomahawk and long knife in his hands.

"It's like that, huh?" I said.

He nodded, a sharp bob of the head.

Lovely.

I kept walking and cut across the parking lot behind the Soi Capitale Bank. A Jeep Cherokee slammed to a stop and the doors opened. The driver was familiar— square head, pale skin, close-cropped black hair, deep-sunk dark eyes that darted away when I looked at him. Three others got out. Big old farm boys by the look of them, moving with the jerky lock step of the possessed or influenced, in battered Carhart jackets with feed caps pulled low over their eyes.

My cell phone rang.

No time for that. I hurried across the parking lot. The three meat puppets turned to follow me. Dillon taught me the first rule of street fighting a long time ago: You won't be in one if you're not there. But if you have to be there, make them come to you on ground you choose, not them.

In laymen's terms, run like hell. Or in this instance, like Hell was after you.

Running and looking back is never a good idea; either run, or look back. If you do both, then you're likely to run full tilt into a parked Ford F-150 and knock yourself on your ass—like I did. That gave the shambling meat puppets a chance to gain on me.

It also gave me a moment to gather my energy, shift my consciousness and call my spirit allies. In my mind's eye, I saw a whirling shape, like a conch shell in motion, twisting and then opening like a tunnel and through it came some help...

The first meat puppet flailed his arms and clawed at his eyes as a crow that only he (and I) could see flew into his face, turning him; a white tiger bounded into the second, batting him down with her massive paws; the last closed on me as I scrambled to my feet. I ducked between his wild swings and I saw the look of terror and violation on his face, the look of the remotely controlled or possessed, and that sheer human terror held me back, for just an instant, till my self-preservation instincts drove me to stomp the outside of his leg and put him down.

Remotely controlled.

Demonic Dark Forces or the Cabal? Or both? Either way, the controller would be nearby. I looked at the black-haired blockhead sitting in his Jeep.

First In Front appeared in front of me and grinned back over his shoulder. *"Follow me..."*

"Okay, Infantry..." I said.

And I did. When in doubt, attack head-on. *Hoka hey!*

I ran right at the Jeep. The controller, if that's what he was, widened his eyes and slammed the Jeep into gear. He hit the gas, peeling backwards away from me. First In Front *flew* at him, then stopped as though he'd hit a pane of glass. The Jeep backed into traffic and then roared away. First In Front looked at me.

"No," I said. A vehicle in the hands of a panicked pawn was as dangerous as a firearm in a crowd. The three farmhands were sitting up, looking around with the confused look of accident victims.

"It's lifted," First In Front said. *"It went with the controlling one."*

"That's no sorcerer," I said.

"No," Tigre said. She sat and licked one paw. Burt circled and landed in a flurry of black feathers.

"We should go," the crow said. *"You hurt that one, and he's going to get his head clear quick."*

"Who's controlling?" I said.

"Hidden," the three said.

I nodded. "Let's go find him."

I jogged away, First In Front and Tigre bounding along with me, Burt flying overwatch, leaving the dazed meat puppets behind.

My cell phone beeped from an unanswered call. It was from Sabrina.

CHAPTER 8

I squeezed into a back table at Gigi's, where I could see the front entrance and still duck out the back exit. First In Front lounged at an empty table across from me, invisible to all but me, still as a tree. On the sidewalk in front, Tigre sat, her back to the window, an invisible guardian; Burt circled overhead—I felt his watchful presence circling.

It was good to know that my protective spirits were on guard.

I hit redial and after six or seven rings, Sabrina answered. She was smoking a cigarette and took a long draw before she said, "You don't mess around, do you, Marius?"

"What do you mean, babe?"

"You've got an extreme case of extreme addiction. Adrenaline junkie." Another long draw on her cigarette. "Maybe you were a biker in another life."

"Could be," I said. "Was I the biker or the bitch?"

She laughed that deep throaty laugh. "You could never be my bitch, honey. Though I'd let you try it out."

I felt her shift gears and drop into an altered consciousness as she channeled the information she'd found for me. "You have a complex situation, Marius. I'll try and keep it simple. I know how you get confused. You're right about past lives...there's history here. An old curse. We can unravel it, it's having a hard time sticking to you anyway. You've fought this sorcerer. It's a he. You've fought him before. Several lifetimes. Black hair, pale skin, dark eyes, square head, right?"

"Yeah. That's him."

"You should see him in a Nazi uniform."

"He play dress-up?"

She laughed. "Could be. But he was one in the war. Goes further back, too. Atlantis. He's a Son of Belial."

I sighed. "Couldn't be easy, could it?"

"No, baby," she said. "That's the lot of a Son of the Light."

Yes. It is.

"Go on," I said.

"You've thwarted him over and over. He's obsessed by you and how you've beaten him time and again. Every time he thinks he's beaten you down, you fool him again and again. You know that great gift you have? For pissing the bad guys off? You've mocked him and defeated him repeatedly...so he's obsessed with you. He's fooled so many others...but not you. He's so full of hatred, and he takes pleasure in hurting. He's a bad one."

"Demon?"

"Yes. He's willingly possessed. Made a bargain, they're bound together in an ancient pact. That's where his strength comes from. It's also his weakness. He's a control freak, so he struggles against the demon's agenda while at the same time playing along. That's his dilemma. He's not yet perfectly possessed, may never be. He thinks he's smarter than everybody including his demon. But in this, they both want the same thing: your downfall. For him it's personal. He comes back lifetime after lifetime to get even. But he hasn't, so he keeps coming back. The demon? I didn't get too close . . . it's a bad one."

She took another long drag on her cigarette. I heard her exhale slowly. "You're high on the Dark Forces hit list, Marius. Because of your Work. How many souls have you rescued? How many have you brought to the Light? Each one of them is a failure for the Dark. And they keep track. So the score sheet is getting unbalanced, and they sent a heavy hitter for you. Wouldn't be the first time, if I recall."

"What's the Nazi thing?"

"He was there," she said. "In the concentration camps. An officer. I saw that clearly. In his last incarnation. The sick pleasure of that is fresh in his mind. He loved being in control, able to hurt others whenever he wanted to. But he died. Badly. Terrified and alone. And that, my friend, brings us to the Cabal."

"Oh, great," I said. "The news just gets better and better."

"We've both run across them before, honey," she said. "Once you're in the Machine they'll never forget about you. They hate shamans. All of us. Because they can't control us and what we do on behalf of

the Light. More of the Sons of Belial are incarnat-
ing; the stage is being set here in America for an
epic replay of Atlantis. So where do they end up?
Banking, politics, cops, military and spooks, computer
companies . . . What are they doing? Same things they
did before. Manipulate, confuse, muddle . . . they're
setting the stage for the final showdown between the
Sons of the Light and the Sons of Belial. And they
all work with or for the Cabal."

"Military. Intelligence. Law enforcement," I said
heavily.

"And armies of snitches," she said. "Legions of
the possessed or controlled. This one must be strong
with a very powerful demon if he can remote-control
four humans."

"At least one of them seemed conscious of it."

"His soul was fighting it, then?"

"Yeah," I said. I remembered the look of desperate
fear, the violation apparent in every line of the man's
face. My Work was to prevent that, to confront it and
stop it. And I felt rage rise in me as the attack on
me had, at least in that man's part, been forced into
an otherwise innocent bystander.

"What else, sister?"

"What else?" she said. "It's not clear. To me, anyway.
There's always a cloud around you; your spirits protect
you with their shielding and it diffuses your presence.
You're hard to find and fix unless there's a positive
connection. You shrug off any attempts otherwise."

"Were you able to see through to the outcome?"

"With you there's always two paths, Marius—the red
and the black. You walk the razor's edge, like we all
do, but you more than most. You'll be tempted. You

have to be aware of your reactiveness, your desire to lash out. It's your style, you know? Kick the cart over, piss on it, set it on fire."

She laughed, coughed. "Personally, I love that about you. But it pisses people—or entities—off, and keeps them pissed off. Not good when you're dealing with people who come back time and again to try and even the score."

"I work on compassion," I said.

"I know you do," she said. "I know. You put it into action. It's not an abstract principle or idea with you. You practice it. It's your path. You've got that whole Bodhisattva thing going and you bring that energy into the world. It's a gift. People are grateful you do it . . . most wouldn't or couldn't deal with the things you have to deal with every day. You get big power, you get big challenges. You work on compassion, but you have a fiery temper. Your work is to heal and protect, but you love a good fight. So there you have it."

"How do I take him out, Sabrina?"

"Do what you do best, Marius. You won't be able to depossess him. He won't give his permission. But you can draw him and his demon out and in the confrontation, the Law of the One gives you the absolute right to self-defense . . . you can do whatever you need to in defense of yourself . . . or others. He's coming after you in any way he can. He's coming. In every possible way."

CHAPTER 9

When I have people coming for me, which is, unfortunately, a common occurrence in the life of a Warrior of the Light, there's one place and one person I reach out to...

I was sitting with Dillon in his lair, watching my friend prepare for what we both felt hanging out there. When I'd shown up, he'd already been getting ready. He just pointed me at a chair and went about his business.

I watched him run a silicon cleaning cloth over the metal and plastic furniture of a folding stock Yugo AK-47. When he handled weapons, or was working in harm's way, he had a certain look on his face, an intense, almost studious face while he dealt with the problem at hand. His energy, and the guides around him, invisible to him but not to me, were both of the most intense warrior kind. He'd been a special operations soldier in the Army's Special Forces, since he took particular care to distinguish between special operations, Special Forces and other special-operations-capable organizations. Those distinctions were lost on me till I'd met him; I'd never been in the military—in this life, anyway—though a part of me and my past lives resonated with that. Dillon and I had a past life there, too—the easy familiarity with which we worked together, in harm's way or not, was testament to that.

He set the cloth down on his worktable, then adjusted the simple sling and hung the AK around his neck. He swung up a few times, aligning the sights with the short rifle punched out taut against the sling. With it hanging down, he could swing it up and punch it out and align the sights almost as well as if he'd extended the stock.

"How you going to conceal that?" I said.

He grinned, put on a three-quarter-length leather overcoat, bulked up in the shoulders, over his black turtleneck. You could see the black strap of the rifle if you were close enough, but it didn't draw your eyes, it just faded into the black. The rifle hung down but the coat was long enough to conceal the short muzzle.

"You look like an extra in *Saturday Night Fever*," I said.

Dillon stepped smartly into a disco step, pointing his finger at the sky and began to sing, "Ah, ah, ah, staying alive, staying alive . . ."

"I sure hope so."

"We will be," he said, paused. "No lycans on this, are there?"

"I hope not. Cabal has some for their special forces."

Dillon considered that. We'd tangled with lycans before. Not pretty.

"Standard ammo we're running in this is brass and lead, steel core and an exposed steel tip. That will knock down any Dark Siders that react to iron."

"No faery in this. They don't work this way or with demons."

"I wasn't thinking of them," Dillon said. He shrugged. "I've got silver made up in a separate mag if any lycans show up."

"You rolled some silver bullets?"

He tilted his head at the Dillon loading press (no relation) over in the corner.

"This place looks like Baghdad at Christmas," I said. "Crossed with a Wiccan supply house."

He laughed. "It works."

"I appreciate it, Dillon."

When his eyes lit up and his teeth pulled back, he looked more like a lycan than a nontransformed lycan did. "I figure it's my part in the fight."

"You've earned your place in the Light. And then some, brother."

"So have you, Marius. So have you. So. What's the plan?"

"Plan? I don't need no stinking plan!"

"You're Yul Brynner, dude. I get to play McQueen."

"I'm *part* of a plan, but I don't have *a* plan."

"That's really comforting," Dillon said. "I'd like to know which way to shoot."

"I hope we won't have to shoot at all."

"There you go," Dillon said. "Being all hopeful. What's the fun of being the best backup to the best shaman, excuse me, practitioner if I don't get to shoot some Dark Warriors once in a while? And I kinda doubt we're gonna miss that opportunity, the way things are going."

Planning has never been my strong suit. I have a Zen-like approach to living; stay in the moment. Shamanic practice reinforces that. Or so I told myself on occasions like this or when rationalizing my expenses in the face of my bill collectors. So the plan, right? They—a series of undead and possessed, remote-controlled or outright possessed, hunting me down to do bad things to me ranging from killing me to torching my spiritual essence in some fiery corner of the Dark Realms—they are looking for me, right? So let's make it easy. Let them come to me instead of spending my meager resources chasing them. Draw them out into the open and while my backup slows them down or takes them out, I search backwards to find the Controller, the one with the capital C.

It's like doing a demonic depossession. When there's a true demonic presence, it's hitched to a controller, a higher level demon, who in turn is hitched to another demon all the way down the line to the biggest baddest demon of all. If you want the Dark Forces out and to keep them out, you must backtrack to the main entity, and then step aside while the Archangels do the work of taking that demon boss to the Place of Confinement and the Womb of Transformation.

So I went with my default plan: kick the bad guy's cart over, set it on fire, and see who comes running.

I gestured Dillon close. We both closed our eyes. I took out my good rattle—a stretched leather ball filled with maize kernels, the handle an old piece of worn birch—and began to rattle gently, setting my intention and calling my power animals closer. The steady rhythmic rattle activated those places in my energy, my spirit, and cleared out all distraction so that I might shift from the Middle World into the Other Realms—

—and I'm on a grassy hillside, looking over a beautifully forested valley, a sinuous river winding its way through, a hawk circling overhead . . . to my right, white tiger, to my left, black crow . . . off in the distance I see darkness gathering on the skyline . . . light stabs down from the sky, a brilliant beam of light that shines on me, to my left and right, above and below, from within, the Light within me like a portal . . . because that's what I am in the Great Game, a portal for the Light, and the more that I channel, the more I am seen . . . on both sides . . .

I felt the attention shifting towards me. Sending up the Light is like issuing a challenge to the Dark— "Here I am . . . come and get me . . ."

My power animals laughed. "Never the easy way with you, Marius . . . can we kill them with kindness this time?"

I began to come back . . .

Dillon opened his eyes. "I *felt* that one."

I nodded. "Somebody else might have, too."

Outside, we both heard car doors slamming shut.

Dillon grinned his crazy grin. "Guess it's show time?"

"Yep."

Dillon's been a warrior for many lifetimes. When it's time for a fight, he runs to the sound of the fight, not away. He was already bounding up the stairs while I was still shaking off my journey trance. I grabbed a handy long-gun, a cut-down Remington 870 stoked with Dillon's hand-loaded buckshot, and chased him up the stairs. He was at the front window, peeking cautiously through the curtain gap.

"Four," he whispered. "Stacked up. Like cops . . ."

The heavy tread of boots at the doorway and then, without pause, the crash of a kick against the door.

Somebody's foot was going to hurt.

If they were human, that is. Dillon had steel fire doors mounted in reinforced frames front, back and side. It would take more than a few undead kicking those doors to get inside.

"We'll go out the side," Dillon said. "We'll flank 'em."

"Is that a real term? Flank 'em?"

Dillon's grin got even more feral, if that was possible. "Find 'em, fix 'em, flank 'em, finish 'em."

"Um, okay."

I followed him through the front room and the kitchen, where he quickly peeked out the window, and then went out the side door.

"Pull it locked, Marius," he said.

I did. The heavy latches fell into place. So no retreat through this door.

We edged wide around the corner of the house. Dillon had his AK up, I had my shotgun ready, every other step I looked back to make sure no one came up behind us.

In front, one man in plain clothes kicked again and again at the front door. The three behind him, also in plain clothes, held pistols to cover the front windows. Plainclothes, acting like cops . . . but none of them uttered a word.

The last man in the stack saw us. He raised his pistol and started shooting—no warning, no announcement—in our direction.

It was his last action.

Because all of a sudden it got like Quentin Tarantino meets John Woo.

Gunfights at close range get violent very suddenly. It's often over before you know it, too fast for conscious recall, or else it's one of those that hang in front of you in slow motion.

This was a slow-motion event.

I saw the ejected casings hanging in the air above the pistol from the guy shooting at us. He was focused and intense as he concentrated on his sights (not a good sign since zombies don't have the fine muscle coordination necessary to shoot well with a handgun); I watched Dillon's leather jacket crinkle (one of those weird details you remember after a fight) as he shifted his weapon mount and fired *pow-pow-pow* three fast shots from the AK and hit that first shooter, whose look of sudden surprise and his arms outflung reminded me of that picture from the Spanish Civil War. It was time for me to get in the fight, so I let fly with the 870 and Dillon's custom buckshot (a .45-caliber ball on top with 00 buck beneath) and watched the door-kicker spray red and stagger back off the steps before he fell out of the line of fire.

Dillon aggressed on them, a steady cadence of aimed fire, crouched over his rifle and walking like Groucho Marx in an experienced roll of heel and toe, me to his right, *boom-boom-boom* of my shotgun before it ran dry and then I cleared my Glock and continued shooting...

Silence, then.

Everyone was down except for us.

The shooting part was done.

But the fight wasn't over.

The ground shook. The grass of Dillon's lawn lifted and pulled itself into a larger than man-sized form, a man made out of the lawn.

I was still disoriented from my journey and the loud shots ringing in my unprotected ears. And I still couldn't help but think, *The Lawnmower Man?*

Dillon watched his lawn rearrange itself into a huge green opponent. Two glaring red eyes rimmed in black appeared in the head.

"I think it's your turn to lead," he said.

The entity turned towards me, and I felt anger rising like a red tide within me.

What I do both is and isn't what is thought of as "magic." Magic involves combining your intention and emotional content in partnership with entities and powers in the Other Realms to get specific results: money, sex, power, secrets. Shamanic Light Workers are primarily Travelers: we go into the Other Realms and gather information, retrieve that which has been lost or stolen and bring it back. We put in that which has been taken and we take out what doesn't belong. And for that, we work with our allies, our guides, our power animals—but there's a fine line that we walk between the use of that energy and what we call sorcery, the exercise of power-over, controlling—and that's what we were running into here: controlled humans and a thought-form, something constructed with intention and filled with hate, that Dark energy overriding the life it was controlling.

To a shaman, even the grass and dirt has life and spirit. To override that in the service of the Dark...

That just pisses me off.

This thought-form looked like the Pillsbury Dough Boy run through a sod farm. It swung a rusty length of pipe in one paw.

"There goes the sprinkler system," I said.

Dillon considered that. "Should I shoot this thing?"

"Wouldn't hurt."

Dillon opened up. Divots of grass and dirt flew like a bad day on the driving range.

The thought-form lumbered forward and swiped at Dillon's head with the pipe.

We both ducked.

"Maybe it would hurt," I said.

"Gee, thanks, Marius," Dillon muttered. He crouched low and tried to get behind the Lawnmower Man/ Dough Boy.

I summoned power; felt the shift and saw the shimmering as the veil between the worlds thinned. Then the grass beneath the thought-form shifted, drew and wrapped long strands and tendrils around the legs of the form, bringing it down. My shamanic vision showed me black lines like puppet strings running from the back of the thought-form, disappearing into a murky gray swirling fog—somewhere back there a human figure, square-headed, familiar...

A massive black crow whipped by my ears and tore at the tendrils.

"... *never the easy way with you, Marius*..."

"Thanks, Burt!" I shouted.

The thought-form rose and stretched out its paws, fingers growing Freddy Krueger-like, swiping at me as I ducked back. Dillon poured shot after shot into it with no effect.

Time for another pass—

—and time to call for the heavyweights.

"Archangel Michael, I call on you, to bring the Sword of Michael here in the service of the Light..." I whispered.

A brilliant flash of white light, hotter than the heart of the sun, brighter than the sum of all days rolled together, and something slicing down—

The thought-form came undone. Tendrils and threads fell backwards into a shrinking gray hole, swirling like dirty water down the drain.

There was only a sadly torn-up lawn and a bent piece of rusty pipe.

And four bodies huddled on the lawn.

Dillon walked to me, reloading his AK. The barrel smoked. There was a sear on his left sleeve from a grazing gunshot or the hot barrel of his own weapon.

"You okay?" he said.

"Yeah. You?"

He looked at his coat sleeve. "Damn. I like this coat. Nothing a Korean tailor can't fix." He surveyed the wreckage of his lawn. "Good thing I don't have neighbors. Guess it's time for the three S's, yeah?"

"Shit, shower and shave?"

"Shoot, shovel, and shut up."

I looked at the rolling cornfields around us, miles from any other houses. "Seems very ecologically conscious to me."

We walked over to the bodies. Despite the damage the bullets had done, they didn't leak much.

"This isn't right," I said. "Back up, Dillon."

I called my spirits close and opened my shamanic vision to encompass the bodies.

... the lines of connection and control hung, floated like tendrils in murky water, tracking back ... were they alive or dead or thought-forms? ... flashes, brief glimpses, and then long rows of stainless steel coffers, glass-fronted, pale bodies floating within ...

"Ah, no," I said.

"What?"

"This just went from worse to worser."

"What?"

"Cabal."

"What?"

"You're getting repetitive, Dillon," I said.

"What?"

I pulled some shells out of my pocket and thumbed them into the Remington.

"Cabal, Dillon. These guys aren't really human. They were grown in tanks, animated by the Dark Forces."

"Grown in tanks? What're you talking about, grown in tanks?"

I looked up at the sky. Down the long road.

Empty.

At least to the naked eye.

"The Cabal grew them. Clones."

"Like *Star Wars*?"

I had to laugh. "Yeah, dude. Like *Star Wars*. Cabal grows them, the Dark Forces empower them. They use technology to embed skills and training in them."

"They're human?"

"It's a toss-up, Dillon. They're grown from human stock, using human DNA, but essentially they have no soul, no Light from the Creator. The Dark Forces breathe a kind of life into them; they possess or inhabit them, but whether they're human in the same way . . . I don't know. They're like zombies, but different."

"'Like zombies, but different?' Oh, dude," Dillon said. "I should have stayed on the boat. Number one rule is: 'Stay on the boat!'"

"'The horror! . . . the horror!'"

Dillon shook his head. "It's murder in this world, Marius. Guess we better find out who they were, since we figured out *what* they were." He bent down and took out a credential case from the hip pocket of the closest body. He opened it up. "Department of Homeland Security, Special Agent." He sighed. "Dead *federales*?"

"Cabal, dude."

"I'm gonna need another long talk, Marius."

"Let's clean up your lawn first. You still got that chipper in back?"

"Why do you pray over them if they're not human?" Dillon said.

We washed our hands after spreading the bloody new mulch into his big compost pit.

"Not for me to decide whether they have souls or not," I said. "I leave that up to the Creator. Just my default. Enemy or not, I honor them and wish them passage to the Light. I do it for you and me, too. Keeps the karma where it's supposed to be."

Dillon considered that for a long moment, his stillness a marked contrast to his fluidity in a fight. He nodded and handed me a clean towel to dry my hands.

"So, what now?" he asked.

"They're moving on me hard, which begs the questions: Why do it this way? Why send Feds after us instead of a midnight attack by the undead or the demonic? Where is the controller?"

"These are Socratic questions."

"Your liberal arts education is showing."

"English degree's got to be good for something."

"You got an English degree?"

"Yes, Marius, I *gots* an English degree. To use the vernacular."

"Every day I learn something new about you."

"Every day I learn something more about you, and frankly, it scares the crap out of me."

"There's that," I said. "Scares me, too. Most days. I think they want to tie us down here in the Middle World. If we have problems with the cops in this world, it degrades our ability in the Other Realms. So we're going to have to measure twice and cut once. We'll get more action like this. But this controller and the Cabal . . . this is different."

"Refresh me on this Cabal thing."

I sighed. It always feels strange to say the words out loud. All the layers of reality come together in a strange way. It's tin-foil-hat territory to the uninitiated, but to those of us who actually experience it—and live to tell of it—it's as real as any other inanity of daily "ordinary" life, like mortgage foreclosures and Happy Meals.

"It's a war, Dillon. Conflict. The essential conflict. Dark against Light. It's been playing out since the dawn of time. There are those who rejected the Light and were tossed down. There are those who stayed with the Light. Some of them come down into the Darkness to rescue those who want to return to the Light. The Dark Forces only rarely can work directly against us; they have to work *through* us. Just like the Light works through us. We're all portals and we all have the choice to work with the Dark or the Light. We struggle with that, all of us—it's the blessing and the curse of Free Will. Those that choose what the Dark Forces offer—power, influence, money, sex, whatever—provide a channel for the Dark and make themselves into a tool to use against the Light. They try to corrupt and squash the Light wherever they go."

Dillon nodded. "Okay. So how do the Feds fit in?"

"You know the story of the bank robber who was asked why he robbed banks?"

"Refresh me."

"When he was asked, he said, 'Because that's where the money is.' That's why the Feds. That's where the power is. Cabal infiltrates at a key level where they can influence power and act without fear of getting caught. They're afraid of discovery."

I rubbed my forehead. This was giving me a headache.

"Cabal's been around in one form or another for a long time," I said. "There's always been humans who work in allegiance for the Dark Forces. Nazis were a good example. The creeping fascism in this country... maybe another. So where do they hide? In plain sight. Behind classification, need to know, law enforcement and military and security. Not all of those are Cabal; some of them are good people doing necessary work. But it's hard to tell sometimes. The intelligence and military people have a vested interest in the Cabal agenda—they get influence and control in exchange for technology, help, whatever..."

"Man, this is way over my head and into the yard," Dillon said. "Just tell me who to shoot when it comes time, okay? We're going to need heavier weapons if I'm going to be fighting animated lawns."

"Somewhere, someone or something is thinking the same about us," I said. I felt a sudden brush against my neck, a heaviness that lingered till I called on the Light...

CHAPTER 10

"You put them in the chipper?" Jolene said, aghast. "A wood chipper?"

"Dillon's got that whole permaculture thing going on. Organic compost and all that..." I said.

"Marius!" She shook her head. Leaned back in the comfortable chair she'd staked out in Gigi's. Crossed one long, Armani-trouser-clad leg over the other. Laughed the laugh I live for.

"It has a certain twisted symmetry to it," she said. "Organic matter returned to organic matter..."

My attempt at levity faded into worry. Her energy was cloudy and disturbed. She was worried about me, and as a powerful intuitive herself, she felt the energy swirling around me, the weight of the Dark Forces probing for me.

And she knew I was worried about her.

Here's the thing: deep down, beneath my feminist exterior, I'm a sexist pig.

Sorry.

I love women. I celebrate women. I love sex with women. I worship and venerate the Divine Feminine.

But hand in hand with that open love and respect of the Feminine Power comes the fierce protective instinct of the Masculine. Yes, Jolene is a full Priestess of the Wiccan Circle, a powerful sensitive and intuitive in her own right, and she is a woman.

My woman.

That activates something deep inside me, a fiery part that rises up bloody handed if there is even a hint of a threat to her.

And that brings up her own fierceness in reaction, because if ever there was a woman who went her own way, who prized the independence she'd fought for her whole life, it would be my Jolene.

"How does this connect, Marius?" she said. "Something about the woman you worked on?"

"I'm not sure. I've journeyed on it, but with the Cabal involved, it's murky. Maybe this sorcerer was connected in some way to her father."

Jolene pursed her lips, drawing a fine array of razor-edged lines around the red pout of her mouth. "I'll look into it."

"No!"

She gave me the Look.

"No, really, Jolene," I said hastily. "It's best not to draw attention with this...I don't need to be distracted worrying about you. Just be conscious of your own protection and shielding. I'll be away for a while..."

Inwardly I groaned as she straightened, then leaned forward, her brilliant blue eyes blazing.

"I won't be rescued nor will I be told to sit on the side, Marius," she said in a clear, scarily calm voice.

"You don't tell me what to do in matters of the Way—or anything else. Ever. How does that make me feel? 'Oh, poor me, I'm so fragile, I'll just sit at home and darn while my big manly man goes off to do battle with sorcerers, undead mercenaries and crooked cops'? I don't live that way. As you should know by now."

"Um, I didn't mean it like that..."

"I hate it when you stammer. Really. You said what you said. I say what I say. I'll look into this myself. Whether you choose to acknowledge it or not, I'm already involved. With you. Remember that? We are joined by the Power of Three and I make my *own* decisions about what to do when someone I love and join with is under threat."

"Ah, okay, look..."

She fixed me with a basilisk glare. "No."

That heated me up. I know, it's crazy, but she's crazy sexy when she's mad. I almost said something, but then that would have immediately led to something physical, for better or worse, so I chose discretion.

This time.

A faint whisper from my guides..."*Chicken*..."

I took a deep breath.

"I respect you and your work, Jolene. You know that. As sure as the breath we both breathe. Okay? Here's the thing: this is already a violent fight. Dillon and me, we've been down this road before. And yeah, so have you. I know this. This is focused on me. I need to keep my mind in the fight. And yes, it's a character flaw, and I'm painfully aware of it, but I can't concentrate when I'm thinking or worrying about you. I can't help it. It's my nature."

"Like the scorpion and the frog."

"Sure. Whatever. You in this makes me more vulnerable."

"What?"

"It's warrior strategy, Jolene. You're my distraction. You're my weakness. That's how they'll try and get to me. They tried the straight-on frontal. All it did was add to my body count and Dillon's compost pile. But with you . . . they'll try to get at me through you. It'll add fear and uncertainty . . . you know how they feed on that."

She studied my face, sat back, touched one finger to her drink. I saw understanding in her.

"Yes," she said. "I know what they feed on."

"Will you do this for me? Please? It will help me get through this. Just stay out, look to yourself. I know you can take care of yourself. I need you to be my safe harbor if I need one. I mean, when I need one," I added in a hurry.

She got up and went to the counter. "Johnny?" she called to the extravagantly tattooed and coifed rockabilly manager. "Would you get me a refill please?"

"Sure," he said. "House?"

"No. The Guatemalan organic."

He decanted some for her and dropped me a knowing wink as she turned back to join me at the table.

Thanks for that, Johnny.

She eased into her chair, all black-clad lissome length of her. A waft of her perfume, heated by temper and the body I knew so well, filtered my way. I grew a raging erection which didn't help my overall discomfort.

She studied me over the rim of her glass.

"I'll leave it alone," she said. "For now."

"Thank you."

She nodded, turned away, stared into space, sipped her coffee.

I took the cue and leaned back, tasted my too-cool coffee, afraid to move to get a refill.

Faint and far off, I heard laughter ... *"Women, can't live with them, can't live without them ..."*

No lie, G.I.

Beard's Plaisance is a park on the southwestern curve of Lake Harriet. It's overlooked by the crowds that circle the lake on foot, on bikes, on skates or skis—in the winter the long hill is popular with local kids who plummet and swoop down the hill on sleds. But it's most often missed, even by the people who live nearby. There's a stand of old trees at the top of the hill, and then a long grassy expanse that drops sharply down to the Parkway, bordered on one side by a tennis court. These hills that ring the lake are built of rubble dragged there by the glaciers; when they melted they created the lakes, and the debris fields around these last pockets of ice created the hills.

The Lakota Sioux, who lived here long before Minneapolis was a thought in the heads of the white men, kept seasonal encampments on the shores of this lake. The hill that Beard's Plaisance is part of is where the Sioux medicine men and women lived; it's the place where they had their gatherings to share their insights from journeys into the Spirit World. There's a long tradition of honoring the sacred here. Just a block away, where the most senior medicine people lived at the apex of the hill, the missionaries built a church. It burned down at least three times, the most recent in a fire ignited by a dramatic flash of lightning during a service. It was only after the Lakota medicine people were called in to do a healing and a clearing of the land did the atmospheric and fiery disturbances cease, and the Christian church morphed into a nondenominational house of worship that, depending on the night, housed Christians, Wiccans, Lutherans, and Unitarians as well as a rotating cast of other spiritual practitioners.

So it made sense that I was drawn here often, especially when I needed to commune with the nature spirits, here in a sacred spot bordered by roads traveled by those who did not see what I saw. I'd done ceremony here that even the passers-by didn't notice; it was as if there was a cloak of invisibility wrapped around the hill, especially at the top amongst the stand of trees. There's a minigrove there, a loose ring of mature trees off to one side, with a low hedge of shrubs between the grove and the street. It made you essentially invisible if you sat in the circle.

I sat cross-legged on the grass. Dillon stood off, far enough away to watch me and still see all the approaches, a short-barreled rifle, illegal as can be, in a padded tennis racket case slung over his shoulder.

My spirits beside and around me, and my warrior brother standing by.

I was as safe as I could possibly be.

I prefer to use a real drum when I can, but one thing I've learned is that sometimes it's to one's advantage to keep a low profile. Drumming in public can draw unwanted attention, especially if you are trying to remain hidden from view. So one of the benefits of modern technology is the iPhone or the iPod—I used my iPhone and its headset to provide me with the full sense-surround experience of drumming in a

completely private way that allowed me to focus on
the nuances of my journey instead of drumming and
stopping to explain what I was doing to the curious.

I opened my tobacco pouch and offered a pinch to
the four directions, to Father Sun above and Mother
Earth below, pressed a coin into the earth for the
earth elementals, and offered up thanks to all the
helping and compassionate spirits. I visualized the
container of sacred space surrounding me, and called
on the Archangel Michael to surround me and cloak
me in his protection, so that I would not be seen by
the Dark Forces—for my intention was to seek my
opponent in the Other Realm.

I tapped on the twelve-minute short journey drumming track that Sandra Ingerman provided along with
several others in the companion CD to her great book
Shamanic Journeying. I closed my eyes, and let the
flute lead me into the drumming portion.

*. . . and I rose up out of my body, hovered over it for
a moment, the steady heartbeat of the drum vibrating
through me, saw and felt the brilliant Light of angelic
protection, and I rose up, Tigre and Burt and First In
Front with me, as always, and we traveled—Middle
World—flying through the air and in the vision that is
not-vision, we saw a swirling, like a tornado of black
and gray, above a shabby town huddled on the prai-
rie, and beneath, a great rift in the very fabric of the
Mother, Mother Earth, a rift through and around the
town, focused in, followed my intention, and there in
an office, sitting at a desk, a man with a square head,
black hair fading to gray at his expensively trimmed
temples, gold cuff links in a custom shirt, two younger
men, his sons, all of them the same, hunch-shouldered*

*with hidden fear, terminally possessed...we tracked
backwards and there were lines of control, like mari-
onette strings, drawing away and then down, tangled
in a horrid symmetry like that of a dangerous spider's
web, and hidden away behind that, another portal...
Tigre blocked my way, merged with and into me,
adding her protection, as did Burt...First In Front
stood before me, and then I saw...dark upon dark,
a black hole shaped almost like something human; the
gravitational pull of the darkness tugging at me like
that you feel on the edge of a pit or looking over the
guardrail of a bridge, feeling gravity and the desire to
fall come over you...and that expanded...the desire
to fall...the Fall...and I knew then what I saw...*

Fallen...

*...and those dark beings turned and, through the
protective fog that surrounded me, I felt their vision
piercing my veil, and I was drawn back, protected
from the dark essence that reached for me...*

*...information unfolding in me like a snapshot, full
of details that I needed to turn my attention to...*

...Fallen...

I was back in my body.

I opened my eyes, thumbed off the music. Took a
deep breath and exhaled slowly.

"I offer up thanks to Archangel Michael and the
Mighty Warriors of Light on Earth, to Creator God and
all the helping and compassionate spirits, I offer up
thanks to my beloved protecting and guiding spirits..."

"*...You're welcome, Beloved...*"

I closed my circle, stood.

Dillon came to me. He looked puzzled and concerned.

"You okay, man? You look like you just got slapped with a two-by-four."

"I feel like it."

Dillon scanned the area. "Let's not tell the tale here, bro. Let's go get you some coffee."

"Good idea. Gigi's. Meet me there."

"I'll follow you." He paused. "You want me to drive? You don't look so good."

"I'm not. I'm okay to drive."

I got into my Toyota, started it, stared out the windshield. I pulled out and drove around the Parkway till I hit the Rose Garden, turned right and took it up to Bryant and parked behind Gigi's. I went in and nodded to the women at the counter, took the table deepest in back. Dillon came in, looked at me, went to the counter and returned with two steaming mugs of black coffee. Set one down in front of me after sizing up the only other table, a middle-aged lesbian couple who smiled and nodded at us.

He sat across from me. "You want to tell the tale?"

I sipped my coffee. The hot brew scalded my tongue, a welcome pain that cleared my head, made way for the caffeine.

"So?" Dillon prompted.

"You ever hear the story of Hell Hollow?" I said.

"The movie?"

"No. Not yet, anyway."

"So . . . ?"

"You ever been over to Decanter?"

He laughed. "Not if I can avoid it. It might not be the asshole of the world, but you can smell it from there. What's Decanter got to do with this?"

"You know the feeling over there? That oppressive

feeling? Stink of the soy processing plants, an economy tanking, everybody looks beat down, weird people everywhere, just a general bad feeling?"

"Yep. There was an article about it a few years ago in the *Star-Tribune*. Highest unsolved homicide rate, completely corrupt government, murder, drugs... lovely place."

"Decanter has a long history of being cursed," I said. "Of Dark Forces. The city was built on Indian holy ground. Part of the town itself, the courthouse and the downtown, is built right on top of Native American burial grounds. The original settlers plowed the ancient mounds down, tore up the burial grounds to build there. And ever since then, there's been lots of dark sorcery there, all kinds of weird shit: incest, murder, strange sex stuff, drug dealing, corruption, you name it..."

"All the more reason to stay out of there."

"There's a gateway there, Dillon. A portal. A portal for the Dark Forces. In a place on the edge of town, where the old town cemetery adjoins what used to be the Native American burial ground. It's called Hell Hollow. What's going on *here* started over *there*. Who came here is from there. Came through there."

"Dude, that's not a place we want to knock around," Dillon said. "It's just a bad and ugly place. I don't want to be running afoul of what passes for law over there."

"I hope we don't have to. They're moving over here... there's something here they want."

"You?"

"Not just me. There's something else going on here... something they want to quash."

"Like what?"

"I don't know." I thought for a moment, and then the images from my journey reappeared...

...a dark form pressing against the dark fabric of space-time, like a face beneath a taut sheet of black latex, pressing, straining...

"I think they're trying to open a portal here," I said.

"Why?"

"Confluence. If you weaken the very material of the barrier between the worlds...think of Decanter as a big gaping hole into the Dark Side—and they can come through there. Think of Minneapolis as a place of the Light...and the fabric between the worlds is bulging here. Get it to tear between here and Decanter, that makes the portal way bigger...big enough for something else to come through."

"What's so big it needs forty miles of room to come through?" Dillon said.

"The Fallen," I said. "The heavy hitters of the Dark Forces. The Fallen Angels."

"Oh, sweet suffering Jesus," Dillon said.

"Yes," I said. "We'll need His help. We'll be doing His work."

"What are *we* going to do?" Dillon said. "A small time gunfighter and the local shaman? We should be calling every shaman in the country here. The Pope! The Vatican! Jews for the Preservation of Firearms Ownership! Gurkhas! Whoever will come!"

"We've got help coming, Dillon," I said. "I've been shown this. But right now, it's you and me, buddy. You and me and the Legions of Light, the Mighty Warriors of Light on Earth. They work through us. All of us who carry the Light. You, me, all those who choose the Light..."

Dillon shook his head in exasperation. "You take care of the shaman stuff, Marius. I'll take care of the shooting part."

I nodded. It was clear we were going to need both.

CHAPTER II

I'm sometimes asked about the difference between a shaman and a sorcerer. Without getting into semantics, the short answer is intention. A shaman travels to the Other Realms to gather information and to commune with the spirits and deities on the behalf of others; a shaman travels with the intention to facilitate healing, to learn, to find things, to help others. A sorcerer does the same thing, but with the intention to hurt, to harm, to act out of self-aggrandizement or ego.

Intention is everything.

It's a fine line. The razor's edge.

My friend Marcus once pointed out to me that it's like *Star Wars* and the Force. George Lucas got it right. The path to the Dark Side is paved with good intentions...but it's the path of impatience, of anger, of rage, of hurt, of sorrow—all part and parcel of human existence. We need to find our way past all that. That's why the shaman's path is so perilous.

Because in the search of power to help others, we can be seduced along the way to take the easy path, the expedient path, to give into anger and reaction.

Anger can be useful. It's the Creator's Gift to us to call us into action when it's appropriate. But acting while in anger is a dangerous place to be when you're working with the spirits. Everything we do is vibration and energy—and while anger and rage can surely get things done, the long-term repercussions will just as surely come back to bite you in the ass.

Or kick your door down and shoot you in your bed.

Or worse, snatch your soul essence while you're in the Other Realms.

I got up off my couch and went into the kitchen to fetch myself another Negra Modelo beer, went back and stared out the window at the park. The beer was good, actually great. It cut through the dryness in my mouth that had afflicted me since my last journey.

It helped wash away the dry ashy taste of fear.

A big part of the shaman's work has to do with fear: his own and the management of it in others. Many New Age shamanic practitioners tend towards a Pollyanna view of reality, clinging to the belief that everything in the Other Realms and this one was fuzzy and warm and nice and safe. The practitioners who were Called and honored their Path, who went forward and did their own work—as hard as it might be—found themselves somewhere along the Path where they had to deal with their own dark fears, because Spirit has a way of manifesting in a very real way those dark things within us we don't want to acknowledge. Demons, dragons, evil . . . inside every human there's a piece that resonates with that, and the harder you repress and deny it, the more it persists—"What you resist, persists . . ."—and the Dark Forces sniff for that and go for it, because that's how they make entry.

So why was I spending a sunny day inside drinking beer and dwelling on this?

Because I'd come to the realization that the real danger in all of this was the focus on me and my weaknesses.

And that scared me. Badly.

If you're Called to be a Light Worker, or you self-identify as a Warrior of the Light, then you're taking a stance. A position in the Great Conflict. The War between the Light and the Dark. The more you do your Work, the more your Light will shine. And the more you will be Seen . . . and once you've been Seen doing the Work, sooner or later, the Dark Forces will turn to shut down your Light, slow you, take you off the board, knock you out of the game.

How do you shut down a Warrior of the Light?

Not easily, but the basic strategy is to find his or her weaknesses and exploit them, work your way through the list of the deadly sins (one thing the Catholics surely got right) and see what resonates within the targeted shaman. But if the shaman finds the courage, he can work through his stuff and eventually, ideally, evolves to where there is no more resonance for the Dark Forces to find.

Ideally.

One thing I was taught early on, and I've embodied the truth of, in this Work, you want to be pure, but not *too* pure. I welcomed the liberation from the need to be perfect, but more than once I've caught myself relying on that adage to justify my avoiding self-work.

That's the danger for me. That's why this was coming to me now. In the guidance that came through my recent journeys, in the myriad past lives I've lived, somewhere back there was a powerful sorcerer, one who'd gone as far down the Dark Road as one can. I'd come back from that, worked through it, but the Laws of Karma and Balance are inescapable and everything that happens we are responsible for. How we relate to events, how we choose to act, that's what provides us with the opportunity to relieve ourselves of the old burdens. To choose to do things differently.

That's what was in all of this unfolding around me. The chance to do things differently.

That's what this was all about for me. While there was a call to action, wrapped up in that call was the clear message to heed *how* I went about it, because this was the opportunity to do things differently than I had before.

Or get sucked into the same old way of doing it.

I felt that draw.

A sense of righteous anger . . . righteousness . . . that's the draw. To be and act angry, to justify it through righteousness, because you're doing it—at least in your mind—on the behalf of others. Anger is seductive. It gives the sense of immediate and palpable power, even though it's an illusion, a semblance of power. Real power is settled and grounded. A filling in. Power-Full.

A knock on the door shook me out of my navel-gazing.

I peeked out the window. It was Maryka Owen, the woman I'd done a depossession with. That seemed a very long time ago.

I went to the door and opened it.

"Hi," I said.

She tugged at her hair with one hand, wrapped a strand of hair around her finger. "I'm sorry for not calling. I needed to see you, so I came right by..."

"Sure," I said. "It happens like that sometimes. C'mon in."

I waved her into the front room and settled back into the couch. She sat in my armchair, leaned forward, knees pressed together, long fingers intertwined in a tight knot on her thighs.

"What is it?" I said.

"I've been feeling much better..."

"That's good."

"But this friend came to see me, from over in Decanter..."

...and I felt the knowing and the soft voice of my guides... "This is how it opens..."

I repressed my sigh. "Yes?"

"...and since then I've had this feeling that there's some entity hanging around since he came over."

"Your friend, is he staying with you?"

"Yes. He had some problems in Decanter. He's going to stay with me till he figures out what to do."

"How long have you known him?"

She thought on it. "Two years. We met at a meditation workshop in Indianapolis."

I closed my eyes. As it often does, information came to me in a big packet, a ball of energy...

Tigre and Burt... Tigre curled beside a huge tree, Burt perched on a low-hanging branch, First In Front seated cross-legged with his back propped against the tree.

"Here's the connection," First In Front said. He held up his old scalping knife and gestured. "This is where it starts..."

Burt flapped his wings and rose into the air, his talons grabbing the fabric of the sky like a curtain and pulling it back... into the black... black, black, black. Far off in the black, two glowing spots of red that rushed forward and became enraged eyes in a sea of black... a flurry of images, one after another rolling into a steady stream... images from Atlantis, medieval images, figures twisting in flames, rolling forward... long black ships hanging in the air, long threads running down from them to humans far below... the main streets of downtown Decanter as seen through a sepia filter... and below the streets, tormented souls pressing up against the concrete and the buildings... the disincarnate, human and otherwise, walking the streets, sitting in waiting rooms, in courthouses, in offices... and near the graveyard on Long Street, on the edge of Decanter, a pulsing invisible to most, a pulsing against the fabric of reality, like the image of a sheet... the Dark Portal. And all around it the cast of characters... the possessed... lawyers, bankers, cops, deputies, school teachers, the everyday people of a seemingly everyday town... all of them looking down at the pulsing blackness beneath their feet and far above their head, a similar pulsing, a pulsing from the Light they ignored... and then the image of an old man, running, out of breath, and behind him, laughing, some of those same faces...

I opened my eyes and murmured, "Thank you" to my guides.

Maryka cocked her head, puzzled.

"I think I should meet your friend, Maryka."

"Now?"

"Yes," I said heavily. "Now."

CHAPTER 12

Anthony Boardman was older than me, probably in his early fifties. He was big-framed but shrunken, as though he'd been ill and hadn't filled out. His face was pained and I saw the energy around him that told me he dealt with some chronic illness...

Cancer...

Yes. He had that look.

"I used to be a Reiki practitioner," he said. He dipped his head to his coffee cup when he sipped, like a bird pecking into a tall glass of water. He looked around at the other tables. "I stopped when I got sick. I want to go back to it, but I feel as though there's a part of me that's gone away..."

"Soul loss is common when you go through major illness," I said. "Did you do chemo?"

"Yes," he said. He nodded. "I've heard of you. Shamanic work interests me. I have friends who've done it. Some of them combine Reiki and shamanic. Seems like it blends well."

"It can," I said. I looked at Maryka and then back at him. "Maryka tells me you had some trouble in Decanter?"

"Yes," he said. "Some trouble with a neighbor that turned into something else. Do you know Decanter?"

"I've been over there quite a bit," I said. "Done clearings. Lots of bad energy in that place...lots of things going on beneath the surface. Literally."

"You know the history there?" he said.

"Some of it," I said. "Burial and holy land to the Sioux...white settlers built right on top of it. Long history of strange disappearances, massacres, madness, crime...just plain ugly."

"Just plain ugly," he repeated thoughtfully. "Yes. It's a corrupt place, energetically and politically."

"Tell me your story, Tony," I said.

He twisted his lips sourly. "It was one of those things you don't think anything about, at first. I had this apartment in Decanter, nice neighborhood, on the South Side, not far from Holy Cross Church and School. Quiet building, just six units. I lived there by myself while I was recovering, just out of the hospital. Mostly older people in the building. Working folks. The apartment above me, this young guy moved. I spoke to him a few times. He seemed like a nice enough guy, he was a school teacher.

"But he was strange. Always staring at me, talking to himself. I heard him complaining a couple of times, to someone else, about me. From his apartment. He didn't like the smell of my cooking or I played my music too loud. It was strange...he never said anything to my face, but he'd say things loud enough for me to hear. I didn't give it much mind at first, but after a while it began to wear on me. It was his energy..."

"It was dark?" I said.

"Yes," Tony said. "Very. I didn't catch it at first. Then I noticed how he looked when he watched me. If he knew you were looking at him, he'd smile, look like an all-American boy. But if you caught him, he was different... his eyes were dark, he had this hate-filled look, that sideways sneaky thing you see in kids that have gone their whole lives lying and never been caught."

"Father of Lies," I said.

"I hadn't thought of that," he said.

"Felt it though, didn't you?"

"Yes."

He sighed and went on. "I noticed some other people his age hanging around, and then this older man started coming by. His father, by the look of him. I heard the kid complaining to his father about me."

"You never did anything? Never spoke to him?"

"Nothing. I left him alone. I was polite when I passed him in the hall... nothing that a normal person would find offensive."

"Normal being the key word."

He laughed. "That's right." His face darkened suddenly. "One day I was sitting in my front room. I spent a lot of time sitting in my recliner and meditating and working on my healing visualizations. I heard someone screaming outside and when I looked it was this kid..."

"What's his name?" I said.

"Bryant. Bryant Eichmann."

"Eichmann? Like the Nazi?"

"In more ways than one."

"Go on."

"It was like he was having a schizophrenic episode...he was ranting and raving about me outside my window...like he wanted me to come outside. Then some young woman came by and made him go up into his apartment. About an hour later someone knocked on my door. It was his father."

Tony paused to sip his coffee. His mouth twisted as though it had suddenly gone sour.

"He was just like the son?" I said.

"Worse," Tony said. "Everything about him...eyes, even how he smelt...something was just wrong about him. What made it so uncomfortable, though that word doesn't do it justice, was how arrogant he was, like everything he wanted was already decided in advance."

"Decided about what?"

"He wanted me to move out. He said I was disturbing his son, his son was special, his son was sensitive. He was important, he knew people, he was a banker... Nothing about me being an invalid, nothing about me minding my own business...it was all about him and what he wanted..."

I nodded. I got that. The self-centeredness, the whole service-to-self orientation before anything or anyone else, is the single most significant indicator of deep-seated possession and allegiance to the Dark Forces.

Evil.

The second most significant is the adherence to the Lie. Satan got his handle as the Father of Lies for a reason. A brilliant theological writer named M. Scott Peck wrote a book called *People of the Lie* which was his take on that indicator of evil, how to define it and how to identify it in others early on.

"What else did he say?" I said.

"I told him the truth. I wasn't bothering anyone. He was the one with the problem."

"I take it he didn't like that answer."

Tony laughed. "No. He didn't."

"And then ... other things started to happen?" I prompted.

Tony stared at me, his eyes sunken and surrounded by bruised flesh. Deep in there I saw a flash of something staring back at me, something quickly hidden, and I felt my guides gather round me ...

... Possession, cording, curse, thought-form ... tended. Definitely tended ...

That meant that somewhere a demon or a sorcerer— or both—were watching through Tony's eyes, tending the possession through an energetic cord.

I drew a deep breath and silently called on the angelic realm, the Mighty Warriors of Light on Earth, and Michael and Uriel, the two Mighty Archangels who honored me with their assistance. I felt the energy shift, a brightening, and saw through my half-closed eyes the darkness above and behind Tony ease as the angelic realm arrived, and awaited the Work that was yet to be done ...

"Yes," Tony said. "I saw his father hanging around with someone else. They were searching outside the apartment building. Like they were looking for something or someone."

"This was while you were at home?"

"Yes. I was always at home. Then I started hearing them outside my door. They'd stand out there and talk about things that could happen, how people could fall down stairs and get hurt. Then someone went through my laundry and some of my clothing disappeared."

"Do you remember what disappeared?"

"Some underwear, boxer shorts, and an old T-shirt."

"Did you ever find them?"

"No."

This was shaping up to be something more than run-of-the-mill possession. Clothing, especially natural fibers worn next to the skin, build up an energetic charge. After so much immersion in a human energy field, they become infused with the energy. So if you have a piece of clothing that someone has worn for a long time, you have a piece of that person's energy. A sorcerer can work with that energy, treat the clothing as though it's part of you, since for energetic purposes it is part of you until it's cleared by time or sunlight or direct focused intention.

Tony wasn't just the victim of an active possession, he was the victim of a curse—a focused one deliberately made with skill and knowledge and technique; a curse tended now by the maker of it, and somewhere, that maker was becoming agitated. I saw, with the shamanic vision that is part of my Gift, a ripple in the energy field of the suffering man seated across from me, a ripple reflected in the muscles of his face, a ripple like the subsurface passage a great white shark might make on a moonlit ocean, late in the night . . .

"How long ago was this, Tony?" I said.

"About a year."

"What happened to prompt you coming over here?"

Tony looked at Maryka. She nodded in support.

"It stepped up," he said. "It got worse. They were coming by all the time, especially at night. They'd stand outside my window, outside my door, talk about killing me . . ."

"Are you sure it was them? Were you hearing it or did you see them too?"

"It was them. I took their pictures. I recorded them with a digital video camera."

"Who was it?"

"The kid upstairs, Bryant, and someone named Christian. I think it's his brother." He paused. "You know what's strange? I think they were twins . . ."

I cringed inside. The Cabal . . . the place where weird science and the paranormal intersected with conspiracy theory and the bloody back corridors of Realpolitik.

Clones. Like the ones I'd run through the chipper.

"So they were twins?" I said.

"I think so," Tony said. "They weren't alone . . . there were policemen sometimes."

"Local?"

"Yes. I think the father . . ."

"Do you remember his name?"

"Wilhelm," Tony said. "His friends called him Will."

"That's a good German mouthful," I said.

Tony didn't think that was funny. "I had dreams about that, too. I dreamt I saw them in a concentration camp, dressed up in Nazi uniforms, laughing, standing on a platform looking down on people, sorting out the weak from the strong, the men from the women, the women from the children . . ."

He blinked back sudden tears.

"Horrible dreams," he went on. "I saw them tossing children into the flames. Laughing while they did it."

I paused. "And the police?"

"The father, he had something to do with them."

"I thought you said he was a banker?"

"Yes. But he also had something to do with the police."

"Okay. What else?"

He went on. "I just had this feeling something bad was going to happen if I didn't move. They kept coming around. They didn't care who saw them. The other neighbors were afraid to say anything. It got to the point I couldn't sleep at all. I went for days without sleeping. So finally I left. I came over here and stayed with Maryka. I had the first good sleep I've had in I can't remember how long. She told me about you and what you'd done for her, and I just knew I had to talk to you."

My coffee had grown cold and my stomach sour. Not a good combination. Nor were the signs before me. Creator had sent this to me, as Creator does. A true practitioner doesn't advertise or solicit, he trusts that the Creator will send him those who need the special kind of help we provide and that what we do will be in accordance with the Divine Plan.

What I felt right now reminded me of an interview with Mother Teresa, the sainted Catholic nun who worked with the poor and with lepers. The interviewer—well meaning but insipid—had asked Mother Teresa how she was able to summon the strength to deal with what she saw every day. But before the elderly nun could answer, the interviewer answered herself and said, "I suppose God never sends you anything you can't bear, right?"

Mother Teresa's acerbic reply was this: "Yes, I suppose that is true. That's why I pray every single day that God not have so much faith in me."

I identify with that. Especially right now.

I hid my apprehension. I do that well. "What can I do to help you, Tony?"

"Can you work on me?" he said. "I could really use your help."

I closed my eyes. "Yes. I can help you."

When I opened my eyes, Tony's relief was visible in every line of his face.

"What do I have to do?" he said.

I looked out the window at the sky, then at my watch. "What's your schedule like today?"

"Wide open all day," he said.

"Maryka?" I said.

"I'm free..." she said, puzzled.

"The reason I'm asking is that if Tony wants you to be available, could you be? To stand in support of him and tend to him after we get done?"

"Of course," she said. "I can do that."

"Okay," I said. "I need some time to pull things together. Maryka, bring Tony to my place around seven-thirty tonight."

"We'll be there," she said.

"Good," I said. "I need to talk to some friends of mine. I'll see you later."

I sat there, lingering, while the two of them left. I swirled the dregs of my coffee in the cup and watched my clients leave.

"*...you know you can talk to us any time...*" came the soft and familiar and loving voices that were with me always.

"I know that," I said out loud. There was no one sitting near me to be disturbed by the sight of a disheveled shaman talking to himself. "But I want to give you the attention you deserve."

Soft laughter. *"Oh no, I think he wants something..."*

"You think?"

"Oh, absolutely."

I walked out the door and First In Front appeared beside me. I was struck, as always, how other people on the sidewalk seemed to sense his presence and move out of his way; sometimes they'd stand aside with a puzzled expression as though they could almost see my invisible but ever-present companion.

"I'm thinking ceremony," he said. *"You thinking ceremony?"*

A big crow circled overhead, cawed once, flew away into the west. I stopped to stare up at it.

"Yes," Burt said. *"Absolutely. Time to gather power and allies. This is much darker than it appears."*

A deep sibilant purr, like a powerful engine idling, heard through layer upon layer of velvet. *"Oh, Marius,"* the soft feminine voice said. *"Always your best work when it's another calling upon you for help..."*

"That's his risk," Burt said. *"He'll start thinking he's special or something..."*

... more laughter, loving laughter...

"Oh, he thinks that," Tigre said. *"But I'll give him this—he does the best he can."*

"Gee thanks," I said. "Glad you see that."

"Excuse me?"

I started. The woman next to me held her daughter by the hand and waited for the light to change.

"Sorry," I said. "I talk to myself all the time."

She laughed. "Just don't start answering yourself!"

The light changed and we all stepped off the curb.

Slam—I felt an invisible body push into me, a flash of white moving fast, and I reached out and grabbed the woman and her daughter and yanked them back hard—

—a pickup truck tore through the intersection, so close that its side mirrors whipped past my face; it never touched the brakes as it sped off, leaving only a glimpse of a tense face glaring straight ahead, hatred simmering off it—

"God!" the woman shouted. "That asshole blew right through the light. He almost hit all three of us!"

"You okay?" I asked. My heart pounded in my ears.

"Yes . . . thank you." She looked at her daughter and then at me. "Thank God you were here."

I looked up at the sky. A crow circled far above me. "Thank God He was here."

"Yes, shaman," Burt said . . . soft laughter. *"It's a full-time job watching out for Marius Winter."*

"Job security," Tigre said. She curled up on the hood of my 4Runner, sunning herself. First In Front sat cross-legged beside her, his coup stick and his war knife resting in his lap. He held the knife in his right hand, straight up, and like a reversed spotlight a beam of light descended from the sky, illuminated his blade, and flowed through him into my car, down into the earth . . .

I stepped into the Circle of Light around my car and felt warmth and the sudden release of pressure I'd been unaware of, the lifting of that dark attention that comes from a shielded presence, a Dark Force watching me, tracking me . . .

"Yes," First In Front said. *"Ceremony and Allies. Who you gonna call . . ."*

Wasn't gonna be Ghostbusters.

CHAPTER 13

Ceremony is a big part of the shaman's work. Spirit—the Great Spirit and its manifestations as individual souls and spirits, all of those pieces that collectively make up the Presence of Creator God—provides guidance to the shaman when it's time for a ceremony; we get specific instruction as to what to do and when for whom. Our job is to translate that information and instruction into action. We have to journey to the spirits along the path of the Divine and return with that information, and use it to create the Sacred Space that contains the Work.

The Sacred Space that brings and holds and heals with the Divine Light of Creator God.

Rituals have a general sequence that rarely varies, though the specifics are always dependent on Spirit's guidance. The shaman, his assistants (if any) and all the participants need to be cleansed and cleared, as does the space in which the Work will be done. The shaman sets out the boundaries of the Sacred Space, the Circle, and calls in the Powers from the Four Directions to seal the space and fill it with light and energy. Then the Work is done, and thanks offered up, and the Circle opened to release the spirits and the energy back to the Creator.

Easy, right?

It can be, but not always.

Part of the shaman's training is to pay close attention to the specific instruction offered by the spirits . . . and that requires discernment—sorting the wheat from the chaff, the static from the clear signal. Discernment in processing information from the Other Realms is often the biggest stumbling block for a shaman.

Creator knows it's been a stumbling block for me.

"More than once, Marius," Tigre purred. *"Right on your face."*

Yes. Well. As I've said, no point in arguing with the Divine Feminine in any of Her Manifestations, especially the big-clawed and big-teethed kind.

So that's the ritual.

Then there's the participants.

Me, of course, since Creator had sent me this particular job. Maryka and Tony. But I wanted more help. Knowing when to ask for help, and who to ask for the specific help needed, is another big educational milestone in the ongoing training of a shamanic practitioner.

Every practitioner has his or her version of a Little Black Book of contacts; mine was just like the *Mission: Impossible*, a list of the very best to be called upon as needed. It's a small list but heavy duty. That sparked commentary from my peers, who agreed that "heavy duty" was what came my way. Some of them chided me for loving the drama of the big fight; I had to sit with that for a while. When I journeyed on it, I was shown this: all of us Called in the Light have Work to do, and no job is greater or lesser or any more dramatic than any other—it's all of value. Me, I figured the Creator needed a hardhead who would tackle the big dirty dark jobs and that was why He made me the way I am.

Or so I tell myself.

My healing room was ready. The table set with clean linen, fresh water and flowers on my altar, a new bundle of sage and sweet grass and a lighter placed into my abalone shell; everything clean and fresh.

I was ready. Rested and clear after a period of meditation and light journey, a shower and a meal of salad and an excellent piece of raw sirloin cut into thin strips like sushi. Raw. The quality meat helped ground me, though it revolted some of my peers.

Pure . . . but not too pure.

Works for me.

A knock at the door.

"... *who you gonna call? Ghostbusters! Who you gonna call? Ghostbusters!!*"

"Thanks, Burt," I said.

I'd called them on short notice, but they all came without question. I felt a swelling and a gladness in my heart as I looked at them gathered on my step: Jolene, the love of my life, carrying with her all the gravitas and power and wisdom of a Full Priestess of the Circle; Dillon, relaxed and bulky under his leather car coat bulging with weapons; and, just getting off her Harley in front, Sabrina, shaking loose her violet hair as she took off her helmet.

We were Four. One for each Direction, one for each Power, one for each of the Archangels who stand at the corners of the Creator's Throne.

Sabrina swaggered up my walk with a big grin. "Hope you got good beer on ice, Marius. Gonna be a thirsty night."

Jolene turned to greet her with a hug. "Hello, Goddess."

Sabrina squeezed her hard. "Jolene. I'm amazed you still put up with this wild man."

"He's not so bad," Jolene said. "You look amazing."

Sabrina laughed, then looked Dillon up and down. "Hey, big boy. Is that an Uzi in your pocket or you just glad to see me?"

Dillon grinned. "AK. And yeah . . . I'm glad to see you."

"I'm between big bad daddies, Dillon. I think you should go home with me." She paused. "Really."

Dillon swallowed his stammer. The rest of us laughed, me most of all. Who wouldn't quail in the presence of a goddess, especially when she was eyeing him like a piece of fresh meat dangled in front of a predator?

"*I love her,*" Tigre said. "*She is so who she is. True Self . . .*"

"*Warriors all,*" First In Front said. "*I welcome them . . .*"

Burt cawed into deep laughter. "*Ah, they're all batshit crazy, just like this one. Like attracts like.*"

Jolene closed her eyes and smiled. "Greetings, blessings and thanks to all who walk with us here."

I felt the joy and smiles of my guides.

They love her too.

"You are all most welcome," I said formally. "Please

enter with my thanks to all of you and all who walk with you, for coming when I called, and for coming to be in Service to the Light."

Jolene entered, paused. "I am here. I am Jolene and I walk with the Goddess. I am here in Service to the Light."

She passed within.

Sabrina was next. "I am here. I am Sabrina. I come in Service to the Light and to the Great Spirit of my ancestors. We are all kin in the eyes of the Creator. *Aho* . . ."

Dillon looked at me. I inclined my head to welcome him in. He came in and stopped. "Uh, I'm, uh, Dillon. I'm here to . . ." He paused for a moment, and then the voice that was great within him rose up, the voice of his warrior guides. "I'm here to protect. To watch over those in Service to the Light. I am grateful for the opportunity to serve and to stand between those who heal and those who would harm. Thank you."

Sabrina and Jolene double-hugged him. Dillon blinked in surprise, his eyes suddenly watering with the emotion flowing to him from two women he worshipped and the invisible spirits around him, who welcomed him and his warrior energy into this space.

I shut the door. "May all who enter here in the Service of the Light be blessed and protected. I am grateful, I am grateful, I am grateful."

We are Four.

And to borrow a line from Pink, "Let's get this party started."

It was interesting to witness how each of my allies' roles emerged when Tony and Maryka arrived. Jolene laid a gentle hand on Tony's arm and ushered him in; Sabrina studied the two and then closed her eyes in communion with her guides; Dillon checked the street outside and then locked the door and followed us all into the healing room.

Each in accordance with their True Self.

What's that?

Your True Self is you as you came into the world—an energetic being, a soul, a spirit, a fragment of the Great Light that is Creator God. You came here with a mission, a purpose, a job to do in the greater Work. But that Divine Light can get shifted, transformed, muddied, when you're in the body and the flesh slows down the processing of information and guidance. Your body is a great gift, designed to provide you the opportunity to learn and experience the things you cannot while in Spirit.

That's where the whole piece about temptation, seduction and wandering away from your mission comes from. Some of us spend our entire lives in pursuit of what we were sent here to do; some of us never find it. Some of us are dragooned into Service—whether we like it or not—because we were sent here to further the Work.

When you're in accordance with your Higher Purpose, when your True Self is doing the Work you were sent here to do, everything flows along, everything works.

When we start confusing the mundane details of ordinary everyday life and consciousness—paying bills, being pissed at the neighbor, worrying about whether Kim Kardashian's butt is too big or whether you can afford a sports car—with what our *real* work is, that's when things get muddled. That's part of what the Dark Forces' work here is in opposition to the Light Workers—keeping you confused about your Higher Purpose, chasing what's the latest and greatest on TV and in constant debt slavery.

Not to say that you eschew your responsibilities in the Middle World—far from it. The best spiritual practitioners in the shamanic tradition walk a middle road. They do well at their business, pay their bills, raise their kids—and they do their Work as they are sent to do. There are many challenges around that, and that's the place of your personal work, the work you do to keep yourself a hollow bone to be filled with the Presence of the Creator in the Service of your People.

Not an easy path.

But for those who are Chosen, or who Choose to follow the Path, the rewards far outweigh the constant challenge.

I'm reminded of this every time when I'm gathered in the Service of the Light to benefit another.

Like now.

"Are you comfortable?" I asked Tony. He reclined on the massage table, his hands stiff at his sides, while I adjusted the knee bolster beneath his legs.

"Yes," he said.

"Nervous?" I said.

"Yes."

"That's normal," I said. "You're in good hands today. Only the best for you."

He nodded and let his hands loosen. "I feel that."

Maryka squeezed his hand.

"Where do you want me?" Maryka said.

I set a small wooden stool down at the foot of the massage table. "Sit here. You'll help him keep his connection to the Earth and to who he is."

Sabrina touched the lighter to the mixture of sage, sweet grass, copal and palo santo in the abalone shell, breathed lightly and murmured a prayer as the flames kindled the aromatic herbs; she then circled the room and went to each of us, first to me and then Jolene and the others, wafting the smoke with a hawk feather around us, clearing our energy and the room and the space. When she had circled everyone and all the four corners of the room, she set the still smoldering shell on my altar and took her place to my right as I stood at the head of the healing table. Jolene stood directly across from me, with Maryka in front of her sitting on the stool at Tony's feet. Dillon stood on my left.

Dillon looked nervous, but then, he always did in ceremony.

"Just be who you are, brother," I said. "Hold the intention that brought you here. Serve and protect."

"Got it," he said.

Sabrina closed her eyes and gathered her power. I locked eyes with Jolene, and felt the jolt I always did, as the power of the Goddess flowed through the blue eyes of the woman I loved, circulating deep within me. I felt the upwelling of love and connection between us.

And yeah, I was thinking about later . . . one of my teachers had told me, early in my apprenticeship, that after a ceremony, participants tended to be sleepy, hungry, or horny—quite often all three.

I was holding out for all three.

Silently, at first, we all called upon the Powers and

our guides. There was a shift in the energy in the room we all felt, even Maryka and Tony, the gathering of our unseen allies into a room that suddenly felt filled, as a stuffy room feels cleared and filled when you open the window to a strong breeze.

I began the invocation: "Father, Mother, Creator, God, Holy Spirit, Great Spirit, Goddess... I call upon you. I call upon Jesus the Christ, Light of the Creator Made Flesh; I call upon beloved Mother Mary, Queen of the Angels, First Among Healers, Mother of Us All; I call upon the angelic realm, and the Four Archangels of the Presence, You Who Stand at the Four Corners of God's Throne, You Who Stand at the Four Corners of the World... Michael, General of the Lord's Host, Mighty Leader of the Warriors of Light on Earth, I call on you... Uriel, Archangel of Fire, I call on you... Raphael, Archangel of Healing, I call on you... Gabriel, Archangel of the Call, I call on you... I call on Jophiel and Zadkiel, You Who Bear the Lord's Standards, and I call Haniel, the Protector of the Great Mother, and I call Metatron, who once walked among us as a man... I call on the entire angelic realm..."

The room brightened, darkened, then brightened again as clouds dimmed the sunlight outside—or was it the infusion of angelic Light that filled the space? My breath deepened and slowed, and my inner vision filled with light and images...

"...and I ask for your presence and your protection, your guidance and your healing, in the Service of the Light, in the service of your child Tony, who is here today, and I ask, humbly, for your assistance, to use me as your vessel in the transmission of any healing that is in accordance with your Divine Plan...I ask for your protection for all of those here today in Service to the Light...and for Tony and Maryka...it is the Work of the Light we do here today..."

I opened my eyes and saw each of my friends and allies illuminated with a Light from within. Sabrina and Jolene, heads bowed, lips moving silently through their own personal invocations, calling their allies in and close; Dillon's eyes closed, but body poised with the vigilance of the watchman; Maryka's eyes closed, her hands resting gently on Tony's feet; Tony's eyes closed, his breathing deep and slow and steady...

I closed my eyes.

... And in that space behind my eyes, filled with the Divine Light, I saw those I had called: First In Front, in his sacred regalia, knife and coup stick in hand, dancing to gather and deepen his power; Tigre, alert and poised on her haunches, eyes deep as the starlit night; Burt, silent for once, the tip of a spear formation of crows and ravens lined up behind him... and behind my Three, the Mighty Three—Jesus, Mother Mary, and Michael... and arrayed behind Michael were the Legions of Light, the Mighty Warriors of Light on Earth...

"Yes," came the strongest voice that ever spoke through me, Michael, Mighty Archangel. "We are gathered here in Service.... This is how it begins. Let it begin..."

This is how it begins.

In a depossession, there is a process that the possessing entity—lost human soul, soul fragment, thought-form, dark force entity, or sorcerer—goes through at the same time that the possessed human and the depossessionist does.

There's an awareness of the Light, a reaction to it, an activation or disturbance with the entity or being. I saw with my shamanic vision the movement of something dark within and beneath the surface of Tony's energetic body.

Like a shark beneath the surface.

And like sharks, there are always a few pilot fish, attendants, smaller entities. They are the first to come forward, pushed that way by the larger presence beneath. Where there's one, there're many.

"I call on the Angels of the Crossing," I said.

In the Other Realms where I watched from my vantage point with a foot in two worlds, a portal opened—a sturdy wooden gate cross-reinforced with massive metal flanges—guarded by two warrior angels with swords of flame. And through that door came the Light—the brilliant Light of the Creator.

Lost souls, lost humans or other-dimensionals caught in the energy matrix of a human will often leave, spontaneously, and go to the greatest source of Light ... and there is no greater source of Light, other than the direct presence of Creator God, than the Light that shines through the Grreat Gates of the Crossing.

The ripples the reaction causes in the energetic shield can be seen by the naked human eye; a darkness comes and goes across the face, especially in the ocular cavity around the eyes. I saw those come up and depart, some of them human, some of them not, transforming as they entered the Light and returned as their True Selves ... one turned and raised her hand, whispered, *"Thank you ..."* as she vanished.

Those are the easy ones.

All that's required is to open Sacred Space, invite

in the Divine Helpers, call for the Gate to be opened, and hold Space while the clearing occurs.

The not-so-easy ones are those who fear the Light; those who've been deceived by the Three Lies: they are not of the Light; the Light will hurt them; they can never enter or return to the Light.

All lies of the Dark Forces, for we all come from the Light.

Remember what I said about the Father of Lies?

The Three Lies are the first of his children.

"Tony, can you hear me?" I said.

"Yes," he said, his voice soft and dreamy. "I can hear you, Marius."

"I'm going to ask you to help me help you, okay? I'm going to scan down through your body, with you, starting at your head and working down through your face and into your neck, all the way down through your body . . . what I need you to do is stop me when you identify any discomfort or pain, anywhere in your body . . . can you do that for me?"

"Yes."

"Let's start at the top of your head, the very top . . ."

"It feels as though there's something there . . ."

"If it had a color, what color would it be?"

"Dark, muddy, brown . . ."

"If it had a shape, what shape would it be?"

"Like an upside-down bowl."

"If it had a sound, what sound would it be?"

"Fingernails scraping on cardboard."

"And if it had a voice . . . what would that voice sound like?"

"Harsh, bitter . . ."

"Okay, Tony," I said. "I want Tony's True Self to

step aside ... Tony, I'm going to speak directly to that shape with the harsh and bitter voice, and I want you to listen to what that shape says, and just tell me whatever it says, no matter how it sounds ... can you do that for me?"

Tony hesitated, then said in a soft voice, "Yes. I can do that."

"My name is Marius Winter," I said. "I am a Son of the Light and I am here in the Service of the Light. Who are you?"

"It says it doesn't know," Tony said.

"Where do you come from?"

"Far away."

"What color is the Light in the world it comes from?"

A long pause. Then, "It says there is no Light where it comes from."

"You come from the Dark?"

"Yes."

"What is your purpose here?"

"To block."

"To block what?"

"Energy. Light."

"Your work here is done," I said. "You are released, with gratitude, for the lessons you have brought to all of us, and you are free now to return to the safety and the comfort of the Darkness ..."

... *another portal swung wide open, a black hole as dark as the space between black holes on the outermost edges of the universe ... a black hole that sucked light into it* ...

... and it was gone.

"Tony?" I said. "Is it gone?"

"Yes," he said, voice full of wonder. "It's gone!"

The deeper activation was even more visible now; ripples of tension, dark and light, played across Tony's face; muscles twitched in his arms and legs and stomach.

Jolene raised her hands as though offering invisible twin chalices to the sky; Sabrina and Dillon followed suit. A mighty band of energy traveled through their hands to me and through me, enclosing the table in a ball of brilliant white light.

Sacred Space.

"It's time," I said.

My allies gathered close and shed their otherworldly bodies to become brilliant spheres of light, joining with me and infusing me with their protection and their power; simultaneously them and me, I saw through their eyes and mine; and then the merging of the Great Powers with me, the two Mighty Powers that worked through me and protected me, Mother Mary and Michael, the merging causing me to tremble with that infusion of power, shook to the core of my mortal self...

...they joined with me to work through me, because the darkest and largest one of all was coming forward...

Tony choked and coughed. Maryka started to move but I held up my hand and she stopped. Tony's coughing and choking continued.

"I feel like I'm being strangled," Tony gasped.

"I call on Michael and Uriel to enclose this being in a super bubble of White Light," I said. "Enclose this being so it may do no harm."

...asking release is the intention, and it's the intention that mighty helping and compassionate spirits need to work through us...and within Tony, a brilliant light like a massive soap bubble infused with

Light surrounded and encased something dark and struggling within his body . . .

"Tony, let your True Self step to one side," I said. "You don't have to speak . . ."

Tony's voice changed to something deep and harsh and mocking. "I want him to speak."

"Silence," I said. "I'm speaking to Tony and his True Self. Tony, do you want to speak for this being?"

"I'm afraid," Tony said in his normal voice.

"You are protected," I said. "You don't have to speak, but you may if you choose to do so. We will all help you. You are protected."

It's always dangerous when you have an ancient and powerful and malevolent being that assumes or tries to assume control of the client's body. On one hand, when the being who's sovereign in the body by Divine Law—Tony in this instance—participates in the process, he regains some of the power stolen by the possessing being. On the other hand, with a deceptive and powerful being—it's always safe to assume that any being like this can be deceptive, powerful, completely telepathic and not bound to time and space—the practitioner and the client run the risk of losing control or being knocked off the concentration necessary to continue and prevail.

That's a favorite tool of the Dark Forces—distraction.

So we have a being that is telepathic, can see the future, knows what you are thinking before you do, has a host of telekinetic and other powers . . . what makes you think you'll prevail?

You'll prevail because it's *not* you doing the prevailing, it's the Power of the Light and the compassionate and helping spirits working *through* you. It's not you, any more than a beat-up saloon piano is the music that flows through it. You're the instrument and the player is a Divine Being that is also telepathic, can see the future, knows you better than anyone or anything in the universe, is not bound to time and space . . . and loves you and those who go in Service for more than anything.

Me, I bet on the Light.

"I'll try," Tony said.

"There is no try, Jedi," I said. "There is only do."

A ripple of laughter from those around the table as well as those gathered round in the Other Realms.

Tony laughed, a lighter sound. "Okay, Yoda. I'm ready," he said.

I could feel the discomfort of the Dark Force's entity; it hated laughter. There's a saying: "The Devil hates laughter." So do his minions. Especially those who take themselves too seriously and think that all laughter is mockery of them.

"Okay, Tony," I said. "Let your True Self off to the side, and let's see who we have here . . ."

"He says he wants to speak directly," Tony said.

"No," I said. "Through you."

"Okay," Tony said. He began, in his voice, "What do you want?"

"Who am I speaking to?" I said.

Tony's voice changed, became deeper and more precise. "You know who I am, shaman."

"What is your name?"

"My name is not important."

"I would think that it would be. You are obviously powerful. You are obviously here with a purpose. Surely so powerful and important a being has a name?"

My guides closed tightly around me, and around me the Legions of Light, surrounding me and infusing me with their power . . . they only gathered this way when in the presence of something powerful as well . . .

"I have no need of a name," the being said.

. . . and the image of banners arrayed across a vast plain . . . the Sons of Belial drawn up in all their ranks . . .

"Nor do I," I said.

Laughter then, musical and deep and poisonous, from Tony's throat. "First blood to me, shaman. That ego of yours will be the death of you. Do you still count coup, little shaman? Or do you call yourself a medicine man?"

"I don't call myself anything other than a Son of the Light," I said. "What is your purpose here?"

Laughter, soft and amused. "Why, to crush you and yours, of course, Marius. Now, forever, and always."

A ripple in the container of Sacred Space; a sense . . . another gathering, a darker one.

"Your work here is done," I said. "It's time for you to return to—"

"—where I came from, with gratitude for the lessons I've brought you?" Sneering laughter. "You cannot compel me, mortal. I am beyond you."

"There is nothing beyond Creator God," I said. "In the name of Creator God and the Light that works through me, I command you to leave now and return to the place where you came from . . ."

Tony screamed and twisted on the table. Maryka clutched his feet.

"You don't know where I come from, shaman?" the being hissed. "Look in your heart. That's where I came from."

"In my heart is the Light of Creator God," I said. "You may return to the Light."

"I am not of the Light! I return to the Dark! Only for now!" the being screamed through Tony's mouth. Tony twisted as though he were manacled hand and foot. "I am the *First*! I will be *back*! We are coming to *crush you*!"

The room shook like a brief earthquake. Dillon rolled forward onto the balls of his feet, alert; Sabrina caught his eye and shook her head no. A thick roiling form of black smoke seeped from every pore of Tony's body, coiling around his head and neck and shoulders; and from within the smoke, two red eyes glared at me, glared in turn at each of us holding a point in the Circle.

"I *will* . . ." the being screamed. It was cut off by the bubble of Light closing in on it, and on either side of the dark form appeared the brilliant white forms of the heavyweights in the Light, Michael and Uriel, binding him within the Light, and lifting him away, still struggling within the bubble, to the Place of Transformation . . .

Tony let out a trembling exhale of pent-up breath, and sagged back onto the table. He was drenched in sweat. His energetic body was torn and shredded, in need of deep healing . . . Sabrina and Jolene appeared as they are in the Other Realms: Jolene tall and terrible in her gowns of white, surrounded and attended by the spirits, avatar of the Goddess; Sabrina, her hair neatly braided, dressed in a white buckskin dress drawn with ochre images, a rattle in her hand—healing energy radiating from them both, and overarching them the Great Mother, Mother Mary as she appeared to me; the light of the moon flowing through Jolene and into Tony, filling him, infusing him; the spirit guides of Sabrina tending and mending the tears in his energetic being, repairing the body container even as it filled with Divine Light, cleaning out the sludge and residue the possession left behind, lingering like the stench of garbage does even after you empty the can; Dillon as he appeared in the Other Realms, a warrior angel, a long spear in his hand, a sword by his side, ready, endlessly scanning for any threat; my guides, all of them, holding the Space steady for the healing taking place . . .

And when that work was done and silently communicated to me from Jolene, I intoned: "Father, Mother, Creator, God, Holy Spirit, Great Spirit, Goddess, I call on you and I call on all the angelic realm and all those compassionate beings who have worked with us and through us on the behalf of Tony, child of God, and we offer gratitude and love for the work done here in your name. We are grateful, we are grateful, we are grateful . . . and we release with our deepest thanks all of the spirits who have gathered here to support this work . . . may the Circle be opened to the Light of the World and all released . . . with thanks of gratitude and love."

We stood back from the table. Tony opened his eyes, blinked and looked around at us. He looked different. His face was lighter and the bags under his eyes had disappeared.

Tears streamed down Maryka's face.

I helped Tony sit up. "Just take a minute and settle back into your body. Concentrate on the feeling in the soles of your feet, feel all the parts of your body, start from the bottom and work your way up."

"Okay," Tony said. "I feel really...different."

"You look different!" Maryka said. "It's a miracle."

"Thanks to the Creator," I said. "Now, Tony, Maryka is going to drive you back to her place. You'll need to drink a lot of water, way more than you think you need. At least two quarts over the next hour or so. Then I want you to get into a very hot bath..."

"With Epsom salts?" Maryka said. "I have that and lavender essence."

"Perfect," I said. "You know how he'll feel. He'll be tired and weak. If he's hungry, just a little soup or something light like fruit or salad. Your systems needs rest, but you should be able to eat anything you want later on. Right now, lots of water."

I handed Tony a cold bottle of spring water. "Start with this. And just rest. I'll talk to you in a day or two, see how things are going...but right now, just rest. Drink lots of water, eat light today, and do the Epsom salt bath tonight and for the next three nights. Okay?"

"Yes, Marius," he said. "Thank you." He looked around at all of us. "All of you. Thank you so much."

He got up and Maryka steadied him. Jolene and Sabrina touched him lightly as he left the room.

"Marius?" Maryka said as she steered him towards the door. "There's a gift for you in your bowl..."

"Thank you, Maryka."

She closed the front door quietly behind her. Dillon stood by the window, and we watched them get into her car and drive away.

I checked my offerings bowl. A check for five hundred dollars. A very generous gift indeed.

"Okay, all," I said to my friends. "With great thanks to the Creator, how 'bout dinner and drinks on me?"

CHAPTER 14

Bella Italia is a restaurant in the Kingwood neighborhood I like a lot. I liked it because a) Jolene adored it, b) they served massive portions of extremely good, albeit simple, Italian food, c) the manager, a former client, hired interesting and excellent servers and d) that same manager *never* let me pay full price.

Professional courtesy, right?

I did a blessing for the restaurant when it first opened and I came in from time to time to do a tune-up. Any public venue picks up an energetic charge from the people who frequent it; if the venue isn't cleared and attuned from time to time, the place itself picks up a charge and maintains it: happy, sad, light, depressed . . . sometimes even malevolent. For those services I always had a good table, all I wanted to eat and drink, excellent conversation and a sense of being welcomed home.

Just like now.

A big table, Dillon at the head, where I always seated him, though he was always the last to move into his seat; Sabrina opposite him where she could play him like a well-tuned guitar; Jolene and I on the wings across from each other, where we lived and loved as always.

Massive platters of pasta, meatballs and sausages, salad, crusty bread and, of course, vino. Fruit of the vine. Though I rarely drank to excess, I loved the taste of wine and the energy that flowed from it through me.

As did Jolene.

The wine heightened our anticipation about what lay before us yet tonight.

Remember tired, hungry, horny?

We'd worked through the first two.

Jolene smiled, touched the tip of her tongue, pink and live like a cat's, to her wine glass.

"Get a room, you two," Sabrina said. "All that second chakra stuff is making me horny. Dillon, how's your back, baby? Think you're up to taming the wild mare? Riding the bucking bronco?"

We all laughed as Dillon flushed, though you had to know how to look for that change under his olive complexion.

"I wouldn't want to wreck our friendship, Sabrina," Dillon said with mock gravity. "You know, once you've had me, you'd be ruined for any other man. You'd hold that against me."

"Talk is cheap, gunfighter," Sabrina said. She tilted her beer in his direction. "It *is* true that I tend to wear men out in search of the best cock."

The laughter was good. The meal and the wine were good. The company the best.

"Yes," Tigre purred. *"The best. More wine?"*

"I want more of that Italian sausage thing," Burt said. *"Tasty."*

First In Front floated cross-legged in the air, off to one side, as spirit guides do, and smoked his pipe. He eyed Sabrina.

"You know she and I have a history," he said.

Silently, I said, *"And you survived this?"*

First In Front blew a smoke ring at me. It opened into a vision: *Sabrina in her white buckskin dress, a teepee in the background, First In Front laughing with her...*

"Don't be talking to my other boyfriends now, Marius," Sabrina said. "Me and him, that's nobody's business but ours. Besides, I got a thing he likes that you ain't got..."

First In Front blew smoke at me and laughed.

Like I said. The best company.

For those with shamanic vision, the room was busy with our companions, guides and protectors; they like to enjoy, through us, the things that we enjoy—laughter, joy, good food, good drink, sex.

It's comforting to know they are there, our extended family in the Other Realms.

Long ago, in a vision, I'd been shown that friends are the family we choose—in this life. Before we enter the flesh we select who we will be born to for the lessons we need to learn or to unwork the karma from a previous life. In the flesh, we're drawn to people, often people we knew in previous lives, people we have unfinished business with—good, bad, indifferent.

Jolene smiled at me. "Yes. Past life karma here."

See? This is what it's like being involved with a

psychic. There's no hiding anything. *"Honey? Do I look fat in this?"* You can't get a word out without—

"Well?" she said sweetly, tipping her glass at me. "Do I?"

I sighed, hid my grin. "No, Goddess. You do not."

"You might tame this one yet, Jolene," Sabrina said. "I got a bit and a bridle I'll lend you."

"That would be lovely, sister," Jolene said.

They both laughed women's laughter, leaving us mere men out of the joke. Goddesses. We must worship them. Or pay the price. Most times both.

"Yes," Jolene said. "I'm thinking a hefty fee..."

When Light Workers commune together in ceremony, there's a joining at a deep level, a telepathic level, where communication is instantaneous, deep and rich with nuance and much, much faster than normal speech or conscious thought. While this capability exists in all humans, those attuned to the Light and who consciously work in the Light have it much closer to the limen of consciousness—hence this whole psychic thing. The decompression period after an intense ceremony eases the spirit back into the flesh and the reality of the Middle or Ordinary World, even while that telepathic union lingers in the wake of that extraordinary heightened awareness.

Great for spirit work; a wee bit challenging for us mortal men contemplating an enthusiastic night of sheet-swimming.

"There's a lot more going on with that man," Sabrina said.

"Huh?" I said.

She ignored me, as did Jolene, who said, "Yes. He'll need more."

"Oh," I said. "Tony? What do you get?"

"Soul retrieval," Sabrina said. "He'll need some work. And more uncording. You got the demon out, Marius, but Tony has lots of resonance. That was a corded and intentional possession; there's someone out there who was running that and it all ties back..."

That took the wind out of my sails. I nodded. "That's what I get...what we discussed before."

"What's that?" Dillon asked.

"We've got layers here," I said. "Like Shrek. It connects to these multiple attempts and passes at me. There's someone incarnate in the Middle World who's acting as a portal for the Dark Forces..."

"The Decanter thing?" Dillon said.

"Yes," Jolene said. "That is a Dark place."

"I won't go there," Sabrina said. "Love you to pieces, Marius, but that place will drain the Light out of the strongest. I don't want you to go over there."

Jolene silently considered Sabrina, then looked at me. It was unlike Sabrina to be so direct; she was up for anything in the Light and had stood both on her own and by my side in many a journey on behalf of others.

"What do you see?" I said.

Sabrina took a long draw from her beer. Paused. "I see loss, Marius. I see and feel sorrow and anger. I see you balanced on the edge of the abyss. More than that is not clear. But there's danger to you, as always. But also to all who walk with you. More than you've ever experienced."

She stared into space, focused and intense, connected like the Medicine Woman she is to her guides as the information came across. The channel closed, and she blinked rapidly.

"Is there more?" I said.

"Not now, Marius. If more comes to me in journey or dream, I'll let you know." She waved her empty beer bottle at the server, an elaborately tattooed skateboarder named Ev, to bring her another. "Tony will need a soul retrieval . . . I can do that for you, if you want. He'll need some follow-up. But the cording . . . you'll want to track that back. At the end of that binding is the Who. Somewhere along the line you'll get the Why. That will tell you what you need to do."

"Time enough for all that," Jolene said. "We all need to . . . sleep."

Dillon grinned into his beer glass.

"Then we can reconvene, after dream and journey, to see what else has come through for us," Jolene said. She smiled demurely at Dillon. "You sure you're not going home with Sabrina, Dillon?"

Dillon laughed. "I don't know how I'd look on the back of her bike."

"This makes me have to pee," Sabrina said. "Excuse me."

"Me too," Jolene said.

The two women went off, leaving Dillon and me grinning at each other.

"Why is it that women always go to the bathroom at the same time?" Dillon said. "Not just psychic-shaman-type women. Every time you get two or more women gathered together, if one has to pee, they all have to pee."

"Uh . . . because we're all connected?" I said.

"Oh, spin that happy New Age shit on somebody who doesn't know better," Dillon said. "Nice try, though."

We sat for a moment and enjoyed it.

"So what does all this mean?" Dillon said. "For you and me?"

"Means we have to be careful, brother," I said. "There's only so much we know. What we do know, we've talked about."

"Maybe we should develop the situation," Dillon said. "Recon by fire."

"We already did. Someone . . . or something . . . noticed."

"That worries me."

"Yeah."

Jolene joined us.

"Where's Sabrina?" I said.

"Outside for a cigarette," Jolene said. "She said to tell Dillon to grow some and come join her. What does that mean?"

We laughed, Dillon most of all.

"More, you think?" I asked. "Or are we done?"

"I can't fit anything else in," Dillon said.

Jolene smiled. So did I.

"What about Sabrina?" I said.

"I think she's ready to go," Jolene said. "It's been a long day and she's ready for bed. Or bedding." She winked at Dillon. "Dillon? Are you sure?"

Her wicked grin. Oh, Creator God, how I loved that grin.

Dillon just hung his head.

I held up my hand and Ev came right over.

"Ev, I need the check," I said.

She was gamine all the way through. Grinned. "Sorry, Marius. *Your* money's no good tonight. Word from the boss."

"You tell him I accept with gratitude, okay? And

I wish many blessings on him, you and this whole establishment. And Ev?"

I handed her a fifty.

"That's for you."

"Marius..." she said.

"Thanks for your great service."

She dimpled. "And you for yours, Marius. You come back soon." She winked at Jolene. "Make it be soon, Jolene? Okay?"

Jolene touched Ev's tattooed sleeve. "Soon, my friend. Thank you."

"Thanks, Ev," Dillon said. "Marius, thank you. Jolene? You are the Goddess."

"I honor the Divine Male in you, Dillon," Jolene said.

"I'm not sure what that means, but I'll take it..." Dillon began.

A high-pitched shriek shattered the harmony and calm of the restaurant. A woman ran towards the rear of the restaurant, sheer terror on her face.

"Oh, God!" she screamed. "Oh, God, oh, God!"

Jolene snapped her head around. "Sabrina?"

Dillon was already moving. That's the true test of the Warrior Called; they run *towards* the danger, not away. He was moving fast. I hesitated, torn between Jolene and Dillon, and Jolene solved it for me by shouting: "Go! Fast!"

I went.

Fast.

Right behind Dillon.

Who came to a sudden halt, his pistol ready in his hand. I yanked my Glock out.

In the parking lot, Sabrina struggled in the arms of something vaguely humanoid in shape, if a human were ten feet tall and wore a dark veil over its head, wreathed in smoke to dim its outlines, and was surrounded by four men backing towards a van with the side doors open.

The customers in the lot fled in all directions.

The four men weren't really men.

Goat-headed, with long nimble hands that seemed quite comfortable with the M4s tucked professionally into the sockets of their otherwise human-looking shoulders. There was at least one human, from the waist up anyway, sitting behind the wheel of the idling van.

"Goat-headed gunfighters?" Dillon said. "Marius, help me out here...do we need iron, silver or will just plain lead do?"

"I'm thinking go with what we got," I said. "Federal HST."

We lit up the goats.

Parenthetically, the CIA and the Joint Special Operations Command once commissioned a study of the effectiveness of various ammunition. They decided the best source of data wasn't ballistic gelatin but living flesh. But since shooting bad guys in a controlled fashion is frowned upon in the U.S. of A., they chose French Alpine goats.

Why?

A French Alpine goat has the same average thoracic cavity and configuration of the statistically average human male. So the testers tied up the goats and shot them, once for each goat, once for each type of ammo, and studied how long it took to incapacitate or kill the goat.

Before they finished it off—humanely—with a shot to the head.

And among the things the operator community learned was that goats aren't easy to kill.

So Dillon and I could consider our field test of Federal HST 9mm +P 124 JHP a continuation of that study, albeit flawed by multiple simultaneous body shots.

We advanced on the goat formation, our expended brass arcing in a brilliant spray out of our twin Glocks. Dillon had hooked me up with the Dawson Precision +5 Magazine Extension for my G-17 magazines, so I had twenty-two rounds of goodness in each of the three magazines I carried when armed. I fired at the two goat-headed operators on the left, keeping a solid cadence with no pause between shots, back and forth between the two who tracked us while Dillon worked the two on the right.

The goat-headed gunfighters sprang aside nimbly. Their legs angled strangely in their 5.11 pants. Goat legs, too? I hoped they had the same thoracic cavity and they weren't running plates under their shirts.

I watched my rounds hit him in the chest, then furrow red along one forearm that certainly *looked* like a human arm. The goat staggered and had sudden difficulty bringing his M4 on-line. It was running an EOTech and a white light and what looked to be an IR laser on the rail. The implications of that didn't sink in till the lights went out in the lot.

"Dillon!" I shouted. "They've got night-vision!"

My own night-vision in my Mark One Eyeball was shot between the parking lot lights (now absent) and the muzzle flash from the very hot rounds I'd been putting out as an instrument of goat extermination. A string of shots from a carbine-bearing goat came my way; apparently their goat night-vision was built in and they could track their IR lasers without the cumbrance of a head set.

"The bad guys get all the best toys," I muttered as I crabbed sideways for cover beside a beat-up Nissan Sentra.

Dillon took two long steps and then proned out behind a very shiny brand new Dodge Ram dualie pickup, gleaming cherry red. He curled up in an urban prone and continued firing at the goats, one down, two advancing, one missing...

...but not for long.

First In Front led the way, Tigre and Burt hot on his heels, my guides attacking a cloud of black winged forms... a dark veil expanding from the black figure tossing Sabrina into the back of the van... First In Front pointed with his coup stick at...

The Dodge Ram, where a goat poked its head around, the square-shaped pupils narrowed in concentration as it aimed at Dillon's back. I stepped around the truck and pulled the trigger...

...my Glock went *click*.

I dropped the dry magazine and plucked the next one from my Rogers single mag pouch and slammed it into place, then put eight shots—almost as fast as Jerry Miculek—in less than a second and a half into that goat, stitching it from upper chest (thoracic cavity) to right between those square-pupiled eyes, dropping it cross-legged where it stood. Then I turned and continued to fire at the last two goats till my pistol stopped—again—this time with a double feed. I stripped the magazine out and worked the slide, slammed my last magazine into place...

"Dillon! Ammo!"

He reached under his jacket and tossed me a spare magazine, one of probably a dozen he was carrying, knowing Dillon. I shoved it into my hip pocket and turned to the fight. One goat down and the other one hobbling backwards toward the van, still shooting.

It sprang into the back.

"Sabrina!" Dillon screamed. "No!"

The van peeled away. The door slammed shut and the last thing I saw seared itself into my eyes: Sabrina, her hands stretching for us, snatched back in as the door shut.

Dillon aimed at the van, stopped himself.

"We gotta go, Marius!" he said. He slapped his pants for his car keys and ran for his Jeep Wrangler.

I turned and saw Jolene watching us.

"Go!" she said. "I'm fine. Go!"

First In Front was perched on the hood of the Jeep... *"No go..."*

Dillon turned the keys. Nothing. He tried again. The hood latches were loose. I lifted the hood. The engine was seared black, wires and hoses melted.

"What the..." Dillon said.

I slammed the hood down. The goat bodies began to smoke, then exploded into flame. So did their weapons. The flames became white-hot and incandescent. We had to shield our eyes.

After a moment, the flames faded. All that was left were three blackened smears and several puddles of molten metal in a parking lot littered with empty shell casings.

"We have to go!" Dillon said.

"We have to track them," Jolene said. "We must shield ourselves first..."

Anguish carved gutters into Dillon's face. And Jolene's.

And mine.

"I see loss, Marius. I see and feel sorrow and anger..." So she'd said.

She'd spoken true.

CHAPTER 15

My front room had become a war room. Dillon pored over the weapons he kept stored in my gun safe; while I wasn't as well equipped as he was, I certainly kept enough for a serious fight. Jolene made tea in the kitchen and held her counsel.

For now.

I sat and tried to still my mind, to open the channel and work past or through the rage and sorrow and guilt that bubbled in me—as the attacker intended. All those emotions fogged the Light, robbed me of clarity, made me reactive . . . and reactiveness is what the Dark Forces were counting on.

What Sabrina needed—what all of us needed—was clarity and the calm marshaling of our forces here, in the world of arms and bullets and cold steel, and in the Other Realms, where our allies waited.

But I needed to clear my mind to call . . .

"We are here for you, Marius," Tigre said. *"As always."*

"Yes. You always are. You know what I need?"

"Yes," First In Front said. "I can track her..."

Images...from First In Front to and through me... a road...no, a highway...the Interstate.

The road to Decanter.

A farmhouse. Dark. Only a single window lit. On the edge of the town, far enough away where the lights of the city were only a dim glow against the sky, but close enough to see that. A shimmering veil over the house...I was lifted above it, to see a whirlpool of black in the middle of the darkest ocean in the depths of the darkest night, swirling and drawing it in...and there, one brilliant point of light ringed by the darkness...

Sabrina.

Rage rose in me. My intention became...violent. I leaned forward...

...and was pulled back by First In Front.

"This is how they get to you," he said. "You'll rush in...there is much that is hidden there, and of a level beyond you. This is not just you, this is all of us. All in the Light. The rage you feel? That's the weapon they'll use against you..."

Tigre put herself between me and the vision. "All of us who walk the Path will walk with you. You must be wise in how you do this. Karma, preordination and the Great Mystery of God's Plan...you must remember this, Marius. What you want, what you react toward, is not the deciding factor. It's God's Will. Not yours. Not ours."

"It's the oldest trick," Burt said. He circled, the leader of a murder of crows swirling in a clockwise spiral above me. "Play on your love for another. The Light Warrior fights not because he loves the fight, *but because he loves that which is behind him. Or on the other side of what he faces."*

"Love is your strength," Tigre said. "And your weakness. Be strong in your love and measure twice..."

"...and cut once," First In Front said.

I was back in my front room.

Jolene stood with Dillon. She offered me a steaming mug of tea.

"Tell us," she said, "what have you seen?"

Dillon's face was drawn taut in a war face. He was locked in a cycle of vigilance, scanning the room, looking out the window. He circled Jolene and me like the planet of war.

"Marius?" Jolene said.

She held her power in check and waited. She was concerned for me, but like a carefully banked flame, there was the fierce Dark Mother, the protective and destructive aspect of the Goddess.

"They took her to bring me running," I said. "There's a portal there. A farmhouse outside of Decanter. Rings of the possessed and Dark Beings. At the center is the place where they plan to rip the fabric between the Other Realms... where their allies are stacked up at the door."

"How is she?" Dillon said.

"She's alive," I said. "Being Sabrina... she'll fight them. But there's a powerful Dark Being there..."

"That's what took her?" Dillon said.

"Yes."

"The goat things?"

"Soldiers."

"Yes," Jolene said. "From both Cabal and Dark Force."

"Who's controlling them?" I said.

Dillon backed up a step as Jolene's power came on her and her voice deepened as she spoke. "The Fallen control them and the humans, who fool themselves into thinking they are able to control the tools of the Dark. The humans have made bargains, negotiated what they believe are deals. The Dark honors nothing. The Dark honors no one. The Dark lies and seeks to quash all that is good."

She stared through me, no longer completely Jolene, the love of my life, who lay with me all through the nights, but an avatar of all that is powerful and pro-creative from the Goddess Herself.

"Marius," she said. "This way is fraught with danger. But you must go. Dillon, you must go, too, and you must be careful... your anger is how they will trap you and you must follow Marius's lead, no matter how strange it appears. You must both go now. They expect you. Sabrina cannot hold out alone against what is gathering there. She needs us. We will be aided..."

I couldn't hold the words back. But I tried. "Jolene... you can't come with us..."

Ever kneel in front of a wood-burning stove and open the door when the flame is at its highest and hottest? Ever feel the gentle warmth turn into a raging blast of heat right in your face? Take that feeling and multiply it by, say, ten thousand or so... then double it again.

That would be a rough approximation of what I felt blaze out of Jolene's eyes.

"You do not decide." Her voice was overwhelming. "The Goddess decides. The Goddess will have me remain here, in the flesh. I will support Sabrina till you arrive. And *all* of us will travel with you."

What she was saying was she'd go into the Other Realms while Dillon and I raced, heavily armed, to Decanter...and that she'd hold off *all* the Dark Beings, including at least one of the Fallen.

By herself.

"Uh, Jolene..."

Try a blast furnace with a megaton yield H-bomb. In your face.

"The Goddess commands." The voice that came through her came from a place and a being much further than my front room.

There is no arguing with the Divine.

I bowed my head. "In accordance with the Divine Plan."

Dillon trembled. He didn't understand or see what was going on. He just needed to run to the fight.

"Marius?" he said.

"Let's rock and roll, gunfighter," I said. "We'll leave everything else to the Goddess."

She didn't smile. Her face was shadowed like the graven image of every avatar stacked back up and through Mother Mary to Isis and to the fierce flame that burns in the hearts of all mothers.

"Go, warriors. Go with blessings as you go in harm's way. Bring our sister home."

We went.

My 4Runner rattled like Arjuna's chariot on the eve of battle. Jolene's car had fried and died in the parking lot outside Bella Italia, but mine had been parked safely in front of my house, so it was still running and had a full tank of gas.

Our chariot was ready.

We were gunned up and ready to roll.

I ran a Glock 17 with a Dawson +5 in the mag-well and three reloads on my belt; in the foot well behind my seat was a semiauto Daniel's Defense M4 with an Arredondo dual mag coupler holding two PMAGs of Hornady TAP 5.56 goodness. That would do for Middle World baddies. I had a five-inch Smith & Wesson 627 revolver, the Jerry Miculek Custom with the eight-round wheel, in a shoulder holster, and a small dump pouch full of speed loaders for it. Each wheel contained bullets of silver and iron and lead for those baddies from the Other Realms, prancing around on backwards legs or otherwise. I also had a Super Soaker full of holy water: natural water infused for twenty-four hours with the peelings of nine oranges, blessed in the name of Jesus and Mother Mary. It was like napalm to Other Realms bad guys, especially vampires or werewolves or the genetic clones of those used by the Cabal.

Dillon ran his full war belt. His Glock rode in a Talon Tactical dropped-and-offset speed holster; the Glock itself wore a Trijicon RMR milled into the slide with suppressor irons, a Dawson mag-well to fit his customary Dawson +5; he had a speed rack with four reloads on it, and what was left of his belt space held two spare PMAGs in Kydex speed pouches, a blow-out kit, a dump pouch and a seriously big Bowie knife. He wore a simple Eagle three-mag pouch across his chest, the Velcro folded back for speed, and the war bag at his feet was full of spare magazines for his LMT SBR—completely illegal, chopped and seared for full-auto, a thirty-inch bundle of "I don't give a fuck" with a white light mounted on one side of the rail and an IR laser on the other. He had NODs mounted on a beat-up skateboard helmet and an identical one—his backup—for me. Mine had a decal of a red arrow pointing forward that said DANGER IN FRONT.

No shit.

We each wore a simple leather pouch. Jolene had draped them over our necks in a simple ceremony as we left. The pouches each contained a small card with the picture of the Virgin Mary, another with the image of Michael the Archangel, and a small stone infused with the blessings of the Goddess and Mother Earth.

Like all Warriors of the Light sent to stand in harm's way, we went with the full blessing—and protection—of the Goddess.

"You know what I forgot?" Dillon said.

"What?"

"Bottle of water."

"I got. Far back, behind you, the small ice chest. Warm, but it's wet."

Dillon twisted around and half-climbed into the back and fetched us two bottles. He handed me one.

"Best place to store water is inside yourself," he said.

I gulped mine down in a hurry. My mouth wasn't dry from just thirst. "Throw some in the go-bags will you?"

We'd have to stop short and take a piss, but it's always a good idea to enter into a fight as well hydrated as you can be. Getting shot at—or fighting demons—is thirsty work.

The highway between Minneapolis and Decanter is dark. No lights for long stretches; the faint glow of lights from farmhouses and the occasional offramp over the fifty miles were the only sources of light. There wouldn't be much in the way of Highway Patrol on a weekday night as the clock approached midnight; after two A.M. there'd be some cruisers out looking for drunks. We'd avoid the main city. My guidance dovetailed into my Google Maps search, which showed an isolated farmhouse—just as I'd been shown—on the south boundary of Decanter. We'd do well to avoid Decanter at night; the police department was full of the possessed and the corrupt, and Dillon and I, to the possessed or other pawns of the Dark Forces, would gleam in their Dark vision like beacons in the night.

My headlights bored a tunnel through the night, just like the tunnel I traveled through...

...in journey. Tigre bounded beside the car, her long white legs an effortless flow; the light in her eyes brilliant...and feral. Burt flew above us, the point man in a long V-formation of crows and ravens, each in a dark gleaming rank, the same formation as the angels, when called to war...and when I glanced in the rear view mirror, First In Front, in full war regalia, sat with his eyes closed in prayer, his coup stick in one hand, his war knife in the other, arms crossed on his chest...

"Warrior..." a soft female voice. I looked at Tigre, who cut her eyes to my front. A beautiful glowing image of a woman wrapped in blue and white who said... "Warrior, the Space is held. Look for unseen help and allies...You will be tested..."

...a deep and sudden warmth in the center of my chest, as my heart swelled with recognition of that voice...

Dillon's voice called me back. "Marius? You're drifting, dude..."

I shifted the wheel slightly and eased back into the lane.

"Sorry. Tranced out. Happens sometimes."

"I know. We've got to keep our mind in the game."

Yes. We did.

CHAPTER 16

We parked the 4Runner off the gravel road that led to the farm; the last mile we'd crept forward on idle, lights out, windows down, listening to the night sounds as we inched closer to the house huddled against the night sky. Walking in was the best way to sneak up on these people; connection to the Earth helped me and my allies keep a cloud around us, hiding us from vision in this world and the next—getting out, well, we'd worry about that when we got that far.

One thing at a time.

I'd learned to trust Dillon's lead in these things. He was silent, crouched forward slightly, his LMT at a low ready diagonal across his front, his NODs tucked up out of the way, as our eyes were ready for the darkness.

I touched his shoulder, stepped to one side, opened my pants and emptied my bladder. Always a good idea when you know things are going to get hairy.

Dillon held security, then when I stepped aside he did the same.

Bladders empty, magazines full.

Time to go to work.

We knelt and watched the long driveway. The house gleamed at the end of it. One light on upstairs; a hint of light from the basement windows.

Of course they'd be under the ground.

A sense of foreboding. Weight on our chest. A chill at the back of our necks, and a sense that an unseen vise was closing around our heads. The Dark Forces cast a cloud, and that cloud can fog your mind, your thinking, even your vision and your hearing. But when you recognize it, you call on the Light...

Michael, beloved Archangel, I call on you and the Mighty Warriors of Light on Earth, to fill and infuse me with your Divine Love and Protection...

Like a bright camera flash from within, the fog lifted and our clarity returned, and that which was slipping in like a dark fog was repelled...but it was still out there...

"Marius, follow me," Tigre whispered.

In my Other World vision she took point, padding along the right edge of the driveway...above us Burt circled, as implacable as a drone in the Middle World, and right beside me, where he always was in the fight, First In Front, his eyes narrowed and intense...

Dillon scanned left and right, his carbine muzzle tracking with his eyes, and I saw him lean in, hurry the pace up...

...in the Other Realm, he was a warrior whose long stride was lengthening as though to gather speed for the first throw of the javelin he held...

Sabrina?

Tigre shook her head no—"Stay focused, Marius. We hold the space. As does Jolene. This is Middle World. We can only work through you and her—Jolene is holding them."

And my stride began to lengthen, too.

And Tigre began to sprint . . .

And so did we all.

And the first of the Dark Guardians turned in the front yard and ran towards us—

—a gigantic three-headed pit bull, maybe three or four hundred pounds, the size of a small cow. But fast as a pit bull.

Ever see a pit bull run?

Dillon broke to the right, I broke to the left and . . .

. . . in the Other Realms, a murder of crows descended on the black hole shaped like a three-headed pit bull . . .

. . . we started pouring bullets into the Cerberus on steroids rushing at us. Dillon worked full auto; he walked the rounds onto the charging pit bull, which flinched, but kept on coming; I rolled my trigger fast-fast-fast-fast and saw at least two hits; the EOTech was fast as can be for this kind of action, but the pit bull wasn't slowing down and it was close enough to see the size of its teeth in each head, the eyes rolling red, the teeth the size of a child's pinky, crooked in a "c'mere baby" fashion, and it looked like there might be an extra row or two in there, just like a great white shark and . . .

"Marius the bullets aren't . . ."

Working? Yep. Dad gum it. Pesky Dark Side entities, which didn't forebode well for our already compromised entry, but these things happen when you bring the fight to the Dark Forces door. I grabbed my Smith Revolver and did my best Jerry Miculek imitation, set the front sight on the three-headed pit bull and pulled the trigger *bang-bang-bang-bang* ... the .357 hand loads shot flame like the Sword of Michael at the End of Days and the alloy of silver, lead and iron struck the pit bull as it launched into an impossibly long leap, necks outstretched, jaws gaping wide with multiple rows of teeth...

...and each bullet strike on the Other Realms flared brilliant blue-white, the white of the sun at the height of the day, the brilliant White Light of the Creator, striking down the Darkness...

And the three-headed pit bull fell and skidded to a stop right at our feet, four huge smoking holes in its body.

"Nice shooting..." Dillon began.

The heads reared up and snapped at us. We sprang back. The center head snapped and continued to snap, and the two side heads dug in and dragged itself along at us.

That's why an eight-shot revolver is a good idea.

Three shots to the heads and one more to the body, dump the casings, speed loader in.

But now the lights were on in the house. The lights were on, and somebody's home...

We replenished mags and advanced on the house.

The second wave sprang out of the door.

Literally sprang.

Like those pictures of centaurs dancing along, except these bad boys had goat heads. They'd dispensed with their clothing. Below the waist, they had goat legs and massively engorged penises flopping back and forth, human torsos wrapped with what looked like Mayflower Trading Company plate carriers and mag pouches (how do they get all the best gear?), M4s tucked into their shoulders and the goat heads scanning...

The lights went out in the house.

Full dark.

We dropped our NODs into place, and saw the IR lasers aimed from their platforms. Apparently those goat heads had their purpose; maybe goats can see infrared, or maybe it was a custom mod configured for the Dark Forces by the black-lab geneticists and biologists. We weren't modded by the black labs, but we had the best NODs Dillon could steal. Problem with IR lasers, as any recent generation of shooter with time in the Sandbox can tell you, is that it works both ways. Fine if you're fighting people who don't have the technology; not so fine if you're careless and assume they don't. They had IR, so did we—but we could see it with the NODs, and we could put our EOTechs right over the source of that beam we saw *without* switching ours on and—

—ever heard of "shooting fish in a barrel?" We were shooting goats in the dark.

Of course, they shot back.

Oh, and Hornady TAP works *awesome* on goats, or goat-humans, or goat-taurs, whatever you call 'em.

Dillon was systematic, in the zone. He worked the trigger on full-auto, no sear-designated controlled burst for him; he liked the finesse required and he could tweak out a single round, a double hammer, a triple burst or light 'em up with a full magazine while dancing sideways like a tango dancer shadow-dancing. He'd worked out a short burst of three to four per goat which dropped them decisively; they tried to converge their IR lasers on us but we were moving in tandem, enough space between us to keep them from tracking us both at the same time and enough firepower to keep them from concentrating.

I kept up the cadence, as Dillon had coached me and never let there be a lull in the fire just keep working the trigger and the brass arced over us both like the Rainbow Bridge of Asgard and track the targets across their front, tracking back to service them some more if they hadn't already fallen out of my sight picture, and then tracking them down to the ground, a couple more anchor rounds in them, their blood black in the NODs.

A flare of gunfire from one of the darkened windows and Dillon met it with a full magazine worth of full-auto that chewed up the window frame and lit up whatever was standing there.

And then a moment of stillness, when we realized all the goats were down, and the *click* as we inserted fresh magazines, our boots clinking amongst the fallen brass.

Wave three met us on the run, pouring out the door, crouched over their M4s. Men, or at least they looked like men—

"Cabal clones," Tigre murmured... *"Hurry, Marius, you must get in and downstairs..."*

A formation of crows flew at them and First In Front leapt forward—

In the First War of the Angels, and in the War That Is Upon Us, the Angels of the Presence of God, the Faithful, have a battle cry. They stand in glowing ranks, the V-formation, and at the tip of the spear of the very vanguard of the Creator's Army, stands the General of the Lord's Host, who always leads from the front, and it is his name they cry as they charge forward—

"MIIII-KAI-ELLLL!"

Dillon and I were abreast and the fire we unleashed was withering the sickles in the wheat and the tares.

Cabal clones are capable of independent thought, of passing for humans, though they are easily muddled by the Light of the Creator when focused with intention, and the sound that issued from Dillon's mouth and mine was an ancient one, one with a visceral energetic connection and meaning to those of the Dark—and it was the battle cry of those who wrought their undoing.

We were almost to the door, our wake littered with expended cases and the fallen carcasses of the soulless. The last clone fell. His vest said DHS. Among the other fallen were vests that said POLICE, SHERIFF, FEDERAL AGENT, SECURITY.

They needed one that said CABAL.

In the Other Realms, that's what it looked like.

The door frame exploded. Literally. The wood framing ignited and blew outwards like det-cord wrapped around an old-school breaching charge. The door splintered and sent hot fragments pelting us and into the yard.

Dillon and I fell back a step, arms up to shield our faces. I had some fragments lodged in my face, but my Oakley goggles had protected my eyes.

At least from the fragments.

In the door was the demon who'd taken Sabrina.

And it had taken off the veiling hood it wore in the parking lot.

I could see why it wore a hood.

Remember Medusa? How she froze all those who gazed upon her, turned them into stone? This guy looked like Medusa on her worst day crossed with one of those giant pit bulls on rabies. Or maybe like the Balrog from *Lord of the Rings*. But worse. And the face shifted...

...the bully that tormented you in grade school... the face of a murderer in a TV show...the glare of a mass killing shooter captured, looking back over his shoulder at the news cameras...the face of nightmares past, present and future, constantly shifting...every bad thing we'd ever been afraid of, shifting across its face, and then it raised its hand and...

We were blown back like cartoon characters across the yard, tumbling end over end.

But we held onto our weapons.

Dillon rolled to his knees, fired a burst at the demon on the threshold.

Nothing. No joy.

He looked at me. "You're on point, Marius."

Gee. Thanks.

The demon wasn't advancing. It held its point at the threshold. Which meant there was probably a containment barrier there, an energetic leash if you will, to prevent it from running amok to and fro. So we had to get past it, which meant through it or... around it.

We got up and as it raised its hand, I saw...

...in the Other Realm, Tigre throw herself in front and lunged at it...

"No!" I shouted.

"Tend to your fight in your realm, shaman," she

whispered as though in my ear. *"I love you for want-ing to stand in front of me, but it is my job and task to stand in front of you. Go quickly . . . Now!"*

And we dashed for a side window as the demon batted and wrestled with something unseen to Middle World vision. The window Dillon had shot full of holes looked good enough. I stuck my head in and looked into a much-shattered front room, old and musty, and the demon wrestled to our left . . .

Dillon knelt and I stepped on his knee and went through, then reached back and pulled him in. We both took some small cuts so maybe it was the scent of blood that caused the demon to turn and glare at us.

"Don't look at it, Dillon!" I shouted.

The demon was struck from behind, and I saw . . .

. . . Tigre batting it with both paws, teeth sunk in at the base of its neck, First In Front circling, his knife glowing from that which issued from the demon's guts, Burt swarming in followed by a murder of crows, filling the room . . . and swarming around a stairway that led down, down, down . . .

The fifth wave showed up.

All three of them.

The first one was young, maybe nineteen, tall and slim and blond, wreathed in black, full sleeve tattoos; she had moon and crescent earrings that gleamed like her oversized incisor teeth protruding from disturb-ingly full lips and the scent . . .

"Vampire succubus, Marius, beware the smell, watch Dillon . . ."

"Dillon! Step back . . . don't look at them, don't smell them . . ." I shouted.

Her companion was a boy about the same age,

dressed much the same, feminine and languid in his motion, his fingers sporting long artificial claws of razor-sharp metal, dragging them across the wall like Freddy Kreuger and humming a child's lullaby...

The last one was like a matron, middle-aged and thick, with black holes where eyes would have been. Her incisors protruded like a boar's, and she clacked them and held up both hands where a single hornlike razor-sharp claw extended like a Dark Side Wolverine's...

"Steel and silver, iron and lead, Dillon," I said.

They sprang up and bounced off the walls and ceiling, the pack of three working to split us up to finish us off. Dillon and I pressed back to back.

It was time to open the Super Soaker.

I felt just like John Malkovich in *Red* when he got to open the pig.

I sprayed an arc around us that misted the air; vampires are fast, inhumanly so (pun intended) but they hit that mist of sacred water like Wile E. Coyote into a brick wall. Vampire screams are like bat calls, but amplified—the sound hurt our ears, reverberated in the room.

It will repel them, but it won't kill them unless they are immersed in it, and even then not right away. A vampire—and their shape-shifting kin, the werewolf—requires an infusion of silver and iron and cold steel, administered and repeated as needed.

Time for my Jerry Miculek Smith Custom.

Nothing like a .357 hand cannon to say "Old School."

In the fight, when you're aligned with the Light, and in the right, there's a sense of being and not-being, a sense of being a portal for the Mighty Warriors of Light on Earth, who guide us, who strengthen our hands for battle, and guide us. I'm a fair shot most of the time, and I get plenty of practice on Dark Siders, but even on my best day I never shot as fast and as accurately as I did just now *BOOM-BOOM-BOOM-BOOM-BOOM-BOOM-BOOM-BOOM click* . . .

Oh, how I hate *that* sound . . .

I dumped the expended casings and grabbed for a speed loader . . .

. . . just as they sprang again, teeth bared, the matron in front, leaking from two massive glowing holes in her chest, but still full of fight; the young female looking down at the three holes in her torso, staggering forward; the male with a sear alongside his head and another graze on his shoulder—must have missed one. Dillon grabbed the Super Soaker, the sling still around my neck, and pulled me off my reload as he sprayed another arc around us, almost fast enough to slow them all, but the matron was on him and then she curled back and shrieked so loud I felt something give in my ear. Dillon twisted the Gerber Mark II fighting knife that had appeared like magic in his hand, cold steel blessed by the water running down his hands, and the matron vampire sprang back, both clawed hands gripping her midsection, one of her extended claws gouging a track white and then red along Dillon's jaw, and I dropped the speed loader and fumbled another one out, a little bit of panic welling up in me and . . .

. . . *First In Front reached out his hand and steadied mine. "Take your time . . . fast," he whispered as he guided my hand into inserting the speed loader and twisting the cylinder shut and then aligning the revolver at the young male springing at me, his mouth opened wide, leading with his teeth . . .*

...which shattered as I put several .357 hand loads in his mouth and down his throat and out the back of his head.

His head shattered, too.

One down, two to go. The young female bounded, but it seemed with the last of her energy, and I placed one round carefully between the dark holes of her eyes—she would have been so pretty—when she turned and ended her existence.

The matron stood across the room. The demon struggled with Tigre behind her. The matron leaked her essence from gaping holes and the massive wound Dillon's knife had opened up in her.

"Shaman..." she hissed. "You're on a journey you will live just long enough to regret."

Boom!

A hand load cratered her face.

Three down, but the demon turned...

...and was snatched down by a white tiger, tireless in battle... "Hurry, Marius. Hurry downstairs..."

"You up?" I said.

Dillon sheathed his knife, checked his weapon. "Good to go."

"Let's roll."

We went downstairs.

In shamanic training, when a practitioner is first taught to journey, the first journey that we make is one to the Lower World. It's classic, simple, and fairly safe while under the supervision of a good teacher-shaman. You journey to a place in the natural world where there's some sort of entrance to the Lower World, you travel down through there, through a tunnel that twists and turns and eventually you arrive in the Lower World. The Lower World looks like the Middle World—except there are no trappings of the "civilized" world we live in. It's all about Mother Nature. Mountains, lush forests, oceans, streams, animals and spirit beings. It's the home of benign and helping spirits, at least at the first levels.

But in the map of the Lower World, there are regions to explore deep and dark below even that surface, and part of the training of the shamanic practitioner is to venture there with the allies one finds, or who find you, because each nook and cranny of the Other Realms can hide a secret, a spirit or an insight that can help—or kill—a shaman.

These stairs were like that tunnel, leading and twisting down.

This staircase wasn't shaped with human intention; it twisted and turned upon itself, crossing over, though always down and the roof dropped down and became one of earth, dripping moisture, crisscrossed with strange veins that looked as though they pulsed with blood or some other fluid.

Like being inside an intestine.

The air stank, had a thick substance to it that left a nasty-tasting film in our mouths.

There were no Guardians upon the stairs.

That worried me.

Dillon's breath rasped.

"You okay?" I asked.

"Yeah," he said. "Good enough." He paused. "I'm scared, Marius."

"I know, bro. I know. Me, too." I took a deep breath. Fear is the mind-killer, as a great writer once wrote. I called and I was answered...

...Michael, stand with us and strengthen us in your Work, lend us your courage and your strength and your Divine guidance in this Dark Place...

And like that, it lifted, and we felt infused.

"Felt like someone lifted a pack off me," Dillon said.

"It's just all the ammo you've run through."

He laughed. "No such thing as too much ammo."

"Word, that," I said.

Faint and far-off, down the staircase, a scream.

A woman's scream.

Sabrina.

We ran. Towards the scream, down the stairs, our knees aching with the impact and our boots clattering and pounding on the wooden stairs that became steps carved out of living stone, and yet the staircase turned and turned again, and again...

Another scream.

From a woman we both loved.

And the stairs ended in a cavern, the way illuminated by glowing globes mounted in the wall, a sickly pale light in each nook, the passageway twisting...

...and then opening into a chamber.

In the middle of the room, a raised dais. Tied up, spread-eagled, Sabrina twisted against the red cord bindings that held her. She was naked. Her spread legs were pointed at a deformity in the rock that shaped the chamber, a deformity that pulsed like a scabbed-over wound with a vein beneath it. In a loose formation around the dais, centered on the one I'd come to find, were what appeared to be men.

And there were Guardians here.

Not one, but three—huge, twelve feet tall and muscled accordingly with bodies that would make a bodybuilder swoon. Faces human-appearing, handsome beyond handsome, but with an evil oiliness and sly-ness that repulsed.

The horns didn't help.

Demi-demons.

A step up from your run-of-the-mill worker demon, roughly equivalent in the Dark Side way with a demi-god, half-elven or half-angelic, half-human.

And Fallen.

Further powered by a Fallen somewhere close by, probably on the other side of that portal, ready to cross when the right energy was there and, from the appearance of it, the energy of rape and murder under dark sacrament was what they had in mind.

We were there just in time.

Dillon was already rolling forward, and I felt his energy shifting, the rage rising in him, overriding his fear to become something elemental, something older than primeval, the fiercest flame of all, the Divine Male in defense of the Divine Feminine, a friend in defense of another, a father for a child...

"Dillon! Stop!" My voice rang with something much greater than me, something much larger, and I felt the presence of the angels gathering at our sides, at our backs...

He stopped.

The closest demon laughed. "Don't stop him, Mar-ius." The voice was male, confident. "Let him run. You're always saying in accordance with the Divine Plan...this is part of the plan. Divine, isn't it?"

Demonic laughter from all three.

Behind them, the ring of men laughed. And in the center, the block-headed gray hair I'd last seen in an expensive business suit. To either side, men with the greasy look of the small-town politician, and at least one officious public official, probably a sheriff or a police officer.

Possessed.

"Welcome to the party, Marius," the one in charge— or so he thought—said.

"How are you, Will?" I said. "Tossed any babies in the fire lately?"

He didn't like that, but he hid it fairly well. One of the demons looked at him and laughed mockingly. He didn't like that, either.

"Not lately. But the night is young. Figure we'd warm up with your tasty little biker bitch friend here, then move onto you and Mr. Shoot-'Em-Up there. We might let him live so he can explain all those dead law enforcement officers upstairs. Make for an amusing day in court, I think."

"Marius..." Dillon growled.

Sabrina raised her head. She was clouded, maybe drugged, definitely fogged by a Dark Veil.

...And then I felt Her... the One who worked through the One I slept with each night... a brilliant white light descending on Sabrina, around her, and I saw, as though through a brilliant porthole window lit with light, Jolene, face drawn with fatigue, lines furrowing her face as she concentrated and surrounded Sabrina with light. I had the sense of dark things throwing themselves against the shield wall Jolene held even as she breathed more life back into Sabrina...

...and I felt my own rage rise up, the heat of the righteous anger coming up in me, and I raised my hand and called upon the Powers...

... and was shown how it had happened before, so long ago, and now the opportunity to choose differently, how long ago the rage I'd felt in the defense of those I loved, those I'd sworn to protect, and how that rage had fueled the power I'd been given, the power I'd been gifted with, and how the rage transformed it into a weapon, the most powerful of all. But once I'd done that, there was no returning, the path of rage and anger led me down the Dark Road...

"Choose differently," Tigre whispered, from far above where she wrestled with the demon on the threshold...

... First In Front touched his coup stick to my shoulder, and I felt his strength flow into me...

... Burt nodded as he settled down on the floor, his head tilted to one side...

And I brought it down, dialed it back like a rheostat, took a deep breath, let it settle down through me, down through the soles of my feet, down into Mother Earth...

... and there let the energy be grounded, let it settle, connect with the Mother and let her strength and wisdom flow up through me...

... And a stillness came over me, the stillness that comes in a forest in the space between strong breezes, when the hush settles; the stillness between heartbeats; the stillness of the 'twixt and the 'tween.

Power gathered. At my back, to my sides. The Presence of the Light.

And the Mighty Warriors of Light on Earth.

"Not me, Creator God, but you through me, in accordance with your Plan," I whispered.

My chest swelled...

... and a huge burst of light issued out of my chest,

*like a flash suddenly ignited, and the Light held open,
as I was the portal, and in the brilliant glare of the
Light, I saw issuing forth the Warriors, who leapt at
and engaged the three demi-demons . . . the possessed
humans throwing up their hands to cover their eyes,
others stirring at their backs . . . bodyguards?*

"Dillon!" I yelled. He'd already sprung forward, a
killing light in his eyes. My shout didn't slow him; he
grabbed one of the humans, an obese man in a Mason
County Sheriff's uniform, lieutenant's bars on his collar,
and head-butted him, knocking him cold, and then Dillon was beside Sabrina, his blooded knife in his hand
slashing at the cordage, pulling her up and throwing her
over his shoulder, grunting with the effort, as Sabrina
was no small woman and she was practically unconscious.

Shots from behind the cluster of humans, and then
several more goat-soldiers and Cabal clones emerged
from a side tunnel. I worked that trigger—a Geissele
SSE—like there was no tomorrow, smoke curling from
my barrel, and serviced the targets before they could
get completely clear of the tunnel's mouth, stacking
'em up so the following echelons tripped over the
bodies in front of them, more good shooting.

Dillon staggered past me and headed for the stairs.
I covered him and backed towards the stairs . . .

*. . . the demi-demons were swinging great swords of
flame, hammering on the shields and swords of the
Angelic Warriors of Light, one of whom turned and
looked at me and mouthed the words: Run, Marius,
we will hold . . .*

And that made me want to run *to* them, my beloved
brothers . . .

"*Run!*"

The blast of angelic communication lifted me and turned me and sent me up the stairs, right behind Dillon, huffing and swearing as he staggered up a step at a time.

"*Run!*" *Burt shouted, his brethren swirling around him...*

"*Run!*" *First In Front shouted, demon blood running from his war knife, his coup stick matted with demon flesh and brains...*

"Run!" I shouted.

Dillon jogged up two stairs, stumbled and fell. "God, Marius," he gasped. "I can't run up these stairs with her. How we gonna get her out of here..."

He was agonized. It's just biology, part of being in the meat...he was in good shape, but we'd just fought our way down into an antechamber of Hell, and now he was carrying an unconscious woman up at least the equivalent of five stories' worth of stairs, on the run, with demons snapping at his heels.

"Do the best you can," I said. "I'll hold them."

"You can't..."

"Get her out of here, Dillon! You're stronger than me; you can carry her, I can't. I'll hold them here and fall back after you. Give me your spare mags."

"What about the demon up top?"

"Dude, one crisis at a time, okay? Let's get up there first. Go!"

He slung Sabrina across his shoulders in a fireman's carry, wrapped his off arm over her dangling arm and gripped her leg, propped his LMT in the crook of his strong arm and started up, huffing—

—there was movement at the bottom of the stairs, and I welcomed them with a good long string of shots,

then misted the air with holy water and fell back to
the next landing, Dillon already working his way up
to the next—

—bounding up the stairway at me a goat-soldier
and a vamp, the vamp a full-body male, strong and
springing from wall to wall, I dropped my M4 in the
VTAC sling and drew my revolver *boom-boom,* two
shots did in the vamp but the goat-soldier got off a
burst that ricocheted off the wall, at least one graze or
maybe a through-and-through on the meat of my leg,
I turned the revolver on him *boom-boom,* four shots
down, hope they don't send any more vamps this way;
working backwards I stumbled and sat down hard on
my ass, which saved me since there was a burst of fire
over my head, courtesy of an IR-equipped goat-soldier,
and I got another .357 into his center of mass, punching
a ragged hole in that very nice Mayflower chest rig—

—Dillon had paused on the upper landing; I could
see his shoulder laboring; it was hard physical work
anyways, especially after the fight in, but we had to
move—

"Dillon! RUN!"

I slammed another speed loader of my hand loads
into the .357 and started jogging up; the body count
had slowed down the pursuers, though I wished I
had a . . .

"Dillon!"

Pant, huff, pant, huff, "What!"

"You got any hand grenades?"

Pant, huff, pant, huff. "Yeah. Wait one."

Thump, thump, thump . . . rolling down the stairs
to me. An M-46 frag.

"You got any more?"

Pant, huff, pant, huff. "Yeah, gimme a minute..."

Thump, thump, thump, thump, thump, thump... two more.

All righty then.

Two turns down the cautious approach, light and nimble, goat-footed almost, a soldier came up.

I doused one grenade in holy water, murmured a quick prayer over it, pulled the pin, counted one, two, throw it!

And threw it down the stairs.

Way too hard, as it bounced right past their point man and rolled further down...

...and I hurried up the stairs—where the heck was that thing—and then...

Crack!

The overpressure compressed my ears, even a floor above, and the screams of goat-soldier shredded with holy-water-soaked shrapnel rose.

I ran.

Dillon was leaning against the wall. He looked as though he'd run a marathon.

"Marius, you take her, I can't anymore..." His legs were shaking with the effort.

The stairwell was wider here, we were only two levels beneath the house. Above, I could hear the battle between Tigre and the demon still raging...

"Hurry, Marius, you must get clear..."

My white tiger.

Burt swirled past me, a wreath of black smoke that sprouted brother crows like feathers; they filled the stairwell beneath me and bounding up the stairs behind came First In Front, a warrior's grin on his face; he stopped and waved me on.

I got up next to Dillon. There was barely enough room for us abreast on the widening stairs, but it was doable.

"Drape her over both of us, Dillon."

He let Sabrina slip and kept one arm around his neck, I draped the other around mine and we staggered up the stairs—

—one flight, one more—

—and then we were entering the house, which was shredding to pieces right in front of our eyes, *Tigre and the demon still tangled up, shredding the house in the Other Realms and in this one*—

I doused the two remaining hand grenades in holy water, pulled the pins with my teeth with my best John Wayne panache, chipping a tooth in the process, and then tossed both grenades down the stairwell, turned to Dillon and . . .

The entire house lifted, shook, shattered into a million pieces of lumber, brick and plumbing, and Dillon and I and Sabrina were tossed like rag dolls in the hands of a furious toddler, end over end, to land in a heap in the field, a good twenty-five yards from the shattered foundation of the farmhouse that was no more. Debris landed all around us, but not on us, thanks be to God.

"Dillon?" I said.

A moment, and then his voice, utterly spent and still wheezing. "What?"

"I'm glad you're alive. Sabrina?"

"She's here. Breathing. Not hurt that I can see."

"Dillon?"

"What?"

"What the hell did you put in those grenades?"

"Nothing."

"Frags won't blow a house up like that." I paused. "I mean, will they?"

"Maybe they hit a gas line."

I pushed myself up. In the ruins of the house, straining at the end of an invisible leash, the threshold demon raged at us, like a guard dog barely restrained.

Tigre stood above me. She was covered with demonic blood, but looked otherwise unscathed.

"How do you do it?" I thought.

"If you were a woman, you'd understand," she said. She licked a paw and groomed herself. *"You need to go, Marius..."*

I pushed myself all the way up, reached down and grabbed one of Sabrina's limp arms and looped it around my neck. Dillon looked on the verge of a heart attack.

"You know, I love her," he said.

"I know. So do I."

"How can a woman weigh that much and not be fat?"

I laughed. "You better look at her now, Dillon. She finds out you even thought that, you'll never see her naked again."

We staggered off, our unconscious medicine woman between us.

A sudden brilliant light illuminated us, the smoldering wreckage of the house, everything—fields, road, everything—for at least a quarter of a mile.

I looked up.

A gigantic glowing disk hovered above, moving slowly, like the Empire's battle cruiser in *Star Wars*.

Dillon looked up. Looked at me. Looked at Sabrina. Sighed.

"Marius ... tonight I've shot it out with goats, clones, demons, possessed humans, fought my way into Hell and back, carrying a heavy-ass woman I love dearly, been blown up, shot, stabbed and almost drank dry by a vampire. *The last freaking thing I need now is a freaking flying saucer!*"

"Uh ..." I didn't really know what else to say.

We were moving, but a blast of light descended from the saucer and tore up the road in front of us.

Just like the house behind us.

That's what we would call a clue.

So we stopped.

"You got any grenades left?" I said hopefully.

"Nope."

The saucer descended. Landing gear extended and it touched down. It hummed and glowed with light. A port opened in the side, and a long ramp extended from it, all the way to the ground in front of us. A backlit figure, humanoid, stood at the stop of the stairs and then descended to stand in front of us.

Human. Late thirties, early forties. Black hair closely cropped, burly, fit and very tall, a cylindrical head like an artillery shell, white skin, a neatly trimmed mustache and several expansive saber scars across his face.

The Nazi Wehrmacht uniform was pretty sharp, and his knee-high leather boots gleamed with fresh brushing.

His voice had, as you might guess, a heavy German accent. "My name is Otto Skorzeny," he said. "Come with me if you want to live."

CHAPTER 17

Okay...so we're in this flying saucer...

That sounds strange.

Let me back up and start again.

A shamanic practitioner, by definition, must be able to grasp and participate in at least two different realities—at the same time. Someone much smarter than me, in the ordinary reality, said that the sign of true genius is to embrace simultaneously two different and opposing perspectives. Someone else said that's the sign of true mental illness and psychosis.

So you make your choice and you live with it.

Me, I hew to the shamanic view. I was Chosen for this Path. I had to learn how to embrace at least two realities at the same time.

Or I would have gone mad.

That happens to neophyte shamans or apprentices or people Called within a society that doesn't know what to do with shamanic initiation except to define

it as illness and try to legislate or medicate it out
of existence. Like our society—rife with sorcery and
curses, controlled by people who deny that—despite
the overwhelming evidence from traditions much older
and deeper than our own that show us the way.

So there's what Michael Harner calls "ordinary
reality." That's the world where we have to pay our
bills and our child support and alimony, stop at red
lights, talk over the fence with our neighbors, watch
mindless TV, be a good citizen and neighbor.

And then there's "nonordinary reality." That's the
reality the great indigenous cultures all over the world
define as the reality that surrounds and permeates us,
the reality that is just a dream—or journey—away.
The Other Realms, the Realms of the Upper, Middle
and Lower Worlds, the Realms of powerful spirits,
malevolent and benevolent ones, the world of magic
and insight, of healing and sorcery, the Realms where
shamans—good, evil, competent, incompetent, student-
apprentices, masters (though they dislike that term)—
traveled to gather information and power to further their
agendas or the agendas of the Great Powers or to do
healing or divination or other work on behalf of others.

If you like the duality of that model, then "nonordinary" reality is where you might put phenomenon
like flying saucers, the Cabal's military involvement,
time travel, age regression and other topics most often
found on conspiracy theory websites or the "New Age"
section of the bookstore.

But like anything else, you have to practice discernment to filter out what the truth is. In the Middle
World especially, there are sorcerers—often called
politicians, reporters, media people—who manipulate

perception to deceive and distort and muddle. The advertising industry was one "beneficiary" of the expertise in propaganda developed during the Third Reich by the visionary Joseph Goebbels in the service of Adolf Hitler—the Big Lie.

Remember what I said about the Father of Lies?

I was privy to a discussion, at a teaching, by one of the best shamans in the country, a brilliant, beautiful, and gifted teacher and practitioner, and the leading exponent of "compassionate depossession"—utilizing the Light in a gentle fashion, more in alignment with the belief of the Tibetan Buddhist than, say, traditional Christianity, to do releasement for the suffering being (i.e. possessing spirit) as well as the client with the presenting symptoms. She was responding to one student-practitioner who was mocking a belief in flying saucers and especially aliens or extraterrestrials.

"So you believe and practice a modality that accepts spirits and powers, but you deny a reality where aliens or extraterrestrials might exist? How do you draw that line?" the teacher asked.

Willing suspension of disbelief aside, as any good reader of urban fantasy or science fiction does, do you accept *everything* or do you reject *everything*?

I look for the Middle Way in all things.

I've seen and experienced enough things that can be defined as strange, bizarre or insane—and I have no need to convince others that I've seen or experienced something. My belief is mine and I don't force it down the throats of others. And those the Creator brings to me generally are satisfied with the evidence of their own personal experience, which may be completely different from my own.

Which brings me back to the flying saucer.

Any depossessionist who practices long enough will run across extraterrestrial or extradimensional beings. Extraterrestrial possessions are often experiments run remotely—or lost ETs without a way to phone home. So in essence the same procedures used in a standard depossession apply—we help them find the Light of their home, and away they go. They are Spirit, or energetic beings.

More rarely, a practitioner may encounter clients who have experienced, or may have him- or herself experienced, physical encounters with ETs, including abductions, experimentation, and, yes, flying saucers or other aircraft.

Some of these are Cabal interventions/experiments with technology given to them by ET or extradimensional beings (extradimension is a fancy term for the inhabitants of the Other Realms; in the Cabal's case demonic, in those aligned with the Light, angelic . . .); some are genuinely ET—not always benign, either. But key to having a workable comprehension of this end of the phenomenon spectrum is accepting, up front, that a human will never completely understand the mind and thinking of an ET . . . unless that ET is also human.

Does that open a Pandora's Box?

It sure does.

But back to the flying saucer . . .

"So here we are," I said, "in a flying saucer piloted by Hitler's bodyguard and personal assassin, one Otto Skorzeny, escaping from a portal that leads to Hell, leaving in flaming wreckage behind us one farmhouse, dozens of dead goats and clones that looked just like local law enforcement, a number of seriously pissed off demons and the closely controlled humans who make up the infrastructure of a seriously cursed town . . ."

"You missed the part about batshit crazy," Dillon said. "This is all . . ."

Skorzeny laughed. "You have good humor. I like this."

I had to admit, I kinda liked him, Nazi or not. He had, after all, plucked us off the battlefield where who knows what was about to happen.

"*We know what,*" Tigre opined. She was curled up in one corner of the spacious cabin of the saucer, which was disturbingly retro in design, like a '40s dirigible run through *Architect Digest* and run through the latest technoware from Akihabara in Tokyo. "*He is your unlooked-for ally . . .*"

Burt perched on the back of one of the luxuriously upholstered seats and cawed once. Then tilted his head and said in his best Brooklynese, "*Yep.*"

First In Front hovered over Sabrina, looked at me and nodded . . .

So a legendary Nazi commando, long dead, appears in a flying saucer and plucks me and mine off the battlefield. Okay.

"So now what?" I said. "What do I call you?"

"Otto," Skorzeny said. "Or Ed. As you wish."

"Ed?" Dillon said.

"My American name."

"Ah," Dillon said. "I thought I was confused before."

"I like Otto," I said. "May I call you Otto?"

Otto tilted his head to one side, a surprisingly delicate movement in so big a man, but then, he was flying the aircraft. His hands were huge, oversized frying pan huge, and they rested in what looked like molded cutouts on the armrests of the command chair in the cabin. It appeared that small, precise movements of his fingers controlled the aircraft.

"Of course," Otto said.

"There's so much I want to ask you," I said.

Otto laughed. "I enjoyed that film very much. Classic. *The Day the Earth Stood Still*. Yes?"

"Dude, you're the *real* Otto Skorzeny? Not a clone? You're the guy? The one who flew a paraglider in to rescue Mussolini?" Dillon said.

"You are a student of history?" Otto said.

"Military history, yeah," Dillon said. "You're the Patron Saint of modern Military Special Operations."

"Ah, you flatter," Otto said. "Yes, I am the real Otto Skorzeny."

"Look, not to interfere with the military fanboy thing, but let's stay on task here—where are you taking us?" I said.

"I am returning you to your home in Minneapolis, Marius," Otto said. "Your woman requires your assistance." He looked at me. "You are a fortunate man to have such a woman. She is very powerful."

The lights of Minneapolis grew in the dark; he'd followed the highway straight back, the glow of the ship somehow hidden from eyes below.

"How do you know this?" I said.

"We will have a long conversation, Marius. Probably many. Right now, you must return to your home." He looked at Sabrina. "There is a greatcoat in the panel behind you."

Dillon opened a panel and found a full-length leather greatcoat inside. He draped it over Sabrina, who was now completely unconscious.

The craft lowered, hovered over my house, right below, the lights on.

"Step into that chamber, there," Otto said, nodding towards what looked exactly like an old elevator from a '40s musical. His huge hands were delicate on the controls.

Dillon and I lifted Sabrina into the chamber.

Otto looked over at us. "Till we meet again, my friend. I will return in a less ostentatious conveyance, yes?"

He pushed a button and the chamber door closed.

We descended in a cone of light and were left on my back lawn, all three of us. Above our heads, only the stars . . . and a wrinkling of the night sky's fabric as something big and unseen flew away . . .

"Cloaking device," Dillon breathed. "Just like the Romulans."

"I don't know if we've gone where no man has gone before, but I think Gene Roddenberry would have given his left arm to go where we just went." I said.

Standing in the rear door, framed by the light behind her, was Jolene.

"I left the lights on for you," she said.

I swept her into my arms. Or words to that effect.

She was exhausted. Long lines on her face, dried sweat and/or tears on her face, her dress damp with perspiration, long arms and legs trembling.

But she was my Jolene.

She pulled away, her hand lingering along my cheek and jawline, then touched Sabrina's head.

"Bring her in, set her in the bedroom," she said.

We carried Sabrina in and laid her down in my bed. And only then did she blink open her eyes. She looked up at Dillon, at me, then at Jolene; down at herself, naked, and the black leather greatcoat she wore. She ran her hands over the rich leather.

"Damn," she said in a shaky whisper. "Musta been *some* party..."

CHAPTER 18

Dillon and I sat on the floor, backs against my couch, our weapons spread out in a greasy array around us; the shower ran long from the bathroom where Sabrina stood and let cleansing water run over her; Jolene came in from the kitchen and handed Dillon and me each a mug of fresh-brewed steaming coffee, then went and brought one back for herself, slid cross-legged with boneless grace into a seated posture, yogalike, across from the two of us.

She had aged, my beauty, and that filled and topped off the reservoir of rage and anger that had driven me at some point during the night. Her face was drawn with fatigue; long lines running beside her mouth that seemed to have grown overnight, a streak of gray hair along the front of her red mane, a boneless hunch, round-shouldered, the posture of the terminally fatigued or beaten . . . and as though she could read my mind—she probably could, fatigue or not—she

straightened herself, took two deep breaths, and a
clarity seemed to emerge from within her, settle her
straight-backed and once again the proud and strong
Priestess of the Great Mother.

She sipped her coffee and stared at me over the
lip of the mug.

It was almost, for a moment, like it had been.

From the shower, barely muted by the fall of water,
muffled sobs.

Dillon began to get to his feet.

"Leave her," Jolene said. "I'll see to her. She needs
to be alone right now."

"I . . ." Dillon said.

"Yes," Jolene said. "I know, Dillon. But she needs to
be alone for now. She'll be with us when she's ready."

The shower shut off.

Jolene nodded. "Soon."

"So what now, Marius?" Dillon said. "I just, I just
don't, I just . . ."

I took a long hot pull off my coffee and focused
on the simple warmth of it in my belly.

"First we drink our coffee," I said, "and see to
Sabrina. All of us stay together right now. And then
we'll sit in Circle and seek guidance. But right now?
Drink coffee. Clean guns. Check the wards and boundaries and protection. Rest." I looked at Jolene. "Yes?"

She nodded. Once. Rose without using her hands,
the blossoming of a red and white and black-garbed
flower, left the room. I heard muffled words and the
homey sound of women in a bathroom.

"It's all like a dream," Dillon said. "Is it always
like this?"

"Yes," I said. "In the 'twixt and the 'tween, when

the Other Realms open up, in the area between where we go to fight, it's always like this. A dream and a not-dream. Nonordinary reality."

"The whole Otto Skorzeny thing?"

I shrugged. "Just as real, or not, as everything else we saw and did, Dillon."

"He said he'll be back. To talk to you."

"If it's in accordance with the Creator's Plan, he will be. If not, he won't be."

I drank my coffee. Jamaican Blue Mountain. That was real. Or real enough.

We cleaned guns. Reloaded magazines and moon clips. Refreshed holy water. Sharpened knives.

The women were alone in the back of the house and we left them be. Their work was the work of the Goddess, the Divine Feminine, and ours, tonight, was that of the Divine Masculine, the protective principle of the universe.

"Oh, Marius," came the soft tigerish voice I loved so much. *"You're so serious..."*

"Should be," Burt said. *"Big night's work. And it's just the beginning..."*

And they were gone, or rather, gone silent.

First In Front was there, sitting in my recliner, watching me and Dillon at our tasks. As always, his knife seemed scoured and sharp, and he seemed still and focused, his eyes gleaming bright with the White Light of the Creator radiating from him like a stove carefully banked.

"It is the end of the beginning," he said. *"You came close tonight, to the trap they set for you."* He nodded yes in response to my silent question. *"Anger and rage, the fuel of the fighter, the warrior... you have to*

beware. And you must watch for Dillon, because he doesn't understand or know, he only trusts you and follows your lead. Be careful where you lead, Marius. The path is perilous..."

And he was gone.

Spirit guides are never really gone—they are with you always. Most times, when they seem to disappear, it's you and your junk that blocks the channel. Junk being the stuff we need to work through—distraction, anger, Dark Forces interfering, all of the long list of things that are obstacles on the way back to the Light—and that junk interferes with *our* reception. The Creator always knows and is always connected to us; or to be accurate, we're always part of the Creator. But the exercise of Free Will allows us to disconnect, to be separate, to feel and experience that we are separate. And the exercise of the Return to the Light leads us back to the full and direct experience of God the Creator, and the connection of all of us.

We are all related.

We are all connected.

Sometimes, when our spirit guides go away for a while, it's for us to examine our relationship with the Creator and our guides, and in the silence the appearance of absence brings, to develop a new appreciation and integrate the lessons we've learned.

And sometimes we all need a break.

I looked at our prepped gear. All ready to go. I didn't have the military experience Dillon did; he'd gone in harm's way as a solider and as a military contractor and for a while, as a bodyguard—the way of Middle World war was familiar to him.

Me, I learned as I went along, and brought along

the skill set gifted to me by my warrior guides and *"Yes, we are all warriors,"* they whispered, and just as Dillon had learned some of my way, I'd learned some of his.

So we were ready for both worlds.

Outside, light grew through the trees in the park. In the Koran, it says that night ends when you can tell the color of two strands of string, one white, one black. It was that time.

Jolene led Sabrina into the front room. Stood there, holding her hand. Sabrina was wrapped in one of Jolene's terry cloth bathrobes, her hair still damp from the shower. Strength had returned to her. The toll of the night was calculated in her eyes. As in Jolene's.

I could tell they wouldn't speak of that. Nor would they need to. All would be shared in journey.

Jolene gestured for Dillon and me to follow her. We did, into my healing room. Jolene had moved the treatment table out, and so there was space for the four of us to sit on the floor, at the four points of the compass.

"Now," Jolene said. "We'll join in sleep and dream. In the light of the day. Together we will rest and heal."

"I'll stay up," Dillon said. "I'll watch over you all while you sleep."

I opened my mouth and Jolene silenced me with a look.

"Beloved," Jolene said to Dillon. "You will rest with us. I've been shown that you all are safe. In our sleep we will be watched over, by the Mother and all of the helping and compassionate spirits." She paused, and smiled the smile that no man could resist. "Dillon, even the mightiest warrior needs rest. Today you have earned that. Please."

He hung his head and nodded.

We all joined hands for a moment of silent prayer, and I felt a wave of fatigue sweep over me. We turned so that we faced outwards, lay down with our heads facing into the center of the circle we made, joined hands.

As the light of day grew against the drawn curtains of my healing room, the darkness of complete rest grew and I fell into a deep and, for a while, dreamless sleep.

CHAPTER 19

I woke with the heaviness in my bones that told me that I hadn't moved at all while I slept. There was no light against the windows. I'd been asleep for a long time. I blinked and rolled onto my side. Dillon was still asleep. No Jolene, no Sabrina, but the clatter coming from the kitchen told me someone was there.

I got to my feet and went to the bathroom.

Then into the kitchen. Sabrina wore a set of designer sweats, courtesy of Jolene's overnight closet stash. She considered me, her hair drawn back tight, eyes and face grave.

"There's coffee," she said.

"How're you doing?" I said.

She nodded. "I'm good, Marius." She took a deep breath. "I'm not ready to talk about this yet. But... thank you. Thank you."

She turned away so I couldn't see her face, filled a mug of coffee, handed it to me. I took it and avoided her face, honoring her wishes, touched her shoulder.

"Dillon still sleeping?" she said.

"Yes." I grinned. "You wore him out."

She laughed, a flash of the old Sabrina there. "I've shown him mine, now he's gonna have to show me his."

"Uh, my name's Paul, and that's 'tween y'all . . ." I said.

She filled another mug and went into the healing room, came back out with it.

"He's too cute when he's sleeping," she said. "I'll leave him alone . . . for now."

"Where's Jolene?" I said.

"She went home," Sabrina said. "She wanted to get cleaned up, get some fresh clothes, and pick up some groceries. And," she said, grinning, as she headed me off on the next words on my lips, "she said not to worry, and to just rest, she'd be fine and she'd be back when she was ready."

She sipped her coffee to hide her grin.

"Gonna have to rein in that old caveman thing, Marius. Don't wanna piss off the Priestess, now."

"Uh, yeah. Okay. Whatever. How 'bout you rustle up the cave*men* some eggs or something, woman?"

She laughed, more of her in that this time. "Already done. Take me about five minutes once Dillon gets up, unless you want to eat and leave your partner to starve? I've got scrambled eggs and some thick slices of ham I found in the icebox, some fresh fruit and made some orange juice. Nothing like breakfast for dinner."

"What time is it?"

"Past seven. You were down for fourteen hours. Did you dream?" she said.

"No," I said. "Not that I remember. I was out."

She nodded. I didn't ask her if she'd dreamed.

THE SWORD OF MICHAEL

I heard stirring, and then Dillon came into the kitchen. Sabrina went to him and gave him a full body hug, long and hard and silent, so hard I heard him exhale with the strength of it. She stepped back, tears streaming down her face, turned away and handed him a mug of coffee.

"Thank you," he said.

She nodded, couldn't speak. More tears streamed down her face. Opened the fridge and took out a bowl of whipped eggs and began to prepare a meal.

I inclined my head in the direction of the front room and Dillon followed me out. We flopped on the couch.

"Wow," Dillon said.

"Yeah," I said. "Best not to ruin the moment."

He looked at me in complete bafflement. "What?"

"Dude, take it from me . . . don't say a word. Nothing. Just be . . . here."

Dillon shook his head. "Marius, I don't know what scares me worse—women or the Dark Forces. I sure don't understand either, but I can handle a straight-up fight. Steering the course with women, well . . ."

I laughed. "Welcome to the club, bro. The only thing I know about women is I don't know, and that I'm here to serve the Divine Feminine. Which means I shut up, most of the time, and just be who I am and hope that's enough."

He held up his mug. "Word. Where's Jo?"

"Took off for home to get clothes and groceries."

"She shouldn't . . ."

"Don't, dude. She'll know and then we'll both be in trouble."

We laughed and laughed. In the kitchen, the homey sound of a woman preparing a meal.

The meal was convivial. A bowl full of steaming scrambled eggs, big slabs of ham, more coffee, some fruit. Sabrina ate little, but sat and sipped another big mug of coffee and watched Dillon and me—okay, more Dillon than me—as we plowed through the food.

Remember what I said about sleepy, hungry, and horny after a powerful journey session?

We'd dealt with sleep and food, and what was unspoken between Dillon and Sabrina was growing with each moment.

"Uh," I said, "should I give you two some privacy?"

Dillon laughed. Nervously I thought. Sabrina grinned a lascivious grin.

"Oh, I don't know," Sabrina said. "What do you say, Dillon?"

"I, uh, I . . ."

I laughed.

There was a loud knock at the front door.

Dillon and I looked at each other, got to our feet. Dillon pulled out his pistol and held it behind his leg and followed me to the front door, stood off to one side and peeked out the window.

Not Jolene.

A very big and very tall man in a long leather greatcoat.

I opened the door and looked up at Otto Skorzeny. Behind him was the darkness of fresh fallen night, fireflies dotting the dark.

"Hello, my friend," Otto said. "I have come for a visit. May I come in?"

"Only those of the Light may enter," I said. "Are you of the Light, Otto?"

"By our deeds we shall be known," Otto said. "I

saved you once, yes? That would make me at least an ally, yes?"

"Are you of the Light, Otto?" I said again. I was aware of Dillon off to my side, his Glock 19 right behind his leg, freshly cleaned, oiled and stoked with the best fighting ammo.

Otto Skorzeny stared down at me. He was dressed in a snug jersey turtleneck, jet black, tucked into pleated black trousers held with an expensive black leather belt and a gold buckle, black socks and expensive Italian lace-ups, also black. The black leather greatcoat and the heavy scars on his face added sinisterness, if such a thing were possible. Danger smoked off him.

"Yes, Marius," he said. "I am of the Light. I have always been of the Light, though for a time I dwelt in the Dark and was used by them. I have returned and I have been redeemed. May I enter?"

"Yes, Otto Skorzeny," I said. "You may enter here."

I stood back. Otto inclined his head once, sharply, in a Teutonic bow, and then entered. Dillon stepped back and looked at me for confirmation.

"You sure?" Dillon said.

"*Yes . . .*" Tigre whispered.

"Yes," I said.

"Good enough for me," Dillon said. He holstered his pistol under Otto's interested gaze, held out his hand and was engulfed in the huge hand that met his. "Welcome, Otto. I believe you are of the Light . . . though you might be the darkest Light Worker I've ever met."

Otto laughed. "This is a good saying. I like this."

Sabrina said it. "Come in. Sit. You are welcome."

Once again, we were Four.

Otto settled into my recliner, facing the window. Sabrina brought him coffee. He looked into the mug, smiled at her.

"You knew I like much sugar?" he said.

She smiled. Dillon looked at her, and then back at Otto. Otto held Sabrina's eyes for a long moment.

"Thank you," Otto said.

"Well," I said hastily. "I'd say, what brings you here, but I think we know that, don't we?"

Otto sipped his coffee, closed his eyes in appreciation. "Do we, Marius?"

That brought a long moment of silence.

"So then," I said, "tell us the tale."

"Where is your woman, Marius?" Otto said.

"Why?"

"I would like to meet her. What she did, last night . . . remarkable. Extraordinary."

"That's her in two words. Remarkable. Extraordinary."

He considered me. "Yes. Exactly."

"She's running some errands."

Otto looked at his wristwatch, elegant gleaming case on a black leather strap, oversized to fit his huge wrist. "Perhaps I should wait till she returns before I begin?"

"It may be some time. What do you . . . feel?"

"I am given to storytelling, Marius. And I . . . feel . . . that time is short. And, as you said, you have many questions."

"Yes. I do."

Dillon looked at Sabrina. She gazed back, inscrutable and distant.

We all sat down, circled once more.

"So . . ." Otto said. "I shall begin . . .

"You know of the Great War...not the Great Wars of this century, which are pale memories of the Great War, the War fought so many tens of thousands of years ago, when the Earth itself was changed...the War between the Followers of the Light, the Path of the One, and the Followers of Belial, the War between the Light and the Dark.

"In Atlantis, so long ago, the descendants of Lemuria had brought with them the sacred technology, the technology of Earth—the masters of sound and vibration, the singing speech, the power of the great crystals—and in Atlantis, their children grew, and two factions grew...those who adhered to the ancient teachings, and the warnings therein, and those who wished to push further, to use the power of the crystals and vibration to change life itself, and to change the nature of time and space.

"To meddle with the work of the Creator, to become like the Creator. To walk the Halls of Time, and track the different timelines. Each timeline grows from a branching point, from a place where a great decision is made—or a seemingly insignificant one. And in the Hall of the Great Crystal was where the Timekeepers dwelt. Specially trained, specially selected, carefully monitored, for the temptation of great power was always in mind of those senior in the ranks—for a timeline can be created—or manipulated—by the intervention of those with an agenda in mind. Dark... or Light. Either way, interfering with the Divine Plan as devised by the Creator.

"And you know of the War...how the planet itself was shattered, the Earth's changes destroyed Atlantis, sank it beneath the waves in three great successive earthquakes, brought on by the meddling...the refugees scattered all throughout the world.

"And the remnants of the sacred technology. The Grid, the Great Grid of energy that connected all the portals of the Timekeepers with the energy lines of Mother Earth itself, shattered by the effects of the War—those that survived had knowledge, and some had bits of the technology, but so many and so much were lost...some was saved, hidden in places that the Timekeepers had seen would remain relatively unscathed, where the ancient bones of the Mother herself would protect those pieces.

"The very nature of time and space was altered in the Great War.

"Fragments of what was were sent, like shrapnel, through the timelines—to different times, in the past, in the future, on different timelines, to manifest. The Great Wars of the twentieth century are racial memories of that which destroyed the Earth; that which presaged the destruction and changing of the Earth itself...."

Otto sipped his coffee. "But you, Marius, and you, Sabrina...you know this. You've seen this, felt it... because you were there. In different bodies, perhaps with different appearances...but you were there."

He nodded at Dillon. "As were you, my brave friend.

"Which brings me to me," Otto said. "And you. And why all this, right now..."

"Yes," I said. "Which brings us to now."

"Yes," Otto said. "I was there as well...for many lives. I came back, as did others. Tossed loose into the timelines. And in the life where you know me, I came back...I lived a normal life, started a career as an engineer . . . in what became Nazi Germany and Austria. And you know something of my career."

"Yes," Dillon said. "You were the first, one of the first, to create Special Operations . . ."

"Not the first, my friend," Otto said. He looked at me. "Long ago, there were units, specially selected, that did similar work. The Timekeepers were such a unit. And among the angelic realm, there are those . . . those who volunteer to descend into the flesh, with all of the dangers there, to do the work in the Middle World directly instead of through others . . ."

"The dangers of the flesh or of the Middle World?" Sabrina said.

"Both, young Goddess," Otto said. "The flesh is not the best vehicle for the transmission of frequency and vibration. It's dense, prone to failure and misdirection. That's the structure of it. And there are the distractions that contribute to that . . ." He looked Sabrina up and down, to Dillon's obvious discomfiture. "The pleasures of the flesh can be a trap as well. Those who descend into the flesh, whether from the Light or the Dark, face distraction that hinder the Remembering, the Remembering of what they have been sent to do."

He smiled. "Dangerous work."

"Not to cut into the story, but you said we didn't have much time," I said. "This is territory we've been over before. Literally."

He nodded once, a sharp Teutonic head bob.

"Then let me pick up the pace," Otto said. "During the Nazi regime, the Dark Forces worked through the portals provided by certain key players in the regime, the obvious ones like Hitler, Himmler, Goebbels, and so on . . . and many of the willing participants in the process became receptacles for the Darkness, which were all drawn to the vortex that the Holocaust created. The Holocaust . . . the Holocaust was engineered to create a massive vortex . . . and to kill a handful of extremely important people."

His face was drawn into a grim mask.

"Among those who died in the camps were the children who would have grown into the scientists who rediscovered, independently, the power of the Grid, the ability to travel faster than light, to walk the Halls of Time. The Dark Forces can see down the timeline, and this had to be prevented . . . they wanted to create the portal through which they can manifest and, once again, exert control over the Earth.

"And the Light sent Light Warriors in the flesh . . . and those who remembered their work did what they could, saved who they could, intervened where they could."

"How did being Hitler's personal assassin and top commando work on behalf of the Light?" I said.

Another sharp Teutonic nod. "Excellent question. I was tasked to assassinate Churchill, Roosevelt and Stalin. Did that happen?"

"No," Dillon said. "It didn't happen."

"It didn't happen because I was approached by the Allies, and I spent most of the war and the entire rest of my . . . documented . . . life, working for the Allies," Otto said. "I was the most highly placed agent in the entire Allied espionage structure. Right next to Hitler the whole time."

He put down his coffee mug.

"Puts it in a different perspective, does it not?" Otto said. "Agent in place. For the forces of Light."

"Oh, wow," Dillon said. "That's . . . no way. Seriously,

man? The whole time? All the operations, the whole ODESSA thing, Paladin Group?"

Otto slapped one huge hand down on his leg. "You are truly a student of history, my friend. You know all this?"

"Dude, I've read everything there is about you," Dillon said. "All kinds of contradictory things, the whole conspiracy theory thing about you and the Illuminati, the Bush family, Tesla..."

Otto's face hardened. "There is much we can discuss," he said. "At the right time. But what you need to know is this—there are many of us aligned with the Light who are coming into the flesh, awakening back into their missions, right now. Changes are upon us. Upon the entire Earth. And right here, in this place, is where it begins. At a portal to what you call Hell. Where you were last night. I was sent to help you. And, eventually you will all remember a time long ago, when I helped you all," Otto said.

"So where did you get the flying saucer?" Dillon said.

Otto grinned. "So, as the young ones say... 'You like my ride?'"

We laughed.

My phone rang.

I got up and looked at the caller ID. Jolene. I picked up the phone. Silence, then the click of the phone disconnecting.

"What the...?" I said. I hit redial and the phone went straight to voice mail, Jolene's cool voice...

I hit redial again. Same thing. Once more... this time, a click, and then the silence of an open line.

"Jolene?" I said.

Silence. A breath.

In the background, harsh and cruel laughter. Then the click of disconnection.

Jolene.

"What is it?" Sabrina said. "What?"

Otto set his mug down. Precisely. Unfolded from the chair.

"We can take my car," he said.

"Flying saucer?" Dillon said.

"No," Otto said. "Something more in line with what we need right now."

Dillon and I tooled up.

"Do you need..." I said to Otto.

He shook his head, opened his greatcoat wide. Strapped under one arm was an extremely modified MP5K-SD; on the offside, three magazines.

"I have other tools in the car," he said.

I looked at Sabrina. Her face was drawn and pale. A look I had never seen on her face before—fear.

"Sabrina," I said. "You don't have to..."

"She can't stay here alone," Dillon said. "And we need everyone we have."

"She will be safer with us," Otto said. He reached out and took Sabrina's hand. "Come."

Dillon looked as though he'd been slapped. Sabrina looked at him, at Otto. Straightened herself.

"She came for me," Sabrina said. "I will come with you and do what I can. The best I can."

"That's more than enough," I said. "Let's go."

I'd never seen a car like Otto's anywhere but in a movie. Or a comic book. A BMW extensively customized, blending retro look with the latest high-tech accouterments. Like a coupe but a sports car.

It was astonishingly cool.

Also astonishingly fast.

Otto drove like he flew. Fast, sure, confident, huge hands steady on the wheel. In the big back seat, Sabrina and Dillon watched over our shoulders as the road disappeared beneath our wheels. I was not far from where Jolene lived, at least not normally; she was in Windom on the other side of the lakes, in a small house that had once belonged to a university professor. We took the back way into Windom, down 46th to Lyndale and then over into what used to be the Bachman Farm, a small enclave of semi-isolated homes on the edge of the city.

To Jolene's house.

Small yard, lovingly tended. Flowers in pots, a row of beloved rose bushes. A small blue house with big windows and a porch, with two Adirondack chairs side by side where we'd spent many a morning sipping coffee after a night of love and sleep. The house was dark save for a single lamp in the front room, obscured by a light curtain.

My hair stood up on my neck.

Something was very wrong.

We stood in the street. Jolene's house is powerfully warded, though to the everyday passerby there was nothing amiss. There were charged crystals buried along the boundary of her yard; a gleaming crystal hanging from the small oak in front that served as a "waiting room" for any spirits coming to be crossed; an altar and shrine with a statue of Mother Mary, the altar covered with wilting flowers...

"She changes those each day, and each time she comes," Tigre whispered. *"Beware..."*

A dark sense that I had never felt here before.

Otto paused at the edge of the yard. "I will stay here, with the car. Marius . . . ?"

"Dillon, with me," I said. "Sabrina, stay here with Otto."

Dillon looked between Sabrina and Otto, then followed me down the walk to Jolene's door.

First In Front was beside me, Tigre on the other, Burt hovering above, and around us the sense of gathering strength and power,

Because each step seemed to drag, as though we were walking through Jell-O, and my vision seemed soft, blurred, as though the very fabric of the air were softened like gauze, and my heart pounded because the woman I loved was in there, I could feel her . . .

"And there's something else, too," Tigre whispered; First In Front was garbed for war and Burt, for once, was silent and grim . . .

I paused at the door. Listened. Nothing. Tried the handle.

Unlocked.

My heart pounded.

Dillon whispered, "Marius? Do you want me to go first?"

"No," I said. I heard my voice as though from far away, the quaver in it. "I'll go."

I opened the door and entered.

The entryway and front room were dark. The light came from the hallway.

"Jolene?" I called.

"In back . . ." whispered Burt.

Dillon was behind me. Tense as a wire drawn tight. He felt it.

Down the hallway, past the lamp, the only light.

Her bedroom to the right, healing and meditation room to the left. Bathroom straight ahead. The door to the bathroom open. Empty. Door to the healing room open. Empty. Door to the bedroom half-open.

Slowly opening the door.

Dark.

Jolene was in the bed. Naked. Sheets and duvet pulled up to her waist. Her back propped against the headboard, her hands crossed, palms down, in her lap.

"Jolene?" I said.

Her head turned towards us. I could only make out the outline of her face.

"I have what you love most, shaman . . ." hissed the voice that came out of her mouth.

Not Jolene.

CHAPTER 20

Madness, injury, illness, poverty, hardship of every kind—all tests by the Creator to prepare a shaman for the most difficult and dangerous work of all. Despite the proliferation of classes and workshops in depossession, spirit releasement, and exorcism, there are those who choose to learn and apply the techniques, and then there are those who are Chosen and Called to this work. In the words of one great practitioner, those that are Called are "dragooned into the Service of the Light..."

Willingly or not.

Yes, we are honored by being chosen, and yes, we know that in some way and on some level we chose this Path, and yes, we are human and sometimes wonder about the toll it takes.

But we are grateful for the opportunity to be of Service.

That doesn't lessen the danger. In fact, the more

experienced the practitioner, the greater the challenges. The brighter your Light shines as a result of your personal work, the more you see . . . and the more you are seen. You become like a beacon, and in the way that a lone porch light on a dark street draws insects and other creatures of the night, you draw . . . things . . . to you.

Spirits, lost souls, elementals, sprites, those of the Other Realms, the curious, the playful . . . the malevolent.

And when you self-identify as a depossessionist, as one who can open the Portals of the Crossing, then you will draw those who want or need to cross . . . as well as those who seek to trap and ensnare those lost ones who want to return to the Light.

Or those who have been lied to about the Light.

I was told a story, early on in my training, about a famous shaman who went to work on behalf of his dearest friend. His friend was dying of cancer. The shaman was distracted by a demon during the ceremony. His friend was cured of cancer. But the shaman died a few days later . . . of massive cancer that had jumped from his friend into him. There are many cautionary tales in the tradition about the dangers of shamanic work for those who are called to work against the Dark, who must go into the Dark and Light the way to return for those lost souls, or to lead the dead across into the Light.

Madness, depression, physical ailments . . . and of course, possession.

Can a depossessionist be possessed?

Of course.

Part of the initiation and apprenticeship of a depossessionist is recognizing the signs of obsession and possession by a spirit, to become familiar with the character flaws and darkness within our own spirit and soul, the parts that resonate with the Dark Forces or the Lost, the parts that draw them in—the parts that cling to those.

Those of us who are called will be tested.

Not all of us pass the tests.

Nor do the tests ever really end.

One of the greatest dangers is becoming complacent, arrogant, cocky, overconfident, mistaking ourselves with that which is great which moves through us. The run-of-the-mill depossession, if there is such a thing, is a lost human without malevolent intent, who is clinging to a live human for the semblance of life that comes through to the spirit, because they don't *know* that they are dead. And so the depossessionist need only light the way and encourage them to cross, often with the help of their beloved departed who wait for them on the other side of the portal.

With Dark Force entities, those with malevolent intent, who mean to harm and obsess and possess with deliberation, it's much harder—but all can be crossed or transformed with the power of the Archangels and the Light of the Creator.

Remember when I said the more you see, the more you are seen?

Be seen as someone who lights the way for the dead and the dead will flock to you.

Be seen as someone who will challenge the Dark Forces directly, and the Dark Forces will seek you out.

And the greatest challenge to the depossessionist is the possession that is aimed directly at him or her, by one that is fully telepathic, not bound to the laws of time and space, who has intelligence and malevolent intent and who finds the weakness...and we *all* have weaknesses...and takes all the time needed to exploit it.

What about protection? Yes, we are protected, by our spirit allies, by the angelic realm, by ceremony and technique.

And it's the weakness *within* us that allows that entry, the beachhead or foothold in our energy that a possessing being can take hold of. Sometimes it's karma, or past-life debts; sometimes it's crossing the wrong entities; sometimes it's just part of what we were sent here to do.

The possibility is always there.

It can come about in a moment of anger, a moment of weakness, or as a result of a slow accretion of mistakes. Shamanic practice is all about power, the cultivation of that through spiritual allies and practice— and that power can disappear in an instant if misused, and the protection that comes with it can go away just as quickly.

We all have to sleep, and that's when we are the most vulnerable; in the deepest, darkest hours of the night, when our soul is wandering the Other Realms, and the body, the vessel of our own individual light, is open to whatever might drop in. Maintaining sovereignty against that kind of intrusion, deliberate, careless, or otherwise, is a big part of the ongoing spiritual hygiene a dedicated practitioner must develop. For we are sovereign in our bodies according to Divine Law.

But to those who don't abide by Divine Law, it falls to some of us who must keep the Law, enforce it, exercise it as a willing instrument in the hand of the Light, allow ourselves to be wielded like a sword of light in an angelic hand...

...which is really what our task is.

The Dark Forces are sly and knowing about the weakness of the human; they've had lifetimes to study their targets, to figure out their approach; and since the Fall, they've been amassing a store of knowledge about how best to corrupt and bring down even the most high amongst humans.

I don't count myself amongst the most high.

But I know that the Dark Forces keep score and I've been on their radar for a long, long time.

Just like a certain zombie told me not that long ago.

So I'm on their radar. I'm seasoned, experienced, reasonably intelligent and incredibly well protected by my beloved spirit guides, allies and the Archangels who bless me with their assistance. How do you get to me?

Get to those you love.

It's a truism amongst the Dark Forces, whether manifest as an evil sicario in a narco-traficante organization charting out your child's movements, or a demi-demon charting out the past, present and future movements of the people closest to you, that the way to push your buttons is to go in from the flanks, to attack those you love.

The greatest push to reaction, to rage and anger, the Dark Side of the Force as Anakin Skywalker discovered, is the one that justifies that anger and rage in defense of those we love.

And to a true Warrior of the Light, there is no greater Calling than to stand in harm's way before those we love, and we love all who stand in the Light.

Makes target acquisition for the baddies pretty easy, yes?

So a savvy practitioner weaves a web of light, connects his energy and his protection to the Grid of the World, and weaves protection in and around all those he loves and interacts with, creates a great glowing crystal of energy that protects and binds all of those that create the larger mandala of his life. Just as a spider knows when there's the least little tug somewhere in the web, so a practitioner knows when there's a little tug—or a big one—on the web of energy that surrounds his life. His guides and protecting spirits and guardian angels know, too—and their job is to inform and protect him or her.

But sometimes, things get through.

CHAPTER 21

"Jolene?" I whispered. "Oh, my love... Jolene?"

Her lips skinned back. Wolfish. Her canines gleamed. She leaned forward, her perfect breasts barely moving, her hands still limp in her lap.

"Oh, my love," it hissed, mockingly. "Oh, Jolene..." The most evil laughter.

Dillon choked back a sound, like a swallowed sob.

It looked at him. "Like the tits, Dillon? You know you do. Always have. Want a little taste? Here."

It cupped Jolene's breasts, offered them to him.

Rage. Sorrow. Revulsion. Disgust. Heartbreak.

All at the same time.

A huge wave, cresting over me...

"... remember that Wave, Marius? So long ago, and it carried you to your doom. Remember this wave, and choose, choose differently if you will," Tigre was there, seated on her rear haunches, alert, poised; First In Front with Burt on his shoulder, watching...

"Marius?" Dillon said. "What do you want me to do?"

212

"Marius?" it said. "What are you going to have to do?"

I took a deep breath, calmed and centered myself, let my anger and my rage settle down through me, down into my center, down my legs, down into the ground, into the depths of Mother Earth, connecting to the great power at the core of the world, and I called out for the help that is always there for me:

"Father, Mother, Creator God..."

"Silence!" it screamed. "Or I will make her twist in pain you cannot imagine, shaman..."

"...Holy Spirit, Great Spirit, Goddess, I call on you..."

More laughter. "Oh, she's screaming now, Marius... you should see her..." it said.

"...I call on Jesus, the Christ, Light of the Creator made Flesh, and Mother Mary, Queen of the Angels, First Among Healers, Mother of Us All, and I call upon MIIII-KAI-ELLLL..."

And a ripple went through Jolene, like a ripple across a body of water made flesh, and I saw her face, her true face of her True Self, for just a moment, in horrible pain and fear, something I had never seen, and I was shaken...

Boom!

The whole house shook. Literally rattled on the foundation.

Boom!

Again.

Evil laughter.

"Will you exercise power over me, shaman?" it said. "Will you...force me?"

I extended one hand. "I call upon the mighty Archangels..."

The sheets flew off the bed.

Jolene turned in the bed, set her feet on the floor, stood up. And something Fallen gleamed out of her eyes at me. She took her finger and inserted it into herself, slowly withdrew it, held it under her nose, put it in her mouth.

"Yum," it said. "No wonder you keep her for yourself, shaman. So tasty."

"I . . ."

"You cannot, shaman," it said. "She has given herself over. Willingly. She's mine. Now and forever. All for love."

Naked, she began to move in a slow, jerky parody of a soft-shoe dance routine.

"She gave it all up . . ." it sang, ". . . for love. She gave it *all* up . . . for love. She gave it all up, for love . . . of you, of you, of you."

An awkward pirouette, and then a slow obscene writhing, an undulation that began in her hips and flowed through her whole body, a filthy parody of the way she'd moved beneath me or atop me when we were wrapped in love. It grabbed one of the corner poles of the bedframe and turned her buttocks towards us, arching in simulated sex.

"Like what you see, Dillon?" it said. "Your dick is getting hard. I can see it. Want a little taste? She always liked you, Dillon. Loved you, actually. The warrior, the fighter. So pure in your anger. Sometimes when she fucked the shaman, she thought about you."

It came at Dillon, reached out to cup his crotch. "Oh, look, it's all hard. Is that for me, sweetheart?"

"Don't touch me!" Dillon shouted, stepping back.

"Michael and Uriel, I call on you, beloved Archangels..."

"Oh, to do what? Enclose me in the Light? She chose me for you, Marius. Gave herself to me for you. They cannot bind me." It flounced away. "Okay, so I can't touch you now, Dillon." It looked back over her shoulder, wiggled her ass. "But you can touch me. If you want. You can do anything you want to me. If you want..."

"Marius... help her. Do something..." Dillon whispered.

"I—"

"—can do...well, nothing, sweetheart. Not without my consent. And I'm not consenting. Well, maybe I will...but only to Dillon. I'll do *whatever* Dillon wants me to do..."

"I don't want anything you have," Dillon said.

"Oh yes, you do," it said. "You want her. The Jolene. Your little redheaded goddess. You want her back. And you *want* her. Don't you, D? I can call you D, right?"

It stood and looked back and forth between the two of us, fists on naked hips, right in the swell of the hip above the sharp jut of her hipbones.

"Oh, you two are such pussies. Guess I'll just have to get dressed and go out. Find me a *real* man. One who will fuck me inside out and upside down. If you're both really good, I'll let you watch. Maybe I'll *make* you watch, yes?"

It pulled out a pair of black leather trousers. One of Jolene's favorites. Lay on the bed and pulled it on over the legs and hips I knew so well.

"Getting an eyeful, Marius? What you don't know about the little secret recesses of your pretty little

Jolene's head...sometimes she despises you, you know that? You're so politically correct, such a Servant of the Divine Feminine," it laughed its nasty laugh. "Sometimes she just wants to be fucked bad and hard and dirty, Marius. It's always some kind of sacred act with you. She doesn't like that..."

"You lie, demon. Are you afraid?" I said.

It continued to dress. A silk camisole over naked flesh, her nipples erect. Part of me ached for her and I knew the demon was working that second chakra energy on both Dillon and me. I could feel his shame morphing into anger, feeling as though he'd betrayed us both, though it was just biology, his body reacting to the pheromones she was releasing in a great epic spasm.

It laughed at us as it slipped on a pair of her black Jimmy Choos.

"Of you?" it said. "Of course not, Marius. You can't do anything to me. Unless I let you. She gave herself to me for you." It sang its obscene parody: "She gave it all up...for love...of you..."

"In Jesus's name, I compel you," I said.

It shook for a moment, then looked at me. "Why, Marius. You are forcing me against her will. Are you going to use your power to override her choice? Are you going to force me, shaman? Please do. Just like you did before..."

"She did not choose."

"Actually, she did, shaman. When she saw what was coming for you. Gave herself up. And she's a tough one. Seriously tough. Or she was. You should see her in the little antechamber we have just for her. We're all lining up for a taste of Jolene, Jolene, Jolene. Want to come watch? You know where to find us. But in the meantime...oh, did I say that? It's going to get *really* mean, shaman. From here on out..."

"What do you want?" I said.

It laughed. "Oh, now you want to bargain, Marius? Let me guess. You for her? How quaint. How romantic. How utterly *fucking* silly. Seriously. Where's the fun in that?"

"It's always been me you want," I said.

"Oh, but not quite yet," it said. "Her body is so sweet and strong. Supple. Tastyyyyy..."

"SHUT UP!" I screamed.

"Take me," Dillon said.

It turned and regarded him, her head tilted to one side. "Oh, Dillon, do be careful about what you say. And what you wish for. You are very tasty, oh so tasty, the pure white knight, our little knight errant..."

Dillon stepped forward. "Take me. Now. I..."

"Dillon, no!" I took his arm. "That's what it wants to do, to turn us all around. That's not Jolene. It's just her body. The flesh. We have to find her another way, I can't force her..."

"You can make her!" Dillon shouted. "You can drive it out, make it go away! That's what she wants! She didn't give herself to that thing!"

"It wants the contest, Dillon," I said, as gently as I could. "It wants me to use power-over, to force my way in...that's the point. It wants you confused and hurt, it wants me enraged and slashing my way in...because it wins when we do that. So we can't do it that way..."

"How self-justifying, Marius," it said matter-of-factly. "Actually, Dillon, it's because he's a coward. He always has been. He's afraid. That's why he has you, right?

You're the warrior, always have been. Always will be. He's nothing without you. Never has been. He needs you, you don't need him. Do you? Of course not. I..."

"Shut up," Dillon said.

"Oh, baby," it whispered. "I so won't shut up. And soon...you'll beg me not to shut up. So I think I'm dolled up enough, don't you think, boys?"

She turned on her heels, smacked the ass she pointed at us. "I think I'll go out and let some sleazy dirt bag fuck me in the ass. You two can come along...or you can come find me later. If you can."

She turned and brushed past us as though we weren't there. "Oh, and boys...you might *not* want to find me...or her body...if you know what I mean. Later..."

Boom!

The whole house shook.

I heard the back door slam shut.

Silence.

And the sick, slick, oily feeling of the Dark.

"Marius..." Dillon said.

From outside, a bellow tinged in German, "Marius!"

It was time to go. We were going to have to go to fetch Jolene's spirit...and find her body before the demon damaged it beyond repair.

"Marius?" Dillon said. His voice was heavy and broken. "I...I don't think I can do this."

"It's not her," I said. My own voice sounded foreign in my ears. "It's the demon. It will say whatever it knows will hurt or distract you. That's what they do."

"Marius, drive it out of her!"

I had to pause and gather myself. Turn and look at him. "Look at me, Dillon."

He did.

"Do you think I don't want to?"

"You can! Do it! I've seen you..."

"That's what it wants," I said. "That's why it came for her; that's why it says what it says."

"I don't understand."

"I'll explain. Later."

"Now!"

His anger was up, driven by shame and guilt. Great tools for the undoing of a good man—which was why the demon chose that. Of course he would have felt attracted to Jolene—any man with a pulse would. And of course he would have felt guilty about it. And of course at some level, with his unspoken loneliness and need for a woman like Jolene, he had wondered...

That was the point of entry. That's how it got to him.

We all have those. It's part and parcel of being human. That's why depossessionists—those that live through the tests without going insane or otherwise broken—learn to be and stay humble. It's not us—we're flawed, but that which moves through us is not. That which moves through us is the Light of the Creator and that is perfect. Our job, to borrow the phrase from the Lakota, is to be the "hollow bone"; to be a conduit and to do the best we can to move our crap out of the way so as not to hinder the passage of the Light. It's a daily process, and one that can never be taken for granted.

"They've mounted a full-scale attack on me," I said. "On every level. Physical, mental, spiritual, Middle World, Other Realms. That's why they came after all of you. You're my family: Jolene, Sabrina...you."

"I get that," Dillon said. "But I've seen what you

can do, Marius. You can drive it out. You can make
it go away."

"They want me to exert power-over, Dillon. They
want me to use force."

"You always do that!"

"Only with permission. The permission of the possessed, or the family member closest who can give
that permission."

"Oh, bullshit, Marius! It's Jolene! You can do that!"

"I have to journey. If she did..."

I couldn't say the words. Choked back what was
coming up in me.

"You think she gave permission to the demon?
She...why...*why*?"

"I don't know. I have to journey and find out."

"You can't wait!"

"I have to."

Power-over. Force. If shamanism is about alli-
ance with spirits and powers, all of them facets of
the Great Power of the Creator, the One, then how
power is used, or how one is used by power, is the
moral fulcrum that a practitioner constantly balances
on. The definition of sorcery is to use power to work
one's will, especially against the will of another; ethical
practice, practice in alignment with the Will of the
Creator and the Divine Plan, is to act as a healing
conduit only with explicit permission of the person
requesting the healing.

Doesn't mean the ability, power and techniques to
do sorcery don't exist within the ethical practitioner;
it means that discrimination and right choice are
exercised. The techniques and tools, practices and
procedures, of shamanic practice—they are essentially

without ethos. How they are utilized and the choice exercised by the practitioner defines the ethos.

Did I have the ability and the tools to force the possession demon out of Jolene's body?

Yes.

So why not?

A battle like that, inside of a body where permission may—or may not—have been given to the possessing entity, can destroy or kill the body. The spirit of the possessed, if driven out of the flesh, may be wandering in the Other Realms . . . or lost or consumed in some way. And more to the point, in this instance, having me exert force and having my emotional energy attached to the actions, would give the Dark Forces the big entry into my otherwise heavily shielded life; they'd be able to occupy the fulcrum, stand astride and unbalance me.

Tip me into the Abyss.

Which seems like exactly what they had showed up to do.

We left.

Outside, Otto scanned the sky and the street. Sabrina stood close beside him. They turned to us. Saw what was written on our faces.

"Oh, Mother Earth and Father Sky," Sabrina said.

Otto just nodded once, sharply. "So what now, Marius?"

I looked up at the stars. The night sky.

"God only knows, Otto. I don't."

"Where is she?" Otto said.

"They have her," I said.

"Who?" Otto said.

"The same ones we were up against."

Otto pursed his lips. "Ah."

"They took her?" Sabrina said. "Do you know..."

"She's possessed, Sabrina," I said. "Her body went out the back door. It said..."

"It said she gave herself to them," Dillon said. "It said she did it for Marius. For us."

"No," Sabrina said. "She cannot be taken and she would not give herself that way."

"It's a possession," I said. "She's completely over-shadowed."

"Which way did she go? Where is she?" Otto said.

"It said it was going to take her somewhere, and... ah, I can't say it," Dillon said. He stepped aside and retched, a dry heave. His eyes ran.

"Oh, no...oh, no," Sabrina said.

Otto studied my face. "This is how they will get to you."

"They already have," I said. "They already have."

CHAPTER 22

We raced down the streets in Otto's car, Sabrina and Dillon huddled like beaten children in the back seat. Otto steered deftly, his lips drawn thin, the long scar on his cheek gleaming pale. I closed my eyes and called...

"Yes, Marius. This is how they have gotten to you," Tigre whispered.

First In Front floated cross-legged, right outside the passenger window as we sped through the city streets. "How you choose," he said. "Be careful how you choose. Everything hinges on you."

Burt was, again, uncharacteristically silent. He flew right in front of the car, vectoring in on the energy trace left by Jolene...

"Turn left at the next light, go down two blocks, then right," I said.

Otto nodded.

"Where?" Dillon said.

"Sharkey's," I said.

Dillon blew out a long breath. "Oh, that's just fucking great."

Sharkey's was a notorious blue-collar bar that hosted at least one motorcycle club and a number of hangers-on, great blues and rock bands that played behind a classic wire mesh fence to prevent beer bottles from hitting them. It was the last place I would want to go, and Jolene—my Jolene—knew it only from reputation and the occasional tale told . . . by Sabrina.

"I can't handle this right now," Sabrina said. Silent for a moment, then a loud laugh from her, "But I guess I will, right? Right? At least it's someplace I know."

Dillon shook his head. "Why do you go there, Sabrina?"

"Because it's simple and uncomplicated. I don't have to be a practitioner, I can just go in for a bump and a beer, take a guy home. Simple. Uncomplicated."

"There is nothing uncomplicated about you," Otto observed. "It is not casual—casual sex. Especially for those such as you."

Sabrina stared out the side window and was silent.

Sharkey's: a sprawling parking lot, part dirt from a vacant lot with the fence torn down, part cracked asphalt sprouting greenery. One-story, brick-fronted, metal front door with two huge black men perched on stools. Otto pulled right up in front.

"Is this wise?" I said. The car brought plenty of attention. So did Otto. As did Sabrina. Dillon and I were just side acts to this circus.

Otto got out and we followed in his wake. He held up a handful of bills—hundreds by the quick look I got—and whispered something to the two bouncers.

They took the bills, nodded, waved us past.

First barrier.

They didn't even pat us down, though one of them gave Sabrina a big leer as she passed him.

More Sharkey's: heavy wooden tables, too heavy to pick up and fling, ringed by battered chairs, a low ceiling with slow-moving fans, packed with burly men in feed caps and jeans, women bursting out of halter tops and tight jeans, lots of beer and shots in hand, the elevated stage protected by metal mesh, jukebox blaring '80s heavy-metal rock, cocktail waitresses ducking in and out of the crowd, a group of bikers in cutoff denim jackets with motorcycle club patches.

The jukebox switched tunes. "Dirrty," by Christina Aguilera and Redman. Rocking-hard stripper music. Good thing they...

A woman climbed up on a table, accompanied by loud cheers.

Jolene.

"Oh, fuck," Dillon said.

She began to beat out the song, pumping the beat with her hips, and all the way across the bar it looked out of her eyes, leered and waved at us. Surrounded by a growing band of men, she began to roll the silk camisole up over her flat, toned belly, undulating to the increasingly frenetic crowd of men around her...

Sabrina ignored the men who waved to her in the room. "Marius, this will be a gang bang in a few minutes. We need to get her out of here."

"This is not a good place for a fighting solution," Otto said.

First In Front, twisting through the crowd, invisible to the eye but the patrons moving out of his

*way as though they sensed his coming...whispering
in Sabrina's ear...*

Maybe a minute into a three-minute song, and already the men were chanting, "Take it off, take it off, take it off!"

Sabrina grinned, grabbed Dillon by the hand and said, "Throw me up there."

"What?" he said.

She pointed at the table next to the one where Jolene's body writhed. "Toss me up there. But 'don't tell the elf,' right?"

He looked at her, puzzled, shrugged and handed her up onto the table. Sabrina threw back her hair and screamed, *"Yeeeehawwww!"*

And broke into her own beat with the song.

And took it up a notch. She beat Jolene's body to the punch by stripping off her sweat top and shaking her large breasts to the riff by Redman.

And the crowd parted like the Red Sea before Moses's staff.

Or something like that.

Not that Jolene—Jolene's body, I reminded myself—wasn't a showstopper, but Sabrina was a known quantity in this bar, and she was getting naked and wilder faster than Jolene's demon, which was still getting a handle on her body...

And Sabrina was surrounded nearly instantly by the crowd howling for her as she began to work the waistband of her sweat pants around and down... and she inclined her head sharply at Jolene's body, suddenly abandoned...

Dillon's jaw dropped. I had to shove him out of the way. "Help me get her, Dillon!"

Otto watched Sabrina as he might have studied Mussolini's mountain.

We elbowed a few of Jolene's faithful out of the way, and the demon glared down at us.

"You can't compel..." it began.

Dillon reached out and grabbed her ankle, tugged hard. It landed hard on her ass. "Oh, let me help you!" Dillon said. "Too much to drink?"

"You can't force..." it began.

"He's not," Dillon said. "I am."

He brought his hand around in a short sharp arc and the open hand caught her right on the tip of her jaw and snapped her head around. Her eyes rolled up in her head as she slumped, unconscious, and Dillon caught her, slung her over his shoulder and turned, so fast that the other men were still trying to figure out what just happened.

He said, "Let's get the hell out of Dodge."

We made for the door; I was on point, and I shouted to Otto, "We'll be back for..."

He held up one shovellike hand to silence me. Reached under his coat and pulled out his MP5K-SD. The crowd clustering tighter around Sabrina didn't even notice. He did something to the muzzle and the short suppressor came off and went into his pocket. He looked up, then fired a burst full-auto into the ceiling.

That, the crowd *did* notice.

We were at the door and stepped aside just as the bouncers came running in, leaving the door free and unguarded. Jolene's body was limp between us. I turned and looked back.

The crowd parted before Otto, who walked up to the table and offered Sabrina his hand.

"Come, my love. Your chariot awaits," he said.

Sabrina jumped down, breasts jiggling. Otto swept his greatcoat off and draped it over her shoulders, his MP5K ready in one hand. Then he offered his free arm, and Sabrina tucked her hands into the crook of his arm and he swept through the frozen and silent room to meet us at the door.

"We shall go, yes?" he said.

"Yes," I said. "We shall go. Let's do like the shepherds and get the flock out of here."

CHAPTER 23

"Is it usual for her to be out this long?" I asked Dillon. He had way more experience than I did in the art and science of knocking people unconscious, but Jolene's body and the inhabiting demon hadn't stirred once during the drive from Sharkey's to my house. We'd laid Jolene's body out on my table, bound it with sacred sea salt and amethyst crystals, topped at the head of the table with a crucifix and at the foot with a figure of Mother Mary, a sheet emblazoned with the crest of the Great Mother of the Wiccans lay across her.

"I don't know," Dillon said. "Most people, they wake up in a few minutes. Some drunks, they stay out. Only if there's a concussion..."

"Did you give her a concussion?"

"I don't know, Marius. I don't think so, but someone as fine-boned as she is..."

I fought the anger in me, another layer of the seething mass inside I tried to settle. Another layer to the onion, another tangent in the multifaceted attack the Dark Forces had orchestrated.

And I still didn't have the name of the demon behind all this.

But I did have a name.

Wilhelm Eichmann.

A not-so-good German name.

We stood in my healing room, loosely ringing the table, not yet a Circle, but soon. Sabrina was relaxed, happy almost, for the first time since we'd fetched her back. I guess stripping in her favorite bar and being escorted out at gunpoint by a badass long-dead German commando suited her. Dillon, though, was another story. He'd slapped Jolene—or to be more precise, her body—into unconsciousness, watched the other woman in his life stripping in front of a bar full of bikers be rescued by his personal hero, and the events of the last two days were taking a huge toll on him.

Otto, though . . . more solid than solid and with a style all his own.

Arms crossed, head dropped, deep in thought—or in communion with his own spirits and guides.

And I still hadn't gotten around to asking him the question on all of our minds: how come he wasn't dead?

Or was he?

"We have a lot to talk about," I said. "One of these days."

Otto considered me. "I have a friend. American. He served in the American paratroopers. He has a saying I enjoy. 'You got the talking part done.' I like this saying."

"I don't understand."

"The time for talking is past, Marius. We must act. Quickly. Things are happening all around us. We must retake the initiative, we must not only respond. Jolene's soul is in danger. Sabrina has been attacked. Dillon is under attack..."

"What do you mean?" Dillon said. "Attack? Where?"

"They attack you in the way they always attack, my brave friend," Otto said. "They prey on what you have in you, in what we all have in us. They prey on your guilt, your jealousy, your envy, your loneliness...your humanity. That is how they attack you. They seek to split us apart."

Dillon looked at Sabrina who gazed back, calm and unafraid, at Otto.

"Like in the *Lord of the Rings*, right?" he said. "The splitting of the Fellowship. When the ring worked its evil on the men, right?"

Otto was puzzled. "This I do not understand. *Lord of the Rings*? Fellowship? What is this thing?"

The three of us laughed.

"When it's all said and done, Otto, we'll have a movie marathon. Then you'll get it," I said.

"Start with *The Hobbit*," Sabrina said.

"And then all three of the *Lord of the Rings*, extended versions," Dillon said.

"Extended versions all the way," I said.

"Hmm. Yes. All right. When we are...done." Otto inclined his head at Jolene. "So how do we approach this problem, Marius? We all stand ready to help you."

I considered that. It was late night, the best time to work in the Dream Time, in the Other Realms. But this depossession would require more than me; I was the target and would be most vulnerable. And of course the Dark Forces wanted that uncertainty in me—so I couldn't give it to them. While I was the most experienced depossessionist, Sabrina was a powerful and gifted healing practitioner . . . Dillon could hold the Space, and Otto . . .

"Otto . . ." I said. "Are you skilled in journey technique?"

He studied me.

. . . and my guides gathered round me . . . First In Front said, "He is powerful in the Other Realms, Marius . . . cloaked and hidden, carefully banked like a fire in the dark of night . . . he is your ally . . ."

"But not all is shown," Tigre said. "This is for you to decide, to exercise the right discernment . . ."

Burt said, "Measure twice. Cut once. Use what you have, because all have been guided to you . . ."

"But beware," First In Front said, "because there are Dark Forces prowling . . ."

"Yes," I said. "I've been shown."

Otto didn't need to say anything, but he did. "Tell us what we must do, Marius."

There was a gleam of headlights outside my house, and then the blue and red flicker of light bar lights.

More than one set.

Dillon peeked out the window.

"There's a SWAT team out there," he whispered.

I looked out, and Otto peered from the other window. Not the locals. These were black Suburbans.

Feds.

"Now who the . . ." I said.

I saw the raid jacket on one of them. DHS. Department of Homeland Security. And standing back, in a raid jacket that said RESERVE OFFICER, was a sneering man I recognized so well: my old friend Wilhelm Eichmann.

"We've got a problem," I said.

Dillon started for the front room, where his guns were.

"Don't," I said. "They'll want us shooting, and we're not..."

"No," Otto said. "We must not fight. The women will be caught in the cross fire, and we will all...no. I will speak to them."

"What?" Dillon and I said simultaneously.

The SWAT team formed up on the run, making the snake and inching up on my doorway. No announcement, and more than likely no knock—they were coming in. Other Suburbans across at the park, and at least one long gun mounted up across the hood of the vehicle, a sniper watching us. From the street behind me, on the other side of my backside neighbor, blue and red flickering lights.

Surrounded.

"What can you do?" I said.

"More than I want to," Otto said. "But if we wait till they enter, anything can happen..."

Happens all the time. After all, when the dust settles, the gun smoke clears, who's to say who shot first?

Only the survivors.

And we were heavily outgunned at this point.

Dillon wasn't having it. I could see that in his face.

"We don't even know if they're really DHS," he said. "They're Cabal, maybe more of those damn goat-soldiers or the clones..."

"This is my home neighborhood, bro," I said. "We can't destroy the whole neighborhood..."

"I will talk to them," Otto said. "Wait..."

He swept by us, went to the door, turned on the

porch lights. The SWAT team froze like a deer in the headlights, or a SWAT team in the spotlights.

"SWAT team!" Otto bellowed. "Officer coming out! Plainclothes officer coming out!"

He opened the door.

Dillon and I looked at each other.

"Plainclothes officer? What the fuck?" Dillon said.

"I don't know," I said.

Sabrina watched. "He's more than meets the eye."

"Yeah," Dillon said. "But is he a Decepticon or an Autobot?"

"What?" Sabrina said.

"Good question," I said. "Or is he an Autobot pretending to be a Decepticon?"

"Or vice versa," Dillon said.

Otto stepped out. Multiple weapons' lights trained on him, and so many red laser dots he looked like a terminal case of the measles. He held a small case open in his raised right hand, the hand so big it hid most of what he held.

"Plainclothes officer!" Otto showed. "My credentials are in my right hand!"

Two SWAT officers converged on him.

"You may enter!" Otto said. "They will not resist. They are unarmed! They will not resist."

They entered hard, sweeping through my front room, shouting "Clear! Clear!" as they moved quickly to the healing room.

"Down! Keep your hands in sight, cross them behind your head, get down!" the leader shouted.

We did.

One of them swept his muzzle across my altar, wiping all of my sacred objects onto the floor.

"Whoops," he said. He crushed a statuette of Mother Mary beneath his boot.

I looked at him. Square head, black hair, black eyes. Eichmann or a clone?

His name strip said "Eichmann."

"You're a credit to your name, Eichmann," I said.

He kicked me hard in the side. "Shut up, Looney Tunes."

"Knock it off!" the team leader said.

"By the Power of the Three," Sabrina started.

"Don't, Sabrina. Let his consequences be his own..."

"I said, *shut up!*" Eichmann screamed.

"Just like his daddy," I said.

"Hey, Winter," the team leader said. "Shut the fuck up. You're under arrest. Eichmann, outside. Ma'am, you'll have to be quiet, too."

He looked up at one other team member. "What you got?"

"Fucking full-auto weapons in the front room, Loot. One of them an M4, and there's at least one hand grenade we've found. Just like the CI..."

"Shut the fuck up," the team leader said. He grabbed the team member by the arm and hustled him into the other room, and began a dressing down I could feel but not see.

CI. Confidential informant.

That means someone had tipped them off.

Wasn't hard to figure out the who or how.

The why was another story, though. Why arrest us and not just kill us?

They picked us up and marched us out; a stretcher team came by and rolled Jolene, handcuffed, onto the stretcher. As they took us out, we passed Otto, arguing vehemently with a man in a raid jacket with the look of the Boss; the elder Eichmann sneered and gloated as we were taken by.

"Enjoy your stay," the elder Eichmann said.

"Somewhere there's a village short its idiot," Dillon said.

"And Hell's short a little minion," I said.

"Shut up!" the elder Eichmann screamed.

"Shut up!" screamed his son.

We laughed.

Because the Devil hates laughter.

I've always hated being in jail.

It's not just the loss of freedom, the being in a cage; it's being surrounded by so much negative energy, by so many of the possessed, both the keepers and the kept, and feeling as though you're at the bottom of a maelstrom, a whirlpool of negativity. The constant din and hum, the simmering violence right beneath the surface, the hopelessness, the gaming of the inmates against each other and the jailers.

This time they had me in a holding cell, after the obligatory fingerprinting and photographing and processing. Apparently I was under arrest for domestic terrorism and plotting terrorist acts; more than one had snickered at "the rock worshipper" in the holding cell.

Eichmann the younger, the cop one, had said through the door, "They say *I'm* crazy? He's the one who worships rocks..."

Apparently the presence of sacred objects, including stones, on my altar prompted that commentary.

"Freedom of worship?" I shouted back. "Sounds like an officially sanctioned hate crime!"

"Shut up, Looney Tunes!" he'd shouted back.

I laughed.

First In Front nodded, and shuffled through a power dance. "Live as though you are dead," he chanted. "Hoka hey, hoka hey ... it is always a good day to die ... hoka hey, hoka hey ..."

There was a vision I had been Gifted once, of the Warrior Angels during the First War of the Angels, when Lucifer, the Son of the Light, was cast down for his betrayal and his rebellion against the One. In the vanguard, an angel, first into battle, who threw himself against Lucifer himself ... Lucifer with his long lance of light, the hooked halberd of the angels, against a warrior angel armed with his sword ... the warrior pierced through his middle, and pulling himself along it, straining to reach the Great Adversary ...

... laughing as he did so.

In the face of the enemy.

The Devil hates laughter.

So I lay down on the metal ledge that passed for a bed and crossed my legs and closed my eyes, letting myself slip into journey ...

... Tigre said, "Stay in your body, Marius ... you are surrounded by the Dark Forces. There are Light Warriors here among them, but you must stay focused and aware, you are in great danger ..."

"He's a hardhead," Burt said. "But God must have need of this particular hardhead, because he keeps coming and coming ..."

... First In Front kept dancing, twirling in a circle, his coup stick glowing in his hand ...

I opened my eyes, made sure I was still in my body, then closed my eyes again and counted my breaths, one, then two, one, then two, for however long it took before the cell door opened up.

It was a long, long time.

Or so it seemed.

The SWAT team leader was there, Otto behind him.

"Get up, Winter," the team leader said.

Otto drooped one eye slightly in a wink.

The SWAT gestured for me to pass in front of him. He escorted us without a word through the processing area, where more than one set of curious eyes followed us. Otto led the way to the exit door, shook the SWAT's hand, and took me outside.

The sun was bright and shining. Midafternoon. Better part of twelve hours in lockup.

"Where's Dillon and Sabrina?" I said.

Otto led me to his car where several local cops stood and stared. As one, they all gave him their back. We got into the car. He started it and drove out of the parking lot, past rows of parked police cars.

"Where's . . ."

He held up his finger, took an electronic device, a meter of some kind, out of the center console. Turned it on as he pulled over to the curb, and studied the meter.

"Say something," Otto said.

"What?"

"That's good," he said. "It doesn't appear that they bugged the vehicle. They had access to it, but it's more difficult than it appears to get into—or around—this vehicle."

He pulled away and started towards my house.

"Dillon is being held on federal charges," Otto said. "Illegal modification of weapons, possession of full-auto weapons without a transfer tax, explosives. I can't get him out—yet—but I'm working on it. Sabrina was released without charges and I put her in a cab to a hotel. I've got it covered. You are released without charges...but there's an investigation pending as to whether you were practicing counseling or medicine without proper licensure."

"How does that work?"

"You're known as a shamanic practitioner," Otto said. "Someone, the same someone who started this, questions whether you're practicing counseling or medicine without a license. Federal charges could apply there, too."

"Not fooling around, are they?" I said.

"No. Won't stick, but they can cause you trouble."

"Where's Jolene?"

"In Carle. In the intensive care unit."

"What?"

"Medically, she's in a coma. She had the bruising on her jaw, which led the investigators to consider that she was struck, but Dillon and Sabrina had nothing to say. Brain activity is the same as a deep coma."

He sighed.

"She's not in her body anymore, Marius. And it may be that when Dillon struck her hard enough, it drove the demon out—for now. You're a depossessionist—there's plenty of stories in the tradition about how an accident or a sharp blow dislodged a possessing entity. Yes?"

Edith Fiore, the California psychologist whose pioneering work in documenting the reality and presence of possessing spirits in her psychology practice helped bring depossession into the light in the twentieth century, recounted several case studies where clients were in car accidents or other incidents that seemed to literally frighten or dislodge the possessing entities out of the host body.

There was a similar technique taught in the Catholic tradition of exorcism, where the exorcist would strike the host with his hand, Bible or crucifix and drive out the demon in conjunction with the Rite of Exorcism.

So it was certainly possible, but it meant that right now Jolene's soul, her spirit, her *ba* and her *ka*, were wandering or, worse, trapped in the Other Realms, subject to the Dark Forces.

As the demon had said.

"Yes," I said. "I have to journey...will you help?"

"Of course."

We were silent for a few moments.

"Otto, how did you get me out? What kind of credentials are those?"

He reached in his pocket and pulled out the credential case. Tossed it into my lap.

"Look for yourself, my friend."

I opened it up. A full-face picture of Otto, identifying him as Special Agent Edward Lansky, Department of Homeland Security, Special Investigations Unit.

"Special Investigations?" I said. "What the fuck is this, Otto?"

"The unit or me?"

"Both."

He nodded, that sharp Teutonic bob.

"Yes. Of course." He turned on 35th, headed towards Lake Calhoun.

"The unit first. Special Investigations. Those investigations of a particularly sensitive and special nature. Which includes investigations regarding...anomalous phenomena. If there is a possibility of a threat to the homeland. And of course, there is *always* the possibility of threats to the homeland. There is a similar unit within the FBI. The rumor of it was the basis for a popular television series..."

"*The X-files.*"

"Yes," he said. "I have seen this. The two agents were drawn from the founding members of the original FBI unit. A man and a woman."

"I'd love to hear about the truth that's out there, Otto, but right now I'm concerned about *you* and who the hell Eichmann is and who he's working with or for."

"My story is a long one, Marius. And very much intertwined with yours. There is the Middle World, and there are the Other Realms. I have been an agent of the Light, working undercover, in this body, since the Second World War. I am here, right now, to help you in this timeline."

"You said you were of the Light, Otto."

He pulled up in front of my house. The front door was shut, blocked off with a big X of yellow police tape.

"I am of the Light, Marius," he said. "I always have been. I work for..." he paused. "I *am* a Son of the Light. Like you. And now, the story you want to hear? We don't have time for that. You need to do what you need to do in order to find Jolene in the Other Realms and return her to her body, to take care of her. The attack has shattered your family here, and you must restore some semblance of order there—and that's a delaying tactic."

"What are you going to do right now?"

"This is your Work," Otto said. "I'm going to leave you now. I will be back once I have released Dillon. I need to speak to the federal prosecutor who is on her

way over from downtown. I will make sure Dillon is
with Sabrina, to watch over her. I will check on Jolene's
status as I can, and then I will return here. I have been
shown that it is the two of us who will decide this."

"Yes . . ." Tigre whispered. Burt circled far ahead,
a single sharp caw. First In Front stood by the door
of my house, waiting . . .

"I'm going to get a few things," I said. "Then I'm
going to journey for guidance on the ceremony. If I'm
not here when you get back, wait for me. I won't go
without you. I've also been shown that the two of us
will work together on this."

Otto regarded me, his face impassive, his eyes deep
and intense. The scar on his cheek pulsed.

"Be careful, Marius," he said. "You are being tested
beyond what most can manage. Stay focused . . . and
wait for me. I know that you wish to go now. I will
be as fast as I am able."

"I'll wait, Otto," I said. "Thank you. For all of this.
And Otto?"

"Yes?"

"I'll want to hear the rest of this story. After . . ."

He nodded. "When this is over, you will know
everything, Marius. I look forward to that discussion.
Till later, my friend."

He pulled away, the heavy German engine fading
into the distance.

I went up the walk to my door. Entered.

They'd trashed the place.

Couch overturned, books swept to the floor, everything upended. The kitchen in disarray, the icebox
open and the freezer contents melting onto the floor.
The bedroom was a wreck, but they had spent special

attention on my healing room. All the pictures, the
altar, the sacred objects . . . ground under tactical boots.
The healing table overturned, and in one corner, the
distinct sharp smell of urine.

The jackbooted thugs of the Dark Forces had left
their mark.

Tigre prowled, her teeth pulled back. It was no
smile. It was a killing looking for a place to happen.
"This is motivated by deep hatred," she said. *"Deep
hatred comes from fear. These are frightened men."*
Burt said nothing, perched on the window sill.

First In Front said it: *"Find your knife."*

"What?" I said. "Knife?"

"Your knife," First In Front said. *"The one you
and I found."*

Ah. I rummaged through the wreckage. Beneath
a pile of paper and the shredded altar cloth I found
the old trade knife in its beaded sheath.

"Your car," First In Front said. *"It still runs. We
need to go to the Mississippi River, where it splits,
near the fort. Bring your knife."*

And the vision rose in me . . .

*. . . a man, a man I knew was me, though he didn't
look the same, sifting through detritus on a seashore,
piles of wreckage and ruin, huddled shapes I knew
were the bodies of the drowned, washed up on a shore
far from where the tsunami had taken place, looking,
looking for something precious . . .*

I tucked the knife into my waistband, hidden beneath
my shirt, and went to my car. It was only a short drive
to Fort Snelling, where the Mississippi and the Minnesota rivers split at Pike Island.

The parking lot was mostly empty.

Overhead, Burt circled, followed by three crows.

A flash of white behind a tree.

And First In Front, in full regalia, waiting for me on the grass.

I followed him. He led me to the hiking trail, along the trees bowed as though in prayer to the path that led to Pike Island. It was a longish bit. I followed the trail to the very tip of Pike Island, where the waters split. First In Front waited for me there, his head bowed in prayer. And I joined him.

"Father, Mother, Creator God, Great Spirit, Holy Spirit, Goddess . . . I call on you . . ." I began.

And the vision grew as though I were watching it on a huge movie screen: *myself in tattered clothing, the remains of white sacred robes, digging with bleeding hands through the wreckage, and laying, with tears streaming down my face, the bodies of the drowned—men, women, children. But searching, searching for . . . what?*

I finished my invocation, head bowed, eyes closed, the vision rising . . .

"Follow the vision . . ." First In Front said.

In the vision I turned and walked along the shore . . .

So I did. There was a tangle of water weeds, dead cattails, and some branches making a mass on the shore, right on the 'twixt and the 'tween, where the water became the shore. I bent over it and began to search . . .

. . . fingers filthy and bleeding, scrabbling through the detritus, something, something calling to me, a glimmer . . .

. . . through the detritus, and buried in there, a branch, probably from the oak tree by the water's edge, where the river had crept up higher, and I brushed it free . . .

. . . caked in mud, tangled in kelp, something long, filthy . . .

I pulled the branch free, it was maybe sixteen inches long, shaped like a sword . . . I knelt by the water and rinsed it clean . . .

. . . a sword, gleaming, like a longer gladius, beneath the filth, as I washed it in the water filled with the bodies and the wreckage of all who had drowned . . .

. . . a long branch, the bark peeling . . .

Take your knife, warrior, peel the bark and expose the skin beneath, the flesh beneath the surface . . .

I took the old trade knife, and skinned back the bark, exposing the pale cambium below. My hand was sure, the knife was keen, and long strips peeled back. There was a natural hilt, where a ring of stubs that might have been budding branches were. I trimmed around the edges . . .

. . . and I washed away all of the filth from the gleaming length of the blade, still keen-edged. But the hilt had been wrapped with leather that had been cut or corroded away . . .

I carried the trimmed and skinned branch back to my car. It seemed as though the walk took no time at all. I drove to the Michael's craft store in Bloomington and went inside.

"You guys still stock that deer-hide lacing?" I asked the girl at the front.

"Yes, sir," she said. "Aisle eleven, all the way in the back, little boxes on the bottom shelf. You can buy it precut, but if you need a specific length, we can measure and cut it for you."

"Thank you."

In the back aisle, a glimpse of a white tiger's tail,

disappearing around a corner . . . First In Front examining boxes of beads . . .

At the bottom, lengths of deerskin lacing. I took the boxes, weighed them in my hand, selected one, paid for it, and sat in my car and tied a rawhide whip handle beneath the natural hilt on the branch.

Perfect.

As though it had been cut just for it.

Now . . .

"In your home, Marius, in the space defiled, carry the Sword and bring the Light," Tigre whispered.

I drove home. Parked the car in front. Went back into the wreckage of my healing room. Pushed the rubble out, all of it, down to the wooden floor. Bare. Still the stench of urine. I fetched a bucket of soapy water, washed the corner down. Then I took from my battered box of herbals a stick of copal and a braid of sage and sweet grass. Lit it all together and smudged myself, the room . . . opened the windows and let the smoke carry the Darkness away and lift the energy.

Now we were ready.

I sat cross-legged on the floor, the carved and wrapped wand across my lap. Lifted it up in both hands, offered it up . . .

. . . and in the image, beside the sea, after I had wrapped the handle once again, I held it up, offered it to the rising sun . . . and then She rose up out of the waters, the Beloved Lady, the Goddess herself, Mother Mary, Isis, the Lady of the Lake . . . Divine and Powerful, and my head bowed as I offered up the Sword, and She raised Her hands, and the Divine Light of the Creator flowed through her, She Who is the Portal through which the Light of the Creator

was Made Flesh, and it flowed into the Sword, and then I held it up, up to the sky, and the power of the mightiest Archangel of all flowed down into it and through me into Mother Earth...and I called out...

"MIIII-KAI-ELLLL!" I shouted, and the vibration ran through me and through the wand I held, empowered by the Light of the Creator, Blessed by the Mother, and channeled through the Power of the Mighty Protector, Michael...

...and there, by the waters, in the ruin of the Old World, the Light descended down and through the blade I held aloft, and through me into the Earth, so disturbed and twisted by the changes, like a Mother writhing in the agony of birth, and the energy restored order to the Grid, while the Earth shook and the sky split open and lightning descended...

...outside, a cloud passed across the sun and then moved, redoubling the light that streamed through the window, bathed me in its warmth, and the wand I held above my head seemed to throb with energy, pulsing down into me, through me...

...and then the vision shifted, and there were my guides: First In Front, Burt and Tigre, sitting patiently, behind them ringed the Mighty Three: Jesus the Christ, Light of the Creator Made Flesh; Mother Mary, Queen of the Angels, First Among Healers, the Portal through which the Light of the Creator was Made Flesh; and Michael the Archangel, General of the Lord's Host, He Who Stands at the Right Hand of the Creator. Behind them gathered all the ranks of the angelic kingdom, triangle upon triangle in formation, the tips of mighty spears, gleaming in the Light...

"Marius," came the Voice, *and though I could not see Him, I knew that Voice...*

"Not you, but through you, not by your hand, but by Mine, as a sword in the Archangel's hand, you will be one of my Swords...

"...you are Chosen...

"And you will be guided, and you will be protected, and you will never be alone..."

I opened my eyes. Lowered the wand to my lap. Such a simple thing. A trimmed branch wrapped with rawhide for a handle. Simple, humble, just a stick, really.

But in the Other Realms, the 'twixt and the 'tween, so much more.

CHAPTER 24

I was finishing a light meal in the kitchen when there was a heavy knock on the front door. Remember hungry, horny, and tired? I was starved. Not horny. And while my body felt the strain in every fiber of my being, I felt sharp and alert, and if there had been fatigue, closing my eyes and letting the energy that radiated from that transformed branch flow from the sky through me into the earth rejuvenated me, reenergized me, lifted me to a whole new level of being.

It was Otto.

Behind him, the late afternoon sunlight hung just below the treetops in the park. Soon it would be dusk.

The 'twixt and the 'tween.

Time to go to work.

"Come in, Otto," I said. "You are welcome. Are you hungry?"

He swept past me. He was garbed for night work: heavy black jersey turtleneck, dark gabardine trousers and low black boots, his long leather greatcoat rustling.

"Yes."

"Come." I led him into the kitchen. There was still raw sirloin, cut into thin strips, left on a platter; I took out some bread from Sun Street Bakery, cut some slices, laid out butter; I put on water to boil and prepared my French press for coffee.

Otto set his greatcoat aside and sat at the kitchen counter, perched on a wooden legged stool like a massive bear in the circus. The nearly invisible black leather straps of his shoulder holster rig held his MP5K-SD, three magazines on the off side, and carefully placed between the first and third magazines, was a thin sheath that held a knife.

I slid the platter across to him. "Try this. You may like it."

He raised an eyebrow, took a piece of thin-cut sirloin and put it in his mouth.

"Yes. Quite good. Very fresh."

"Only way to eat it...before Work."

"I see."

I made the coffee while he ate. Put extra cream and sugar into his oversized mug, slid it across to him, sat with my own.

"So?" I said.

He nodded that sharp head bob. "They are safe. All of them."

"Where?"

"Sabrina and Dillon are in the Marriott downtown. Room's paid for, they have room service, and the room is warded and guarded. The security there is good—cameras, in-house security, and the police have them under surveillance. They know that my people—DHS—are around keeping an eye on them, so I think that mischief will be stayed. At least mischief of the Middle World kind."

He sipped his coffee, closed his eyes in appreciation of the coffee. "Thank you, my friend. This is quite good."

"Jamaican Blue Mountain. Excellent coffee. I like to indulge myself sometimes."

"Yes."

He looked older now. His face was drawn with fatigue, long lines that had been hidden before etched from his eyes down to his mouth, crinkles around his lips. If he actually had been alive all these years—not a clone, not a construct—he'd be over a hundred years old.

I wanted that story.

But some other time.

"What have you seen, Otto?"

He considered that. Smiled wearily but with a hint of his great humor in his eyes. "I am to follow *you*, Marius. To the Gates of Hell and beyond. We are to recapitulate Orpheus, my friend, and descend into the Underworld to rescue the Beloved. Unlike Orpheus, you will not descend alone. And I hope that you will not look back."

He raised his mug in salute.

"I've been to Hell," I said. "Didn't like it."

"An unpleasant place, I agree. What was the nature of your previous visit?"

"Unfinished business on behalf of a client."

Otto laughed. "Your client got great value."

"Just my job five days a week."

"'Rocket Man...' Elton John, yes?"

We both laughed.

"So where do we begin?" Otto said.

"Where we met."

"Ah. Decanter. Truly a gateway...to Hell."

"Where do you park that saucer of yours?"

"Over the city, below the FAA ceiling. Cloaked."

"I need to hear that story, too."

"You will. Perhaps tonight. But darkness falls. And duty calls. Yes?"

"I guess that means we're driving."

"No. Tonight, I think a sky chariot is called for."

Why not? After all, if you're going to storm the Gates of Hell, why not fly first-class?

If you live a tame life, as I do, when I'm not battling demons, Cabal clones, goat-headed soldiers and Fallen Angels, you've probably seen outlaw bikers tooling down the road in formation, hair flying, colors flapping in the breeze, and felt a little bit of trepidation as those dangerous outlaws blew past you. Or maybe you've seen a movie with an epic fight scene like *The Two Towers* when the Rohirrim are coming to rescue the besieged at Helm's Deep, or seen the faces of the Mongol horde assembling on the plains, preparing to loot and pillage a helpless village—in other words, you've probably seen major league badasses assembling and preparing to descend with wrath, wrack and ruin on some hapless foes, right?

If you've never ridden to battle with the Dark Forces in a tricked-out retro '40s flying saucer with Otto Skorzeny, you have not yet *lived*.

I sat behind him in a jump seat that came out of the floor, and watched over his shoulder as we jetted along the highway towards the dim lights of Decanter, the sick yellow glow of the downtown where the ADM corn processing plants punched corn into corn syrup, the favorite toxin of major food manufacturers, and shipped it out via railcar to all four corners of the Middle World.

While I'm sure we could have traveled much faster, there was something appropriate about cruising at not much more than car speed, invisible to the eye—and apparently the radar as well, though there was a heads-up display that showed not only the location of all aircraft but the satellites above, including the ones with look-down capability, and the locations of all vehicles on the road. There was even a FLIR-type insert that showed the thermal signatures of animals and a few humans in the woods off the road.

Full dark was on us, and so even the ripple in the night sky as we passed would be invisible.

We were running light. Otto carried his machine pistol, and he had a satchel full of spare magazines and hand grenades. He had a well-worn Luger tucked into his belt and magazines for that as well tossed into his greatcoat pockets and the satchel. He bore no power-phernalia.

Me, I was running a battle belt Dillon had left at the house. Glock 19 with a Dawson +5 in place, three of them on my belt, and two pouches for Magpuls for my M4, a dump pouch behind, though I doubted I'd worry too much about reloading magazines; I ran a Paul Howe–designed Universal Chest Rig with eight magazines in pouches, four extra pistol magazines, also +5s, and my trusty Smith & Wesson 627 loaded with sacred hand loads. I had every extra pouch and the dump pouch on the chest rig stuffed with moon clips, and a small Maxpedition dump pouch attached on the off side carrying even more. And of course the obligatory Super Soaker full of holy water strapped across my back. Tucked into my belt was the wand I had cut from the tree...and that was that.

Did I say light?

Maybe it just felt that way because I was sitting down.

"*Yes,*" First In Front said. He was in his war gear: simple breeches, stripped to the waist with all his scars highlighted in paint, long lines of paint drawn down his face, hair dangling free and a single war feather tucked into a knotted braid, his coup stick in one hand and a war knife in the other. "*This is good, riding to war. I like this chariot of the sky.*"

Tigre stretched luxuriantly, rolled on her side, heaved and sighed, then winked at me.

Burt said, "*Beats the hell out of driving. I get tired keeping up. This guy's got class.*"

Otto laughed, as though he could hear.

Burt tilted his head, fixed one wise and gleaming eye on me. "*More than meets the eye, Marius...be cautious in all things.*"

My three guides exchanged looks.

What is it I'm missing? I asked telepathically.

"*This is the Test,*" Tigre said. "*Be aware of all things, all interactions, all choices...every action you take tonight will have resonance far beyond what you can see with mortal eyes...*"

"*Let him have his Test,*" First In Front said. "*We are here to guide and protect...*"

"*...and to make sure he's never alone,*" Burt added. *Laughter in the Other Realms...*

...and in the distance, with shamanic vision, I saw the dark pulsing over the entire city, which seemed to have grown like a scab, and off south, the vortex of Darkness there, where the portal was, where we'd descended after Sabrina...

"We will descend shortly," Otto said. "I will anchor the ship above the portal. We'll descend with the transporter."

I had to laugh. "Away party, standing by for transport."

Otto laughed too. "An excellent series. Remind me, when we are through, to tell you about Gene Roddenberry. I worked with him as a creative consultant, uncredited of course."

I was flabbergasted. "Otto, you are a man of many hidden talents."

He nodded, intent on steering the saucer in on the final approach. "Much is hidden in all of us, my friend. You as well, Marius."

There was some sort of illumination that made the seeing through the windshield canopy almost as clear as day, albeit with a purplish tint and overtone. The wreckage of the farmhouse was still scattered about; someone had been out there and strung plastic fencing all around it. There were no vehicles, but plenty of tire tracks. No signs of any thermal signatures: human, animal or Cabal clone.

Otto hovered the craft, touched the panel and all of the controls disappeared seamlessly into the, well, dashboard I guess I'd call it. He stood up and we both went into the transporter booth, which looked a heck of a lot like a '40s-era elevator in an opulent hotel.

He looked at me, nodded that sharp Teutonic bob, and pressed his palm against the control plate.

We descended in a cone of light.

Slowly.

Like Tom Cruise and Dustin Hoffman in the casino scene from *Rain Man*, or Zach Galifianakis and Bradley Cooper in *The Hangover*.

The cone of light disappeared, and we were standing amidst the rubble. Otto pulled a small flashlight with a red lens cover out of his pocket and lit the way. We pulled some of the rubble away and exposed the entrance to the stairwell.

"Let us go then, you and I?" Otto said.

"Like *The Hollow Men*," I said. "I'm a T.S. Eliot fan as well."

Like the evening spread out against the sky, we went down.

The stairwell was littered with rubble, pocked with bullet marks and shrapnel, blood trails and what looked like blood...but no bodies. Char marks seemed as though the Cabal clones and the Dark Forces soldiers were all equipped with a self-destruct mechanism, which made it *Mission: Impossible*-like to recover their bodies and, apparently, their gear. Total deniability.

Too bad, because I was hoping to scrounge some of that Mayflower nylon, since I was a statistically average-sized male and maybe one of those goat harnesses, with a little bit of tweaking, would fit me.

That gear's expensive.

Otto was on point, which was fine with me. All of the ammo and the gear I carried seemed even heavier as we descended flight after flight of stairs, steadily down. The big man moved like a ghost, light and sure-footed, our way illuminated by the deathly glow of the pulsing walls and the red beam of his flashlight. From time to time

I turned and checked our back trail—nothing but the whisper of our passing, and above us the tunnel twisting upwards into darkness, punctuated by empty stairs.

"I was expecting a reception committee," I said.

Otto paused and waited for me to step up beside him. "Yes. One would think so."

I adjusted my chest rig slightly. Listened. Nothing. Only the pounding of my heart in my ears. Otto's eyes seemed to gleam in the dark as he too listened.

Nothing.

"How much further?" he asked.

"Three more levels."

We descended.

At the final turn before the chamber where we had rescued Sabrina, there was a dim glow that came from around the corner. We both paused, weapons at the ready.

"Caution, Beloved . . ." Tigre whispered.

We came around the corner, pied out like the most tactical of the tacti-cool.

Dillon would have been proud.

The chamber was empty. The dais was still littered with a tangle of cordage, and our casings from what seemed like a lifetime ago.

The space on the wall that had pulsed with malevolent force before was smooth and still. Like a mirror, except of stone.

We entered, made our way to that space.

"This is where we enter," Otto said. He laid the flat of his hand against the stone. "This is the entrance."

"Not permeable right now," I said. "Any ideas?"

"I was hoping you would have those answers," Otto said. "That is what I've been shown."

I was stumped, but then, that was irrelevant...
for you will be guided, protected, and never alone...
Yep.

"Wait," Tigre said. She paced back and forth before the portal. "The answer is summoned, and will come..."

...*First In Front stood, arms crossed, holding coup stick and knife. Silent. Grim.*

...*Burt rested on First In Front's shoulder. He wouldn't alight on the dais.* "You know, Marius, you take us to the finest establishments..."

Laughter...

Otto laughed and so did I.

"You can see them?" I said.

"Not as well as you, Marius. But yes."

"And yours?"

He shrugged. "So. What is your guidance?"

In the Other Realms, all three of my guides stood ready. Tigre said, "You carry the Sword, Marius..."

I drew the wand, which seemed heavier than it should, closed my eyes...

And in the Other Realms, I held the Sword... I turned and touched it to the wall...

Which shattered, right here, right now, in this, the Middle World...

...*which it isn't anymore, Marius...*

"Truly," said Tigre, a beautiful white tiger standing beside me.

Otto's eyes widened, if a man of his experience could be surprised. "Astonishing."

She arched her back. "Yes. I am."

"Oh here we go," Burt said. Oversized crow, hopping forward, and a distinct Brooklynese to his voice.

"Hey hey, heya, heya..." came a soft baritone.

"First In Front?" I said in wonder.

He came forward, in the flesh. Tucked his coup stick beneath one arm, reached out and grasped my upper arm and bicep in his strong and calloused hand. Squeezed.

Real.

In the flesh.

He grinned. "You're not in Kansas anymore, Dorothy."

"You won't hit me if I ask you to call me kemos-abe, will you?"

Laughter.

Otto shook his head. "This is something I have never seen before."

"That's saying something," Burt said. "Given your history."

"Yes," Tigre said. "So say we all. Shall we go?"

"You know the way?" I said.

She looked at me. Green eyes, tinged with yellow. Loving eyes.

"Yes, Marius," she said. "I know the way. I have been to Hell before. With you."

"So many stories," Otto said. "Please, Lady. Lead us."

She padded ahead, looked back over her shoulder fetchingly, and said, "Follow me."

Did I mention that she sounds like a young Lauren Bacall?

You do know who Lauren Bacall was, right?

Led by a tiger with the voice of Lauren Bacall, a crow from Brooklyn, a Lakota war chief with a deep Welsh baritone, and protected by Hitler's personal bodyguard and hit man, I crossed the portal threshold into the Gates of Hell.

I love my life.

CHAPTER 25

"So," Otto said. "Just how does this all work?"

"The Sword," Tigre said. Beyond the portal, there was more of the same, except that the tunnel widened out and then became a path carved into the sides of an increasingly wider cavern; the path growing broader as well, with room for Otto and me to walk abreast following Tigre, while Burt and First In Front padded behind, because for some reason Burt was walking instead of flying, which worried me considering the amount of room he had.

"The Sword? What Sword?" Otto said.

"Marius carries the Sword. His wand, or rather, his Sword..." she went on.

Because once we'd crossed the threshold into Hell, not only had my spirit guides assumed what certainly felt, appeared and sounded like the flesh, but my wand had become a metal sword, with a handle wrapped in rawhide leather, that I carried at the ready. I wish I could say I felt and looked like Conan with his sword, but it was more like the young Bilbo with Sting in the cave where he first met Gollum.

"...is a Sword, or rather, *the* Sword of Michael."

"The Archangel's Sword?" Otto said.

"Yes. One of many. Or rather, one of the many facets of the Sword itself. Each fragment contains the whole of the original. That Sword he carries is a channel for all the power of the Archangel Michael—as is each of the other Swords in the World, as is the Original Sword of Michael, which he carries always."

"One is all, and all is one?" Otto said.

"Absolutely," Tigre said. Her voice would render most men to throbbing helplessness, were it not for the fact it issued over awe-inspiring fangs propelled by massive paws heavily clawed. "Quantum physics. String theory. Or whatever flavor of the cutting-edge science you want to call on. That Sword can open the Gates of Hell and transport all of us, in the flesh, into this portion of the Other Realms. It carries all the power of the Sword that Michael used to strike down the Adversary, the same Power that binds him and his."

Otto eyed me. "Astonishing. He is most blessed."

"Yes," Tigre said. "He is. There are few that are Chosen, and all are heavily tested. And it can be taken back. It can only be used with Right Discernment."

"That's comforting," I said.

"Ha," Burt said. "That's why you've got us along, friend."

"Why aren't you flying ahead?" I said.

"Because there's strength in numbers, and there's things flying in here I don't want to run into without you big boys backing my play, you know what I'm sayin'?" Burt said. "And you didn't ask me."

"What, exactly, can we, um, *do* here, Tigre?" I said.

"Anything you can imagine or manifest, if you stay connected to the Light of the Creator through the Sword."

"Can we be hurt?" I asked.

She stopped and regarded me with her loving feral eyes. "We can all be killed or bound here, Marius. As we are in the flesh. As can you and Otto. We can be injured, we can be maimed. But then, so will *anything* we encounter, including the demonic all the way up through the demi-demons up to the big one himself... we are on, as you say, a level playing ground."

"As to tactics," Otto said, as a good commando would, "do all the weapons work?"

"Yes," she said. "And magic or energy casting as well. And the holy water, which is even more potent here than elsewhere. Be sparing with it."

Great. At least we were heavily armed with the right stuff to be walking down the driveway to Hell.

My white tiger continued to lead the way.

Impressions of Hell: surprisingly banal. No Guardians or other denizens, which surprised me...

"All of us," First In Front added.

... and the entry was a widening cavern, with the staircase gradually morphing into a wide, broad path, paved with carefully fitted stone. There was no visible source of light, but somehow the cavern was lit enough so we could see our way as we descended.

Ahead of us, as the path wound round, we saw glimmering lights that grew as we came closer.

"Hey, Otto," I said.

"Yes, Marius?"

"You like to read?"

"Very much so. It is one of my great pleasures."

"Like science fiction, fantasy, that kind of thing?"

Otto found that amusing. "Only the best. As you can see, it's hard to compete with real life."

"True, that," I said. "Ever read Roger Zelazny?"

"Oh, yes. Brilliant author. He was very much attuned to the Other Realms. Did you read the Amber series?"

"Absolutely. Rocks socks. Did you ever read *Lord of Light*?"

"Yes. Of course. I believe that was his first novel to win the Hugo?"

"Actually, that was *This Immortal*. But in *Lord of Light*, do you remember the sequence when the Great-Souled Sam descends into the Hellmouth to free the Rakshasha?"

"Vaguely... wait, yes, of course."

"Take a look around. Remind you of anything?"

There was an alcove in the wall ahead, where a dim grave light gleamed. We were almost abreast of it.

"He's descending on the path into Hell when he comes up next to one of these glowing alcoves and..."

The trapped spirit within the alcove threw itself against the gleaming light that enclosed and bound it.

"Free me, master, and I will lay the world at your feet!" it shrieked.

We stopped and looked at it. Mostly human, though the face was twisted in a constantly shifting display of extreme emotions: anger, puzzlement, pure rage, disdain... over and over again, like a neon sign blinking through its predetermined sequence.

"Life as a sci-fi novel," I said.

"It goes through the same sequence," Otto said.

"Yes," Tigre said. "The dominant emotions in its

previous life. Played over and over again until it somehow masters them and breaks the cycle."

"I guess that's a good working definition of life in Hell," I said.

"It isn't life," Burt said. "It's Hell."

Otto stared. The light from the binding gleamed on his face.

"What are you thinking?" I asked.

"There but for fortune go you and I, my friend."

"There but for God," I said. "And the White Light of the Creator."

He was silent, regarded the bound spirit, who stared at him beseechingly. "Why does it ask us to free it?"

First In Front answered that. "The Sword binds. What it binds, it can unbind."

Otto looked at the gleaming length of metal in my hands, looked into my eyes.

"A dangerous power," he observed.

"The most dangerous," Tigre said. "The power to slay . . . the power to heal. The power to bind . . . the power to free. Dangerous to the wielder, dangerous to the foe. Not for anyone. And not forever . . . at least in mortal life."

"Uh, I wish you guys wouldn't talk as though I'm not here," I said.

Tigre laughed. "Follow me, boys."

And led the way.

Otto lingered, staring at the bound spirit, then followed behind us.

As we descended, a light began to glow in the Sword. A pale blue glow at first, that began at the edge and the point and then began to deepen in color, becoming almost cobalt, brilliant enough to light the way, almost enough to dazzle my eyes. Tigre looked back over her shoulder (OMG, what a...feminine... power...) and smiled, if the baring of massive fangs and crinkling eyes meant the same thing in a tiger as in a human female.

"The power grows," she said.

"Does this mean...orcs?" I said.

"We will meet something very similar, soon," Tigre said. "The power grows as we descend. The Power of the Light grows from two poles: complete Light and complete Dark. We're descending into the Dark, and as we approach that pole, the Light of the Creator grows to match it. You're a Light Bearer, a Path Finder, a Sword of Michael, Marius. This is *your* destiny."

I held the blade up above my head, just like Luke in *Star Wars*. My guides and allies all paused for a moment. Otto stared up at the sword, at me, then bowed his head in respect.

"If you're done channeling your boyhood fantasies," First In Front said, "we have a friend to rescue."

"Yes," Tigre said. "We must hasten."

She lowered her head...and then she grew... to the size of a midsize Mack truck. Now I'd seen this before in the Other Realms...but to see it with physical eyes, smell it, touch it...that was a whole 'nother thing. She flattened out on her belly, tilted her head and whispered, "Mount me."

Um, remember what I said about the young Lauren Bacall? Imagine that whisper...I'd say it was overwhelmingly arousing, but I wouldn't want to incite her anger. Don't mess with the Goddess in *any* of her incarnations or manifestations, that's my rule.

"Um, ah, yes, absolutely," I said.

And I don't think it was my imagination that I saw a sly grin come across that fierce visage before she turned away to keep her eyes on the descending trail.

We slid up onto her back, me in front, First In Front behind me, then Otto, facing rear for security. Burt flapped his wings.

"Love you to pieces, sweetheart, but this ol' crow is gonna hang onto his dignity and fly," he said.

And in the way of power animals and guides, he flapped his wings and hovered just above, eyes up, our own aerial surveillance and acquisition platform.

Tigre came up off the ground. Her fur was silken beneath us, pulsed with her breath and the *pounding-pounding-pounding* of her gigantic heart.

"Hang on, boys," she purred. "It might be a bumpy ride."

She began to bound down the trail, in long, loping leaps that ate up distance, more and more in each bound...

"Hey, Otto," I said.

"Yes?"

"Did you read Zelazny's *Creatures of Light and Darkness*?"

"Of course."

"Steel General?"

He laughed. "My favorite character of all. You are thinking his mount?"

"Yep."

"Perhaps someday they will make a film of that novel. Epic in reach. One of his best and often overlooked."

So there we were, loping down into the bowels of Hell, mounted on the back of a gigantic spirit tiger, me, a Lakota war chief, Hitler's best commando and a big black crow...

I so looked forward to telling that story to Jolene.

That thought brought a welling of emotion up in me. I'd kept it buried, but that's a dangerous thing for a practitioner...

"Shaman," Burt said.

"Medicine Man," First In Front said.

"Light Warrior," Otto said.

Tigre laughed. "Hardheaded mortal."

Like I was saying, a dangerous thing for a practitioner to do, keep emotions buried—emotions provide the charge for the Work, or they can—and buried emotions are like land mines, nuclear land mines, that can go off with little or no warning. Part of the ongoing task of the Light Worker is working to keep the channel clear, that's to clear out the stuff that comes up and out with life. None of us are perfect; that's the point—it's the constant process and the journey that is the destination.

So we have to work on our stuff constantly.

But back to anger and rage, borne out of fear... I feared for her. And that enraged me. And I had to let that come up so that it can be released and transformed. Use it. Release the energy. Easier said than done. Transform it into love, which means I had to get past the fear and connect with the deep love I had for her...

"And she for you," Tigre said.

"Yes," I said. "And she for me."

"Mind on the ball," First In Front said.

"You play ball?" I said, surprised.

"We Natives invented it, white man."

Um, okay.

The alcoves that held trapped souls and spirits grew more numerous, began to stack up in rows above one another, each glowing like a light, making the way brighter, though we passed them in a blur: there were glimmers of faces, hands clawing at the bindings, some huddled and staring... all of them calling out variations on "Free us! Free us!"

Ahead, a widening in the path, like a mezzanine (some part of me was giddy with thought, wow, I'm at the Mezzanine of Hell), a widening that grew, and lined up across the path, barring our way, small figures that grew, and grew, and grew...

...the first line of Guardians, Dark Side issue.

Battle.

I raised the Sword. Brilliant blue light rippled across the edge and the point. I pointed it at the growing ranks, and Tigre redoubled her speed, wind howling at my face and blowing my hair straight back. I felt like Gandalf leading the charge of the Rohirrim in *The Two Towers*, except with less hair.

The line grew.

Goat-soldiers. Big ones. The industrial strength and size. About six feet on their hind legs, running all the cool-guy gear—Mayflower nylon, M4s, and...

...enormously oversized penises.

Not to gross you out, but like the size of a baseball bat on steroids, with a spiked ball on the end. Like a mace, but made out of man parts.

Behind the ranks, stood one massive Archdemon—goat-headed, and this guy had an erection, sprouting spikes from the end, like a fire truck ladder.

And a huge double-headed ax.

Game on.

Tigre smashed into the line like one of the Oliphaunts in the battle for Minas Tirith in *The Return of the King*. Long lines of fire arced up at us, but I waved the Sword and a brilliant bubble of blue light surrounded us and it turned back the bullets.

The line shattered, tried to regroup and swarm us, but I waved the Sword and the goat-soldiers fell back, like mosquitos against an electric swatter, sparking as they fell. Some of them snatched at Tigre as she burst through them, swatting them aside with great sweeps of her gigantic paws, First In Front slashed at them with his war knife, cutting them away from their tenuous holds on my white tiger's fur, Burt led a murder of crows again and again on the scattered and broken line of the goat-soldiers, Otto fired short, discrete bursts from his MP5K, taking out goat-soldiers in a steady accretion of loss . . . every swinging dick.

The Archdemon held up his hand, and Tigre stopped.

The goat-soldiers held their fire, and Burt and his brethren circled our heads.

The Archdemon clopped forward. His erect phallus bobbed slightly, well over our heads. The ax was held at port arms across its chest. No firearms, but then, he was on his home turf, so firearms would've seemed, well, superfluous.

"Marius!" it said. The voice—it seemed like a male voice—was rough and gruff like the hair on his chinny-chin-chin, hearty like a demented frat boy's at the end of a long drunken night. "So glad you could make it. I've been wanting to meet you for oh such a long time . . ."

"You have my name," I said. "Who are you?"

It grinned. Huge teeth and then an obscenely long tongue appeared and licked its lips, like a Rolling Stone poster sprung to life.

"I have a name, human, but I won't give it to you." He tapped the enormous phallus with his ax. "This will tell you..."

"Let me guess," I said. "Big Dick? Enormous Prick? Or just This Way to the Asshole?"

"SILENCE!" the demon bellowed.

We all laughed.

"Definitely a big dick," I said.

"I am *lust* incarnate! I am Asmo—" it began.

I cut it off. His speech, I mean. With a blast from the Sword. Asmo-Big Dick took two steps back and fell on his big ass.

Much to the astonishment of his minions, my allies and companions, Big Dick His Own Self, and... yes, me.

"Anything you can imagine, visualize and will into existence," Tigre said. "Be careful what you wish for..."

"I can wish for a little more of that," I said.

Asmo-Big Dick stood up. While it hadn't affected his erection any, a little bit of stuffing had been knocked out of him, and he was less sure... and that uncertainty radiated out to his followers, who held their fire.

And a little bit of stuffing was knocked out of me, too. Like I've said before, it's not me... it's that which moves through me. And having the Archangel Michael's Sword—or one of them—is a pretty heady thing on any day; knocking an Archdemon down with focused intent and the wave of the Sword is pretty heady on any day as well, only doubled (okay, maybe tripled) my pleasure.

That's the danger.

Pride is the great danger, the deadliest of the sins, the rock upon which we will founder. The practitioner that starts taking credit for the Work the Creator does *through* him or her is a practitioner that may find himself sans power and allies when he needs them the most—humility is the most necessary attribute, and that is like wisdom: it comes from experience, which comes from making mistakes.

I had to rein myself in, manage the Power, manage the *experience* of the Power, and not mistake that Power that moved through me like music through a piano for being me, the beat-up old saloon piano.

"Time for less smack talk and more smackdown, demon," I said. "Move aside. We are here on business for the Light."

Ol' Asmo didn't like that.

I held the Sword up and said, "Not my will, but yours, Creator. Strike in accordance with your Plan, not mine."

As they used to say on *The Sopranos*, "Bada boom, bada bing, ain't no big thing."

Just a bolt of blue lightning punching a smoking hole all the way *through* one hellishly endowed Archdemon, and torched about a third of his shaft on the way through. Not that he seemed to notice as he toppled.

His followers scattered, nary a shot in our direction.

Tigre rumbled with satisfaction beneath us; the purr of a contented elephant-sized tiger is an astonishing thing when you are seated upon it.

"Not as difficult as I expected," Otto said.

"He is only the first," First In Front said. "There

are seven. He is the first, and the least among them. This was only the beginning of the test."

I turned to face him. "This you've been shown?"

"Not my first time at the rodeo, white man," he said. "You've got a long road ahead of you yet. And then the return."

"Let's not put the cart before the horse," Burt said.

Tigre rumbled. And began to descend, leaving the scattered bodies of the goat-soldiers, every swinging dick of them, behind us.

"Do you see what is coming next?" I asked First In Front.

"Much the same as you were shown, Marius. There is a sequence, each Guardian progressively more difficult, and along the way, there will be at least one that resonates with some deeper aspect of yourself," he said.

"This was Asmodeus, the Archdemon of Lust," Otto said.

"That would explain his, um, equipment," I said.

"Common with Dark Siders," Otto observed. "If the Seven Guardians are aligned with the tradition, we should encounter next Gluttony, Greed, Sloth, Wrath, Envy, and finally Pride. That gets us to the Throne Level."

"That's where she is?" I said.

"What were you shown?" Tigre said.

It's strange, being in the Other Realms in the flesh, with my spirit allies and guides in the flesh as well. The knowledge that they conveyed to me through themselves was, well, just available to me. Like you know that apples are red and crunchy, the sky is blue, and grass is green—without even thinking about it. You just know.

"Yes," I said. "She'll be there. We will have to fight one of the Champions."

"Which one?" Otto said.

"Not clear," I said. "Who do you think?"

"One of the Fallen, I fear," Otto said. "Those are the Dark Side's Champions. And you are a Sword Bearer..."

"You have known others?" I said.

"Yes," Otto said. "Those that were taken up, and those that fell."

"I'll add that to the list of stories we'll tell someday soon," I said. "Anything I need to know right now?"

"Nothing you don't already know," Otto said. "There is a weakness in the Seven Great Sins that you will resonate with, more than one...the Power that moves through the Sword magnifies all things and repels the Dark, but you can fall prey regardless...if you allow yourself."

"Wasn't Lust," I said.

Tigre laughed, a deep throaty womanly laugh that chilled me—in a good way.

"You love women, and Woman, Marius," she said. "Your sexuality is channeled in a healthy fashion with a woman you love. You... *appreciate* women, but you don't fall prey to lusting after them and pursuing the wrong types. At least, not anymore."

Spirit guides. No hiding the truth from them. Especially those representatives of the Divine Feminine.

"So who's up next?" I said. "We looking for Gluttony? Who would that be?"

"Starts with a B and ends with a bub," Burt said. "No lightweight, either."

❖   ❖   ❖

The path wound round and round. The alcoves for the soul-lights were stacked high and packed deep, each one a container for a tortured being, each one alone and cycling through the emotions that had captured them there. The ones on the level of Lust were, well, inventive at best, sad and sickened at worst. I tried not to look at them.

"Well, here we go," Burt said. He was above us with a flock of ravens and crows, acting as our own personal Predator and Raven coverage. "Told you he's no lightweight."

Starts with a B and ends in a bub, as in Beelzebub, Archdemon of Gluttony. I'd say Lord of Gluttony, but that might be a bit too grandiose.

As in big.

But maybe not.

Beelzebub . . . Ever see the carved happy Buddhas? The one with the jovial fat-faced Buddha and a huge round belly atop pillarlike legs? Okay, take that image, put a greasy face with yellow eyes and fangs protruding over wrinkled lips, the head the size of a president's on Mount Rushmore, sitting atop fold upon fold of greasy yellow brown meat stacked high like the Michelin Man after he'd been locked in a truck full of Twinkies for three months, a spare tire that would end world hunger if rendered down for fat, and with a gigantic much-gnawed limb of some kind of gigantic creature as a club. Swarming around him were foot soldiers, bulbous things with enormous bellies and huge gaping maws for mouths, all sprouting teeth and long tongues, clubs the weapons of choice . . .

. . . from time to time Mr. B the Unhappy Buddha would drop his club on a mass of his own minions, reducing them to mash, and the rest would swarm the mash like cockroaches on a donut at lights-out.

Which gave me an insight into our fate should we stumble at this particular threshold.

Tigre slowed to a trot.

"Best not to take this one lightly," she said. "He is more than he seems and contains much power for the Dark."

As we approached the next landing, the landing of Gluttony, BiggityBub's minions formed lines, five deep, in front of us. They were Super-Sized and no Happy Meal—the heights varied but averaged at least twelve feet, and probably close to half a ton of meat on the hoof. No cutting implements, only the cudgels and clubs for rendering meat into mash . . . and those oversized maws sprouting teeth.

I felt as though I'd fallen into a Pieter Brueghel painting crossed with a screenshot from the Fellowship in Moria, except instead of a flaming Balrog, I had an obese demon swinging his meat.

Tigre stopped short. Her breath was like a bellows.

The other sounds took a while to sort out. There was a steady grinding which issued from the mouths of the lesser demons; a wet sound, of sweaty meat flesh rubbing against each other, the occasional explosion (literally) of a foul fart.

They didn't say much, but then, they didn't need to.

Beelzebub spoke. His voice was huge, but not what I'd expected. He had a sweet, almost simpering quality to his voice that was at serious odds with his appearance. But then, demons are known for that, yes?

"Marius Winter, Marius Winter," Beelzebub said. "And in such fine, fine company. How tasty! We have your tiger, your crow, your Lakota war chief and you brought along Otto Skorzeny! Hello, Otto, so nice to have you here. Perhaps we'll have you to dinner."

The massive maw split in a semblance of humor.

"Or for dinner, haw haw haw!"

"HAW HAW HAW!" echoed the ranks of his minions.

"We require you to make way," I said. "We must pass."

"I'm aware of that," Beelzebub said. "Your desire. Tell me something, Marius . . ."

The voice was rich and sweet, cloying really, like an unskilled baker's attempt at a fine pastry, too much sugar and poor-quality flour baked unevenly.

" . . . have you ever considered just *asking* to pass? It's so very very rude to tell me, here in my home and place of employment, that you *require* me to make way. I'm very busy, you know. Lots of mouths to feed and all that."

The huge belly rippled with laughter.

"Not that there's much here to feed my hungry children," it went on. "Not more than a few mouthfuls, except for that pretty little tiger of yours. I might make a nice centerpiece out of her."

We considered each other.

"Hunger, Marius. Have you known hunger? Of course you have. At least, appetite. Hunger of the senses, too . . . that's what this is all about, yes? Your hunger for your woman, your sweet Jolene . . . not lust, no that's too *nasty* for you, you're too *good* for lust . . . but hunger? Sure you hunger for her . . . else you wouldn't risk your soul and the souls of your companions for her. Because that's what's on my table tonight . . ."

"Not quite yet," I said.

Belly laughter. Ripples of fat like waves in a stagnant pond, and the odor that was released each time was near to unbearable.

"Oh, certainly, not quite yet. Of course. So you are like viands on the shelf?" Beelzebub's laughter grew. "It would please me to taste you, Marius. A soul like yours, so many experiences, so many lives, so many different flavors of experience. Tasty. It's not just the meat of your body which you so foolishly brought with you here—and that of your friends—but that which ensouls the body, that very tasty substance. You're like fine aged meat to a human... and I enjoy the taste of human," it said.

While it talked, its minions inched forward. If it was distraction, it was poorly executed. Tigre flexed her paws and the huge claws slid out, scored the rocky path.

Beelzebub smiled even wider.

"Not your first visit, I understand," it said to her.

"No," she said. "It is not."

"Our first meeting."

"It is."

"The White Tiger," it said. "Quite famous, in some circles."

"We require you to make way," I said. I raised the Sword.

Beelzebub appeared unimpressed. "Oh, yes. That."

He raised his club and all his minions raised their weaopns.

The Sword rained blue lightning on the ranks of Gluttony's soldiers. The smell of seared meat rose above them. More appeared, excreted as though from Beelzebub's very pores like grains of meat or pus from a wound. The lightning rained all around Beelzebub, but his meaty club seemed to draw the lightning, smoked it down to ashy bone, but still the club was like a lightning rod . . .

. . . instead of bounding into the fight, Tigre bounded *over* the minions, landing lightly after sailing over the milling ranks, without us firing as much as a shot. She landed and faked right, went left, then leapt over the club of Beelzebub that came whizzing past us, then under us, and we sprang for the path beyond when suddenly Beelzebub appeared as though transported from where he'd been, right in front of us and we ran right into the belly and bounced backwards, all of us tumbling even though Tigre turned in midair and landed on her feet, then reared up onto her hind legs and swiped at the impossibly fast form of the Lord of Gluttony, who was almost dainty in his blinding speed, like the dancing hippo from that Disney movie.

Otto tumbled end over end, but with skill, judo or jiu-jitsu type training, and came up with his MP5K aimed at the milling herd of Gluttonous minions who just now were realizing we were behind them, significantly so, and engaging their boss—

—but it told me something that First In Front sprang in front of me, pushed me back just as Beelzebub swiped with that impossibly fast club, and Tigre was lunging and swiping at him, that just maybe this fat gourmand of human flesh and soul was more than he seemed—

"You think?" Burt said as he swarmed past with his fellow crows, swirling around Beelzebub's eyes to rob him of his vision—

I thought of Jolene.

Yes, I hungered for her, but not of flesh alone. I was here as more than a man in search of his woman; I was no Orpheus in search of his Eurydice, I was here as... a Sword of Michael.

I raised the Sword. "MIIII-KAI-ELLLL!"

A blast of blue light from the Sword rained across the shield that Beelzebub had raised, but as the blue light ran down like rain on a windowpane, it cut and scored the earth away around the Archdemon's feet, till the very earth gave way beneath its feet, toppling it to its side, though it snatched at the sides of the sudden sinkhole that had appeared with its impossible speed—

—and Tigre struck at one of its hands, while it flailed its club with the other; First In Front, fluid, the knife flashing in his hand, cut at the demon flesh, the blade leaving sears of bright red fire that ran like blood down the Archdemon's arm; Otto placed single shots, precise, dead center of the ugly teeth-rimmed flower that passed for a maw with each of the minions, conserving his ammo because I sensed that he also saw this as a very, very long night's work....

—and I raised the Sword once more, and a series of pulsed blue lightning bolts struck the Archdemon in his huge belly, creating smoldering holes that forced it further down, and then it tumbled free, lightning raining down on it, like the Balrog tumbling down off the broken bridge, and its club flailing, catching Tigre hard on one forearm. The snap of shattered bone was loud in my ear as was the roar of pain and sudden rage, something I'd never heard before, and she was limping away from the crumbling edge of the sinkhole, and I realized that we were all on the *wrong* side of the hole; the same side that held a huge horde of hungry mouths, and I looked up at Burt, who nodded as he dived toward me. He grew suddenly huge, like the Eagles in *Lord of the Rings* or the Ravens of Randall Flagg in *The Stand*, and he and his murder of crows swooped down, plucking us up and carrying us across the widening hole, with several of them swooping up my beloved tiger, wounded now, and depositing us on the other side. We ran, but Tigre could not. So Burt and several of his fellows picked her up and flew her right ahead of us, like a squadron of Black Hawks transporting a tiger, and we ran further down the stone path, leaving the gape-mouthed horde of Gluttony falling into the widening hole behind us—

"Going to be difficult getting back across that," Otto said, breathing evenly and smoothly as his long legs ate up the distance.

"We'll have to consider an alternate route," I said. "Or alternate transportation."

We stopped to regroup. Tigre sat on her haunch, her maimed right front paw broken with the bone protruding halfway between the paw and the first major joint.

"This doesn't look good," I said.

Her face was genuinely twisted in pain, and her sides heaved as she panted. I'd never experienced this before; in journey, my guides and allies were, well, indestructible, and regularly encounter and defeat enemies—though Archdemons were not a common occurrence, and two in a row pretty well unprecedented.

"When we are in the flesh, in this realm, we are as vulnerable as you are," First In Front said.

I knelt beside Tigre, examined her leg. Her eyes gleamed into mine.

"Anything I can visualize or imagine, as long as I am aligned with the Sword and right intent . . . right?" I said to her.

"Yes," she said.

I'd never heard pain in her voice before.

It shook me.

I felt a tide of rage rising up in me.

Test.

That's what it was.

Wasn't it?

I took a deep breath, settled myself. From the walls and the very roof above us gleamed millions of trapped souls, cycling through the emotions that bound them, a reminder of what it took to be free, to be unbound. Connect to the Light . . . with healing intent.

The Sword grew even brighter; redoubled again, then again . . . brilliant blue light, cobalt in its density, so bright that everyone else stepped back.

I touched the flat of the blade against Tigre's wounded leg.

Blue light pulsed into her leg, illuminated each individual hair of her fur, like an X-ray we could see right into her bone and muscle structure, blue light pulsing through it, down to the cellular level, each cell illuminated in brilliant blue light . . .

I felt the Presence of the Archangel himself, flowing through that Light into Tigre's leg, and then the Presence I most loved, She who always appears in blue and white, Queen of the Angels, First Among Healers, Mother of Us All, Beloved Mother Mary, and her healing Light channeled through the Sword, through me, combined with my intention, cleared of the anger and rage that had fueled me, for once a clear channel here in the antechambers of Hell...

Tigre convulsed once, then relaxed. Before our eyes the leg straightened, lengthened, smoothed out, even her fur curled into place...

And the Light was banked.

For now.

"How are you?" I said.

Tigre extended her paw like a woman admiring her expensive manicure. "Better than new," she said. "So this is what it's like for those mortals so blessed." She regarded me, then Otto. "That is one of the great gifts of being in the flesh. You mortals are blessed beyond your knowledge. This is the only time in my entire existence I've experienced; and it may be the *only* time. Appreciate your gifts. Now I understand..."

Otto said, "This night is full of revelations."

"The night is young, to paraphrase a mortal of my acquaintance," Burt said.

"We have promises to keep, and miles to go before we sleep," First In Front said.

"And miles to go before we sleep," I said.

"Stay Frosty," Tigre said. "Mount up, boys."

"I don't know that one," I said.

"John Wayne," Tigre said.

"I've heard of him," I said.

"You bet, pilgrim," she said. "And Marius?"

"Yes, Goddess?"

"Thank you."

"No need to thank me..."

"Yes," she said, serious. "There is."

We mounted up, and descended further into Hell.

CHAPTER 26

I'm fond of random digression, even when engaged in epic quests, and I reckon that a frontal assault on the Gates of Hell would qualify as epic. When I was in college, one of my required classes was an advanced literature class in which we read John Ciardi's translation of *The Divine Comedy*. I'm sure you had the same class, so I won't recapitulate the plot, but what I remember most was the debate over the geography of Hell. What I liked about the Ciardi translation as published by Penguin was that they had the good sense to include a map of Hell, which even then, long before my Call, I committed to memory. The overall configuration was that of an ice cream cone, wide at the top and steadily narrowing down, to the deepest chamber where Satan himself was bound in chains by Michael the Archangel.

Thus far, it was pretty much like Dante Alighieri called it. This was something that I'd be shown in journey and vision; authors, popular culture and mass media often portrayed truth, even dangerous truths, in ways that the mass of people could assimilate them. Dante was like the Stephen King of his time and he certainly helped shape perception, in the same way science fiction, fantasy, and film helped shape perception of what was going on in our world and time—sometimes years in advance.

Makes me a little nervous about the recent fascination with zombies and extraterrestrials.

There were more tunnels branching off the main path of descent, tunnels that led deeper into the darkness illuminated by the corpse light of trapped souls; the main path was broad and plain to the eye. What struck me most was the absence of traffic; I suppose at some level I imagined Hell to be busy with demons and devils going to and fro on the Dark Force's business. But in my previous journeys, I'd found it to be much the same, though in the way of shamanic travel I'd gone directly to where I needed to go and done what I needed to do. Traveling in the flesh, literally, accompanied by my spirit guides and protectors who were *also* in the flesh—something completely different.

I looked at the Sword in my hand.

The instrument of my transformation, and that of my companions.

I wouldn't let myself think of what might come after. There were other Guardians to get through, by deception or force, and then the final contest, whatever that might be, that would lead to the rescue of Jolene... and then there was the healing she would need, and then there's the whole part about coming back.

But one thing at a time. One crisis, one obstacle to be dealt with.

And another one coming up.

Hell, like I said, was an ice cream cone. We descended, the winding of the tunnel became narrower; each of the Guardians we'd encountered held a post on what was like a mezzanine. One of those loomed close and I could see the ranks of gleaming soldiers lined up—waiting for us.

"Ah," Otto said. "These look interesting."

Ranks of soldiers in gleaming black armor, highly polished, with a white V and a black slash down the middle. Looked just like a business suit as we got closer. Humans, or human-looking enough, a variety of faces, all different but with one common characteristic—the overfed taut-skinned face of the completely possessed, the self-satisfied look of the banker, the lawyer, the stockbroker, successful and untouchable.

Maybe not.

Ranks upon ranks, and behind them, sitting on a raised dais on an opulent throne covered by a canopy, another Archdemon. Too far to see him well.

As we approached, the ranks opened and made a passageway directly to the throne.

Tigre continued forward.

"Is this wise?" I said.

"We cannot go around," she said, "so we must go through."

Otto said, "This reminds me of a great deal."

"I imagine so," I said.

Tigre slowed her stride, a steady and majestic parade of powerful and sacred flesh through the ranks of soldiers. The ranks closed up behind us, but the way remained open. Burt had called his fellow crows back into himself, and perched on my shoulder. I found the grip of his claws comforting. First In Front was uncharacteristically silent.

"What are you thinking?" I said to him. It seemed strange to have to ask.

"This one," he said. "This one cost the Native Peoples dearly. I know him of old. Be careful with him, Marius."

"Who are we up against?" I said.

"Mammon," First In Front said. "Lord of Greed. He is powerful here and in the Middle World."

We approached the throne. The ranks closed up behind us. The throne was before us. It looked like a customized Aeron executive chair, with an enormous number of adjustable points, a control panel sprouting monitors off to one side and an incongruous mug holder which steamed. I smelled coffee. Good coffee.

"Jamaican Blue Mountain," Mammon said. "Your favorite, right? May I offer you a cup?"

Mammon looked like a very tall human dressed in an extremely expensive black business suit, white shirt, open collar, no tie, like Richard Branson on a dress-up day. Huge coiffed mane of black hair swept back with a double streak of white on both sides, clean shaven, perfect teeth. Eyes as black and deep and merciless as those of a great white shark.

His head was very square.

"No, thank you," I said.

"Are you sure? I get the best of each crop. Brought in special. I know it's your favorite . . . and Jolene's. That's her name, right? The little redhead? Jolene?" Mammon said, sipping his coffee from an exquisitely crafted porcelain cup.

"Yes," I said. "Her name is Jolene."

"Mmm," he said, savoring the coffee. "Tasty." He paused. "The coffee, I mean. Not your... Jolene. I wouldn't know. At least, not yet."

He regarded me, sipping his coffee, then leaned back and crossed his legs.

"You know, Marius," Mammon said. "We all work for someone, right? I work for someone, you work for someone..." He inclined his head at the Sword. "A powerful someone. So at the risk of offending you, I'll just say that we have something in common. We both work for beings who might be at odds with one another. And at this point in time, we're placed in conflict with each other."

Another sip of coffee, and then a long moment with his eyes closed, savoring the coffee or something else. "Doesn't have to be that way, Marius. We can make a deal and you can get what you want, and we can both tell our respective employers that we've done our job, and everybody leaves happy... and unharmed. No disrespect to you, what you bear, and who you travel with, but the prospect of significant harm grows with every step you take on this path. So a reasonable person might consider an offer and make the best out of the situation, instead of perhaps forcing it to the place where certain irrevocable actions would need to be taken. Perhaps you see my point?"

My allies and my guides were silent.

I turned and looked back at Otto, who had shifted sideways to watch behind us and still hear the discussion. He was grave and impassionate. I turned back to Mammon. My call.

"What do you want?" I said.

"What do *you* want, Marius?" Mammon said.

Tigre growled deep inside her, a vibration beneath us. Mammon looked at her with amusement.

"It *is* his call, tiger," Mammon said. "You do not control him. From what I've heard, he's not easily controlled. Marius, what is it that you want?"

So simple a question, and yet not.

"Jolene. Returned, unharmed. And passage back to the Middle World. For all of us, unharmed."

"Not difficult," Mammon said. "For me. What are you willing to exchange for that?"

"What do you want?" I said.

"Ah, so much," Mammon said. "That's the point of being me. I want it *all*—every single drop. So, more to the point, what do I want from you?" He considered this for a moment.

"I could ask for your life, but then, I could take that. I could ask for your soul, but I doubt you'd do that. You could give it, but then you'd find a way to take it back since you're probably not going to be satisfied with that simple swap. Even a romantic such as yourself. Forgive me for that, by the way. No insult intended." He smirked.

"So what does that leave me? Life, no; soul, unlikely. From where I sit, I see two possible options: the Sword, and your Service. Am I missing something?"

"Sorry. Nonstarters on both," I said.

Mammon stared at me. I felt as though I were staring into the twin barrels of a double-barreled shotgun in a dimly lit room. "Excuse me?"

"The Sword doesn't enter into any of it. Nor will I serve you or any other Dark Force. At all. So this whole discussion is a nonstarter."

"Nonstarter? Interesting phrase. I thought we had started a discussion."

"You did. I'm ending it."

Mammon laughed. A rich and decidedly cruel laugh. "Oh, Marius. Your childhood love of cowboy movies is showing. Do you remember, as a child, how you sat glued to the floor, staring at that lovely flickering screen, watching *The Lone Ranger*, *Rawhide*, *Bonanza* ... all those grand old cowboy movies? And the cowboy, valiant to the end, a man of his word ... and of his gun ... 'Well, podner, you started it, but I'm a-gonna end it—'

"And then you had to go and make it worse with your addiction to samurai movies. Remember the first time you watched *Seven Samurai*? You cried. Really, Marius. How embarrassing. The valiant samurai, giving it all in service to his lord; or dying heroically for his comrades. Your love of those antiheroes has colored your response to the world. What was it that your ... teacher Betsy said to you? 'You have to give up the drama to mature as a practitioner ...' Have you done that yet, Marius? You love the drama, you love the high risk ... Who do the other ... shamans," he laughed at the word. "Who do they send their high-risk possessions to? You, of course. And you never turn them away. You are cut and shot and cursed and slimed, for peanuts and whatever tips they deign to throw into your empty jar ... and right now, Marius, you refuse to bargain for what you *claim* you love most in the entire world ... your little redheaded Wiccan. Shall I show her to you, Marius? To remind you of what you are bargaining for? Here ..."

He waved his hand, and one of the monitors on

his sideboard swung around to face us, blew up large as a movie theater screen.

Jolene appeared on it, her eyes wild, her hands pressed as though against the inside of the monitor, tears streaming down her face . . . "Marius! Marius! Help me, oh help . . ."

The image disappeared as I stepped forward, the Sword rising in my hand.

"Ah, ah, ah!" Mammon said, swinging the monitor back into place. "Mind that Sword, Marius. I don't think He Whose Name We Do Not Mention would approve of you swinging it about in such . . . rage. Would he?"

I stopped.

"Marius," Burt said softly. "Measure twice. Cut once."

Mammon laughed. "Be silent, Old Crow. I know you of old. Notice how quiet they are, Marius? They know it's your—how do you Christians say it—cross to bear? This is not the Middle World. This is not the Upper World. You are in Hell, my friend. And here, in Hell, there is One who rules and those of us who administer his rule. I administer. So. What shall it be? Will you strike a bargain with me? You don't like what I'm asking, counteroffer. That's the nature of the game."

"It's the game they want you to play, Marius," Otto said. "It is the buying and the selling. He's turning it to his . . ."

"Shut up, Nazi," Mammon said. "You've made plenty of bargains yourself. To save your pathetic skin, and your family, and your precious little soul. Commando . . ." he sneered. "Plucky little engineer with your dueling scar. Take care not to interrupt your betters again or I'll sear a scar down into your soul to look at for all eternity."

Otto remained silent, but I could feel his fighting anger heating behind me. First In Front strained without moving, like an attack dog on alert.

Mammon was amused by his silence. "Nothing to say, War Chief? You sent me many a soul in your time. So much anger . . . it amuses me to see you reappear as a spiritual counselor. That's what you do, right? Spiritual counsel? Perhaps from time to time you whack some hapless being with that coup stick or shove that knife into them."

Mammon turned his attention back to me. "Interesting company you keep, Marius. Interesting choices. We are defined by our relationships, are we not? Who we choose to associate with. You could associate with a different class of people." He shrugged. "But this grows tiresome. So. You reject what I want and you offer nothing up. So, what does that leave us? A dispute. A dispute you don't want to negotiate out of. You may have noticed that you are significantly outnumbered. Not to dismiss the power of that Sword you carry . . . but perhaps its owner told you it can be taken from you? Were you aware of that? And here, of course, you and your . . . spirit guides . . . can die. In the flesh."

He smiled. "In your tasty, tasty flesh. Or perhaps I could have Jolene fetched and you could watch her die first. In the most horrible way you can imagine . . . I'd say that I could imagine, but that would be, oh, overkill." He laughed. He leaned forward. "What say you, Marius?"

"You watch much TV?" I asked.

"What?"

"TV. You watch it much?"

"No. I own the souls of most producers and have

an interest in all the networks, but I don't have time to watch."

"Figures. Ever watch *Firefly*?"

Mammon laughed. "Oh, that's rich. A tired little band of misfit thieves, puttering around the universe in a broken down spaceship? Is that how you see yourself? Which one are you? The romantic captain? The secretive preacher? Or the whore? You amuse me, Marius. Perhaps I should just keep you and take your Sword. You could be my jester, keep me laughing each day. I could make a rug out of your tiger, and boil your crow, skin your Injun and gas your Nazi, you think?"

I grinned. "I collect one-liners, Mammon. And, as you may have noticed, I am blessed with many gifts. You know which one I have to admit to a certain amount of pride in?"

Mammon leaned forward, rested his elbow on his knee and cupped his chin in one hand, a complete parody of rapt attention. "Do tell, shaman. I am *so* fascinated..."

"I've been told I have a great gift for pissing bad people off."

Mammon roared with laughter, echoing within the cavern. His ranks of execu-clones laughed too, toadies following the lead.

"That's rich, too rich," Mammon said. "And? The one-liner?"

I looked around at my allies. Winked at Otto. Patted Tigre on the neck. "I aim to misbehave."

"What?"

I was still, calm, slightly amused and not the least little bit pissed. Kind of the perfect mental state to channel the power of the Archangel. So I lifted the Sword and just blasted Mammon, Lord of Greed, dead center in his face.

He *flew* backwards as though sucker-punched, tumbling end over end backwards, leaving his fancy Aeron chair smoking and spinning.

Wow.

Game on.

The ranks of execu-clones attacked in an orderly fashion and were decimated in a disorderly fashion. Tigre batted them aside, scattering them; First In Front slid down to fight on foot, spinning and whirling, striking with his coup stick and slashing with his knife; both weapons glowed brilliant with the Light and each stroke sent dozens of greedy corporate minions tumbling away ablaze; Burt circled and struck with precision, joined by dozens of his spirit clones, and Otto abandoned his usual precision and emptied magazine after magazine into the ranks of the Greedos.

I held the Sword up and a brilliant ball of Light surrounded all of us, expanded out like the blast wave of an atomic device; scattering the ranks of the corporate possessed far and wide, leaving them in smoking, huddled heaps all across the cavern floor.

"Let's do like the cowboys and Indians..." I started.

"Not so fast, Marius. He's not done..." Tigre said.

I turned and saw Mammon. He'd returned. The human mask of his square head was burned away, and what was below was the true face of a servant of the Dark Forces. Skin the color of burnt meat, and black eyes with a pinpoint of red flame at the center over a mouth permanently twisted into a mocking sneer. He held a long lance in his hand, that looked like a

Mont Blanc pen on steroids with a razor-sharp point. Probably signed up plenty of lost souls with that one.

What was left of his legions of minions circled round us, careful to keep their distance. The Sword flamed its entire length, seemed longer somehow.

Mammon pointed his lance and red flame lashed out at us, crackled on the blue light of the shield wall the Sword held around us. I extended the Sword, pointed directly at Mammon's eyes like a good fencer, and whispered to myself, "Not my will, but yours through me, Creator..."

A pulsing stream of brilliant light ran from the tip against the red energy shield that appeared around Mammon, like a fire hose of light, beat at the shield... Mammon raised his lance and launched red lightning bolts at us, which dribbled down the shield of Light held around us, the container we traveled in, and meanwhile the steady pulse-pulse-pulse of the blue light hammered on his shield... irresistible... and his shield exploded in red fragments that rained down like shrapnel, and wherever pieces of it struck, it singed the stone and burned, and there was a screech of torture and torment, and Mammon was struck directly by the brilliant blue light, and for an instant, superimposed on the image was another image, an ancient image, of Mammon and a mighty Archangel on the battlefield, Mammon struck down by one stroke of the Sword, and then Mammon fell, collapsing in a heap burning with blue light...

The Light in the Sword pulsed.

"Hurry," Tigre said.

We mounted and she bounded around the smoldering heap of the Lord of Greed, and left his level shattered and covered with the wreckage of his dealings.

CHAPTER 27

We hurried down the winding pathway. The trapped souls were reduced to silence by the vigor of our encounter with Mammon. Or maybe they were just stunned that we'd made it this far.

I was.

"Some resonance there, yes?" Tigre said.

"I guess so."

"What do you mean?" Otto asked.

"Resonance. Something in Mammon resonated with Marius. Or did. Perhaps not now," Tigre said.

"He's not done," Burt said.

"He was struck down," First In Front said.

Tigre was the one to clarify it. "Yes. He was struck down by the Sword. But in this Realm, only one being can completely undo Mammon. And that is his master. If the Archangel himself were here, yes, Mammon would be undone forever. But Marius is here as his emissary. He is undone for now. But he may return. And those beings never forget. And they never forgive."

"Lovely," I said. "Who's up next?"

"Is there any way we can bypass any of this?" Otto said. "Tigre, can you perhaps just...fly? Fly us straight down to where Jolene is held? Burt?"

Tigre bounded, the ride as smooth as a classic Caddy on a clear stretch of well-maintained highway. I felt like I should have a fedora and a Hawaiian shirt on, puffing an Arturo Fuente with Son House on the sound system, tooling through the desert somewhere, maybe on my way to Vegas.

Wow. Maybe I took a hit to the head.

Tigre laughed long and hard. "Oh, Marius. Maybe 'Willie the Wimp' instead, some classic Stevie Ray?"

"I don't want to think about any Cadillac coffins, Goddess."

"I like the style," she said. "I'd take that ride any day."

"What are you speaking of?" Otto said.

"Classic Stevie Ray," I said. "You like?"

"Who is Stevie Ray?" Otto said.

"Stevie Ray Vaughn," First In Front said. "Electric rock guitar. Very good. Only white man who could play as well as Jimi Hendrix."

"That's racist," I observed. "Eric Clapton is pretty good."

"I'm Native American," First In Front said. "I'm the original oppressed minority here, and as that representative I restate my case—no white man played as well as Jimi Hendrix."

"This is a musician?" Otto said.

Burt laughed. "Not much of one for electric rock are you, Otto? Please don't tell me you're a Wagner fan!"

"I am indeed a fan of Wagner," Otto said. "And yes, I enjoyed that scene in *Apocalypse Now*."

We all laughed at that.

"We need theme music," I said. "I wish I had a boom box."

One materialized.

"Be careful what you wish for," Tigre observed.

It was an *epic* boom box. I mean, better than anything I'd ever seen. As a matter of fact, I couldn't figure out how to . . .

"Just wish it," Tigre said. "Instantaneous manifestation. In this realm. So please . . . be careful with what you wish for."

"I wish for . . . 'Bad Company.' By . . . Bad Company."

Presto, zoomo, whammo—just like that.

"I was born . . . six-gun in my hand . . . behind a gun . . . I'll make my final stand . . ." I sang.

"Please," Burt said. "Don't ruin it."

So we descended further into Hell, accompanied by a boom box booming out the long, live version of "Bad Company" by, yes, Bad Company.

Made me wish I had a beer . . . a Negra Modelo.

"No," First In Front said. He knocked the bottle away just as it appeared in front of my face. "No firewater till we're done, Marius. Too early to be celebrating."

"This is interesting music," Otto said. "Would this be considered rock and roll?"

"Dude, when we get a break, you're going to have to tell me how you've lived through the sixties and not heard this stuff," I said.

"I enjoy Elvis Presley," Otto said. "I am not familiar with these musicians. Elvis, he is rock and roll, yes?"

"Yes," I said. "He is most definitely rock and roll. Dead, though. Great loss."

"Oh, he's not dead," Otto said. "Just in retirement."

"Ah..." I said.

"Head in the game," First In Front said. "We are approaching another landing..."

"Otto, if you know where Elvis is, we may have to take that saucer of yours and make a visit..."

"Certainly. It would be my pleasure," Otto said. "He is an interesting conversationalist. Very sharp, for someone of his age."

I just shook my head in disbelief. Could this journey become any more bizarre?

We turned onto the landing.

"Marius?" Tigre said.

This was...interesting. Instead of the usual lines of troops, we had assorted demon types lolling about, mostly supine with their heads propped up on their hands, quite a few dice games going on, some sleeping and napping. No one seemed too excited about our approach. And no one appeared to be in charge.

"Think we can just pass through here?" I said hopefully.

"We can try," Tigre said thoughtfully.

Ever see a tiger try to be discreet? No? No wonder. It's not in their nature. Apex predators can certainly blend in, lie in wait. But discreet? Uh, not. Her idea of "just passing through" was to stride right through the huddled masses yearning to be, well, maybe free, but huddled nonetheless. Hey diddle diddle right up the middle, as a good infantryman would say—I thought of Dillon for a moment, and said a brief prayer that he be safe and sound with

Sabrina. The slothful demons barely slouched out of the way.

"Who's the Lord of Sloth? Next in line in the Seven Deadly Sins?" I said.

"Belphegor," Burt said. "Lazy bastard."

"Kind of the point, isn't it?" First In Front said.

"Which one is he?" I said. "Hard to pick out anyone in particular here."

Tigre passed through them all. Nothing barring our way.

"Well," I said. "That was—"

Not exactly nothing barring our way, but lying in front at the passage down was a huge demon, slack-faced, slack-bellied, on his side in a position of classic repose, his head held in his hand.

Belphegor the Slothful.

"Whaddup, dude?" Belphegor said. He sounded like a teenage Malibu skater with a head full of dope.

"Nothing, bro," I said. "Just passing through. You mind?"

He took his time answering. I could almost hear the bong bubbling.

"Mind? Uh, like care? No, I don't care, bro. I might could have to *do* something, though, y'know. And that's just, like, fucked up, y'know? I'm all mellow and you're coming through and I gotta do, like, something . . . if I could remember what that was . . . uh . . ." Belphegor sounded like he'd really gotten into the primo.

I looked around at all his troops, such as they were. Not much interest if they were actually supposed to be guarding this pass. Downright slothful. Belphegor pushed himself slowly into a slouched sitting position, legs crossed, like a '60s-era Deadhead in midday buzz. I was waiting for Jerry Garcia to show up.

"We'll just get on our way, bro. Thanks for being cool, see you later, right?" I said.

Tigre started around him, giving him a wide berth. His eyes rolled up in his head and he collapsed directly in front of us, like a bad case of demonic narcolepsy. She gave him a wider berth and his eyes popped open and he rolled on his side. It seemed as though his head had grown larger, if that was possible, and his eyes were the size of a couple of '60s-era VW Bugs.

"Ah, dude?" Belphegor said. "I don't think you're gonna wanna go this way, like, I'm not supposed to, like, let you, y'know? So you need to go another way. Like away. Far away."

"Definitely, dude," I said. "We're working it. We can't go back that way, so we're just gonna go up here and cut back, y'know? Through the tunnels? Don't mean to harsh your mellow or mess with your day, y'know? We totally gonna go far away. Just right over there." I pointed past him, where he'd actually have to turn over and look.

"Ah, cool, bro, thanks. I mean, y'know, makes it easier, and I'm pretty tired, kinda crashed out, you know what I'm saying?" Belphegor muttered. He laid his head down and went to sleep.

We slipped by quietly, then picked up speed and continued on our way.

"Not bad," Otto said.

"It does not seem possible for it to be so easy," First In Front said.

Burt circled us. "Don't look a gift horse in the mouth."

"No resonance," Tigre observed. "You are anything but slothful, Marius. Nothing to engage, perhaps."

"Maybe," I said. I hefted the Sword. "The Sword works in mysterious ways."

The Sword gleamed blue, as though in answer.

We descended.

CHAPTER 28

"What do we have left?" I asked.

"Wrath, Envy... Pride," Otto said.

"Lovely," I said.

Tigre was silent. We passed in a blur the stacked lights of trapped souls. We were remarkably unscathed. Tigre wounded, but healed; the rest of us unhurt from our encounters with the Guardians of Hell. I wouldn't let myself think of Jolene or what she might be enduring; that would only feed my anger and rage and that was the trap I needed to avoid. All of this could be seen as a snare for me, a snare designed and built specifically for me—but I saw now it wasn't me... it was the Sword.

A dangerous gift to have, to carry, to wield.

Tigre picked up speed. All the better for me. I don't do well with waiting. I wanted to pass all of this and go directly to the confrontation I knew was waiting for us, down at the bottom, at the Gate itself.

Ahead a landing. A significant gathering of soldiers, in a V-shaped formation, the point of the V facing us. Tigre slowed so we could assess them. Rank after rank, human faces, garbed in armor much like angelic armor, but darker, cheaper looking somehow. We drew close and came to a stop. Human faces. Eyes blackened holes, staring at us, sucking at us, pulling at our energy. Staring at us, and more than a few staring at the Sword that gleamed bright blue in my hand.

They did not move.

Tigre whispered, "Hang on, I think I'll..."

The ground shook.

"Hold on," I said. "Wait."

The ranks parted. An Archdemon came forth.

Long narrow face and squinty eyes, covetous eyes that roved over us, lingered on the Sword. Tall, like all of them, clad in a semblance of angelic armor. Armed with a sword of his own, though surrounded by soldiers with spears. I wondered if any of the deeper layers actually bothered with firearms at all.

"I am Leviathan," the Archdemon said. "And you are the Sword Bearer Marius. And your little company."

"Yes," I said. Didn't seem any point in denying it.

He drew his sword. "Give me your Sword."

"No," I said.

If it was possible, his face twisted even tighter, as though a series of internal cords drew tauter.

"I have been ordered to ask you to give it to me first. If you do not, I will take it from you," Leviathan said.

"Good luck with that," I said.

He raised his sword. It looked like a poor copy of mine, but much, much bigger.

"You have much," Leviathan said. "And I will take

it all from you. And cast you down and grind you beneath my heel. You don't deserve any of it, much less that Sword. Your sole purpose is to bring it here, to me, to my master. And he won't be bothered with the likes of you and yours, Marius Winter. No matter what you have done, or think you have done."

His sneer was epic.

I raised the Sword and Leviathan raised his. I slid from Tigre's back and as I stepped forward, I grew— much as I did in journey, with each step I grew—till I looked Envy in the eye.

We crossed swords.

The Sword was, in proportion, much the same dimension and size of the classic Roman gladius. The gladius wasn't designed for fencing; it was a purpose-built killing tool designed to be utilized with a shield and within a formation, used to cut legs out from beneath an opponent while tying up his blade with the shield, and then stabbing him while he lay hamstrung on the ground. A long-term study by a military historian shows that most of the opponents of the Roman legions bore two distinctive wounds: one to the outside of the leg, cutting the knee and the ligaments that supported the leg as well as the great vessels; then a coup de grace administered to the head or else a thrust through the neck.

A fencing match, bare sword on bare sword, was better suited to the supple fast blades of classic fencing. This called more for the technique of the Bowie knife, the fourteen- to eighteen-inch blade of the American West, which I had some familiarity with courtesy of Dillon and some long afternoons in the sun playing with wooden Bowie knives and fencing masks.

I circled to the outside, the ring of steel, weaving

the point of the Sword in a figure eight to catch the eye of my opponent. My allies stood and watched me, silent. I feinted to the low line, then entered with the blade flipping up in an extended back cut, the razor edge of the Sword hooking like the claws of a raptor across Leviathan's brow, drawing a burning line that dripped yellow-ochre blood.

"Ahhhh!" he screamed, and slashed wildly at me as I backpedaled out of his reach.

The Sword gleamed even more brightly. Lightning flashed out of it, was met by bolts of red from the sword that Leviathan swung wildly as I ducked back and away. A blast of red grazed my side, singed my clothing, burned me. I hissed in pain, leapt forward and brought the Sword down in a long chop; Leviathan ducked his head to one side like a boxer slipping a punch and I took his ear.

Leviathan slapped one clawed hand to his ear. The glare from his eyes was a blow; I held the Sword up to shield me from the envy and hatred that burned from those eyes.

"All eternity you shall twist for that, shaman," he said.

His sword arced through a hissing figure eight as he encroached on me, I backed off at an angle, conscious of my footing, and I saw my chance—I feinted high, as though to chop over his guard, and then dropped low as he entered, hoping to catch me on my feet, but I continued to drop—and cut hard at his knee. The Sword didn't slow as it cut through demon meat and bone, searing as it went; the sound of it was like the sizzle of fresh meat dropped into a hot pan.

Leviathan's leg collapsed in two pieces, and like a great tower crumbling down, he fell to the wounded

side, flailing with his sword. I sprang over him, and
he spun on his back slashing at me. While I had him
engaged, I moved towards his head and all his attention was focused upwards; Tigre and the rest mounted
upon her back sprung over his sprawled and ruined
legs past him. I hacked at his sword, then spotted an
opening and severed two of his claws, just like Isildur
removing the One Ring from Sauron—and I sprang
away. Otto waved for me to catch up and he caught
my arm as Tigre raced past. He swung me into place
just like a SEAL on a Zodiac pickup; I twisted in
the air, sudden aerial grace courtesy of the Sword,
and dropped into place on Tigre's neck, just like the
Fedaykin atop a worm in *Dune*.

Tigre bounded away, leaving Envy crippled behind
us, screaming in rage, flailing with his blade.

"That felt strange," I said.

"Single combat," Tigre said. "The Test is evolving.
That was Envy. Little resonance for you there. You
have Wrath and Pride ahead. We will do what we can
to support you, Marius—but it may be that our task
is to bear witness and hold Space for you."

"I will fight beside you," Otto said. "No matter."

"*Hey nah hey, nah hey, heya . . .*" First In Front
began to sing a war and death song I'd heard before.

"We will all fight if we must," Tigre said. "But we
may not be allowed . . . or able to. This is for Marius.
And the Sword."

"Not our plan," I said, "but Creator God's. His
will, not ours."

"Yes," Tigre said. "Otto? You understand?"

He was silent.

We descended.

CHAPTER 29

Burt circled around and landed on Tigre's shoulder as she trotted along, tireless.

"Not just a landing ahead," he said. "Almost like a plain. Drops down to the bottom of this cavern. There's an army there waiting for us, where the path opens up onto the plain."

"What's on the other side of the army?" I said.

"More army," he said. "And in the distance, the Gates."

The Gates to Hell.

"Well, then" I said. "Let's go."

Tigre said, "Yes."

We went.

Around the turn and arrayed where the path became a broad plain, there was an army. Behind the army in the distance I saw the red glow of the Gates of Hell, surrounded by black walls.

Red and black.

The colors of the army facing us.

The colors of Belial.

Drawn up in broad ranks, opened in the middle, facing one another, an army clad in black armor with a red trident on their chests, a red flag with a black trident flying above them. Standing facing us, between the two broad ranks and blocking our passage down between them, an Archdemon.

Tigre slowed, stopped at a distance from him.

The Archdemon tilted up his visor in salute.

"Hello, Marius," he said.

"Hello, Satan," I said.

Satan. Or as he is sometimes known in this realm, Amon, Lord of Wrath. His face, what could be seen through the raised visor, shifted constantly: my face, the face of countless anonymous humans, a leering visage with eyes of red, a single glowing red eye, a cat's face twisted in hatred, the cruel beak of a bird of prey, constantly shifting, human, animal, human, animal, the one constant an eye or eyes, gleaming red, and the sense of heat radiating off him, like a blast furnace carefully banked, ready to consume all that passed or entered it.

Satan-Amon, Lord of Wrath.

"Enjoying this trip?" Satan asked. "Not the same as journeying, is it?"

"Different trip, same territory," I said. "And some of the same players."

"Yes. What was it last time? You fetched back the soul of that drunken Irishman, father to your friend. He'd wandered here and was ensnared. What did you leave me, that time? A stone?"

"I don't recall at this time," I said. "Perhaps. He wasn't supposed to be here. But then, none of these are."

"No. All of mine are supposed to be here. I'm aware of your need to rescue, Marius. One of the many flaws in your eightfold armor. They all made choices, they all have consequences. I am a consequence, enriched by their choices."

"Helped along the way by you, of course."

"Of course. For every mewling one you rescue, ten thousand you pass over. You're like a child who takes satisfaction in plucking one grain of sand from the sea while countless others drown. Remember that, Marius? Remember how many you left behind beneath the waves?"

The curling huge green wave, breaking over the crystalline towers, the screams of those running hopelessly before the waves rushing towards them, and I was running *towards*—

"We do what we can, Satan," I said. "Not our plan."

"That's your little litany, what keeps you more or less sane, isn't it?" Satan said. "'Not my plan, but yours, Creator?'" He laughed. "The same Creator created me, Marius. Ever think about that? Maybe this is just the vanity of a mortal gifted with things beyond his grasp or comprehension. Worse than throwing pearls to swine is throwing Divine Power to a mortal. Especially to you, little shaman, hustling back and forth, retrieving souls, guiding those who wandered my way courtesy of their misguided beliefs and self-judgment, seeking *healing*."

He sneered the last word.

"Healer. Hah. You're just like me, Marius. You take their souls, just in a different way. They are all so *grateful* to you, so thankful as they drop their pennies into your empty little jar, and you turn away, so humble, and inside you're counting the days till your rent is due, or where you can buy the cheapest cuts of meat.

"You don't seek it out for healing, little shaman, little Marius. You seek it out, you seek me out, because you're so angry. Angry about how it ended, angry about what you did, and what you didn't do. Angry about being a coward, Marius, angry about leaving some behind because you were afraid, angry because you want to strike out but you do not, because your puling *guidance* says not to strike in wrath, not to be angry . . . that's why you're weak and a coward, Marius, you won't use what you have to do it right, so they all died screaming your name, and you never came, did you, Marius? . . . Did you?"

He drew his long great sword, put it point down in front of him, crossed his hands on the hilt and leaned forward.

"You never came, Marius. Not then. You failed. As you've already failed now. Here. For your little *Jolene*—and all of your friends there behind you, those who stand silent right now, they'll get to witness your failure once more. This is where your Lie gets exposed, Marius—where the Lie of you and what you are, what you proclaim yourself to be—that Lie is opened up."

"You're not the Father of Lies, Satan," I said. "You're the bastard stepchild of Lies."

Heat began to radiate even more from his armor, which took on a reddish-black tinge as it heated. As did his blade. Tiny flames began to pop along the edge and point, and small tendrils of steam and smoke appeared to emanate from the blade itself. His eyes narrowed and I felt the blast furnace of his gaze.

"You already failed, Marius," Satan said, "in your

quest for your little Jolene. You know why you failed? She gave herself for you. She was shown what was going to happen, and she said, 'Take me.' She gave herself willingly, because she knew you were weak. That you couldn't take what was coming your way."

"No," I said. "Lies from the poor relation of Lies. Stand aside and let us pass, Satan. You are nothing and less than nothing before the Sword of Michael."

The ranks of Satan shivered, like a reflection in a body of water as a wind passes over it, at the name of the Mighty Archangel.

"Each time you utter that name, Marius, your bitch screams in pain," Satan said matter-of-factly. "Each and every time. Try it. I'll let you hear her."

Can you remember when you last were enraged, if you ever have been? I'm not talking about pissed, irritated, or even angry.

I'm talking about rage.

The kind that leaves you red-faced, eyes and veins bursting, screaming at the top of your lungs, the kind that leads to you leaping on someone and sinking your teeth into their neck, beating your fists against them till they are pulp beneath you, the kind of rage that beats like an oversized drum right behind your eyes, a drum pounded by an insane drummer as hard and fast as he can . . .

That kind of rage.

Take that and double it.

Then double it again.

And then double it again.

That's what I felt.

The Sword throbbed and pulsed. The blue light was so bright it hurt my eyes, but Satan leered at me, seemingly unaffected by the light. I raised it, my hands trembling...

And held back.

Fought it down.

The answer to wrath... is patience.

"Step aside, Satan," I said. "Or do something with that sword besides lean on it."

"You're something of a swordsman, I understand," Satan said. "The One We Do Not Name didn't give you the full-sized model, I see. More of a dagger on steroids. Commensurate with your rank, probably. You need a shield, shaman. I think I have just what you need."

He raised one hand, and two of his minions came running, bearing a round shield between them, a black and red cloth covering the front of it.

"I want you well equipped for the fight, shaman. I will not have it said that I did not give you every chance. So here's a shield my Master had made, just for you. I think you'll like it. You will find it necessary."

"I want nothing you have. I want nothing from your Master," I said.

"Oh, but you do, don't you? You want your little Jolene back. Well, you can have her, shaman. But you probably won't want her."

"Marius..." Tigre began.

"*Silence, Tiger!*" Satan bellowed. The cavern shook and echoed with his fury. "You have no say in his decision."

"I want no..." I said.

Satan gestured, and his mailed minions pulled back the black cloth and exposed the face of the shield. It was like a window looking into a chamber, round and mounted on a backing like a shield. But you could see into it with depth, like a chamber, and she pressed her hands and her face against that window, screaming silently at me.

Jolene.

Her eyes were mad, and her hair had turned white. Long furrowed lines of pain and sorrow etched her face.

Jolene.

Satan grabbed the shield by its edge in one clawed hand, held it to his face. She screamed silently, her arms crossed against her face as though against a blow. Satan extended his long forked tongue and slowly licked the front of the shield.

He tossed it to me.

"Protect yourself, shaman," he said. "She said she'd take it all for you. Every arrow, every sword stroke, every blow, she said she'd take it for you. She's already taken so much . . . and if you don't let her take it, you'll die. As will all your other friends. And then I'll take your Sword. So much for Marius Winter, little shaman of the central plains, and his little Fellowship of the Carved Twig."

"No!" Otto shouted. "I will fight you!"

He strode forward, his machine pistol ready in his hand.

Satan laughed. "Be silent, worm. Your work is ahead of you, if you live that long." Satan waved his sword and the MP5K burst into a hot splatter of metal and exploding rounds. Otto shouted in pain, clutched his burned hands to his chest, metal and burns pocking his face.

"No!" I said.

I held the shield, turned it towards me, looked into its depths.

Jolene.

She mouthed my name over and over, screaming silently, pounding her hands flat against the inside of the shield, pounding her hands against her head...

Mad. Driven insane.

"Tigre? Is it..." I said.

"Yes," she said. "It is. Part of her soul. Not all of it. But some. It's her."

Jolene.

Satan raised his hand. "Archers!" he shouted.

A rank of bowmen swung in behind him, one from each opposite rank. They drew back black double recurve bows with cruel arrows glinting.

"No!" I screamed.

They launched the arrows. Not just at me. But a volley at my allies as well. I held the shield to my chest, facing inwards, raised the Sword and cast a veil of Light over all of us.

While some of the arrows burst into flames on contact with the Light, there were so many that some slipped through.

They found targets.

One lodged in Tigre's haunch, and she reared in pain; Otto took one in his hand; First In Front dodged the first volley, as did Burt.

But more arrows came right at me.

I swiped with the Sword, and one arrow notched my ear, another parted my hair and left bits shaven free dropping onto my shirt.

"Volley!" Satan shouted.

An arc of arrows climbed high and plummeted towards us. Burt rose into the sky, split into a huge cloud of crows that met the cloud of arrows.

One crow, one arrow, all of them raining down to land with heavy thuds around us.

Burt turned his face to me, fallen, a bolt through his wing.

"Do what you can, Marius," he whispered, in pain. "We will rise to help as long as we can."

He twisted his beak, yanked out the arrow. Real blood leaked from the torn bone and wing, matted his feathers.

"To me, brothers," the crow called, and those that were left rose into the sky, Burt wobbling in flight but he rose—

"Volley!" Satan shouted.

And another cloud of arrows rose to meet the crows, each arrow finding a crow, their thin line crumbling, tumbling from the sky, thudding again and again into the ground, a piece of the essence of crow cut down...

Satan pointed his sword at Tigre and at First In Front trying to remove the arrow from her haunch as Otto was pierced again, this time in his shoulder.

I ran to them.

First In Front waved me off. "They will get all of us. Attack him!"

Burt tumbled out of the sky, landed beside me, arrow in his breast. He turned one old, wise eye to me, then looked skyward. The last of the crows fell, and arrows descended like black rain. An arc of them fell towards me and without thinking, I threw the shield up and several pierced the front.

"Aaaahhhh!" Jolene screamed.

Satan smiled. "Now you can hear, shaman. Make your choice. Use that Sword or lay it down and run away. I'll let you live, and you can take your little mad woman with you. These others... they stay."

"Aaaahhh! Marius, oh Marius, please no . . ." Jolene screamed.

I could not bear to look.

Satan smiled at me. Lifted his sword of flame. Pointed it at me. Fire lashed out, set Tigre's fur aflame, knocked First In Front back. Otto held up both his wounded arms to shield himself from the fire.

"Volley!" Satan shouted once more.

Another dark cloud of arrows rose into the air and descended down on us, pinning Tigre and piercing Otto and First In Front.

Satan laughed. "Always the coward, Marius. Always the coward."

The rage took me. I lifted the Sword. Blue flame crackled its length, sparked off it. I pointed it at Satan and a line of pulsing blue flame lashed out at him.

Casually, he lifted his sword and red flame blocked the blue.

"You are not the Archangel, mortal. You're a porter. You carry his bags. You do not have the power in this place. And your rage?" Satan laughed. "As mewling as everything else you do. Die screaming with your woman, shaman. But not till I'm done with your . . . allies."

He pointed his sword and Tigre burst into flames.

Her back arched and she screamed, a sound I'd never heard before, a sound I'd never imagined. Unlike anything I'd ever heard in this life or all those that came before.

"STOP! NO!" I screamed.

Arrows descended. Otto screamed in pain. First In Front shouted his defiance; "*HEYA, HEYA, HEY*—"

He choked, and I saw the arrow protruding from his throat.

For the first time, I felt the Sword go limp in my hand—I did not know what to do. Arrows thudded around me. Jolene screamed from within my shield, an endless litany of "Marius, help me, Marius, help me, Marius, help me . . ." Tigre twisted in the flames, blackening, her eyes beseeching me; Otto was on his knees plucking arrows out of himself; and First In Front was singing his death song and drawing out the arrow from his throat, flinging it down and preparing to charge Satan himself . . .

The rage took me.

I lifted the Sword, blue lightning descended, and a blast wave rippled out from me, incinerating arrows in flight, and the wave of light crashed into the ranks of Satan's army, who huddled behind their shields; Satan himself just raised his sword and a shield wall of red flame protected him.

Like the wave, so long ago—I'd saved all that I could, more than expected, but there were still others there, and I turned back and the Faithful who went with me, we ran *towards* the wave, the wave rising up over the Island of the Faithful, the wave breaking the Tower of Healing, the Hearth of the Great Crystal, the Halls of the One, breaking the buildings that had stood for so long, crushing beneath those green waters so many who were loved: fathers, mothers, brothers, sisters, elders, children . . . and I had run so hard, and I saw them, there in the Tower, the Priestesses holding the Space, holding it back against all odds, against all hope, and we tried and we tried, but it was too late, and even as the wave washed down, crushed me in a dizzy swirl of green with the weight of the raging waters, my rage rose, shattered my Spirit, and

I returned again and again, as my dying thought was, *Save all that you can* . . .

So many times I descended into the flesh, to save all that I could . . . time and again . . . but always the rage betrayed me, the anger, the fierce fire with which I had tried to turn back the icy waters that descended on me, and the lesson, over and over again, was that the rage was powerful, the rage could turn it back, for at least a time, but that was a mortal thing, the power of Satan and his master, Belial, was the power of rage, of wrath . . .

. . . and the other side of it was patience, was compassion, and even now I raged against that, where was that on the battlefield where all that I loved lay dying, wounded, burning, screaming in pain for me to help them, and I alone against the armies of Belial . . .

And that voice came through to me . . . *guided, protected, and never alone* . . .

And I remembered that sequence in the *Bhagavad Gita*, when Krishna explains to Arjuna, to strike without hatred, to strike with love, to be the instrument in the hand of Creator God, not to be the fuel of the fight, but to be the Vessel for the Transformation, and I remembered that which sustained me on so many battlefields through so many lives, all the way back to the first battle . . .

And I whispered to myself, through a mouthful of my own blood, "Not me, God, but You, through me . . ." and I felt myself raise the Sword and turn the Shield, and the Shield grew to cover us all, and I held the Sword high and shouted the battle cry that carried us on that first battlefield . . .

"MIIII-KAI-ELLLL!"

Clarity fell over me, a strange calmness, as though I were removed from my body and yet not; the brilliant blue light of the Sword became like that of the sun, and from my chest a brilliant white light emanated, the white light at the heart of the sun, the Divine White Light of Creator God. Satan's ranks quailed, and even Satan was shaken behind his shield of flame.

Arrows burst into flame or lodged in the Shield, grown large and curved over our heads, big enough for all of us.

I waved the Sword from side to side, and the ranks of Satan's army flew backwards, tumbling. I pointed the Sword directly at him, and said, "Not my Will, but Yours, Creator God. Let me be the Sword in Your Hand."

As though the light of a thousand suns was unleashed, a beam of White Light shattered the shield of red fire around Satan, staggering him back. His army was in disarray behind him.

"Go!" First In Front shouted. "Go!" Otto pressed at the blood gushing out of himself, but dragged himself close to Tigre and threw the shredded bloody remains of his shirt to First In Front who swatted at the smoldering fire covering Tigre. Burt was bloodied and still, one eye gazing upward.

I held the Shield and the Sword and advanced on Satan.

He was staggered. Injured, even, his eyes fading in and out of the constant kaleidoscope that was his face. But he raised his sword and ran to meet me.

His first blow fell on the Shield, and I heard Jolene scream. I turned that sound down in my head, tuned it out, let the Light of Michael shine through me, and it was his hand on the Sword, moving in a brilliant mosaic of light, cutting, slashing, piercing, burning all over Satan, blocking his sword in an array of sparks,

throwing blue lightning on him, hammering on his big
sword again and again, forcing him back. The litany of
screams and beseeching cries from within the Shield
grew louder, but I let the pain of that wash over me,
focused on filling myself with Light as I feinted high
with the Sword and then came in under his counter,
cutting at the Archdemon's knee, catching him on the
hinge of his armor, the Sword of Michael parting his
Hell Armor like a Spyderco on a thread. But he back
cut at me. The Shield, screaming in pain, saved me once
more (Jolene...) as his Hellblade slammed into it, and
then I saw the line of attack, the angle, and I thrust,
a straight thrust, hard. The point went in between his
helm and gorget, at an angle, the blade following. A
sudden explosion of blue light emanated from every
joint and angle from inside his black and red armor, a
sudden stagger, and then Satan dropped his sword, fell
to his knees, and I withdrew the Sword and brought it
down in a vicious cut at the neck, and then a whirling
explosion of black and red and blue and white...

Stillness.

Satan's armor lay disjointed in front of me, smoking
and red with heat, his sword as well. His army fled
in disarray or lay in smoking heaps on the battlefield.

The armor was empty, his sword abandoned.

I raised the Sword of Michael. A blue column of
light emerged from above, illuminated and surrounded
me, spread out like a blast wave from the sword...
all the way to the Gates in the distance.

The field was ours.

Broken weeping from the Shield. I turned its battered surface towards me. Oh, my beauty, my Jolene...
she was bloody and burnt and pierced with arrows,

on the floor in a heap, her white hair strewn like ancient straw, weeping, weeping...

The rage, the rage had gone.

There was only what needed to be done.

I ran back.

Tigre twisted in pain, her fur burnt away and the skin blackened, broken in great red rents. Otto was unconscious, bleeding out from multiple arrow wounds in his neck and shoulders, his hands and face burnt and pocked with shrapnel from his exploded machine pistol. Burt was huddled and still, pierced through with an arrow.

First In Front was on his knees, his hands held high as he prayed. Blood ran from his head, from his hands, and he prayed in Lakota and the words were burned into me: "Take me to your breast, Creator, for today I have stood with my brothers and my sisters, I have stood in the face of great Evil, and I have stood not because of me, Creator, but because You are strong in me, and I am grateful for the opportunity to serve you, Creator God, and I ask that you make my place ready there, among my ancestors, and tell them that I did not dishonor them on this day..."

"Not yet, my friends. Not this day..." I raised the Sword. "I call on you, Creator God, and I call on Jesus the Christ, and Mother Mary, Queen of the Angels, and the Mighty Archangels of the Presence, and I call on you, Michael, and I ask for your presence here, at the Gates of Hell, to Light our way, and if it is in accordance with your plan, to bring healing and relief to those who have stood here this day, I plead for this, Creator God..."

And White Light descended and filled all of us...

CHAPTER 30

I opened my eyes. I was sprawled facedown on the ground, the Sword in my right hand and the Shield in my left. I tested my body for injury. Nothing that I could feel, just a great feeling of lassitude. I rolled to my side, pressed myself up to my knees, then my feet.

First In Front was on his knees, hands held out in prayer. Uninjured, at least to my eyes.

Burt stretched his wings, flexed them in. A nasty scar, but it didn't seem to hamper his wing function.

Otto was on his feet, stripped to his pants. For an old guy, he was in awesome shape. He'd picked up a couple of doozies for his scar collection; a pockmarking of black, healed, burn spots and multiple arrow entries.

Tigre...ah, Tigre, my beautiful tiger. She was singed and stiff with tight new flesh, and her fur was spotty and matted, but she was on her feet and apparently with no pain.

I turned the Shield to look into the front.

Jolene.

Her hair was white, her face still furrowed with lines. But there was some of her old calmness and serenity returned to her. She too was scarred by the arrows and the flame and the sword of Satan. But she bore those scars with dignity.

"Jolene?" I said.

"Yes, my love," she said. "Yes."

I could not speak.

"Thank you, Marius," Tigre said. "For all of us. And thanks to Creator God for the healing that you channeled for us all, for our work here is not yet done."

"I am ready," First In Front said. "We must go."

"We have Jolene," I said.

"No," Tigre said. "We do not. We have a soul fragment, a soul piece. Her soul is there." She pointed one paw at the Gate in the distance. "We must have all of her before we return. This soul retrieval is only through when we confront the final Guardian, and we take Jolene intact out of here."

I looked once more at Jolene in the Shield. She nodded, once. I took a deep breath, exhaled.

"Then we go," I said. "We go straight to Hell."

Burt laughed. "Oh, how many times have I heard that."

We laughed. Weak laughter, then growing.

We were back.

Otto went past me. Stood over the shattered armor of Satan. Bent and picked up Satan's sword.

"I'm surprised I can handle it," he said.

I was too.

"Be careful, Otto," Tigre said. "Perhaps you should leave that as it is."

"It is the best weapon out here," Otto said reasonably. "And I am poor with a bow."

He swung it experimentally several times, thrust with it. "I may not be able to throw lightning or call the fire, but I think I can swing this Hellblade."

"Suit yourself," I said. "Time for us to go. We have promises to keep..."

"And miles to go before we sleep...yeah, yeah, yeah..." Burt said.

We trudged towards the Gates of Hell.

CHAPTER 31

We were a battered company, limping our way across the plain to the Gate that grew in our sight. We all walked, as we could not bear to ask Tigre to carry us on her scarred and matted back. Otto held the sword of Satan on his shoulder like a rifle. Burt would fly ahead, then land to rest and wait for us to catch up. First In Front marched proudly ahead. I carried the Shield slung across my back, the Sword ready in my hand.

The plain was flat stone. Nothing grew here. There was a path of sorts, and we crossed onto it. The path was laid with flat stones. Each stone was the face of the soul traps we'd seen on our descent, except these were all laid flat and flush together, carefully fitted so there was barely a crack between them. Faces pawing up against the surface, as though trying to reach through and grasp our feet, mouths moving in pleadings that were silent, for once, and I was grateful for that.

I don't know where the light in Hell comes from. It was just . . . illumination. Maybe from the stones, because the cavern vanished away above us, the distance we had descended invisible to our eyes. Or maybe it just *was*, like the feeblest glowing of a poor lamp in a dingy basement.

For once, we were all silent, alone with our thoughts.

Nothing like death and resurrection to somber you right up.

I said nothing to the Jolene soul fragment in the Shield on my back. From time to time, I heard soft sounds coming from there: weeping, choking, murmured prayer.

They'd driven her insane, and yet she was healed, this part of her.

I didn't want to think about what might be before us.

The Gates of Hell: The path ends before two massive metal doors, taller than even your run-of-the-mill Archdemon. The metal is black. There are no locks or gaps in the doors; no window, no portals.

Just the end of the road and double doors that open into the darkest Pit of the Underworld.

We assembled there, well clear of the door swing. Stood. Breathed. Prayed.

"Should we do something?" Otto said.

"Reasonable question," I said. "I don't know. In journey, I just passed through. Here, in the flesh? I don't know. Tigre?"

"We wait," she said. "The one we're waiting for knows we are here. When he's ready, the doors will open."

"Marius, you know how to play pinochle?" Burt said.

"No."

"Too bad. You could do some of that instant manifestation stuff and rustle us up a table and some cards. We could kill some time that way," Burt said.

"I saw a velvet painting in a pawn shop that looked like that," I said. "So there's this crow, a tiger, an Indian, a German and a practitioner sitting at the table, playing cards . . ."

"That sounds like the beginning of a poor joke," First In Front said.

"What is a velvet painting?" Otto asked.

"You know how you have all those kitschy pictures of men in lederhosen and girls in dirndl dresses in all the cheapest bars in Germany?" I said.

"Yes. I dislike them," Otto said.

"Velvet paintings are like that."

"Oh."

Otto swung Satan's sword and tested it with a few obviously expert thrusts, parries and cuts.

"You were a fencer, right?" I said. "That's how you got your first facial scar."

"Yes," Otto said. "Renommierschmiss. It is considered honorable to duel with an edged weapon and collect such scars. Or it was when I was young."

First In Front nodded. "Among my people, we look to the warrior with all his scars on the front. Like this one," he said, inclining his head towards me.

"Yes," Otto said. "All of his scars come from facing his enemy."

I turned away. I didn't want to think about the final enemy we were to face.

The sound of tortured metal. The high-toned squealing of massive metal moving against stone. The gap between the two doors grew as they slowly swung open, foot by foot, in a slow ponderous swing.

We all fell silent and watched the doors open.

It took some time.

Finally the doors splayed open. Darkness.

Have you ever been way out in the country, maybe in the mountains, far from any city, on the darkest night, maybe the dark of the moon, driving a car, and turned off the headlights? The transition from brightly lit to absolute darkness is a physical blow against the eyes, an assault on the vision—this is what looking into the Darkness behind Hell's Gate is like.

So black it sucked light into it, an absolute blackness, the heart of darkness, darkness that seemed past even the possibility of light, of even the faintest illumination.

Hell Gate.

"Marius?" Tigre said. "I cannot see what is beyond that threshold. I do not know what will happen if we cross into it."

"Ditto," Burt said.

I looked at First In Front, who stared back, the implacable warrior gaze of a Lakota war chief and a sacred medicine man.

"I do not fear the Dark," First In Front said, "for I am of the Light."

I nodded. Looked at Otto.

"I have come far with you, Marius," he said. "And we are not yet through."

I unslung the Shield, looked into it at the much-scarred soul piece of my beloved.

She stared at me unafraid. Nodded once.

Consensus.

I nodded again. Stepped forward. They fell in on either side of me, making the V formation of birds in flight, or angels at war. I held the Sword high.

And marched through Hell's Gate.

Crossing the portal was a tangible, physical sensation. It felt as though we were pressing through some thick aqueous membrane, something that held us back to a certain point, but then snapped and let us through, sealing us in. All of us crossed into and through the barrier, and I held the Sword, which gave off a brilliant blue light, illuminating the long hall in which we stood, even to the end of it, where something huge was chained to a throne on a raised dais at the end, details wreathed in shadow.

The Fallen.

Something approached us down the hall. Manlike in shape, still wreathed in shadows. Closer. Closer. Closer.

It was a man. Not tall, hunch-shouldered, with erratic, sharp, jerky motions to his arms and legs. He stopped short and waited for us to approach him. He flinched as the Light of the Sword washed over him, but stood there as we walked closer and fully illuminated his features . . . and a very neatly pressed Nazi uniform.

"Hello, Adolf," Otto said.

Adolf Hitler had his arms crossed behind him. His facial muscles twitched constantly, giving a Charlie Chaplinesque tweak to his small mustache. He nodded once, sharply, the whole Prussian-Teutonic nod thing.

"Otto Skorzeny," Hitler said. "Betrayer. Why have you returned?"

"You know why," Otto said. "I see you are still chief lackey to the Fallen. Lackey, this word you understand, Marius?"

"Yes, Otto," I said. "I understand lackey."

"You are to follow me," Hitler said. "I will take you to him."

"Lead on, lackey," I said.

"I require..." Hitler began.

"You require to do your master's bidding," I said. "So lead on and be silent."

Hatred blazed in the depths of the black holes that passed for Hitler's eyes. He turned, stiffly, and with that strange jerky walk led us down the featureless hallway to the Throne of the Fallen.

A dais. Raised of the same black metal that formed the doors. The same black metal that formed the throne. The same black metal that formed the chains, the leg irons and wrist manacles that held the Fallen.

Lucifer. Also known as Belial. Son of the Light. Lord of the Darkness.

Michael's brother, cast down and bound here till the Creator released him.

The perfection of a chiseled human body, the size of a five-story building, each muscle and sinew showing, with just a slight bit of extra flesh at the middle to add verisimilitude to the likeness. A classic Greek face, a dimpled chin, sharp cheekbones, but then the eyes...

The eyes.

I expected Darkness and Flame. The red and the black.

Instead, human-looking, blue and huge...weighted with sadness. Heartbreaking sorrow. Or so it appeared.

On his shoulders, the shorn stubs of sheared wings, with a few white pinfeathers still remaining.

He looked down at us gathered at the foot of his throne.

"Marius Winter," Lucifer said. "Welcome to Hell."

What do you say to that?

I thought silence was best, or maybe it was just because, for once, I was at a loss for words.

"And you have brought the Sword," Lucifer said.

"Yes, yes he has," Hitler said eagerly. "He has it and now we can..."

"Shush," Lucifer said gently. Hitler's mouth slammed shut as though slapped.

"He's very eager, isn't he?" Lucifer went on. "The Sword that Binds can also Unbind. True, yes?"

"That is not my purpose here, Lucifer. There is only one who can and will unbind you," I said.

"The Sword," Lucifer went on, as though I had said nothing. "The first time since I was...brought here, I see the Sword. I once had one just like it, you know? All of us did. All who stood in the Presence. As I once did. It was taken from me...by my brother. Perhaps there's something of it in that fragment you carry. Perhaps.

"Do you ever wonder why you were Chosen, Marius?" Lucifer went on. "Why you would be Chosen to join the handful of mortals who carry part of the Sword? I wonder. I'm not allowed to know, you see. Once, when I was joined in the Light with my brothers and my father and my mother, I knew everything. All of the Divine Plan. But now...I do not. I only see bits and pieces. My part to play, if you will. And I see you in this part, Marius Winter, shaman of the plains, Bearer of the Sword of my brother, whose name I am not allowed to utter here, Seeker in the Darkness, Light Bearer...Path Finder."

He laughed, a booming presence, yet strangely empty of any true happiness.

"Path Finder. That would be you. So few descend here who can return. You've been here in spirit, but now, now you are here in the flesh. You and your party. All for a woman, yes? Is that what you believe?"

"We are here to retrieve the soul of Jolene LaMoore. We are here to return her to her life after you and yours took her," I said, as formally as though I were reading an indictment.

"I find that amusing," Lucifer said. "Her name. Jolene. Derived from the French for pretty, perhaps derived earlier from Norse for Yule. The birthday of your ... well, the Light of the Creator Made Flesh. I'm not allowed to say his name, either. Inconvenient. And her last name ... is that a joke, I wonder? LaMoore. *L'amour*, the French word for love. Pretty love. Is that what you came here for, Marius? Your pretty love?"

Behind the sad blue of the eyes, something dark and cruel peeking out around the facade.

I raised the Sword.

"Not yet, shaman," Lucifer said. "Be careful here with that. Certain things, once done, cannot be undone. Would you like to leave here with your pretty love? And all of your friends? Or would you prefer to stay here for all time, in the Darkness, with me?"

There was a massive slam that shook the stone beneath our feet and a blast wave of air rippled our hair and what remained of our tattered clothing.

The door had slammed shut.

"I understand you are fond of movies, Marius. Actually, I know this, because peering into mortal minds is one thing my ... brother and my father ... left me. A particularly exquisite form of torture, perhaps? Or their idea of mercy? Who knows. I can no longer peer into their minds so I must amuse myself by peering into yours. Do you remember that movie *The Watchmen*? From the comic? That wonderful scene where the character is imprisoned, and after brutalizing one of his fellow inmates, turns and screams at his fellow inmates: 'I'm not in here with you, you're all in here with ME!'"

The last word was shouted and echoed through the chamber, which, despite its vastness, felt very small with those echoes.

"Eternity is a very long time, Marius," Lucifer went on, in his semblance of a normal, calm voice.

Hitler was hunched up, his shoulders under his ears. "Master, we, I mean, Master . . ."

Lucifer looked at Hitler and silenced him with an eye blink.

"A very long time," Lucifer said. "So perhaps you'll see something that will influence your thinking. After all, so few mortals have ever made this trip in the flesh. And while you have come here in journey . . . this time you are subject to binding of the flesh as well as of the spirit. Here. By me. For here, I hold Dominion, bound or not."

I held my tongue.

"Wise," Lucifer said. "Or else the cunning of the cornered fox."

He gazed at each of my companions, one after another. "Powerful allies . . . in the Middle World. Here, well, that remains to be seen." He drew a massive breath and exhaled.

"Bring out the woman," Lucifer said to Hitler.

Hitler scurried away, mouth moving nonstop though no words came out. He went around the corner of the dais and vanished into the dark.

A long moment.

And then he came back around, leading Jolene on a chain. She was in an otherwise immaculate white gown that covered her from chin to the ground. Her hair, completely white, pulled back in a tight pony-tail. Her eyes were empty sockets. Where her mouth would have been was a pale expanse of scarred flesh. She followed, like a cowed dog on a leash, unable to see or speak.

I felt the red tide of rage coming in on me.

"She is a bit worse for wear," Lucifer said. "Very stubborn, and very strong. Willful, too. And more than a bit arrogant, or at least she was. I doubt that now. As one of my followers said to someone at Abu Ghraib, 'It's biology. Everyone has a breaking point.' Even one such as she."

Hitler tugged the leash to and fro, and Jolene stumbled along, head down.

"Steady," Otto whispered from beside me.

Lucifer studied him closely, leaned forward, smiled. "I remember you well, Otto Skorzeny. So much about you . . . but I require your silence now."

Otto raised his hands to his mouth . . . or where his mouth had been. A seamless expanse of flesh from below his nose to the jaw. Sealed.

"And you others . . ." Lucifer mused.

Black metal manacles and chains appeared around the wrists and ankles of Burt, First In Front, Tigre, and Otto.

Everyone except for me.

"I cannot bind a Sword Bearer, Marius. But I can certainly bind everything you hold dear and love in the world," Lucifer said.

"And I can call on the Light of the Creator here," I said. "I hold the Sword."

"Yes," Lucifer said. "You can. You *may* be able to unbind them. Perhaps you should try?"

Otto strained against his chains, throwing his head violently from side to side in a silent no. I looked at them, the metal that held the chains and manacles together... the same metal that held Lucifer in place.

"Oh, I think you see the dilemma," Lucifer said. "Are you thinking that if you unbind them... you might unbind me? Certainly a possibility. Though of course, then you'd have your allies and your woman. And the Sword. Shall we see?"

Otto struggled, to Hitler's amusement. Hitler saw me looking, and rattled the chain that held Jolene. I heard a hiss from the Shield on my back.

"Yes," Lucifer said. "With both of them, you may be able to repair her. After a fashion. Though I don't think you can do it here. You'd have to be elsewhere. Out of my Dominion. And you, of course, can go. But these others... they'd have to stay here. Much like Persephone and Hades, yes? Except all your beloveds will be in the one place where you can guarantee that they will endure undying torment till the End of Days."

Lucifer laughed, a peal of a gigantic bell.

"Shall we try the unbinding, shaman? Think of the story you will be able to tell. How you went to Hell and unbound Lucifer. I'd let you tell that tale, though you'd probably have to fictionalize it a bit. Maybe as an urban fantasy, that's what they call it these days, yes? And of course, the world might change a bit... what say you? Shall we give it a go?"

"No," I said. "I think not. I think I will contest with you, Lucifer. Because you are the Father of Lies, lies in all things. If it's true that I can unbind you, perhaps I can add to your binding. Or perhaps the Sword has other plans for you. Maybe this is your ending. What do you see, Fallen?" I held up the Sword, pulsing with blue light. "I see the Light of MIIII-KAI-ELLLL!"

Lucifer screamed. Hitler fell to his knees and clapped his hands over his ears. The entire chamber shook and rocked; dust settled around us, and there was a huge clap as though of thunder. Lucifer tried to raise his manacled hands to his own ears, but the chains were too short.

"Aaaahhhh!" Lucifer screamed, his torment echoing in the chamber.

I rushed to Otto, raised the Sword and slashed down on his chains. Sparks flew, but the metal was untouched. I tried it with Tigre. The same. I turned and went to Hitler, who cowered down in the fetal position, his hands pressed tight over his ears. I struck at the chain that bound Jolene.

Nothing.

For a long moment, Lucifer twisted against his chains. Then he opened his eyes.

"So now you know a little more," he said calmly, as though nothing had happened. "The contest is not over. You must fight my Champion. If you win, you take your woman and your allies and you will leave. If you do not, you, the Sword, and your allies remain here forever. Except for one. I will release one to return to the Middle World, so that what happened here will be known to all. To all, Marius. You will serve as the object lesson to those who trifle with me and mine. And that one will bear witness. Do you understand?"

"I think you got the talking part done, Lucifer. Arm your lackey. He'll need more than his sharp uniform and little mustache," I said.

I was looking forward to kicking the shit out of Adolf Hitler. Seemed to me I might have missed that in a previous lifetime.

Loud peals of laughter, and Lucifer didn't even try to hide the malicious humor in it. "You are such a fool, Marius. Such a tool. Your ego is such that you see yourself as an instrument in the Hand of the Creator . . . you are a tool for any who can get to you. You think the Creator has use for such a blunt instrument? I think not. I call forward my Champion to crush you. Now."

I turned and faced Hitler. "You like movies, Adolf? Ever see that masterpiece *The Unforgiven*, directed by the one and only Clint Eastwood? Great line in there: 'He should have armed himself, he's gonna decorate his saloon with my friend.' So I'll paraphrase Clint, Adolf, though I dislike mentioning you and him in the same breath: best arm yourself if you're gonna decorate this chamber with my friends."

Adolf leered at me, orclike in his glee. "Oh, I'll see you crushed, vain mortal. I'll see you ripped to pieces while you watch me rip your little toy here . . ." he rattled the chain. "And I'll see you stripped of that Sword."

I tipped the Sword and stepped to him. "You're not much of a Champion, Adolf."

"He's not the Champion," Otto said.

I spun on my heel, backing to keep Adolf in my peripheral vision while I looked back.

Otto's chains were gone. His mouth had returned. His recent scars vanished. And he had grown to the size of your standard Archdemon. Satan's sword was held firmly in his hand. The shredded clothing he'd worn had disappeared to be replaced by what looked like a gladiator's loincloth, bound at the waist with a golden belt that looked like the Ouroboros.

"Otto?" I said.

His eyes were still human. Sad and trapped. But determined.

"Yes, my friend," he said heavily. "I am Lucifer's Champion."

CHAPTER 32

"Otto! No!" I said.

My other allies strained at their chains, helpless in Lucifer's Dominion.

"I'm sorry, Marius," Otto said.

"How is this?" I said.

Hitler laughed. "What a fool you are, Winter. You'll have all eternity to ponder that question."

"You fought beside me, you saved my life and my soul, Otto," I said. "How is this?"

Lucifer laughed and laughed. "Pride goeth before the Fall, as was written, little shaman. Welcome to your undoing, your binding, and the celebration of my unbinding."

I raised the Sword. "I think not, Fallen. Otto?"

"He is a betrayer," Lucifer said. "He always betrays. It is his purpose, his method, his reason for being. He betrayed Hitler, he betrayed me, ultimately he betrays all who trust him. And he is so, so trustworthy, is he not? Trustworthy enough for you, to be at your side, to make sure that Sword made it all the way down here, past all the Guardians, past all the trials, to be sure that it arrived safely . . . here. Right here. Where I called it and where I need it."

Laughter, demonic beyond demonic.

"How else to get a Sword Bearer here? Were you more experienced, you would have known how to use the Power of the Sword to fetch your little wench back, but no, you always go for the drama, don't you, Marius? Something about the romantic appeal of storming into Hell with your allies, like the Rangers at Normandy, or the Charge of the Light Brigade, or 'Mad Dog' Shriver's last stand . . . so you had to bring it here, all the way here, where I can call upon it . . . once your dead fingers are pried from it . . . to unbind me and mine. So that we may return in triumph to the Middle World, pour out of the portals to reclaim all that is rightfully ours, and to do so long before my brother realizes it. Possession is nine-tenths of the law, yes?"

Demonic laughter.

"So to speak," Lucifer said. "So to speak. So. Champion. Shall I tell them of your seduction? How you were seduced? Or would you like to tell it? I might enjoy hearing you relate the details of your downfall—pride, fear, love of a woman, love of children . . . all the good things that make up a good man, turned and corrupted— you are one of my finest pieces of work, Otto Skorzeny. Courage turned and twisted . . . so brave in facing me, so craven in your downfall . . . but like someone else said, 'It's all biology' for those of you born into the meat. And you are all meat on my table . . ."

Demonic laughter, deep into the marrow of my bones.

"What say you, Champion? Would you like to explain to your friend, your friend of many lifetimes? Did you know that, Marius? Otto here was your lieutenant in the Guardians of the Faith, you oh-so-elite in the Service of the Light, in Atlantis. He ran with you, beside you, without question, to your death ... and his. Life after life, the two of you met and partnered, faced down death together, saved so many lives ... and always the seed of resentment, the hatred well hidden that leads to betrayal, deep in Otto's heart. You're always so blind to those you choose to befriend, Marius—you overlook what it's like to be in your shadow always, to be the second banana (an appropriate metaphor for a reasonably intelligent ape) to you—to watch you save the day and sail away with the fair maiden ... each and every time."

Lucifer reached as though to stroke his chin, came short because of the chains.

"Perhaps not this time," he said. "Perhaps Otto will walk away with a reward. Otto? Would you like the woman? A bit damaged goods, I'm afraid, but perhaps you can put her right. So to speak. Would you?"

Otto trembled. Was silent. Could not meet my eye.

"Ah," Lucifer said. "The humiliation of the strong made slave. Something he should be used to by now. You would think, wouldn't you? How about you, Marius? Are you ready to be made slave? I have so much you could do around the place ..."

Otto.

I raised the Sword. "He'll be freed either way, Lucifer. You cannot bind the Sword. Nor me. Not while I draw breath and the Sword has Light."

I advanced on Otto. "I'm sorry, my friend."

"As am I," Otto said. "I am so sorry. No matter. If it is meant for me to win this day, I will see Jolene released and returned. I swear this."

"Be silent, slave," Lucifer said. "You can promise nothing. Do as you are told."

"You *promised* me!" Otto shouted. "And I hold you to that!"

Lucifer smiled and licked his lips as though savoring a particularly tasty treat. "Oh, well, there is that. First you must defeat the Sword Bearer...Champion. And of course you'll have your reward. I promise."

Hatred and rage in Otto's eyes. His scar pulsed with his heartbeat. He turned towards me, raised his sword in the classic salute. "On guard, my friend. May this unfold as it is meant to."

I raised my Sword and he lunged forward. I parried in fourth and ducked aside wishing for an additional foot on the end of my blade—which immediately appeared.

"That's useful," I said.

And I prayed silently that the hand of Michael guide his Sword as I crossed blades with Lucifer's Champion, my friend and ally, Otto Skorzeny.

And our blades went *snicker-snack, snicker-snack*. Lunge, riposte, beat, parry, cut, back to en garde, repeat as needed; Otto was by far the more experienced fencer, and the blade of Satan had an energy of its own, the red fire against the blue light, but my hand was guided by something, someone much larger than myself, whose wisdom and guidance and experience and love flowed through me, quenching the rage that had roiled in my heart, rage at the twisting of a good man. The lesson was burned into my soul;

the only way to defeat the Dark Forces was to keep love and Light in one's heart always, to move through the rage and the anger to the still, white, calm space within, where a hand much greater than ours would wield the weapon without passion, without hatred, without anger. As the blades whirled around us, a ring of steel, a mesh of razor edges and needle points, it was as though there were a movie overlaid over us, images of lives past...

Otto giving a briefing in his Wehrmacht uniform, me in an American paratrooper uniform listening intently...

...the edges bound as he beat the blade and lunged at my face, narrowly missing it as I ducked and back-cut at his hand...

...the two of us beneath the Eagle of an Imperial Legion, marching through the hinterlands of the Empire...

...and Otto enraged, hammering with both hands like an ax down on my upraised Sword, for I would not bring the Shield into play despite Jolene's pleadings...

...the two of us in frontiersman's garb, accompanied by an Indian warrior band, stealing alongside a red-clad British detachment, somewhere in the American wilderness...

...and an unexpected kick to the chest, not enough that he be good with the steel but deadly with the integration of blade and hand and foot at close quarters, far better than me, Marius, but it wasn't me, Marius, in this fight it was the...

...two of us in vinyasas, speeding over the land, and raining fire down on the assembled troops on the plains below us...

"MIIII-KAI-ELLLL!" I shouted.

The Sword gleamed with blue fire and hammered on Satan's blade, knocking Otto to his knees. I returned his kick with one of my own, straight under his blade and into his chest, knocking him back, stumbling and tripping—and then I held my blade high...

"Otto! Fight him..." I said.

He scrambled back to his feet. "I cannot. I cannot. He holds what I hold dear. As he does with you. I'm sorry, Marius..."

He charged me, changing his fencing style to a whirling scythelike approach of figure eights, hacking and hacking at me. I ducked to one side, slapped at his blade and thrust into his side, felt the Sword cut into meat, searing with its blue light.

"Aahhh!" Otto shouted. He slashed, bashed the Sword away, slashed at my inner arm, nicking me and drawing red blood, human blood, that ran down my arm and spattered across the black floor. My wound closed and, for a moment, a part of me exulted that, man, I was *just* like Wolverine.

Never get cocky when you're fighting the Champion of Belial, especially when it's Otto Skorzeny, one of the modern masters of Special Operations and deception.

He hesitated as though injured far worse than he was, and then back-cut impossibly fast with his edge. I ducked, lunged forward, watched him dance back and beat my blade down and come in the high line, aiming for my collarbone with a lunge designed to pierce my subclavian artery. I felt the tip touch me, stumbled back, and fell.

Flat on my ass.

Otto didn't hesitate. He stomped in and pressed

the tip of Satan's sword directly against my neck; the length of it gleamed with fire barely contained, lit his eyes with red highlights.

"Otto," I said. "Fight him. Fight it down. You can do this...of anyone, only you...you can do this."

He stared at me.

Lucifer/Belial's laughter pealed throughout the chamber. "Oh, how elegant! My Champion, pinning my brother's Champion, and the appeal to his higher nature...how perfect! Marius, you missed your calling. You should have been an author of penny romances, a writer of soap operas, something of that sort. How dramatic! Is this the denouement? Do tell!"

"Otto," I said. "You must do this. Only you can. Together, we can find those he holds...we can free them...but you must be the one who fights free. I cannot do it for you..."

"Why?" Otto shouted. "Why? You help everyone else, why not me? Why can you not do it for me?"

"Free will, brother," I whispered. "You must choose, or unchoose. I cannot do it for you."

His hands trembled. His face was drawn in the fierce Teutonic visage of the Odinic warrior. Ready to thrust.

"I'm sorry, Marius. It is my nature. I have to..."

I knocked his sword aside and rolled clear, came up with the Sword ready. "No worries, Otto. I know what it's like to be a slave to my nature."

There was no hesitation, for the Sword had a mind and a life of its own. Steady pressure, constantly banging and cutting, pressing Otto back all the way to the dais, his back pressed against the metal. I lunged and when he ducked his head, as I knew he would, I flipped the blade and slapped him hard with the flat, stunning him just long enough for me to round-kick his knee and yank him to the ground, lever the sword of Satan out of his hand, and now we were reversed. He was pinned, and I held my Sword and his, one to his neck and one to his chest.

"It's one of the Great Lies, Otto," I said. "The Lies of Belial, Lucifer, Father of Lies. The Lie that you can never undo the covenant he forces on you. That the contract is irrevocable. That's the Lie, Otto. He cannot bind you. He tries. But he cannot. What he holds of you can be released. Can be set free. And you can be the instrument of your own freedom. Remember when you entered my house, Otto? I asked you. And you said you were of the Light. You would not have been able to enter were you not. The Light of the Son of the Light that is Lucifer is Dark. And you are not. You are of the Light."

I leaned on the blade and stared him right in the eye. "Choose."

"I cannot. I cannot," Otto choked out.

I waited. I stared. Even Lucifer was silent.

"Yes," I said. "I see that you cannot. And I cannot make that choice for you. So I must take your life."

"Yes," Otto said. "You must. I am sorry, Marius."

"So am I, Otto."

I leaned on the blade.

Then lifted it and stepped back. "Get up."

"What? You cannot, Marius! You must finish me!"

"Ah, I don't think so. Get up."

Otto scrambled to his feet.

Lucifer bellowed. "FINISH HIM!"

"You don't give me orders, Lucy." I handed Otto the sword of Satan.

"We can either go on with this or you can join me, Otto. Together, we can do this."

He held the sword, looked up at Lucifer looming above him.

"Remember who I hold!" Lucifer-Belial shouted.

"I do," Otto said. He turned to me. "I choose the Light of the One."

"That's all I needed to hear, brother," I said.

I raised the Sword. "I call upon the full Power of the Mighty General of the Lord's Host, MIIII-KAI-ELLLL!"

A blue blast of light, the heart of the sun made even more brilliant, burned inside the chamber.

White Light poured out of my chest, and there in the chamber was the likeness of the Mighty Archangel, illuminated within and without, Michael, standing before his bound brother—

—Lucifer screamed in rage—

—Hitler curled up in a ball—

—the chains binding Jolene, Tigre, Burt, First In Front exploded into blue sparks.

I grabbed the blinded Jolene by her hand, the Shield slung over my shoulder, Tigre knelt and we all leaped on her back.

"Get us out of here, Tigre," I shouted.

The Archangel Michael stood between us and his bound brother. Blasts of atomic red and blue between them.

Tigre bounded down the long passageway to the doors.

"Marius, the . . ." she began.

"Doors?" I pointed the Sword and the bolt of blue lightning that came from above shattered the doors and Tigre sprang through the rubble of the collapsed doors.

Inside, there were brilliant flashes of blue and red, red and blue, and parts of the tunnel collapsed, hiding that within from those of us without.

Dust settled, though the rock itself pulsed with the fury exchanged inside.

"He is still bound," Otto said.

"Yes," I said. "And still Lord of this Dominion. So we need to call on some help..."

I knelt. I held the Shield in one hand, the Sword in the other. Otto led the blind Jolene to the Shield, where she grasped it with one hand, and Otto held the other. Tigre leaned against the German, and First In Front grasped her shoulder in one hand and held out the other for Burt to perch on; he spread his wing to touch my shoulder.

We were in Circle.

"I call on you, Father, Mother, Creator God, Great Spirit, Holy Spirit, Goddess... I call on you, Jesus the Christ, Light of the Creator Made Flesh, and I call on You, Mother Mary, Queen of the Angels, First Among Healers, and I call on the Mighty Archangels of the Presence, Raphael, Archangel of Healing, Uriel, Archangel of Fire, Gabriel, Archangel of the Call, and Michael, Archangel of Protection, I call on you and I ask for your help on behalf of your beloved daughter, Jolene, I ask that she be joined once again and be made whole in accordance with your Divine Plan, that she be healed, and that all of those who have traveled this road in Service to the Light of Creator God be healed and made whole..."

And the most brilliant Light of all descended around

us, filled us and infused us with gleaming golden Light, and as the Light filled me from the inside out, till all that was Marius Winter dissolved into the Light, I heard Burt say in his definitive Brooklynese: "Lucy, I'm home! And *you're* in *big* trouble...."

As we all dissolved into the Light and the laughter, I saw Him grinning at me, waving for me to follow him as I always have.

"C'mon, Marius," Jesus said. "Time to go home."

CHAPTER 33

I opened my eyes. I was on the floor of my healing room. I sat up. The wand I'd carved was in my hand. There were burn marks on it I didn't remember making. Jolene was on the healing table. Sleeping on the floor beside her were Dillon and Sabrina. Curled up in one corner was my Tigre, fully restored and unharmed. Burt rested on her shoulder. First In Front was laid out full length, his head propped up on Tigre's haunch.

Otto stood guard at the door.

We studied each other.

The others stirred.

Otto held one huge finger to his lips, and shook his head no.

I went to Jolene's side. Her face looked calm and beautiful and rested. There was a shock of gray in her red hair. She opened her eyes.

"Hello, beloved," she whispered.

I hugged her. I held her. I loved her.

❖   ❖   ❖

Bella Italia had reserved the back room for us. We were a boisterous party; we were loud, proud, and out of control. The bar tab alone would probably cause the Inspector General of Homeland Security some fits when Otto submitted his credit card voucher.

"I don't understand why I don't remember," Jolene said. "When I journey on it, there's ... nothing. Like a black road, but nothing on it. I've never experienced that before."

She'd kept the gray streak in her hair.

Dillon and Sabrina exchanged glances, said nothing. Otto looked to one side and grinned.

From the corner of my eye, I saw the flash of a white tiger's tail disappearing around the corner to the ladies room. A man at a nearby table looked up: First In Front in an expensive business suit with no tie, a cowboy hat parked on the table. Tap-tap-tap at the window and there was a crow from Brooklyn ...

All my loved ones.

All of them home.

Home again, home again, home again home.

"There're some stories to tell, I'm sure," Dillon said.

"I don't know," Sabrina said. "You know what they say."

"What's that?" I said.

"What happens in Hell, stays in Hell."

After the laughter, Otto and I stared at each other, till the others noticed and fell silent.

"I'm thinking there's an unfinished part of the story," I said, "but I'll leave it be. For now."

Otto nodded once. "Yes, my friend. For another time."

The following is an excerpt from:

GENTLEMAN JOLE AND THE RED QUEEN

LOIS McMASTER BUJOLD

Available from Baen Books
February 2016
hardcover

Chapter One

It was a good day on the military transfer station orbiting the planet Sergyar. The Vicereine was coming home.

As he entered the station's Command-and-Control room, Admiral Jole's eye swept the main tactics display, humming and colorful above its holo-table. The map of his territory—albeit presently set to the distorted scale of human interests within Sergyar's system, and not the astrographic reality, which would leave everything invisible and put humans firmly in their place as a faint smear on the surface of a speck. A G-star burning tame and pleasant at this distance; its necklace of half-a-dozen planets and their circling moons; the colony world itself turning below the station. Of more critical strategic interest, the four wormhole jump points that were its gateways to the greater galactic nexus, and their attendant military and civilian stations—two highly active with a stream of commercial traffic and scheduled tightbeam relays, leading to the jump routes back to the rest of the Barrayaran Empire and on to its nearest neighbor on this side, currently peaceful Escobar; one accessing a long and uneconomical backdoor route to the Nexus; the last leading, as far as forty years of exploration had found, nowhere.

Jole wondered at what point in the past

double-handful of years he'd started carrying the whole map and everything moving through it in his head at once. He'd used to consider his mentor's ability to do so as something bordering on the supernatural, although the late Aral Vorkosigan had done it routinely for an entire three-system empire, and not just its smallest third. Time, it seemed, had gifted Jole easily with what earnest study had found hard. Good. Because time bloody *owed* him, for all that it had taken away.

It was quiet this morning in the C-and-C room, most of the techs bored at their stations, the ventilation laden with the usual scents of electronics, recycled air, and overcooked coffee. He moved to the one station that was brightly lit, letting his hand press the shoulder of the traffic controller, *stay on task*. The man nodded and returned his attention to the pair of ships coming in.

The Vicereine's jump-pinnace was nearly identical to that of a fleet admiral, small and swift, bristling more with communications equipment than weapons. Its escort, a fast courier, could keep up, but was scarcely better armed; they traveled together more for safety in case of technical emergencies than any other sort. None this trip, thankfully. Jole watched with what he knew was perfectly pointless anxiety as they maneuvered into their docking clamps. No pilot would want to make a clumsy docking under *those* calm gray eyes.

His newest aide popped up at his elbow. "The honor guard reports ready, sir."

"Thank you, Lieutenant Vorinnis. We'll go over now."

He motioned her into his wake as he exited C-and-C and made for the Vicereine's docking bay. Kaya Vorinnis was far from the first of the techs, medtechs, and troops from the greatly expanded Imperial Service Women's Auxiliary to be assigned to Sergyar command, nor the first to be assigned directly to his office. But the Vicereine would approve, which was a charming thought, though Cordelia would doubtless also make some less-charming remark about how her natal Beta Colony and a like list of advanced planets had boasted fully-gender-integrated space services since forever. Personally, Jole was relieved that he only had to supervise the women during working hours, and that their off-duty arrangements here on-station and on the downside base were the direct responsibility of a rather maternal and very efficient ISWA colonel.

"I've never seen Vicereine Vorkosigan in person," Vorinnis confided to him. "Only in vids." Jole was reminded not to let his long stride quicken unduly, though the lieutenant's breathlessness might be as much due to incipient heroine-worship, not misplaced in Jole's view.

"Oh? I thought you were a relative of Count Vorinnis. Had you not spent much time in Vorbarr Sultana?"

"Not that closely related, sir. I've only met the count twice. And most of my time in the capital was spent running around Ops. I was put on Admin track pretty directly." Her light sigh was easy to interpret, having the identical content to those of her male predecessors: *Not ship duty, dammit.*

"Well, take heart. I was put through a seven-year rotation in the capital as a military secretary and aide, but I still caught three tours on trade fleet escort duty afterward." The most active and far-flung space-based duty an Imperial officer could aspire to during peacetime, culminating in his one and only ship captaincy, traded in due course for this Sergyar patch.

"Yes, but that was aide to *Regent Vorkosigan* himself!"

"He was down to Prime Minister Vorkosigan, by then." Jole permitted himself a brief lip twitch. "I'm not *that* old." And just kept his mouth from adding, "...young lady!" It wasn't merely Vorinnis's height, or lack of it, that made her look twelve in his eyes, or her gender; her recent male counterparts were no better. "Although, by whatever irony, my one stint in an active theater of war *was* as his secretary, when I followed him to the Hegen Hub. Not that we knew it was going to end up a shooting war when that trip started."

"Were you ever under fire?"

"Well, yes. There is no rear echelon on a flagship. Since the Emperor was also aboard by that point, it was fortunate that our shields never failed." Two decades ago, now. And what a top-secret cockup that entire episode had been, which, glued throughout to Ex-Regent Prime Minister Admiral Count Vorkosigan's shoulder, Jole had witnessed at the closest possible range from first to last. His Hegen Hub war stories had always had to be among his most thoroughly edited.

"I guess you've known Vicereine Vorkosigan just as long, then?"

"Nearly exactly, yes. It's been . . ." He had to calculate it in his head, and the sum took him aback. "Twenty-three years, almost."

"I'm almost twenty-three," Vorinnis offered, in a tone of earnest helpfulness.

"Ah," Jole managed. He was rescued from any further fall into this surreal time warp by their arrival at Docking Bay Nine.

The dozen men of the honor guard braced, and Jole returned salutes punctiliously while running his eye over their turnout. Everything shipshape and shiny, good. He duly complimented the sergeant in charge and turned to take up a parade rest in strategic view of the personnel flex tube, just locking on under the competent and very attentive supervision of the bay tech. Exiting a null-gee flex tube into the grav field of a station or ship was seldom a graceful or dignified process, but the first three persons out were reasonably practiced: a ship's officer, one of the Vicereine's ImpSec guards, and Armsman Rykov, the only one of the new Count Vorkosigan's personal retainers seconded to his mother, in her other hat as Dowager Countess. The first man attended to mechanics, the second made a visual and electronic scan of the docking bay for unscheduled human hazards, and the third turned to assist his liege lady. Vorinnis tried to stand on tiptoe and to attention simultaneously, which didn't quite work, but she dropped from Jole's awareness as the last figure cleared the tube in a smooth swing and flowed to her feet with the aid of her armsman's proffered hands.

Everyone snapped to attention as the color sergeant piped her aboard. Admiral Jole saluted, and said formally, "Vicereine Vorkosigan. Welcome back. I trust your journey was uneventful."

"Thank you, Admiral, and so it was," she returned, equally formally. "It's good to be back."

He made a quick initial assay of her. She looked a trifle jump-lagged, but nothing like the frightening dead-gray bleakness that had haunted her features when she'd returned alone almost three years ago from her husband's state funeral. Not that Jole himself had been in much better form, at the time. The colonists of Sergyar had been entirely uncertain if they were going to get their Vicereine back at all, that trip, or if some stranger-lord would be appointed in her place. But she was wearing colors again now, if subdued ones, Komarran-style trousers and jacket, and her unmistakable smile had warmed to something better than room temperature. She was still keeping her tousled red-gray hair cut short; the fine bones of her face held out, like a rampart that had never fallen.

Her left hand, down at her side, gripped what appeared to be a small cryofreezer case. Lieutenant Vorinnis, like any good admiral's assistant, advanced upon it. "May I take your luggage, Your Excellency?"

Cordelia cried, sharply and unexpectedly, "No!" twitching the case away. At Jole's eyebrow-lift, she seemed to catch herself up, and continued more smoothly, "No, thank you, Lieutenant. I'll carry this one. And my armsman will see to the rest." She cast a quick head-tilt toward the girl, and a plea of a look Jole's way.

He took the hint. "Vicereine, may I introduce my new aide, Lieutenant Kaya Vorinnis. Just assigned—she arrived a few weeks after you left." Cordelia had departed six weeks ago to present the Sergyaran Viceroy's Annual Report to Emperor Gregor in person, and incidentally catch a little of Winterfair Season with her family back on Barrayar. Jole hoped that had been refreshing rather than exhausting, although having met the Vorkosigan offspring, he suspected it had been both.

"How do you do, Lieutenant? I hope you will find Sergyar an interesting rotation. Ah—any relation to the young count?"

"Not close, ma'am," Vorinnis replied, an answer Jole suspected she was tired of offering, but she did it without grimacing here.

The Vicereine turned and delivered a few well-practiced words of thanks to the honor guard. Their sergeant returned the traditional, "Ma'am, yes, ma'am!" proudly on their behalf, and marched them out again. Cordelia watched them go, then turned with a sigh to take Jole's arm proffered in escort.

She shook her head. "Really, Oliver, do you have to do this every time I transit? All I'm going to do is walk from the docking bay to the shuttle hatch. Those poor boys could have slept in."

"We never did less for the Viceroy. It's an honor for them as well as for you, you know."

"Aral was your war hero. Several times over."

The corners of Jole's mouth twitched up. "And you're not?" He added in curiosity, "What's in the box? Not a severed head—again—I trust?" It seemed too small for that, fortunately.

Cordelia's gray eyes glinted. "Now, now, Oliver. Bring home one dismembered body part, *once*, mind you, *once*, and people get twitchy about checking your luggage ever after." Her smile grew wry. "But that we can *joke* about that now...ah, well."

—end excerpt—

from *Gentleman Jole and the Red Queen*
available in hardcover,
February 2016 from Baen Books